Andr... and u... ...ge. He has travelled
widely, and worked for a time as a librarian in
London, but gave up his work to concentrate
on his writing. He has published a number of
successful books, including the much-praised
The Second Midnight and *Blacklist*. He now lives
in Gloucestershire, near the Forest of Dean,
with his wife Caroline and their children.

BLACKLIST

'It really does deliver, with that vital element of
compulsion. Satisfyingly packed with moral
ambiguities and delightfully devoid of stereo-
types . . . excellent.'   VENUE

'Another cracking yarn, totally riveting . . . one
of Britain's most accomplished young thriller
writers.'   THE CITIZEN

THE SECOND MIDNIGHT

'An ingenious idea . . . echoes of le Carré.'
                                                      PUNCH

'Sharp, vivid, intriguing: an excellent novel.'
                                              YORKSHIRE POST

'First-class adventure.'   IRISH TIMES

ANDREW TAYLOR

Toyshop

Fontana
An Imprint of HarperCollins*Publishers*

First published in Great Britain in 1990 by Collins

This edition first issued in 1991 by Fontana,
an imprint of HarperCollins Publishers,
77–85 Fulham Palace Road,
Hammersmith, London W6 8JB.

9 8 7 6 5 4 3 2 1

Printed and bound in Great Britain by
HarperCollins Book Manufacturing, Glasgow

For Robert

ONE

I was in bed with my brother's wife when they came to tell me he was dead.

It was a Sunday afternoon. The sky outside the window was the colour of snow that's been lying too long by the side of a busy road. We'd reached the talking stage; Anna wanted to discuss my performance. Even then I knew that what we had done was a mistake. Not just for me – for all of us.

'Wolfgang's more inventive,' she said. 'And he's got more staying power.'

'Good for him.'

'On the other hand, you're more considerate.'

I tried to look pleased. Talking was a mistake too.

'A woman likes that, you know. It's a shame you couldn't sort of combine.'

She shook a Marlboro out of the packet and waved it like a wand. Anna, my brother once told me, believed in magic. Maybe she thought that somewhere in the world was a spell that could make my brother and me merge into a single person.

No, not a person. Just a lover. Anna wasn't very interested in people.

She lit the cigarette with the Dunhill lighter he gave her when he last came home. She leant across me for the ashtray. The bed creaked. A massive breast brushed against my eyes.

Years ago, when he was drunk, he'd told me that Anna had breasts like torpedoes. Now they were more like tired balloons.

But she was still very attractive, especially in her clothes. I had always envied my brother: Anna looked like every adolescent's fantasy of a mature woman. Her hair was the colour of dark honey. Usually she wore it in a coil at the back of her head. Now it spilled over the pillow and over my chest. It occurred to me that in my old fantasies she never talked.

'How can you bear to live here?' she said.

'It's all right.'

'But it's so tiny. And you can hear everything your neighbours are doing.'

Apparently she hadn't realized that the transmission of sound worked both ways. A few minutes before she'd been screaming her head off.

'I'm lucky,' I said. 'I've got a separate bedroom. And a shower.'

I knew I wasn't lucky. I just had Wolfgang as a brother. He had arranged for me to get an apartment that would usually go to a married couple. A privileged married couple. The block was only two years old. The central heating worked. I even had a view of the railway line.

'You could do a lot better. If you wanted to. If only . . .'

'I'll get the drinks.' I eased my arm away from her and swung my legs off the bed.

'You never listen.'

I glanced back at her. 'You're wrong there. I always listen.'

'Don't be silly. You know what I mean. Wolfgang says — '

8

That's when they knocked at the door. A double-knock, loud enough for all the neighbours to hear. Not the sort of sound a friend would make. Even Gustav from downstairs was quieter when he came to complain about the volume of the music.

Suddenly Anna's face was no longer beautiful: it was fat, white and stupid. Panic had smoothed away her individuality. I grabbed my jeans.

'Don't answer,' she whispered.

'The light's on. They can see it from the road.'

Anna reached for her clothes, most of which were scattered on the end of the bed. I rescued my shirt from her.

Another double-knock.

'Where's your car?' I hissed.

'A couple of streets away. For God's sake, answer it.'

So we were in with a chance — if no one had seen her come in. I tucked in the shirt and went into the living room, closing the bedroom door behind me. There were two glasses beside the brandy bottle on the table, and her handbag was on the armchair. Fortunately her coat was hanging in the closet. I put one glass and the handbag in the wastepaper basket, and tossed a newspaper on top of them. Then I opened the front door.

Two men were waiting in the corridor. They were dressed alike in smart overcoats and grey hats.

'Herr Herold?' the smaller one said. He had a soft voice and one of those thin, sensitive faces you associate with romantic poets. 'Herr Gerhard Herold?'

I nodded, faking a yawn. 'Sorry — I was taking a nap.'

'Lieutenant Arendt.' He held out a warrant card. 'And this is Sergeant Voss.'

When I saw the card, I tried to keep the surprise out of my eyes but I don't think I succeeded. These men weren't Vopos, they were Stasi.

'May we come in?' Arendt asked, returning the card to his pocket.

'Of course.' I stood back from the doorway. 'This way,' I added, not that my flat offered any choice. They'd caught me off-balance: I'd been expecting the People's Police, not State Security.

Three was a crowd in my living room. Voss shut the door. Arendt glanced around the room, noting the bottle and the solitary glass, the paintings, the dirty plates stacked by the sink in the kitchen corner, the records and the books. My private life was like a card index; he flicked through it with an ease born of long practice.

'Do sit down,' I said. 'How can I help you?'

Arendt pulled out one of the hard chairs at the table and lowered himself onto it. I followed suit, making more noise than necessary because I thought I heard a movement in the bedroom. Voss ignored the one remaining chair, an armchair, and leant back against the door. He was a big man with a lot of excess hair in his ears and nostrils.

'I'm afraid we have bad news,' Arendt said. His face wore the same expression of impersonal sorrow as the doctor's had when he told us my mother had only a few months to live. 'Really we should tell Frau Anna Herold first, but she's not at home at present. I don't suppose you know where she is?'

'Anna?' I shivered; I think my body understood before my mind did. *Anna first, then me . . .* 'Is it Wolfgang? Is he okay?'

'I'm sorry,' Arendt said. 'Your brother is dead.'

10

You can never tell how you will react to the sudden death of one you love. I suppose I would have predicted shock or sorrow; if I'd thought a little harder I would have come up with disbelief or even guilt. But none of us works like the textbook model.

Instead I listened to a goods train rattling over the points outside and the sound of Gustav's television beneath my feet. There was a ring-mark on the table-cloth where Anna's glass had been. The solitary ciga-rette in the ashtray had a smudge of pink lipstick on the butt. Everything was fuzzy, like surroundings half-sensed in a dream.

And I thought, with the sort of clarity that hurts, *he'll never find his Lenné Triangle now.*

Part of me despised her for staying in the bedroom, and part of me was grateful.

Anna lingered there even after Arendt and Voss had left. On the surface she was impulsive, but she had inherited the caution that characterized her father. Probably caution was at least partly behind her choos-ing me: she would have thought I could be relied on to keep my mouth shut. I wondered if Arendt had noticed the lipstick on the cigarette. It no longer mat-tered very much, not to me.

The footsteps receded down the corridor. Gustav changed channels on the television. Usually I don't smoke, but I wanted a cigarette. I opened the bedroom door.

She was fully dressed and sitting on the edge of the bed. No tears, of course. The room smelled of Chanel, cigarettes and physical exertion.

'I don't believe it,' she said. 'Not Wolfgang.'

I knew what she meant. Wolfgang was one of those people who seem indestructible.

'You heard it all?'

Anna snorted. 'Such as it was. They weren't exactly chatty. Who were they?'

'Stasi.' I watched her eyes narrow. 'Can I have a cigarette?'

She gave me one and took one for herself. 'I've got to go,' she said; but she made no move to leave. I sat down beside her on the bed. When she flicked the lighter I stared at the flame.

'A fire?' She snapped the lighter shut. 'What sort of fire?'

'They didn't say. Only that it was an accident.'

'Horrible.' She blew out a stream of smoke. 'Imagine – watching yourself burn.'

'You'd probably suffocate first,' I said. I hoped it had been quick. Maybe he'd been asleep and death had taken him unawares. A kind way to go.

'It's a mess. Why weren't they Vopos?'

I shrugged. Maybe because it happened abroad. The Stasi would have been the first to hear. What will you say?'

'When they catch up with me? I'll think of something. I know – I drove out to see Great-aunt Luise. Then, when I was nearly there, I realized it was past visiting hours. So I drove back.'

I almost laughed. It was such a typically neat solution: almost impossible to disprove and it would look good on the record. So much better than scandalous conduct with your husband's brother.

Caring for the elderly is a social virtue. It didn't matter that Anna only visited Great-aunt Luise when Wolfgang dragged her there. Nor did the possibility that Arendt wouldn't believe her. In the German Democratic Republic we spend our lives playing

12

a complicated game; and the first and most important rule is that you must appear to play by the rules.

'It's tragic.' She swallowed noisily to suggest that she was in the thrall of strong emotions. 'And what we were doing makes it even worse. I . . . I shall never forgive myself.' She gulped again and glanced at me. 'No one must ever know.'

'I won't tell them if you won't.'

She bared her teeth at me in the sort of smile that makes you think of wolves scenting prey on a frosty night. 'You're involved as much as me.'

'I know. But you've got so much more to lose.'

My anger caught me off-guard. What was in her mind was so blindingly obvious: she wouldn't be a highly eligible widow if it became known that she had been screwing her brother-in-law just after her husband's death. But it was an unkind thing to say and I wished I'd kept my mouth shut. For all I knew she was grieving under the surface, in some part of her she would never show to me. In any case, it would be stupid to antagonize her.

Anna had reached the same conclusion by a different route. She patted my leg in a sisterly sort of way. 'We mustn't quarrel, Gerhard.' This time she sniffed to indicate the presence of sorrow; she was never very subtle. 'There's no point. And Wolfgang would have wanted us to be friends.'

In fact Wolfgang had wanted Anna and me to be lovers.

The last time I saw him was when the two of them came down from Berlin, just before he went back to England. They stayed with Anna's parents, as usual, and paid the duty visit to Great-aunt Luise. And one

13

evening, Wolfgang and I slipped away for a few drinks together.

That evening we talked a lot. He mentioned Anna near the end, when we were in the last bar we visited. Maybe he had planned it that way – maybe he wanted us both to be a little drunk.

We were sitting on a terrace that overlooked the Schwerin See. It was already autumn, and the evenings were too cold for drinking outside in comfort. The terrace was raked by a breeze that smelled of dead leaves. But Wolfgang loved water so we sat there, huddled in our coats and staring at the lights across the lake. In my life the first thing I remember is being with Wolfgang in a rowing boat. I must have been about three. The boat was swaying wildly and all around us was water, glinting like liquid silver. And I remember most of all that I was unafraid, because Wolfgang was there and he would look after me.

'Anna's going to stay with her parents,' he'd said, 'just while I'm away. The Ministry has arranged a temporary transfer.'

'I know. You told me.'

I guessed he was grinning though I couldn't see his face. 'But I didn't tell you why, did I?'

'No, but she did.'

'What did she say?'

'Less lonely for her, and her father's been ill and – '

'It's not that. Or rather that's only part of it. I wanted her here because she's less likely to make a fool of herself again. And of me.'

He paused, which irritated me. Wolfgang liked to seem mysterious, to create tension, and that's what he was doing now. He did it automatically and often just

14

for the hell of it. But there was no need to do it with me.

'Are you going to tell me now?' I said. 'Or have I got time to take a piss?'

He chuckled. 'Anna has strong passions.' He put the last two words in invisible quotation marks, mocking both himself and me. 'And surprisingly little self-control.'

'You mean she'll want to take a lover while you're away?'

'Yes – and she'll find it harder in a backwater like Schwerin where everyone knows her. *And* her father.'

'I won't be your watchdog, if that's what you want. Anyway, it wouldn't work. We move in different circles – you know that.'

'I don't want a watchdog,' Wolfgang said. He left another pause, this time to allow me to catch up with the implication of what he'd said. I knew I was flushing. I sipped my brandy and took one of Wolfgang's cigarettes.

Then I said, 'No.'

He pushed the lighter across the table towards me. 'You'd be doing me a favour, Gerhard.'

'No.'

I felt ungracious as well as angry. I owed him a lot of favours. I owed him my flat, thanks to his influence with Anna's father. I owed him my job, thanks to his influence with Rudolf Bochmann.

'You remember the Conflict Commission?' he said.

I nodded.

'I've never forgotten that, and I never will. It makes us even.'

'Damn you,' I said. He wouldn't even allow me to feel ungracious about refusing him.

'The thing is,' he went on, 'she'll do it with someone. I'd rather it was someone I trusted not to hurt her, not to be indiscreet. And I don't trust anyone but you.'

'You're forgetting something.'

'What?'

'Anna's not interested in me. Never was.'

'You underestimate yourself.' He lit my cigarette for me. On the other side of the flame his eyes were laughing. 'I know that for a fact. She told me. We have a very frank relationship, Anna and I. Of course' – his lips curved upwards in the briefest of smiles – 'the attraction may not work in the other direction. In that case, forget what I said.'

So Wolfgang knew. The smile told me that. It was stupid to feel surprised. No doubt he had guessed from the start. I was in my teens when they got engaged; I probably made it obvious that I fancied her. But that's all it was, then and now. A biological reflex conditioned by . . .

'It's perfectly natural,' he said. 'So don't worry. We're not children any more.'

'I'm not worrying. Anyway, that's irrelevant. The point is, I won't. It just wouldn't work – can't you see that? There's nothing more to say.'

'Okay. But if you change your mind – '

'I won't.'

'If you change your mind, you'll be doing me a favour. You'll be doing us all a favour. Let's go inside. I'm getting cold.'

He picked up his glass and the cigarettes and looked out over the water. Then he led the way into the warmth and light. Inside most people were watching a football match on the big colour TV above the bar. Dynamo Berlin were thrashing FC Union, much to

16

everyone's disgust. We found a table in a booth near the door.

It was then that Wolfgang mentioned the Lenné Triangle.

Anna left me alone at last. I poured the rest of the brandy down the sink and made some tea. That night I didn't get much sleep. Next morning I phoned the office and told Werner Huber that I wouldn't be coming to work today.

He coughed at me for a few seconds. Then he said, 'Why?'

So the news of Wolfgang's death hadn't reached him yet. I was surprised. It suggested that the Stasis hadn't yet told the Party, which was distinctly odd. Usually the unofficial communication system between the Ministry of State Security and the Socialist Unity Party was both fast and efficient; after all, officials of the former tended to be members of the latter.

I explained. Huber muttered the conventional condolences and coughed a little more. I could almost hear the machinery turning over in his mind as he assimilated the fact that Wolfgang was dead. There would be implications. For men like Huber there always are.

'I've got to go over to the Eichler place,' I said casually, just to keep Huber on his toes. Then I topped up the truth with a lie: 'Old Kurt's been asking for me.'

That brought on another fit of coughing. 'Ah – do give him my regards. Or rather my deepest sympathy.'

I was glad to put the phone down.

The Eichlers had a big, split-level bungalow with lakeside frontage about ten kilometres outside the city.

During the night it had snowed again. As I turned into their drive, the sun came out for the first time that day. The garden was a dazzling, unblemished white. Beyond it, the lake was a deep blue. It seemed that the Eichlers' privileges extended even to the weather.

I parked between the two cars already outside: the new Trabant that Anna used and a Chaika limousine. My twelve-year-old Wartburg with its dulled paint and patches of rust lowered the tone of the neighbourhood.

Anna's mother answered the door. The skin around her eyes was red and puffy but her face lightened when she saw me. Suddenly I didn't know what to say.

'I thought I'd better come,' I muttered.

'You poor boy.' To my astonishment Frau Eichler hugged me. 'You and Wolfgang were very close, weren't you? Come and have some coffee.' She pulled me into the hall. 'Anna's in the living room.'

I jerked a thumb at the Chaika. 'Are you sure I'm not interrupting?'

'Don't be silly. It's only Heinz.'

She made the present First Secretary of Schwerin province sound like a favourite nephew. In a sense that's what he was. In our part of the world he was the nearest thing we had to a tutelary divinity; but he owed his position in the province to his predecessor, Kurt Eichler. Eichler still had friends on the Central Committee and the Politburo; he was one of the grand old men of the Socialist Unity Party; so the First Secretary would naturally be in the queue of sympathizers when Eichler's son-in-law died.

'How's Anna?' I said.

'She's taking it very well.' Frau Eichler was still holding my arm and she gave it a tiny squeeze. 'She's like her father, you know. She bottles things up.' She looked anxiously up at me. 'It worries me, sometimes. I wish she'd *cry*.'

'Delayed reaction, probably,' I said. 'I believe it's quite common.'

'Yes, of course. I was so fond of Wolfgang. He could make you laugh. Do you know what I keep thinking? Thank God there weren't any children. After all these years it's a blessing in disguise.'

Her face began to work. I put my arms around her. I didn't know whether she was mourning Wolfgang or the grandchildren she'd never had. Perhaps both. I hardly knew the woman. We had met perhaps five times in the last ten years, usually at family functions where there were so many people that no one had to talk to anyone for more than about thirty seconds. But from the moment I had arrived today, she started calling me by the familiar *du*. Death had made me part of the family.

A moment later she pushed herself away and blew her nose. 'I'm sorry.'

'Don't be,' I said. I meant it. It was a relief to find someone else who cared. In a strange way her grief helped me accept that Wolfgang was dead.

'You're very like him, you know. Younger, of course, and slimmer.'

'There were lots of other differences,' I said.

'It's never easy – growing up in the shade of an older brother or sister. He more or less brought you up, didn't he?'

I nodded. 'After my mother died.'

'And you stayed friends. It's much easier to rebel against parents. I'm talking a lot of nonsense, aren't I? Let's find Anna.'

She wasn't talking nonsense. She was being uncomfortably shrewd.

I followed her along the hall to the long room at the back of the bungalow. The two French windows overlooked the lake so the room was full of light. Anna, dressed in black, was sitting on a sofa by one of the windows. She stood up as we came in.

We acted out a playlet for her mother's benefit. First we exchanged respectful kisses. Then we murmured about how sorry we were, what a tragedy it was and how we missed Wolfgang. For once she wore no make-up; her face was white and strained. For the first time I realized that she'd inherited her looks from her mother.

Frau Eichler left us to fetch some coffee. Anna gripped my arm so hard that I winced.

'No problems?' she hissed.

I shook my head.

A door banged, somewhere in the front of the house. The Chaika's engine fired.

'Arendt was waiting here when I got home last night. I'm sure he believed me.'

'Good,' I said.

'What about your neighbours?'

'Even if someone noticed something, they're not going to volunteer the information. Why should they? Don't worry.'

'But if Arendt starts asking questions – ?'

'Why should he bother?' I pulled my arm away from her and sat down. 'I doubt if either of us will ever see him again. Unless, of course, there's something you're not telling me.'

'Don't be stupid. It's just that – '

20

The door opened. Kurt Eichler shuffled into the room, leaning on his stick. I stood up.

'Good morning, Gerhard,' he said. His voice held the ghost of its old resonance; I was reduced to an audience of one. With his eyes fixed on the lake, he launched into the platitudes the occasion required.

Even now, the old bastard was impressive. He was still a big man, though age and arthritis had diminished the physical presence he'd had in his prime. He had started his working life in Rostock, and he had the heavy torso and thick arms of a docker. Shreds of the power he had once held clung to him; they clothed his condolences with an undeserved significance. Wolfgang, he said, was not only a loss to his family: he was a loss to the Party. More than that, he was a loss to the state. But there was some consolation for those who were left to mourn him: Wolfgang's life would be an inspiration to others.

I stood there, with my head bowed, allowing the oration to wash over me. Eichler was a great one for maintaining appearances. He had never liked me. I was one of Wolfgang's liabilities – and therefore a liability to Anna and, in the last resort, to himself. But the conventions had to be observed.

At last he moved from the general to the particular.

'He will be cremated over there,' he said in a throaty whisper, 'and the ashes will be flown home. Anna feels that would be best. The Embassy will make all the arrangements.' He looked directly at me for the first time, challenging me to object.

'It's Anna's decision, of course,' I said. All that mattered to me was the fact of Wolfgang's death. I turned to Anna. 'Is there anything I can do?'

21

She shook her head. 'Mother wants some sort of memorial service. Do you mind?'

A telephone began to ring. No doubt more condolences were on the way.

'Why should I?'

Eichler grunted. In this instance, I guessed, he would have liked me to object – in a respectful way, of course. Since his retirement, his wife had allowed her attachment to the Lutheran Church to resurface. It was politically embarrassing but there was nothing he could do about it. Among other things a marriage is a balance of power, and balances shift as circumstances change. Wolfgang had found Eichler's predicament amusing.

'Nothing big,' Anna said. 'Just family and a few friends. It would please Mother.'

'The phone,' Frau Eichler said from the doorway.

Both Eichler and Anna turned towards her but she was looking at me. Her face was anxious. When I reached the phone in the hall I understood why. It was Lieutenant Arendt.

'I'd like you to come and see me,' he said. 'This evening – at six o'clock.'

In this country we look after our old age pensioners.

Before the war, the nursing home was a private house. It was built for a dye-manufacturer in the middle of the last century. He chose a site on a wooded hill overlooking the Schwerin See and an architect whose inspiration was the newly-rebuilt grand-ducal palace in Schwerin itself. The result was an absurd little villa in the French Renaissance style. I liked it because it was frivolous. No one has built anything frivolous in this part of the world for over fifty years. But nothing's

22

perfect: the new annex at the back of the house reminds residents and visitors what a serious, socially responsible building should look like.

I timed my visit for the middle of the afternoon. I didn't want to come but I knew that no one else would bother to tell Great-aunt Luise what had happened.

'She's a relation?' the nurse said as she took me upstairs.

I nodded.

She paused on the half-landing, her hand resting on the lion's head on top of the newel post. 'I don't want to alarm you, but she's not too good. The Director would like to see you afterwards.'

'Anything new?'

The nurse shook her head. She had beautiful grey eyes and permanent worry lines between her eyebrows. 'Just winding down. You know? Try not to excite her. No more than fifteen minutes. I'll come for you.'

Great-aunt Luise was sitting in an armchair by the window. Her room was in the old part of the house. It was large, well-furnished and stiflingly hot. She was staring at the screen of a colour TV. The sound was off but the programme looked like yet another documentary about shopfloor democracy.

'It's your nephew, dear,' the nurse said loudly. 'You remember?'

Great-aunt Luise came slowly to life. Her head turned towards us. A smile began to creep across her face. She raised her hand as if she wanted to stroke me.

Then the smile died in its infancy. The hand dropped to the arm of the chair.

'Gerhard,' she said. 'I thought they meant Wolfgang.'

23

'How are you?' I brushed her cheek with my lips. 'You're looking well.'

'I'm dying. As usual.'

'You've been saying that for twenty years.'

The nurse closed the door behind her.

'Because it's true. It's true for all of us, you fool.'

That was indisputable. I nodded at the window. 'You get a beautiful view from here.'

The snow-covered lawns rolled down a little valley to the lake. The hills on either side were smudged with pines.

'We don't get winters like we used to have,' she said. 'When I was with the von Doeneckes . . .'

Her voice trailed away. I wondered what she was seeing in her mind. Horse-drawn sleighs and skating parties? The great hunts they used to have? The von Doeneckes' baroque palace near Neubrandenburg, its windows blazing with lights, marooned like a liner in a white sea?

'I have photographs.' She waved a limp hand in the direction of the bookcase. There was a row of albums on the bottom shelf. I remembered them too well from my childhood. 'I showed them to Wolfgang last time he came. Why hasn't he written lately?'

'He's very busy,' I heard myself saying. 'And I think someone said they've got a postal strike in England.'

I stared at the lake, wishing the words unsaid. I had been determined to tell her the truth. I thought I owed her that at least. But when it came to the point I couldn't do it. She was an old woman. Her life had given her only two things of value: the reflected glory of the von Doeneckes and whatever she felt for Wolfgang.

24

So I stayed for another ten minutes, talking about the von Doeneckes, who were securely dead, and Wolfgang, whom I could not allow to die. For as long as I can remember, these were the only safe subjects with Great-aunt Luise; anything else could unleash her hostility to me. She came to live with my parents after the war that had shattered everything she prized. After my parents died, she stayed with us, endlessly complaining. Wolfgang always knew how to get the best from her: maybe I was too impatient, too willing to take offence.

As she talked about the past, her hold on the present slackened. Her memories were real; I was the ghost. Then, without any warning, I became someone else's ghost.

'You remind me of him,' she said.

'Who?'

'Young Count Georg. The one I was talking about. The brother of the one they murdered. But I've told you that before, you silly boy.'

My skin crawled. She had never used that cooing voice to me.

'But we had our revenge, didn't we, Wolfgang?'

'Yes,' I said. 'I suppose we did.'

'Our little secret.' Suddenly anxious, she glanced at me. 'You haven't told Anna?'

'No.'

'Such a *common* girl. I would have wanted someone better for you.'

Before I could ask her about the secret, she drifted off into an attack on Anna. Wolfgang used to say that Great-aunt Luise was jealous of his wife; and he was probably right. While she rambled, I became Gerhard again; the opportunity was lost. At last the grey-eyed nurse came to relieve me.

Afterwards I saw the Director in her office on the ground floor. She was a brisk, middle-aged woman who ran this anteroom to death with cheerful efficiency; she was also distantly related to Rudolf Bochmann. She wore a white coat; the room was painted white; and the snow outside the big window made everything whiter still. In consequence I felt grubby.

She told me that Great-aunt Luise was unlikely to last through the winter. I told her about Wolfgang.

'You made the right decision,' she said. 'The news of his death could only upset her.'

'She was always much closer to my brother.' I hesitated. 'For a while up there, she thought I *was* him. And then she switched back again. She didn't even realize what she'd done.'

'It can be very distressing for the relatives,' the Director said. 'But you were wise not to try to disillusion her. There'd be no point, would there?'

I shrugged, refusing to commit myself.

'You're lucky in one respect,' she went on. 'She is very – how can I define it? – emotionally independent.'

'That's one way of putting it.' Self-centred and self-sufficient was another.

'In some ways it's an advantage. For her, for you – and even for the staff.'

I got up to leave. The Director came with me to the front door; the courtesy, I guessed, was due to my remote connection with Rudolf Bochmann. Her smile slipped a little when she realized the Wartburg belonged to me. But she shook hands warmly and promised to keep me informed if there were any change.

'And don't hesitate to phone,' she said, 'if you have any questions.'

I had only one question, and the Director wouldn't have the answer: what was the secret that Great-aunt Luise shared with Wolfgang? *Our revenge*, she'd said. Then who was the victim?

Arendt kept me kicking my heels for three quarters of an hour.

At five to six I reported to the uniformed sergeant at the desk. He ticked off my name on a piece of paper and nodded towards the bank of chairs.

There were thirty of them, drawn up in neat ranks of five. I know, because I counted. When I arrived, eight other people were already waiting. By tacit agreement, each of them preserved the largest possible area of space between him and his neighbours. No one talked. Most of them smoked a lot and stared at the big clock mounted above the sergeant's desk. It was better than looking into each other's eyes or reading the posters on the walls. No one came in or went out.

I read the small ads in *Neues Deutschland*. The Wartburg needed a new exhaust but I couldn't find one. Wolfgang could have got hold of it in about five minutes. Then Sergeant Voss tapped my shoulder.

He led me through a door to the right of the reception desk. We walked in silence up a flight of stairs and down a long corridor. All the doors were closed but behind them I heard typing and talking and coughing; once there was even a laugh. Voss knocked on the door right at the end. Without waiting for a reply, he opened it and stood back to allow me to precede him.

I stopped in the doorway. This wasn't an office: it was a small tropical jungle.

Fundamentally the room was similar to a hundred other offices I'd visited and worked in, right down to the standard-issue furniture and the photograph of the President on the wall behind the desk. But every horizontal surface, including the floor, was covered with house plants.

'Come in, come in.' Arendt was sitting behind the desk, partly concealed by a Christmas cactus dripping with pink, frilly flowers.

Voss and I inched along a narrow path that zigzagged through the jungle to a small open space in front of the desk. Two chairs were waiting for us.

'The plants belong to my wife,' Arendt said. 'We've been having trouble with the central heating in our block. Apparently the temperature here is ideal.'

'Have you had them here long?'

'A day or two. They go back tomorrow.'

His mouth tightened, and I felt sorry for the service engineer who'd had to deal with him. In most apartment blocks repairs to central heating systems take months, if not years. But not when one of the flats is occupied by a middle-ranking Stasi officer.

Middle-ranking? If his superiors were prepared to tolerate his turning his office into a temporary greenhouse, it was possible that Arendt carried more clout than his rank suggested. The state does not encourage eccentricity in its servants.

'Now.' Arendt opened a file. 'I'm sure you appreciate that when someone dies, there are often loose ends.'

I nodded.

'Usually we talk to the widow. But in this case Frau Herold is very – ah – distraught, and we thought it might be kinder to have a word with you first.' He looked up suddenly. 'You've no objection, I take it?'

'Of course not, Lieutenant.'

I knew, and he knew that I knew, that the real

reason for his sensitivity about Anna's feelings was her father's position; but neither of us would have dreamed of mentioning it. As I said, we are all playing a game and we all know the rules.

'You were very close to your brother, I believe?'

'When we were young, yes.' I suspected it would be better to err on the side of caution. 'But after Wolfgang married I saw much less of him.'

There was a moment's silence, broken only by a faint gurgle from Voss's stomach.

Arendt sucked in his cheeks, increasing his resemblance to a consumptive poet. 'According to our information,' he said, 'your brother may have been involved in currency irregularities. But perhaps you already knew that?'

TWO

The next day, Tuesday, I went to work as though nothing had happened. My brother was dead; thanks to his indiscretions, my career was on the line; and the only thing to do was to carry on as normal.

I got there at 7.25 and signed my name in the register. Today of all days it would have been tactless to be late. At 7.30 a clerk would draw a red line across the page. To sign below the line was to invite a reprimand that went on your file; to do it often led to dismissal.

Upstairs in our office, Dieter was already at work, breathing heavily through his nose as he collated last month's export figures. I dumped my briefcase on my chair. To my surprise – and relief – there was no one behind the third desk in the corner furthest from the light.

'Sorry about your brother,' Dieter said. 'Life's a bastard sometimes.'

'Yes.' I hung up my coat with unnecessary care so I wouldn't have to see the sympathy in his face.

'Anything I can do?'

'Not really.'

'Do you want to come to dinner on Saturday? Edith's sister promised us some steaks.'

I heard someone coughing in the office next door. The husband of Dieter's sister-in-law was a useful man to have in the family: he was a quality controller at a slaughterhouse.

'I'd like that,' I said.

'Good.' He picked up his pen again. 'By the way, Huber wants to see you. As soon as you get in.'

'What about?'

He shrugged. Dieter had a wife, a housebound mother and two children to support. He was doing rather well in the Christian Social Union and he preferred to keep his nose clean. I liked him a lot.

'Do you want some coffee?' I said.

'Hadn't you better – ?'

'Coffee first.' I took the thermos from my briefcase; the stuff they provided in the canteen was disgusting. 'Where's Manfred?'

'He's with Huber.'

'Talking about me? Do you really not know what's going on?'

'I'd rather not speculate,' Dieter said primly, passing me his mug. 'Besides, I haven't time. I'm trying to organize the quarterly export statistics for the entire combine and – '

'Who got you a new seal for your washing machine?' I said. 'Who got you the leather coat for your wife's birthday?'

The answer to both those questions was Wolfgang. Dieter pushed his sandy hair backwards with both hands; it was a trick he had when he was nervous or embarrassed.

'No wonder your hairline's receding,' I said.

'I don't know anything for certain. Not really.'

'Who does? I'll settle for guesswork.'

'Well, Huber doesn't like you much.'

'That's not a guess. That's an understatement.'

'Your brother's dead, so he can't answer back if someone slings mud at him. And that makes *you* vulnerable.'

'Any more?'

'Huber was in a filthy mood yesterday morning. But after lunch he cheered up. He spent most of the afternoon with Manfred.'

Manfred Schmude, our colleague. I have never met anyone who looked so much like a middle-aged weasel. A year or two younger than me, he was a stalwart of the Free German Youth, the boy scout wing of the Socialist Unity Party.

'He wants my job,' I said.

'Yes.' Dieter flicked a crumb off his desk with a chubby forefinger. 'He was on the phone yesterday . . . Manfred, I mean. He was saying something about Conflict Commission records when I came in. Then he saw it was me and he started talking about Dynamo Berlin.'

Dynamo is the most successful and least popular football club in East Germany. Both achievements are due to the fact that the club's president is the Minister of State Security. Manfred Schmude was a Dynamo supporter.

'That's all?' I said.

Dieter nodded.

I poured the coffee and passed him his mug. He had told me enough. It all tied up neatly with Arendt's little chat last night. Arendt and Huber had their knives out, and they were being encouraged to stick them in me.

Every politician or senior official has his tail of appointees: the little people whom he pulls up behind him, and who push him in return. Wolfgang was part of Eichler's tail. And you could say I was part of Wolfgang's tail.

Since Wolfgang's death I had lost my protective screen. If my brother was about to be posthumously disgraced, Eichler no doubt wanted to distance himself from the connections of his former son-in-law. I was a sitting target for the old man's righteous indignation. I wasn't a Party member – I wasn't a member of *any* party.

I wondered how they would do it. An accusation of incompetence? Failure to meet productivity norms? Or would they try to put together a criminal charge and link me with whatever Wolfgang was doing? The Conflict Commission's verdict was an indelible black mark against me. With our economic system almost every citizen ends up breaking the rules at some time or another; it's very convenient for our masters.

'It's good coffee,' Dieter said. 'I'm sorry.'

I leant against my desk and took a sip of coffee. Dieter must have guessed most of this: he could read the signs as well as anyone, and he knew about my difference of opinion with a Conflict Commission. And yet he had asked me to dinner.

'I just remembered,' I said. 'I'm doing something else on Saturday. Maybe another time?'

'We'll keep the invitation open,' he said firmly. 'You never know.'

'Look, Dieter – '

The door opened a few inches and Manfred Schmude weaseled into the office. A Free German Youth badge was pinned to his lapel. His brown, slanting eyes slid round the room, noting the evidence of an illicit coffee break. I'd expected him to show a little indecent triumph. Instead he looked subdued.

33

'Herr Huber would like to see you,' he said. 'Sorry about your brother.'

I grinned at him just to throw him off balance, and said, 'Thank you for your sympathy.'

Manfred slithered behind his desk and opened a file. Dieter returned to work. I drank my coffee slowly, to annoy Manfred, and tried to work out what the hell was going on. Finally I went to see Huber.

Our section head was sitting in his smoke-filled sanctum — a small, dried-up man with a grey face. The only thing about him that wasn't insignificant was his cough.

'Sit down, Herold,' he said. 'My condolences about your brother.'

I sat down and said nothing. Silence always irritated him.

'Personnel wish to see you,' he said at last. 'On the Director's orders. It's urgent.'

I realized I must have misread Manfred's mood. Personnel had an office on the fifth floor of the building. No doubt they were going to demote me or, if I were very unlucky, sack me. I had half-expected the summons; the only surprising aspect was the speed of the move. Maybe Manfred was upset because someone else was ahead of him in the queue for my job.

I stood up. 'Then I'd better not keep them waiting.'

Huber waved me back to my seat and coughed for a while. Then he blew his nose and lit a cigarette. 'Not upstairs,' he said. 'Berlin.'

Now that was confusing; and at a guess it had confused Huber and Manfred as well.

'When do they want to see me?' I said.

'Four-thirty.'

34

'*Today*?'

'If you leave right away you should manage it. There's a travel warrant waiting for you downstairs. If necessary, the Ministry will sort out overnight accommodation at the other end. You're to ask for a Frau Mauer.'

I swear he was as puzzled as I was. There is a procedure for doing everything, including the removal of unwanted personnel. Deviations from routine were unsettling for all concerned. Huber didn't know how to play it: was I about to be disgraced or not?

'Schmude will take over your work for the time being,' he went on, looking at his watch. 'I'd advise you to hurry.'

He started coughing again. He was still coughing as I left the room, collected my coat, said goodbye to Dieter and walked out of earshot. It was astonishing that so small and so discreet a man should cough with such careless vigour.

The Ministry's headquarters was on the Unter den Linden, not far from the Soviet Embassy. I got there early, only to find that Frau Mauer was based in the annex on Clara-Zetkin-Strasse.

By the time I found it I was ten minutes late. Frau Mauer didn't seem to mind. She was a motherly, middle-aged Berliner who laboured under the illusion that I knew what I was doing there.

'Let me take your coat, Herr Herold. You had a good journey? I'm sorry there's not time to offer you coffee.' As we left the room, I heard her secretary murmur my name into a phone.

Carrying my coat, Frau Mauer led me to the main bank of lifts. In almost any organization the altitude of an office signals its occupier's status. We went up to the top floor. On the way she talked about the weather and the Berliner Ensemble. As we rose, my confusion deepened.

Up there the carpets were thicker and the paintwork and furniture were newer. It was probably my imagination but the inhabitants seemed glossier than down below: the women were prettier and the men more handsome; their skins glowed with winter suntans in place of the pallor that reigned downstairs. Few of the doors had nameplates on them; the implication was that people on this level were too important to need labels.

Frau Mauer towed me into an anteroom with one desk, five armchairs and a glass-topped table with a coffee tray on it. The sole inhabitant of this magnificence was a slender young man in a suit that came from the other side of the Anti-Fascist Barrier.

He smiled at me and murmured my name into the intercom on the desk. Frau Mauer slipped away. Still smiling, the young man put my coat on a hanger and ushered me towards a door beside the desk. All this deference was unnerving me.

'This way, Herr Herold.'

I walked into an office that was twice the size of the anteroom. There was a vast beechwood desk and a big window looking east towards the Hotel Metropol. Standing by the desk and in front of the window was a man who, in silhouette, looked a little like a scrawny chicken: hair swept up at the top of his head; a curving nose; narrow, sloping shoulders; and a prominent rump supported by thin, short legs.

He turned and smiled. 'Gerhard, my dear boy. You remember me, I hope?'

The voice had a faint Silesian accent, blurred by the hint of a lisp, and it took me back over twenty years. The plump face belonged to a stranger. But I recognized the voice.

'Herr Bochmann,' I said, trying to hide my surprise.

'The last time I saw you, you were a schoolboy,' he said. 'Come and sit down.'

There was a knock on the door and the young man came in with the tray of coffee. The china was Meissen.

'Over there, Reichel.' Bochmann gestured towards a table at the other end of the room.

He stood there, still smiling at me, as he waited for Reichel to leave. His immaculate blue suit emphasized his physical peculiarities rather than concealed them. He should have looked faintly ridiculous, but he was too much in control for that. I smiled back, grateful for the breathing space. In those few seconds a wave of memories rolled over me, pushing me back to the house in Pankow. Wolfgang had told me the building no longer existed; they had replaced it with a block of flats in the seventies.

There had been six families in a house designed for one. We moved there shortly after my father died – my mother, who even then was ill, Great-aunt Luise, Wolfgang and I.

Smells that turned the stomach often invaded the bathroom we shared with two of our neighbours. The rumble of the U-Bahn trains made the house tremble. There were rotten floorboards in the corner of the tiny room where Wolfgang and I slept; once we found a dead rat underneath the bed, its fur sparkling with frost. Most of all, I remembered the cold and the damp that seeped through the crumbling plaster and up from the stones of the stairs. Every winter had been a battle.

My mother was on the losing side: she died in that house.

The Bochmanns moved into the attic flat a few months after we arrived. I think they came up from Dresden. They were said to be very poor: both of them had been born in Silesia and their families lost everything when the Poles took over after the war. But Rudolf Bochmann had just got a job at the Ministry of Foreign Trade and he was a Party member, so at least they had prospects. I hardly ever saw him – most of the time he was out at work or at Party meetings. In my memory he was always clattering down the stone stairs, one hand on the wrought-iron rail, the other clutching a cardboard briefcase, in a hurry to be somewhere else. However, he usually found the time to say something as he passed, even if it was only a comment on the weather. At that time, he was a skinny but muscular man with a high complexion and short, black hair. Age and perhaps good living had turned him into a chicken.

In those days it seemed eternal winter. Frau Bochmann was a small, silent woman who tried to keep the cold at bay with a ragged fur coat that hung down to her calves. We met occasionally, usually on the way to and from the bathroom, but she rarely spoke.

There was a baby, a son I think, who made up for his mother's silence by crying most of the time. One night, Frau Bochmann was carrying the baby downstairs to the bathroom. She tripped and fell against the banisters: the baby slithered out of her arms and fell to his death. They said his skull was shattered. Another victim of that damned house. A few months later, we moved away.

Wolfgang told me that Frau Bochmann died, and that Bochmann had married again and produced a brood of chubby children. Over the years, I had heard quite a lot about him from my brother. Bochmann had helped him into the Party and intervened during his career like a benevolent fairy godmother. I am sure my brother gave good value: as Bochmann pulled, Wolfgang pushed.

Bochmann picked up a file from the desk and tossed it face down by the tray. He sank into one of the black leather armchairs and with a wave of his hand invited me to sit opposite.

'I was desolated when I heard the news,' he said softly. 'Your brother's death was an immense loss to us here. More than that, Wolfgang was a personal friend.'

'I know,' I said. 'He was very grateful to you.'

And so, in my way, was I. Bochmann's benevolence towards Wolfgang had spilled over onto me and Great-aunt Luise.

'In a sense, I feel guilty.' He bent over the tray and poured our coffee. His hands were very clean and the nails were manicured. 'It was I who put him forward for that job. If he'd stayed here, it wouldn't have happened.'

'But he was delighted to go.' I hesitated, realizing that here, even more than in Schwerin, the conventions required me to make the ritual noises. 'He felt it was an honour. A unique chance to serve his country.'

'Quite so.' Bochmann sounded a little bored. 'And Frau Herold? How is she coping with her dreadful loss?'

'As well as can be expected. Her parents are being very helpful.'

'The Eichlers?' He passed me a cup of coffee. 'Dear me, I thought the old man was dead.'

That put Eichler in his place: a provincial has-been. But why was Bochmann bothering with me? My brother was dead; I was useless to him. Altruism is not a quality you associate with senior state officials.

'Did Wolfgang tell you much about his job?'

'Of course not,' I lied. Like anyone with an official job, including myself, Wolfgang had been classified as a *Geheimnisträger*, a bearer of secrets, and forbidden to talk about his work.

'Naturally.' Bochmann pursed his lips again. 'I think I can say it was essential to the economy, to the future of this country. He was an obvious choice – a man with drive and socialist vision. Absolutely loyal. Even as a teenager he had those qualities. I recognized them in him when I first met him.' He picked up a cake and glanced at me. 'We used to have long chats in those days.'

'In Pankow?'

'Yes – you remember?'

There was a sense of urgency about the question. Looking back, I realize that my answers to his other questions didn't really matter. But this one did.

'I remember the house,' I said carefully. 'And you, of course. But not the conversations. I was too young.'

In the pause that followed we both finished our coffee. I was getting worried again: it was as if I had undergone a test whose nature and purpose I didn't understand; and I didn't know whether I had passed or failed.

Bochmann picked up the file and opened it on his lap. Suddenly I saw my name. It gave me a jolt. In the

40

GDR everyone has a file, but it is rarely seen by anyone except your section head and the security police.

'Languages seem to have been your strong point at university,' he said. 'Your grades were even better than your brother's.'

I cleared my throat. 'In English and French, yes.'

'Not Russian?'

'I can get by, of course. My Polish and Czech are on about the same level.'

'Curious.'

I knew what he meant. Russian is the one compulsory foreign language on the school curriculum so, in theory, it should be everyone's best second language. I doubted if Wolfgang had ever told him how Great-aunt Luise had bullied us into working especially hard at English and French: 'the civilized languages of Europe – indeed, of the world'. Once, when this country was part of a larger Germany, she had been a governess. After our mother died she made us talk English at home. 'The von Doeneckes often talked English among themselves. Count Georg spent a year at Oxford.' The sheer flexibility of the language fascinated me; and I still read and talked English whenever I could. As a result, I was very nearly as fluent in it as I was in German.

'Recently you've earned some excellent reports from your Director,' Bochmann said. 'The general feeling seems to be that you are underemployed at present. For example, your analysis of the reasons for the short-fall in actual hard currency earnings last year: that was really first class.' His eyes darted at me and then back to the file. 'If it hadn't been for that unfortunate business with the Conflict Commission, you'd have been promoted long ago.'

The case involved twelve bottles of vodka that were intended for the union's Labour Day celebrations. They were found in my possession when they should have been locked in the canteen storeroom. I was hauled up before a court composed of my colleagues; one of Huber's friends was in the chair. Nearly half the GDR's penal cases are handled in this way and not referred to outside courts. I made a public apology and paid a fine; Wolfgang gave me the money.

'Water under the bridge,' Bochmann said with a smile. 'It needn't be a problem. You were very young. And now you've paid your debt to society.'

'I hope so,' I muttered. 'I was foolish.'

Perhaps I had been foolish – but not for the reason that Bochmann thought. And was it water under the bridge? According to the jargon, I had been 'rehabilitated'. But the verdict remained on my file.

'Tell me, why did you never apply to join a political party?'

'I never got around to it,' I said. Wolfgang had often urged me to try. Bochmann was still looking expectantly at me, so I added: 'Naturally I'm in full agreement with all aspects of Party policy. But I thought perhaps the Conflict Commission verdict would go against me.'

'Evidence of modesty,' Bochmann said – slowly, as though trying the flavour of the words in his mouth. 'A self-imposed punishment? A sign of sorrow. A deep sense of personal unworthiness, which, though self-indulgent, has its admirable side.'

'Yes,' I said wearily. 'All of those things.' Plus a simple desire to avoid the mind-boggling tedium, the time-wasting, the hypocrisy and the sycophancy that an active political life entails.

'And no doubt you stayed in Schwerin for much the same reason?'

I nodded. In fact I'd stayed in Schwerin because I liked the comic-opera charm of the old town and the lakes and woods around the city. But to a man like Bochmann it was the back of beyond: a small city in an economically backward, predominantly agricultural area; it was politically unimportant – the sort of place whose only value was as a stepping-stone to somewhere else.

Bochmann pushed aside his coffee cup and patted his pockets until he found a silver case. He took out a small cigar and rolled it between the thumb and forefinger of his left hand.

'The Special Committee for Export Procedures,' he said, 'is about to consider a shortlist of candidates for your brother's job. In exceptional circumstances it has been empowered to sidestep the standard application procedures. I think it would be worth including your name on the list.'

The interviews were on the following Friday.

That left two clear days. I spent the nights at a government hostel, ploughing through a stack of reports and statistics that Reichel, Bochmann's assistant, thought I might find useful.

During the days I was passed from one office to another, some within the Ministry and some outside. I talked to planners, export managers and economic analysts. I was never alone: Reichel acted as my guide, and perhaps as a watchdog as well.

Much of the material wasn't new to me; Wolfgang had told me more than I had realized, both about the economic thinking that had led to the creation of his

43

job, and about the mechanics of the toy trade itself. On one level, he had been a glorified salesman whose brief was to increase the East German share of the British toy market. But he was also pioneering a new export strategy.

I was given a crash course in a subject that officially does not exist: the GDR's economic crisis. The most successful industrial nation in the Eastern bloc is not supposed to have problems. Our difficulties have two underlying causes: the chronic shortage of raw materials and energy sources, and the dependence on a cumbersome system of central planning, thrust upon us by our friends in Moscow. We import raw materials and energy and export mainly industrial products. Since the Arab-Israeli War in 1973 this trade structure has hit a snag: the price of raw materials and energy on world markets has risen much faster than the price of industrial products.

'So what do we get?' Reichel said cheerfully. 'A rising trade deficit. A stagnating standard of living. Domestic shortages because we have to export more to maintain the level of imports we need.' He paused, his face suddenly serious. 'The Politburo is said to be particularly worried about the domestic shortages.'

I nodded. We were on very thin ice indeed. There is an unwritten agreement between the Party and the population of this country. The prices of basic foodstuffs and housing are kept artificially low; the welfare state cossets us from cradle to grave; and there are consumer goods in the shops, which most people can afford. In return, you obey the rules and don't grumble too loudly about the restrictions on foreign travel, the queues and so on. But if the Party allowed that unwritten agreement to be broken, they could have another Poland on their hands. Or worse.

I cleared my throat noisily. 'Foreign debt?'

Reichel looked relieved. 'Somewhere in the region of US$20,000 million. It's a nightmare just finding the hard currency to service that level of debt. The Western banks aren't particularly enthusiastic about lending to us now.'

'The only answer is to increase our share of the export market, preferably outside Comecon countries.'

'In most sectors, our share is actually falling,' Reichel pointed out. 'Toys are a case in point. In recent years we've had to deal with an increasing volume of Far Eastern competition: Taiwan, South Korea, Hong Kong.'

'I know – cheap labour and new technology.' I had been briefed on this an hour before. 'We just can't match their prices or their products. And they react to market forces much faster than we do. But according to the figures, our production's increased considerably.'

'Yes,' said Reichel drily. 'According to the figures. And statistics also show that we've had some success in preventing waste of raw materials and energy. The combine system we introduced in 1980 has been a great improvement.'

I raised my eyebrows at him. 'I thought results were patchy: the factories that were successful before they linked up into combines continued to be successful afterwards. And vice versa.'

'All right. But for God's sake don't mention that on Friday.'

'The system's still too cumbersome,' I said. 'Too much central planning. Too many rigid five-year projections. We're not going to dominate any market until we learn to be more flexible. We've got to respond to the customers' demands. Like the capitalists do.'

'That's it,' Reichel said. 'You can tell the interview panel that, but perhaps in a more tentative manner. You know, with qualifications like "It seems to me" and "There might perhaps be an argument for considering the possibility . . ." You understand? And of course you've got to rabbit on about the socialist context whenever possible. But I'll brief you on that when we go through the questions.'

'The questions?'

'Didn't Herr Bochmann tell you? He chairs the panel, so naturally he'll do most of the talking. There are seven members, but only two others will ask you anything. I've got a full list of the questions, together with guidelines on the answers.'

It was considered expedient for me to join a political party. In fact I discovered I had joined the Liberal Democratic Party of Germany eighteen months earlier and then forgotten all about it.

The LDPG was chosen only partly because its candidature procedure is less formidable than that of the Socialist Unity Party. There was also the consideration that forty per cent of its members are state functionaries like myself, and the fact that the SUP prefers to limit its intake to blue-collar workers and members of the police and the armed forces. As a consequence of all this, it was easier for Rudolf Bochmann to use the Liberal Democrats to achieve the effect he wanted; the SUP is harder to manipulate, unless you are a member of the Politburo.

In any case, the differences are more notional than actual. All the parties and mass organizations of the

46

GDR belong to the National Front. The National Front supports the policies of the SUP. The SUP finds the arrangement convenient: the GDR combines the propaganda value of a multi-party democracy with the practical advantages of a one-party state. The lesser parties act as transmission belts, disseminating SUP policies among non-communists. Additionally, they allow the state to make use of the services of those who may not be entirely committed to the cause of Marxist-Leninism. Dieter, for example, who is a practising Lutheran as well as an excellent economic planner, was sanitized for state use by enrolling him in the Christian Democratic Union.

A few hours after I had filled in the back-dated application form, I visited the LDPG's headquarters in Johannes-Dieckmann Strasse. A senior official explained without a trace of embarrassment that the Schwerin branch had received and processed my application the summer before last. A clerical error had prevented them from notifying me.

The man apologized for the delay. I said he wasn't to worry about it.

On Thursday Bochmann invited me for a drink after work.

We went to the Stadt Berlin in Alexanderplatz. I had been there before a few times – usually when the Ministry was throwing a party for a trade delegation. Essentially, however, all the Interhotels are machines for relieving Westerners of as much hard currency as possible.

If Bochmann wanted to show me how important he was, he succeeded in the first five minutes. He led me to the bar where piped music tinkled offensively. There were a lot of Western tourists, a few Africans and a handful of East Germans. Nevertheless the big room seemed half-empty. Anyone can use the Stadt Berlin, but the prices deter most Berliners, and the waiters have a nasty habit of making it clear that they prefer customers who tip in hard currency. Tipping, of course, has officially been abolished in the GDR.

But a waiter was beside us before we had even sat down. He settled Bochmann in his chair with a solicitude that reminded me of those historical dramas on TV: the browbeaten employees grovel before their Junker master in the first half hour, before the working-class hero ignites the torch of revolution in the servants' hall.

'Your usual, sir?' the waiter purred.

'Yes.' Bochmann turned to me. 'What would you like? They do quite a pleasant malt whisky here. Glendronach, I think it's called. Your brother often had it.'

Who was I to object? I nodded at the waiter, who sped away.

'Has Reichel done a good job?' Bochmann asked.

'Excellent, I think.'

'We'll find out for sure tomorrow. He said you had a few questions.'

The questions I wanted answers for would have made a substantial book. But most of them I couldn't ask.

'Why the toy trade?' I said. 'I'd have expected something that was more central to the economy. Machinery, say, or industrial equipment.'

'That's the whole point. Toys are marginal.'

The waiter served my whisky and Bochmann's French mineral water with a flourish. I waited until he had gone.

'So we're just putting a toe in the water? If we're facing a crisis, don't we need a more radical programme?'

'We need to be absolutely sure that we're doing the right thing. Not everyone is convinced.' He lit a cigar and allowed the first lungful of smoke to dribble out of his nostrils. 'Other Comecon countries have tried similar tactics and the results have been uneven. So this is in the nature of a pilot study. And it's vital that it should succeed.'

Vital for the economy or vital for Bochmann? It sounded as if there were disagreement in the Politburo. When it comes to change, the old men who run our lives can be as hidebound as any of their Junker predecessors.

'Is that why we're starting with Great Britain?' I asked.

He nodded. 'In many ways West Germany would have been a better choice. But our trade turnover with them is about five times greater than with the British. It's too important to put at risk.'

'If it works, what happens then?'

'We apply the same strategy to other countries. In any case, that will be inevitable if the Common Market develops according to plan. And we simultaneously start to broaden our base, to use the same approach for other products within the same export sector: jewellery, musical instruments and so on. If that works we can move into the other sectors.'

'It'll take years,' I blurted out.

He just looked at me. Then, 'Time isn't the only problem. Wolfgang ran into opposition from his colleagues in London.'

'I know. Reichel showed me some of his reports.'

49

Bochmann stared into his water. 'I had a piece of good news today,' he said. 'The first shipment is ahead of schedule. The combine has made heroic efforts to meet Herr Rownall's requirements. He will see that we mean business.'

Rownall, the British importer whom Wolfgang had selected, played a key role in the new import system. All our toy exports to the UK would be channelled through him.

'Does he know – '

'About you?' Bochmann touched the rim of his glass but made no move to pick it up. 'I believe it has been mentioned that you're a candidate.'

'Do you know how he reacted?'

'I imagine he was pleased. They say he got on very well with your brother.'

In my innocence, I thought I understood why I was here. Bochmann needed to keep Rownall happy; he couldn't afford a hitch – say a clash of personalities between the importer and the Ministry appointee – at this stage. Knowing Wolfgang, he had made Rownall into a friend; my brother had the knack of making people like him – animals, too, for that matter. So I had been chosen for the simplest of reasons: I was the nearest substitute for my brother that Bochmann could find. He wasn't to know that I didn't share Wolfgang's aptitude for getting on the right side of people and staying there.

Without warning Bochmann stood up, stubbing out his cigar. 'I have an appointment. But don't hurry away – finish your drink.' He beckoned to the waiter. 'If you do get the job, State Security will want to see you. Nothing to worry about, eh? Not unless there's something I don't know.'

He gave the waiter a note and walked – or rather waddled on his short, thin legs – out of the bar. I thought about Bochmann and State Security, about Arendt and Eichler. Despite Bochmann's reassurance, I was worried. I still had a list of unanswered questions. Ignorance is an excellent qualification for a scapegoat.

'If I wanted to leave,' Wolfgang had said once, 'I could go tomorrow.'

It was the summer before he'd got the job that Bochmann wanted to drop in my lap. He and Anna had come down to Schwerin for the weekend; he'd borrowed a dinghy and, ignoring my protests, had taken me out for a sail.

'How would you do it?' I was concentrating on not being sick and I thought talking might help.

'There's a bar in Rostock. The Baltic Star, down by the docks. A woman who works there has got a brother who does a lot of freight-handling for Deutfracht.'

'What does he do? Stuff you in a container when no one's looking?'

'Something like that, I imagine.'

'Sounds risky,' I said. The boat lurched as Wolfgang went about. I closed my eyes, which made things worse. When I opened them again, Wolfgang was still looking at me, waiting for me to go on. 'The merchant marine must be riddled with Stasi.'

'Everything's risky.' He shrugged away the danger. 'Are you interested?'

'Not really.'

'You ask for Mitzi,' Wolfgang said with a grin. 'And you bring a lot of money, preferably in dollars. You look green. Have some Schnapps.'

I shook my head. 'I couldn't. I'd be sick.'

'Drink Schnapps or defect to the West?'

'Both.'

'It wouldn't work, in any case.' Wolfgang paused for a few seconds. Then he said, with a sudden spurt of anger: 'Have you ever thought what it would be like? Say you got to Denmark and found the West German Embassy. Okay, you'd automatically be a citizen of the Federal Republic. But what then? No money. Having to start all over again from the bottom of the heap. They don't want us any more, not really. And you know what their unemployment figures are like.'

'Who are you trying to convince?' I said.

'But it's true, isn't it? However you look at it, we're between the devil and the deep blue sea.'

I looked around me and shuddered. 'Literally.'

I got the job, of course. They shunted me up two whole grades. Bochmann lisped his congratulations and Reichel took me out to lunch. Then I spent the afternoon with State Security.

The Stasis weren't as bad as I'd expected. They made no mention of the Conflict Commission or of Wolfgang's penchant for private enterprise. Instead, they gave me what I imagined was the standard briefing for GDR citizens going to the West. I was warned about its temptations and told to be perpetually on my guard for the insidious approaches of the fascists; I was told to consider myself as a twenty-four-hour ambassador for my country, though it was emphasized that I had no diplomatic status; and I was given to understand that State Security was just as capable of looking after me in London as it was in Berlin.

Bochmann told me I could use the weekend to set my affairs in order.

So I went back to Schwerin. After Berlin it seemed more dead than alive, and I wondered why I'd stayed there so long; I should have applied for a transfer years before.

I told Great-aunt Luise I was going to London. She thought I was Wolfgang and she said she didn't need to be told things twice. But when I tried to bring up the subject of the secret she shared with Wolfgang, she suddenly remembered I was Gerhard.

On Saturday night I had dinner with Dieter. He wasn't very happy: his car needed a new engine, and he'd heard on the grapevine that Manfred Schmude was getting my old job. I couldn't do anything about the human weasel but I told Dieter he could have the Wartburg while I was away. His wife Edith gave me the largest of the steaks, and I promised to bring her back some perfume.

The following morning I drove out to the Eichlers' house. I didn't stay long. Eichler had had a relapse and was in bed upstairs. Frau Eichler had gone to church. But I saw Anna. She was dressed in black. I wondered uncharitably if that was because she knew that black suited her.

'You've got Wolfgang's job?' she said. 'You devious little shit.'

THREE

In the departure lounge at Berlin-Schönefeld I over-
heard a handful of British businessmen swapping anec-
dotes about the GDR. Most of the stories revolved
around black market operators and obstructive bureaucrats.

'Well, what can you expect?' one of them said with
the air of a man stating the obvious. He paused rhetori-
cally, fingering his short, black beard. 'They're all afraid
of their own shadows. Can't say I blame them. After
all, this is a police state. Makes you thank God for good
old UK, doesn't it?'

Interflug didn't fly to London, so the Ministry travel
section had booked me on a flight to Amsterdam,
where I would have to change onto a British Midland
flight to Heathrow. I am a land creature; I dislike
aeroplanes almost as much as I dislike boats. The seat
next to me across the aisle was occupied by the self-
appointed political analyst from the departure lounge.
When we were airborne he reached across the aisle
and touched my arm.

'Your first trip to London, is it?'

He spoke in heavily-accented German and his breath
was flavoured with whisky. When I nodded, he said,
'You'll enjoy the night life, I'll bet. You lot always do.
Let you off the leash and you can't get enough of it.'

He chuckled. 'The Poles are just the same, you know. But not quite as serious about it.'

A young man from our trade delegation met me at Heathrow. His name was Walter Keller; he wore round, gold-rimmed glasses and he was in a bad temper.

My first impression of the West was a blurred mixture of noise, colour and crowds. Airports, unlike railway stations, are depressingly cosmopolitan. Keller led the way out of the terminal. He didn't say anything until we got to the car, a VW Golf with CD plates.

'I've got to take you to the Embassy first,' he said. 'It'll take another couple of hours, at least.'

'I thought we'd be going to Ealing.'

The Embassy was in Belgrave Square, but the trade section was miles away in Ealing Broadway, on the outskirts of London.

'So did I. But Margarete Klose wants to see you.'

'Who?'

'You haven't heard of Fräulein Klose?' Keller reversed carefully out of the parking slot. 'Well, that's a treat in store for you.'

He drove with a ferocious concentration that discouraged talking. I looked out of the window instead. We came to a motorway where there were too many roadworks, too many cars and too many bad-tempered drivers. It was raining, and everything was unexpectedly seedy. There was no countryside worth mentioning – only wastelands surrounded by industrial sites and half-built housing estates.

I glanced at Keller, who was hunched over the wheel and breathing heavily.

'Do I need a British driving licence?' I said. I knew the answer already; I was just trying to crack Keller's silence. People usually like it when you appeal to their knowledge.

He kept his eyes on the road. 'Non-British and international licences are valid for a year's continuous driving. After that, you need a British one.' He ran the tip of his tongue along his upper lip and then spiced the information with a hint of malice: 'But that won't affect you, of course.'

'Why not?' I said innocently. He must have known my posting could last more than a year.

'I won't talk while I drive, if you don't mind,' he said. 'It ruins my concentration.'

As we got into London itself, the flow of cars congealed into a traffic jam. It was a city of contrasts: bright, modern shopfronts tacked on to ageing façades; old buildings huddled next to new ones; sedate double-decker buses surrounded by swarms of squat black taxis; white people jostling blacks, Asians and Chinese; and everywhere there was litter. I suppose it was colourful, compared with Berlin, and the shops were certainly fuller; but nothing was clean, nothing was uncrowded. The city was smothering itself with rubbish and people and cars.

Keller swung the VW off the main road and took us into a series of side streets. The shops and offices gave way to houses and blocks of flats. The houses grew larger until we turned into a square lined with stuccoed terraces on a palatial scale.

'London,' Keller said in English. 'Flower of cities all.'

'What?'

He reddened. 'That's how one of their poets described it. Makes you want to laugh, doesn't it?'

*

Margarete Klose was a short woman who had a tall room on the second floor of the Embassy. Two huge windows overlooked the square. She had a beechwood desk and a photograph of the President of the GDR, just like Bochmann had. Unlike Bochmann, she gave no sign that she was pleased to see me.

'Klose,' she announced as I was shown in. 'State Security.'

Just like that — no social chit-chat, no indication of her rank or responsibilities, and certainly no offer of coffee. Her voice was low-pitched and full of resonance; it didn't fit her appearance. She was a very thin woman in her fifties, with wispy grey hair that trailed down to her collar. She looked like a social worker I once knew: a woman who spent her life reprimanding feckless mothers.

'Herold,' I said, not to be outdone. 'Ministry of Foreign Trade.'

'Sit down,' she ordered. 'I want to stress from the start that you are in a very delicate position.'

'I'm sorry?'

'Any citizen from the GDR who finds himself in the West,' she said, 'has certain responsibilities. You must avoid social contacts unless they have a professional purpose. You must be always on your guard against journalists. You must rigorously obey the regulations of the host country. You must immediately report any suspicious contacts or incidents to my section.'

I nodded. I'd heard this lecture, almost word for word, from her colleagues in Berlin. My eyes wandered around the room. The only personal item I could see was a small, silver frame on the desk; presumably it contained a photograph. Surely not a boyfriend. A father? A niece? It was difficult to imagine Fräulein Klose having a private life or even a past.

'But your case,' she went on after a short pause, 'is even more sensitive. For one thing, you don't enjoy diplomatic status, which makes you correspondingly more vulnerable.'

'Yes, Fräulein,' I said.

'And for another, the very nature of your job requires you to operate by yourself for much of the time.' She glared at me. 'I advised against that, I may say. I would have preferred the Committee to send a team rather than a single person.'

'But surely, the trade section will – '

'And thirdly,' she interrupted, 'there's the matter of your brother.'

'What about him?'

'The British police wish to interview you.'

I frowned. No one in Berlin had mentioned this. At this stage I wasn't really worried: all I felt was a flicker of distaste. After all, maybe this was standard procedure. But as far as I was concerned Wolfgang's death was in the past. It was something I wanted to forget.

'How can I help them?' I said. 'What's it all about?'

She ignored the question. 'It's extremely tiresome. You are under no obligation to talk to them, but in the circumstances I think it would be advisable.'

'I don't understand this.'

She shrugged, uninterested in my state of mind. 'I'll arrange the meeting, and naturally I'll be there too.'

'"In the circumstances", you said.' I hesitated. 'Are you saying there was something wrong about my brother's death?'

For a few seconds she played with the thin gold ring on the third finger of her right hand. Her mother's

58

wedding band? Her sallow skin was drawn tightly across the bones of her face. They were good bones: at one time she might have been pretty, even beautiful. I had the impression that she didn't like me. It was more than the usual disdain an official develops towards those he – or in this case she – has to deal with. And it wasn't just the fact that I was the innocent cause of her being in an awkward situation. No, there was a personal element, too. It was me she didn't like, not what I represented.

'We will discuss all that at the proper time,' she said at last. 'Goodbye, Herr Herold.'

Keller was waiting for me downstairs. He was smoking a cigarette in a self-conscious way that made me realize how young he was. He was also reading a book. It was *The Waste Land*.

'You like English poetry?' I said.

He shut the book with a snap and stood up. 'I read it because it exposes their cultural poverty.'

His skin was fair, almost translucent – the sort that cruelly exposes its owner's freckles and flushes. Keller was flushing now, and I felt sorry for him. It seemed a shame that he couldn't even read poetry without having to justify it in terms of the socialist struggle against the imperialists.

We got back into the car and he drove me, again in silence, across the city and out to Ealing. He showed me the outside of the Broadway building and told me to report there at 8.30 in the morning.

The flat they had assigned to me was about half a kilometre away in a road lined with trees. It was part of a semi-detached house with a bow window on the ground floor; the walls were covered with pebbledash and had recently been painted white. Keller reversed onto the concrete hardstanding that covered what had once been the front garden.

He didn't help me get my cases from the boot. When I joined him in the little porch, he jerked his thumb at the three bell-pushes on the right of the door.

'The whole house belongs to the Embassy. It's divided into three flats. You're on the top floor. There's an intercom, so you can unlock this door from inside the flat.'

I glanced at the illuminated labels beside the bells: *Stern – Teichler – Herold.*

'Someone hasn't wasted time,' I said. 'Is that to make me feel at home?'

'Eh?' Keller's eyes flicked from the labels to my face and then down to the ground. 'Let me take one of those cases.'

He unlocked the front door and led me down a narrow hall and up the communal stairs. I couldn't see his expression, of course, but I could see the back of his neck. He was blushing again. At the top of the stairs was the door to the flat. Keller had difficulty getting the key in the lock.

'This was my brother's flat, wasn't it?' I said.

'As a matter of fact, yes.' He got the door open at last and plunged inside. 'I thought someone would have told you.'

I followed him in. The door gave on to a minuscule hall with three more doors opening off it. The place smelled stuffy and slightly sweet. I thought I caught a whiff of the aftershave Wolfgang had used.

'Bedroom on the right,' Keller said, 'bathroom straight ahead. Living room here.'

He opened the third door. The living room was larger than the whole of my flat in Schwerin. It had a sloping ceiling and a dormer window. One corner had been partitioned off to form a rudimentary kitchen where you could cook the sort of meals that come in tins and packets. It was sparsely furnished with what I later realized were rejects from the Broadway building. And in the middle of the carpet, stacked on top of each other in descending order of size, were Wolfgang's three suitcases.

Keller shifted his weight from one foot to the other and jingled the two keys. 'There's an inventory on the table. Personnel thought they might as well leave the checking to you. In the circumstances it seemed best, you know. Since he was your brother. Then the Embassy will have the stuff shipped back home. To the – ah – widow.'

I nodded. 'What about food?'

He calmed down immediately. 'You'll find essentials in the refrigerator and in the cupboard beside it. You shouldn't need to go out this evening. But if you do, there are a few shops round the block, and one of them stays open late. Just turn right out of the house, and take the next two rights. Or you could ask the Sterns or Karl Teichler.'

'That seems clear enough.'

'Right, I'll leave you to it.' Keller edged towards the door. 'I'll see you tomorrow, I expect,' he added without much enthusiasm. 'At Broadway.'

'Just a minute,' I said, holding out my hand.

He looked – first at my hand, then at my face. Behind the glasses his eyes were huge and bewildered.

'Shouldn't you leave me the keys?' I said.

It was a bad start.

In their very different ways, neither Keller nor Klose

had done much to make me feel welcome. What I had seen of London was hardly calculated to raise my spirits. The flat didn't feel like mine: it belonged to the pile of suitcases in the middle of the living room. Worst of all were the doubts that Klose had sown about Wolfgang's death.

I didn't know precisely how he had died. I didn't want to. I wanted the whole business to be over and done with.

It took me no more than a minute to survey my new home. The living room window looked through two rows of leafless lime trees to a house almost identical to the one I was in. It was growing dark so I drew the curtains. The bathroom had been designed with midgets in mind but at least it was clean. The boxlike bedroom had a single bed to encourage celibacy and a window that looked down an unkempt back garden to a high fence; on the other side of the fence was a railway line, just like at home.

I unpacked my bags, which didn't take long. My clothes filled less than a quarter of the built-in ward-robe in the bedroom. In the kitchen area, I found some herbal teabags in the cupboard. While the kettle was boiling I looked at Wolfgang's suitcases and thought I might as well get the job out of the way.

Possessions seem curiously forlorn when their owner is dead. I went through each case in turn, checking off items on the inventory. *Pairs of Socks, 8. Toothbrush, 1.* Everything was clean and neatly folded. I wondered who had done the packing. Not the personnel section: the sudden death of one of our citizens would be a matter for Klose's department. Probably Fräulein Klose had delegated the job to one of her minions. Her attitude towards me might have been due to their finding something in the flat that shouldn't have been there. Knowing Wolfgang, I thought it possible but unlikely; he had been too shrewd to make silly mistakes. But he might conceivably have slipped up: maybe there had been a wad of sterling under the mattress or a carton of electronic gadgets in the wardrobe.

It was a job I didn't want to do, but I did it slowly and meticulously. I suppose it was a way of saying goodbye. What would Anna do with the *Pairs of Socks, 8. Toothbrush, 1*? The ancient cultures had the right idea when they buried a person's belongings alongside him. When I'd finished I stored the cases in the wardrobe. They were no longer anything to do with me.

The evening stretched before me, an empty space I didn't know how to fill. I wasn't hungry. I wasn't sleepy. I would have liked to talk to someone but I didn't want the effort of introducing myself to my neighbours downstairs. Instead I let myself wallow in self-pity, thinking that the West wasn't glamorous and exciting: it was boring and lonely.

So I sat at the table, sipping herbal tea and opening the pile of mail that someone had left. People wanted to sell me things: insurance, groceries and a variety of services which ranged from building me an extension to cleaning my car. Other people wanted me to do things for them: attend the local church, write to an MP, or help them to save the whale. The letters at least had the charm of novelty: we don't have junk mail in the GDR.

Then there was a buzzing noise.

It was so unexpected that I knocked over the mug. The buzzing stopped. My first thought was the phone. I picked up the handset but the line was dead. There was another buzz. I realized it must be the entry phone in the hall.

I rushed out there, and fumbled with the unfamiliar buttons. 'Yes?' I said into the plastic grille. There was no answer. I shouted: 'Who is it?' Then I realized I was still pressing a button I should have released. I felt hot, embarrassed and stupid.

A man's voice suddenly filled the hall. 'Mr Peisker?'

'I'm afraid you've got the wrong address.'

'I don't think so, Mr Peisker. Or shall I call you Mr Herold? It's all one to me.'

'What's this about?'

'I think you know. Why don't you come down, Mr Herold? I expect you'd prefer it that way. Perhaps you'd like to buy me a drink.'

The man who was waiting in the porch did an odd thing as soon as I opened the door. He put a finger to his lips in a theatrical invitation to keep quiet.

'Mr Herold?' he said uncertainly.

'Yes. I think you might have been expecting my brother.'

'I can see the resemblance.' He hesitated, chewing his lower lip. Then he backed out of the porch and gestured for me to follow.

Pulling on my overcoat, I joined him on the pavement. I had the feeling that this was better handled by me than by Walter Keller or Fräulein Klose. Besides, I had nothing else to do.

The road was almost deserted. The rain had tailed off to a fine drizzle. The streetlights were on. A couple of cars swished by, spray hissing up from their tyres. It wasn't as cold as Berlin had been.

'Where is he? Your brother, I mean?'

64

'He's dead.'

The man swung round and stared at me. He was wearing a beige mackintosh and a flat tweed cap. 'Are you having me on?'

'Why should I bother?'

'I can think of one reason.'

'I'll buy you that drink,' I said, 'and you can tell me what it is.'

We walked there in silence. I wasn't worried: the man didn't smell like a cop; he smelt like one of Wolfgang's pieces of private enterprise. He steered me round two corners and there, just past the shops that Keller had mentioned, was a pub called the Admiral Nelson. It was a new brick building, with a lot of cars parked on the forecourt. The saloon bar had a nautical décor that relied heavily on anchors, fishing nets and pictures of men-of-war under full sail.

'Ghastly,' my companion said; I think he was referring to the décor. 'A pint of best, please.'

'Best what?'

'Eh?' He looked shocked. 'Best bitter – beer, you know. I'll wait there.'

He nodded towards a table by the jukebox. I was about to ask if we could find somewhere quieter when it occurred to me that perhaps he wanted the noise, for the same reason that he had preferred not to come up to the flat. A moment later, as I was ordering the drinks, it struck me that the secrecy might be as much for my sake as for his.

While I waited for the change, I glanced surreptitiously at him: he was about my age or perhaps a little older; he had a thin, olive-skinned face with high cheekbones; and he was wearing a charcoal grey suit. The raincoat, neatly folded, was on the chair beside him with the cap on top. To me he looked highly respectable, but I was no judge of respectability in this country. When I rejoined him he was smoking a cigarette and tapping his foot to an old Beatles song.

'Cheers,' he said, and swallowed a third of his beer.

I sipped and winced.

'You should have had lager,' he said. 'Your brother always did.'

'What was your connection with him?'

He dug a wallet out of his jacket, fished out a card and laid it on the table between us. *Alan Snape,* it said. *Private Investigations. Personal and Company. Criminal and Civil Cases. Confidential – Reliable – Economic.*

'You're his brother?' Snape said. 'And you really didn't know about this?'

'I've only been in England for a few hours. I hadn't seen or heard from him for months.'

'What happened to him?'

'He was burned to death,' I said. 'It was an accident. I'm here because they gave me his job.'

'You *are* East German, aren't you? Like he was?'

I nodded.

'He said he came from West Germany, that his name was Franz Peisker. Now why would he want to do that?'

'I expect he had his reasons.'

'For example?' Snape ground out his cigarette and answered his own question: 'He thought your Embassy might not approve. He wouldn't give me an address – said he was a salesman; he wasn't sure of his itinerary. Don't phone us, we'll phone you. That always makes me suspicious. And I often find it pays to be curious, especially with foreign clients.'

'So you followed him home one night?'

'Of course. And I checked with the rating authority afterwards. That house is owned by a property company that often fronts for the GDR. I pass the place almost every night on my way here. I saw there was a light on in the top flat, so I rang the bell.'

'Why did you think I was having you on? About him being dead?'

'It's a question of money, Mr Herold. I've known clients of mine go to absurd lengths, just to avoid paying me a few pounds. Some of them were very rich men.'

'Have you had one who burned himself to death before?'

I spoke harshly, and he sat up as though I had slapped him.

'Yes – well, if that's true, obviously I've done him an injustice.'

'I'm sure you can check it,' I said. 'It must have been mentioned in the papers, even if it was only a local one. Or you could – '

'But you'll agree that the circumstances were suspicious. He *had* lied to me. And there's still the matter of my bill. What do you advise me to do? It's not a large sum of money. I could contact the Embassy, I suppose; no doubt they could arrange for me to make a claim on your brother's estate. Eventually. Perhaps we should have another drink while we discuss the options.'

The threat was so gently presented that it took me a few seconds to recognize it for what it was. I pushed back my chair and stood up. From this vantage point I could see a bald patch half-concealed by thick black hair. He looked up at me, smiling. A small businessman,

I thought, just trying to scratch a living: and good luck to him.

He pushed his empty glass towards me. 'They'll use it again,' he said helpfully. 'Saves their washing-up. Why don't you try Foster's? That's what your brother drank.'

I had to wait several minutes to be served. It gave me time to think. *Foster's.* Snape was blackmailing me in such a low-key way that it seemed almost inoffensive. Pay me, he was saying, or I'll make trouble for you. If Klose and Keller were in any way representative, my colleagues in London would be only too glad if Snape got in touch with them. I wondered if it could be some sort of trick. I was a stranger here, and vulnerable. But I could hardly afford to call his bluff.

'Most of the lager's terrible,' Wolfgang had said on that last evening we spent together. 'Foster's is all right. It comes from Australia of all places.'

When I got back to our table, Snape was halfway through another cigarette. I swallowed a mouthful of Foster's. It was a huge relief after the best bitter. If he was bluffing, he had certainly done his preparation thoroughly.

'How much?' I said.

'It's only forty-five pounds,' he said. 'Give or take a few pence. Here – have a look.' He produced a typed invoice with a sheaf of receipted bills stapled to the top lefthand corner. 'As you see, your brother paid quite a substantial deposit. In cash. The money outstanding mainly represents my expenses.'

I laid my hand on the invoice but did not pick it up. 'Expenses for what?'

Snape looked disappointed in me. 'I'm afraid that's confidential. Part of our code of practice, you know.

An investigator's relationship with his client is strictly – '

'I can't pay you all at once,' I said. 'Some now, the rest next week. But first you answer my question.'

The money would have to come out of my subsistence allowance, which was paid weekly in sterling. I couldn't touch my salary – it was trickling into my bank account in Schwerin. Besides, no Westerner in his right mind would accept East German marks.

Snape sighed. If he wanted his money, he must know that I was his only hope. The Embassy would smother his claim in bureaucracy, even supposing it were allowed.

'After all,' I said, 'you know you can trust me.'

His mouth twisted in what was almost a grin. 'Fair enough. I suppose I could say you're the legitimate heir of my client. Or at least his representative. I'll give you a receipt, of course.'

I almost laughed. Instead I took out my wallet and passed him two ten-pound notes and a five. Snape wrote a receipt with a gold fountain pen.

'I must apologize,' he said, 'for doubting your brother.'

'It was perfectly natural.'

'And now – the little enquiry he wished me to undertake. You'll appreciate why I thought you would know about it. It concerned a relative, you see. It was quite a little challenge. He thought she lived in the West but didn't know where. He knew her maiden name but nothing else, nothing for certain, not even her date of birth.'

We had no relatives who lived in the West. Wolfgang and I had no relatives at all except Great-aunt Luise.

'What was her name?' I asked.

'Wilhelmina von Doenecke.' Snape's High German pronunciation was perfect. 'Her married name is Mrs Issler, 43B Rangoon Road, NW6.'

The U-Bahn is cheap and clean, though often crowded. The London Underground is expensive and dirty. 'Best avoided,' I'd been told at one of my briefings, 'in the rush hours.'

I would have phoned if I could. But the number wasn't in the directory at the flat. If Mrs Issler had a phone, she preferred to keep the number to herself. I found a street atlas and looked up Rangoon Road. It was too far to walk. I couldn't afford a taxi and I didn't know how the bus system worked. But according to the map in the atlas, the Underground could get me there by a roundabout but reasonably straightforward route. So I walked to the station at Ealing Broadway and took the Central Line to Bond Street, where I changed on to the Jubilee Line. It sounds simple but it wasn't: London's underground railway is designed to confuse foreign visitors.

By now it was the middle of the evening. There were advertisements everywhere; at least they gave one something to read. My fellow passengers kept themselves to themselves. The only exception was a party of drunken youths who got on at Notting Hill Gate and ran whooping along the carriage. Everyone pretended that nothing had happened. Suddenly I felt homesick; such behaviour would not be tolerated in the GDR.

On the northbound platform of the Jubilee Line, a woman was begging. She wore a light summer dress and plastic sandals. Her legs were bare. In one hand she carried a plastic bag; with the other she tried to restrain two children, aged perhaps three and five.

Against my will, I watched her as she came closer. I think she hated us all, the ones who gave more than those who didn't.

'Can you spare the price of a cup of tea?' she said, over and over again as she passed along the line of passengers. Most of them couldn't. 'God bless you,' she muttered if someone gave her money. She didn't look at them and they didn't look at her. The children had listless, grimy faces, smeared with mucus around the mouths.

'Typical,' said a man in a blue overcoat who was standing beside me. 'No, I won't give you a penny.'

I put twenty pence in the outstretched palm and received a blessing I didn't want.

'You shouldn't encourage them,' the man said. His face was red and, as he went on, the colour darkened to purple. 'Spongers on the state. She'll be getting Supplementary Benefit. She's just collecting enough money to get drunk on. Using the children to persuade the gullible to part with their money. Oldest trick in the book. Damn it, she's probably earning more than I am. You know what I'd do to people like that if . . .'

The train came in, drowning his words.

According to the street atlas, West Hampstead was the nearest Underground station to Rangoon Road. The walk took me about ten minutes, plenty of time to wonder if I were making a fool of myself. I had come here on impulse, for much the same reasons as I'd had that drink with Snape: if Wolfgang had left any loose ends in the private sector, I wanted to tidy them up rather than leave them for Klose to find; and the flat in Ealing was so dreary that I wanted to get away. I suppose there was a third reason: I was so keyed up that any activity was better than none.

71

Of course, Mrs Issler might not be there; and if she were, she might not want to talk to me. I admit I was puzzled, even then. I could understand Great-aunt Luise wanting, for some sentimental reason, to contact a surviving descendant of her employers. Wolfgang probably told Snape he was a relative of the von Doeneckes to avoid unnecessary explanation. But why hadn't he mentioned it to me? Similarly, when I visited Great-aunt Luise and she mistook me for my brother, you would have expected her to have said something about Wilhelmina von Doenecke. But that line of reasoning led to an absurd conclusion: that Wolfgang had his own reasons for tracing her. No, it was more likely that Great-aunt Luise was so confused that she had simply forgotten all about it, and Wolfgang hadn't had time to tell me about it.

Rangoon Road was a side street near a cemetery. Most of it was lined with old redbrick houses. Judging by the cars outside, this was a prosperous area. Number 43B was on a corner near the end, where a narrow alley joined the road. It was smaller than its neighbours and looked as if it had originally been built for another purpose – as a coachhouse or workshop, perhaps. The windows at the side overlooked the cemetery.

There was a light above the door and more lights behind the curtained windows of the ground floor. It was quiet at this end of the road and I could hear raised voices inside the house. Probably the television. I rang the doorbell. I noticed a spyhole in the door, just below the level of my eyes.

The door opened a few inches; it was on a chain.

'What do you want?'

It was a woman's voice and it surprised me twice over: the voice was young, and subconsciously – if illogically — I had expected a von Doenecke to be old, like Great-aunt Luise; second, the voice had an American accent.

'My name's Herold. I'm looking for Mrs Issler. I believe her maiden name was Wilhelmina von Doenecke.'

'Tell him to come back later,' a man's voice, also American, shouted from somewhere in the house. 'We haven't finished.'

'If it's inconvenient,' I said, 'I could — '

'No, come in,' the woman said bitterly. 'Why not?'

The chain rattled and the door swung open. The hall was dimly lit and empty of furniture. The woman had short, dark hair and a face that was drained of colour. She was slender and almost as tall as me.

'I'm sorry to bother you,' I began. 'I would have phoned, but — '

'Get your ass out of here. Now.'

A man was standing in the doorway at the end of the hall. He had a bottle in his hand. The way he held it made it into an offensive weapon.

The woman swung round. 'It's none of your business, Mike. Not any more. Remember?'

He advanced into the hall, slapping the bottle against the palm of his free hand. He was a big man in his forties, smartly dressed in a suit and tie; once he had carried a lot of muscle but now he was running to seed.

'It is so,' he said. 'Just for a while.' He looked at me. 'Now get going.'

'No,' she said. 'He's staying. You're the one who's going.'

He wrapped his arm around her neck and squeezed her against him. 'You never learn, honey, do you?'

She struggled against him, trying to stamp on his

feet and push herself away. He just laughed and told me to shut the door behind me. The struggle was so unequal it seemed obscene: like the prosperous citizen and the beggar at Bond Street.

I said, 'I think you'd better let go of her first.'

He did let go – pushing her against the wall. 'All *right*,' he said, almost gleefully. Then he came for me. The bottle swung in his hand and his feet thudded on the bare floorboards. Suddenly everything was very simple.

I hadn't hit anyone since I'd done my national service in the People's Army and I didn't want to do so now. I threw up my arm just in time and twisted away. The blow connected with the arm just above the elbow. My movement deflected most of the force of the attack. He wasn't prepared for the lack of impact. The bottle slipped from his fingers, fell to the floor and shattered. A red stain spread over the single rug just inside the door. It smelled sweet.

'Ah, Jesus,' Mike said.

So he threw a punch at me and hit the wall instead. Suddenly the fight went out of him. He just stood there, nursing his hand and swaying.

'You'd better go, Mike,' the woman said. 'Or I'll call the cops. I mean it.'

He frowned at her – not angrily but in bewilderment, as if he were trying to work out how he had got himself into this situation. She stepped past him and opened the door. He staggered outside. The cold air braced him. He turned back.

'This isn't the end, sweetheart,' he said. 'Just the beginning. I'll be back. I'll be – '

She shut the door on him, double-locked it and threw the bolts across. I bent down and gathered some of the fragments of glass. They were sticky. According to the label, the bottle had contained fifteen-year-old port.

'Leave it,' she said. 'I'll do it later. Sorry about Mike. I guess I owe you a cup of coffee or something.'

'Thank you,' I said. My hands were full of broken glass. 'Where shall I put this?'

'There's a garbage can in the kitchen.' She moved down the hall towards a door right at the end. There was something so eerily controlled about her that I wondered if she were drunk, too. Then she stopped by the stairs. 'What did you say your name was?'

'Gerhard Herold. Are you Mrs Issler?'

'No,' she said. 'My name's Elizabeth Allanton.'

'But Mrs Issler does live here, doesn't she?'

'She used to.'

'Has she moved? Where?'

Elizabeth Allanton sat down suddenly on the stairs. 'Some punk stuck a knife in her last night. She's dead.'

FOUR

Great-aunt Luise used to quote an English proverb: *East or west, home is best.* In the last hour I had found three arguments in favour of the GDR: the gang of teenagers on the train, the woman and her two children at Bond Street, and what a punk had done to Mrs Issler. A police state has its virtues.

'Aunt Willy was walking back from the bus stop,' Elizabeth Allanton said. 'The police think he was standing in a doorway and just grabbed her as she passed.'

'Why?'

'How do I know? Money, I guess. He took her purse. A junkie or something.'

'You said "he". Does that mean –?'

'It means it's statistically likely it was a man,' she said wearily. 'That's all. There were no witnesses as far as they know. They're not going to catch him. I don't think they're even trying.'

'I'm sorry,' I said.

She looked up at me; her face was slightly puzzled, as if she were wondering about the purpose of my questions or calculating the value of my sympathy. She was still sitting at the foot of the stairs. In this light her eyes seemed green; and they had very long lashes. She had a straight nose, arched eyebrows and high cheekbones with the suggestion of hollows beneath: the face was precise in all its details, like a portrait on a coin. She wasn't exactly pretty. Rather better than that.

'I'll fix that coffee.'

'I can do without,' I said.

But she struggled to her feet. Carrying the fragments of glass, I followed her into a bleak little kitchen, the sort that belongs to someone who doesn't have much interest in cooking. I threw the glass into a blue plastic bin by the back door. Elizabeth switched on an electric kettle and opened several cupboard doors beneath the counter. She had to think about where the cups and saucers were, and it took her a while to come up with a new jar of instant coffee. This wasn't her kitchen.

'So you don't actually live with your aunt?'

'She's not my aunt,' Elizabeth said. 'She was a friend of my parents. I can't find the sugar. Do you want some?'

I shook my head.

'And we're out of milk.'

'It doesn't matter. Do you know where I can find a dustpan and brush?'

'Try the cupboard under the sink. But there's no need for you to do it.'

While the kettle was coming to the boil, I swept up the rest of the glass and wiped the rug with a cloth. The wine was going to leave a stain.

She spooned coffee into the cups and poured in the water. 'Did you know her?'

'No. But I think my great-aunt used to work for her family, in Germany before the war. My brother was over here and decided to trace her. I was hoping Mrs Issler could tell me why.'

'Can't you ask him?'

'He's dead, too.'

She looked sharply at me but all she said was: 'Let's go in the living room.'

This was a thin room that ran from the front to the back of the house. There were two worn Persian rugs on the grey carpet and three armchairs that had seen better days. A glass of port, half full, stood on the shelf above the gas fire. In the alcoves on either side were bookshelves of unpainted pine. Mrs Issler had not left much clutter behind her.

Elizabeth squatted on the rug by the fire. 'Mike's my husband,' she said, holding out her hands to the warmth. 'My almost ex-husband.'

'It's none of my business.'

I sat down in one of the chairs. It creaked beneath my weight.

'He followed me here from New York,' she went on. 'But not because he wants to stop the divorce. As far as he's concerned, it's purely a business trip. He always gets aggressive when he has a few drinks.'

'A lot of people do,' I said gently. She was talking jerkily and slurring the words together. I thought she needed to go to bed with a couple of pills for company, and stay there for about twelve hours. 'You don't have to explain.'

'I've got to get away from here. Not just because Mike's found me. Aunt Willy's landlord wants me out. He lives in the house next door. She didn't own this place, you know, just rented it. Didn't own very much. Kind of weird, when you think how she grew up. All that money. All those servants and houses and rolling acres. Not that she seemed to miss them. The world well lost for Uncle Solly. You know, I envied her that. I'm talking too much.'

'It's the shock,' I said. 'What are you going to do?'

'Find somewhere to live. And then a job.'

'What sort of job?'

'I used to . . .' Then she changed her mind. 'I'll take anything. I'm not picky.'

We sat there in silence for about half a minute, sipping our coffee. She was wearing a jersey and an old pair of jeans. She was probably about thirty but she looked much younger.

'Did Mrs Issler say anything about my brother?' I asked. 'Or about someone called Peisker?'

'No. But maybe she hadn't gotten round to it. I only flew in from the States the evening before she died.'

Another silence. She stared at the fire and I stared at her. *My brother traced Mrs Issler, and now they're both dead. Do you believe in coincidence?*

'I'd better go,' I said. 'I think you need some sleep.'

'Thank you – for everything.'

I stood up and took a deep breath. 'I'd like to ask you some more about Mrs Issler. Will you have dinner with me sometime?'

She shrugged. 'Everything's kind of fluid at present. I don't know where I'll be. Can I call you?'

Some of Snape's caution had rubbed off on me. The phone at the flat might be tapped. 'It could be awkward,' I said.

'Why? Are you married?'

'No.' I knew she had no reason to believe me.

'There's a restaurant near the Underground station,' she said. 'It's called Ruffles, I think. How about Wednesday evening at seven-thirty?'

'I'll try and be there.'

'You don't sound very certain.'

'I wish I could be.'

'Okay. But what happens if you can't make it?'

'Phone the restaurant beforehand. I'll book a table if I can be there.'

'What was your name?'

'Gerhard Herold.'

She wrinkled her face, half-apologizing for forgetting it. 'And how about if I'm the one that can't make it?'

'I'll take a chance on that.' I thought quickly. 'But if it happens, maybe I could write to you and suggest another time. Is there anywhere that would hold mail for you?'

'Write me care of American Express in Piccadilly. Elizabeth Allanton.' She spelled the surname for me.

A moment later I was walking down Rangoon Road. It was natural to think of her and what we had said. I told myself that we had something in common: grief for the dead. Nothing more, nothing less.

Elizabeth Allanton was still on my mind as I fell asleep. One way or another, she's stayed there ever since.

On Tuesday I had my first business appointment. The restaurant was in Cork Street, Mayfair. I was early but my host had got there first.

Sebastian Rownall, the importer whom Wolfgang had chosen, had a face like a partly-inflated football. He bustled up to me as I was checking in my overcoat.

'Gerhard! I'd recognize you anywhere – so like your brother. You don't mind if I call you Gerhard? I'm Seb. Damn silly name, but there you are.'

He pushed a plump little hand towards me. Then he swept me down the restaurant to a table at the back. The place was called Glass and it lived up to its name.

The walls were covered with mirror tiles. The table tops and the bar counter were made of clear glass. The rest of the furniture relied heavily on chrome and black leather.

'I'm delighted they gave you the job. Keeping it in the family, eh? Would you like a drink before we order?' He kept up the flow while we ordered both the drinks and the meal. The lavishness of the menu shocked me and so did the prices. All the time he was studying me, and I suppose I was studying him. A lot depended on how well we could work together.

'I was so sorry about Wolfgang,' he said when the waitress had gone. 'And because of the circumstances I naturally feel guilty – no, not guilty, that's the wrong word: responsible, to some degree.'

He screwed up his face and looked so miserable I wanted to pat him. I also wanted to know what he meant about the 'circumstances'. But before I could ask him, he rushed on to another subject.

'You went to Broadway this morning, I presume? How did you find them?'

'Much as I'd expected,' I said.

'Oh, dear.' Rownall understood at once. 'I hoped they might have come round a little by now.'

Keller had introduced me to the rest of the trade section. My reception there had been more than chilly: it had been a few degrees below zero. If Wolfgang had failed to charm them, there wasn't much I could do. I'd heard a lot of talk about the effectiveness of our existing export system and – in general terms – the folly of pursuing novelty for its own sake.

'Two of the typists were quite pleased to see me,' I said, feeling that I might as well point out the bright side.

'They're so conservative,' Rownall said. 'Still, with Herr Bochmann and the Committee behind us, there's not much they can do.'

Except be obstructive, I thought. Aloud I said: 'I gather the first shipment has arrived.'

He cheered up at once. 'It's at the warehouse. I've got buyers for ninety per cent of the stuff already. Mainly wholesalers, but one or two of the big retailers are buying direct. The dolls' layettes are proving very popular — that's something we need to discuss when we get back to the office. If you could persuade them to modify the packaging, I think we could sell almost twice as many.'

'Would you expect an increased discount?'

'Well, naturally there would be room for adjustment. There's a strong argument for lowering the unit cost to the wholesaler. In the end it's a question of retail level. The Taiwanese have got a very attractive layette on the market and they're trying to undercut us. It's our only real competitor at present. If we can improve the artwork on the packaging *and* lower the price, they won't stand a chance.'

He was probably right. This was one of the situations that the new system had been designed to cope with. It gave us two advantages over the old. We had cut out a couple of the middlemen, in the shape of the Ministry's export organization and the British company that handled most of our exports to the UK; this gave us more room to manoeuvre with prices because there were fewer people requiring a cut from the profits. Secondly, fewer middlemen meant better communications: I was directly in touch with the manager of the combine that produced the toys.

'I had a phone call from the chief buyer at Morganettas this morning,' Rownall said. 'She's interested in bricks.'

'Well, that's good news.' Morganettas was an American-owned chain with about twenty branches in the UK; all of them were in out-of-town locations and organized on supermarket lines. 'But aren't bricks a little old-fashioned for them? I thought they went in for battery-operated lasers and that sort of thing.'

Rownall shrugged. 'They believe they've identified a consumer trend towards traditional toys. So they're launching a new line in the autumn. They've recruited a team of tame educationalists to endorse the products: these toys are good for your child's imagination and dexterity skills.'

Bricks were cheap to produce. We used the softwood offcuts from our timber-yards, which kept the cost of raw materials low, and most of the manufacturing process could be left to unskilled labour. Low production costs meant high profits.

'Is it a firm offer?' I asked. 'Do you know the buyer well?'

'She's called Sylvia Carne. Wolfgang and I had lunch with her last month – Sylvia took quite a fancy to him.' He giggled disconcertingly. 'Actually, we all got rather tipsy. On the way back to the Jag, I fell over outside Richmond station. I just lay there like a stranded whale. We were laughing so much it took me about half an hour to get up.'

I tried to match Rownall's jolly smile. His eyes gleamed and there were beads of sweat on his forehead. I wondered if he were halfway drunk now.

'To go back to the deal,' I said. 'Where's the catch?'

He sobered up. 'There are several. Morganettas want

stringent quality controls in line with recent legislation here. They want an exclusive, of course. They are asking for a twenty to twenty-five per cent discount, based on the original quoted price, plus a guarantee that the price won't go up before autumn next year. And they want their own designers to do the artwork for the packaging.'

'It must be a huge order if they think they can get that sort of discount. What about delivery dates?'

'I was coming to that. Delivery dates are to be written into the contract, with a scale of penalties if you're late.'

We talked about the deal for another fifteen minutes; it carried us through the starter and well into the roast duck. It was potentially important not just for itself but as a way of showing the big retailers and wholesalers that we meant business. Western customers had an array of complaints about East German manufacturers: the East Germans, they said, had a fixed idea of the right buying price, and wouldn't take into account the fluctuating retail levels that dominate Western pricing; our deliveries were often late; our packaging was primitive by Western standards; and – worst of all – we were hidebound. The customers failed to realize how many of our problems stemmed from centralized planning, which often forced us to cling to quotas that were unrealistically high for some products and unrealistically low for others. Part of my job was to convince the customers that in future we were going to operate more efficiently.

'I think we can give them what they want,' I said at last. 'I'll check with the combine and Bochmann.'

Rownall nodded vigorously, his mouth full of duck. All his movements were slightly more emphatic than you would have expected; maybe it was a way of compensating for his lack of height.

'Can I ask you about something else?' I pushed my plate away. 'How did Wolfgang die?'

Suddenly he lost his bounce. Still chewing, he stared at me in astonishment. Finally he remembered to swallow.

'You mean they didn't tell you?'

'Only that it was in a fire. An accident.'

He laid down his knife and fork. 'Wolfgang was my guest at the time. That's why I feel responsible. I've got – I *had* – a boat in Suffolk, moored in the Alben estuary. The *Sally-Anne*.'

No wonder Wolfgang had chosen Rownall, a fellow sailing fanatic, as our importer: he had usually managed to find ways of combining business with pleasure.

'She was a gaff-cutter,' he went on, 'over fifty years old; clinker-built. We planned to go down together on the Friday night, and spend the weekend sailing. Sleep on board and, if it got too cold, go to a hotel. But I was delayed – something came up at home. Wolfgang said he'd go on ahead. He'd been there before, you see, in the autumn.'

'Sailing? At this time of year?' I said.

'Winter's a good time. Bit chilly, of course, but on the other hand there's hardly anyone else around. It can be very beautiful.'

In my opinion only a masochist would rate freezing to death on a windy expanse of grey water as a beautiful experience. My brother had accustomed me to the little lunacies of amateur sailors but he had failed to make me understand them.

'I don't suppose you sail?' Rownall said.

I shook my head. 'But he didn't drown, did he?'

Rownall wrenched himself back to what had happened. 'I'd given him a set of keys. I was going to drive down early on the Saturday morning. The mooring's pretty isolated and it was a filthy night, which didn't help. He had a few drinks beforehand at the nearest pub. And then – well, no one's very sure what happened. They thought he must have lit a match . . .'

'On the boat, you mean?'

'I kept fuel on board, you see, and calor gas. Or there could have been vapour in the bilges: that sort of accident's quite common. There was so much wind and the boat was built of wood – went up like a torch. A farmer on the other side of the river saw the blaze: he raised the alarm. But it was too late. By the time the emergency services arrived, there wasn't much left.'

The waitress came up with the menu. Rownall waved her away.

'When did you hear about it?' I asked.

'In the early hours of Saturday morning. The police phoned. I felt so *useless*. At least it must have been quick. And he was happy, by all accounts: that's something. I talked to Tom Burns after the inquest: he's the landlord of the pub. He said Wolfgang was in great form: a bit sloshed, and looking forward to the weekend.'

'Drunk?' Wolfgang had had the hardest head for alcohol of anyone I knew.

'Well, not incapable. A bit merry. Perhaps that made him careless, I don't know. Do you want anything else?'

The waitress was hovering again. I shook my head. Rownall asked for coffee and the bill.

'My insurance on the boat had lapsed. Still, you won't want to hear about my little problems. It was a bloody awful business all round.'

'Nothing we can do about it now,' I said.

'Why do you think they didn't tell you the details?'

'Maybe they thought I wouldn't have come here if I'd known.' I didn't add *to work with you*, but the words were there.

'Were they right?'

'No,' I said. 'I don't think so.' I hesitated. Suddenly I wanted to know, very badly, how close my brother had been to Rownall. I think perhaps I was a little jealous of him. 'Tell me, did he ever mention the Lenné Triangle?'

'I don't think so.' Rownall frowned. 'What is it?'

'It's a patch of land in Berlin,' I said. 'It doesn't matter. I just wondered. What's the plan now? Back to your office?'

'If you can spare the time.' He seized on the change of subject with relief. 'There are some figures I'd like to show you. And we ought to have a chat about the fair: the British International Toy and Hobby Fair; it's next week, and I thought you'd want to go. Size up the competition, as it were.'

Rownall paid the bill and we took a taxi to his office, which was miles away in Finchley, beyond the North Circular. I was expecting the sort of accommodation that businessmen have in drama series on West German TV: smoked glass, wall-to-wall computer terminals, a flock of alluring secretaries and a small forest of potted plants. Rownall himself, with his trim suit and his aura of good living, reinforced the expectation. In fact he had two rooms above a down-at-heel shop that sold electrical appliances. There were grey steel filing cabinets, two scuffed desks and half a dozen hard chairs. It looked as if someone had furnished the place on a tight budget about thirty years before.

'Sorry about the mess,' Rownall said. 'My secretary left me in the lurch on Friday and I haven't found a replacement yet. And Suzy wasn't the tidiest of persons at the best of times.' He swept a jumble of catalogues and invoices off one of the chairs and dumped them on an in-tray that was already overcrowded. 'Do sit down. Do you mind if I check the answering machine?'

There was an oil painting of a clipper on the wall opposite the window. On the desk were two photographs. One was of a boy, perhaps two years old, sitting on some stone steps at the end of a terrace. The other was a studio shot of a blonde with slanting eyes and one of those misleadingly waiflike faces.

Rownall skipped through the tape. Most of the calls seemed to be from a man called Toughton, who sounded increasingly anxious to get hold of Rownall.

'Is this your daughter?' I asked when he had finished.

'My wife, actually.' His face lit up with pride, and the glow intensified as he picked up the photo of the boy. 'And that's David.'

Someone knocked on the outer door. Before Rownall had time to answer, the handle turned and a burly man strode into the office as if he had a right to be there.

'I was just about to call you,' Rownall said loudly. 'You've come at a good moment.' He turned to me. 'Gerhard, this is John Toughton, who manages the warehouse we use. John, this is Herr Gerhard Herold, who's come to replace his brother.'

Toughton nodded curtly in my direction but didn't offer to shake hands. He had short, curly hair and a broken nose. 'We need to talk,' he said to Rownall.

'Of course we do, John. Gerhard, don't think me rude but would you mind waiting here? Just a tiresome little admin problem. We won't be long, I promise.'

'Do you mind if I use the phone?' I said.

'Be my guest.'

He shut the door between the two rooms. I heard their voices in the outer office. I couldn't distinguish the words but Toughton had a grievance and Rownall was soothing him. It was none of my business. I wasn't sure if Rownall rented space at the warehouse or actually owned it. Whatever the problem was, it was nothing to do with me.

I sat down at the desk, looked up the number for Ruffles and booked a table for tomorrow evening. They were still talking away next door. I thought I would use the interval to make a few notes about my conversation with Rownall; I had to get reports off to Bochmann and the manager of the combine by the end of the day. Among the clutter in front of me I found a pencil and a spiral-bound shorthand notebook.

The pad was open at a blank page. I picked up the pencil and yawned. It had been a heavy meal, by my standards, and I wasn't used to drinking at lunchtime. Instead of making notes I thought about Elizabeth Allanton. I knew I was being foolish. Trying to get information out of her was risky enough; hoping for anything else was like getting down on my knees and begging for trouble.

While my mind was uselessly engaged, my hand was otherwise occupied. I am a compulsive doodler. Generally I start off by shading an area of the paper. Then I look at it and create an outline to match the shading. Usually the doodle turns into a four-legged creature with a vague resemblance to an elephant.

This time I didn't get as far as the elephant. When I glanced down at the paper, I shivered. Suddenly I was no longer sleepy. The palms of my hands were clammy.

When someone presses hard, perhaps with a Biro, as he writes, an impression of his words is often indented on the sheet beneath. If you shade over the indentations with a pencil, the words appear in a pale grey against the darker grey of the shading.

Some of the used sheets of the pad had not been torn off but simply turned over. I leafed through them. The one immediately in front of my doodle was the draft of a letter to the managing director of a wholesalers that specialized in toys and fancy goods. It was dated last Thursday, and across the top was written *Suzy: Please get this in the post before 5.30 – SR.*

I examined the spiral binding. Between my doodle and the previous page was a shred of paper. At least one sheet had been torn out. I turned back to the doodle that would never become an elephant. The words were blurred, like ghosts. I compared them with the draft letter. The '3' in each case tailed beneath the line it was written on; the lower-case 'a's were written as capitals. There was no question that the same person had written them both. I opened Rownall's desk diary at random and found the same handwriting. I shut the diary and went back to the pad.

The draft of a letter, dated last Thursday, on one page and, on the next, an address: *43B Rangoon Road, NW6.*

The outer door shut with a bang. Toughton must have left. I retained enough sense to rip the sheet with the doodle from the pad and stuff it in my pocket. And then Rownall burst into the office, smiling his jolly smile.

I got back to Broadway late in the afternoon. Keller had left a message for me: Margarete Klose wanted to see me at the Embassy at nine o'clock tomorrow morning. On my way home that evening, I bought soup, bread, cooked ham, yoghurt and coffee. Afterwards, on impulse, I went into the Admiral Nelson.

Snape was at the same table by the jukebox. He looked just as I had left him, nearly twenty-four hours earlier. Nothing had changed except me. I went over and asked him if he would like another drink. Beside him on the table was a newspaper folded open at the crossword; about two-thirds of the clues were solved.

'Why not?' His smile faded as he looked at me. 'No – you sit down. It's my round.'

Snape's technique for getting served was far superior to mine: he penetrated the crowd by the bar in seconds. A minute later he returned with the drinks.

'Hard day?' he asked, carefully lowering the glasses to the table.

'Not the easiest I've known.'

I took a long pull on the drink. Snape didn't hurry me. He was a very restful man. I don't know why, but he reminded me of Dieter.

'I expect you're wondering what I'm doing here,' I said.

'You might have come to pay me the balance of the bill. But I'm rather afraid that's unlikely until next week. So – at a guess – you've thought of some more questions.'

'Did my brother ever mention anyone to you?' I cleared my throat, realizing that the question must sound hopelessly vague. 'A friend, say, or a colleague?'

Snape shook his head.

'You don't know a man called Sebastian Rownall?'

'No. Who is he?'

'A man my brother knew.' I wished I'd left Rownall's

name out of the conversation. 'Could anyone else have known of the enquiry? At your office, perhaps?'

'I'm a one-man band, Mr Herold. At present I haven't even got a secretary. If I get a larger caseload than I can handle myself, I employ other people on a temporary basis. I've not been overloaded with work lately.' His voice hardened. 'Besides, I aim to provide a completely confidential service.'

'Sorry,' I said. 'Stupid of me to ask. As you said, it's been a hard day.'

We sat in silence for a while. Then I tunnelled through to the bar and bought us another drink. When I got back he had finished the crossword.

'I have a friend who works for a cuttings agency,' he said. 'I asked her to check your story.'

I shrugged: I could hardly blame him for wanting to confirm it.

'She found it in the end. At least I think she did.' Snape chewed his lower lip, just as he had done when we first met. 'There was a small item in the *Eastern Daily Press*. Not much: a German businessman was believed to have died in a fire on a boat in the Alben estuary. He wasn't named.'

'That's right,' I said.

'But the odd thing was,' Snape told his drink, 'there was no follow-up. Nothing in the *Eastern Daily Press*. Nothing in the other locals. Nothing in any of the nationals. If I had seen the original item, I wouldn't have connected it with your brother. It wasn't even mentioned that he came from East Germany.'

'Is that unusual?'

'The lack of coverage? Yes – I'd have expected rather more, if only in the local papers.'

'Are you implying that someone decided they wanted it kept quiet?'

Snape chewed his lower lip and reached for his cigarettes. 'It's possible.'

I thought: *so much for the glorious free press of the West.*

'When do cover-ups occur?' I looked at him and he looked at me. It was obvious that he wasn't going to answer so I did it for him. 'When it's a matter of national security.'

The interview room was in the basement of the Embassy. It contained a small wooden table, four hard chairs and an ashtray. No doubt there were cameras and microphones as well, but they weren't on public display.

The security man ushered me through the door at exactly nine o'clock on Wednesday morning. Two men in civilian clothes were waiting with Fräulein Klose. The older one looked at me as though I were something unpleasant he had found in his refrigerator. His colleague, a fresh-faced man in his twenties, opened his notebook with a sigh of relief.

Speaking in English, Klose told me to sit down. 'This is Herr Gerhard Herold,' she said in her deep voice. Then she turned to me. 'These gentlemen are Detective Inspector Hebburn and Detective Sergeant Walsh.'

We nodded to one another.

'If I may – ' Hebburn began.

Klose overrode him. 'You may not take notes,' she said to Walsh, who looked startled and then closed his notebook. 'I wish to begin by emphasizing that Herr Herold has courteously volunteered to talk to you because he is naturally anxious to give the British authorities any reasonable assistance in his power. But he is under no compulsion to answer any of your questions, and he may leave this interview at any time. The interview is off the record.'

Hebburn blinked. 'That's understood. Herr Herold, we are very grateful that you have agreed to talk to us.' He blinked again. 'I know this must be distressing for you. We'll try to keep it as short as possible.'

At the third blink I realized he must have a muscular tic. He still looked disapproving; I began to suspect that was habitual, too.

'There's no real doubt,' he went on, 'that your brother's death was a tragic accident. But you know how it is – the police have to tidy up all the loose ends in a case like this. For example, would you have thought your brother was in any way a suicidal type?'

'No,' I said. 'Quite the reverse.'

'Good,' Hebburn said gloomily. 'He wrote to you, I suppose?'

'Very occasionally.'

'Would you say you were close?'

I nodded. 'Fairly. But of course he was much older than me, and that made a difference.'

Klose was watching me, not Hebburn.

'When did you last see him?' the inspector asked.

'In October. He had a few days' leave.'

'Did he ever say anything that led you to believe he might have enemies of any sort?'

'Of course not. People tended to like him. He – '

'Is this really relevant to your enquiries?' Klose asked.

Hebburn shrugged. 'Perhaps not.'

'You have other questions, Inspector?'

94

He blinked at her. 'One tiny thing. There is a suggestion that Herr Wolfgang Herold had been drinking just before he died. Rather more than a suggestion, in fact.'

'He was entitled to do what he wanted with his free time,' Klose said, automatically rebutting a criticism that hadn't been made.

'Of course. All I wanted to establish was that this was not an abnormal pattern of behaviour. Would you care to comment, Herr Herold?'

'My brother liked a drink,' I said cautiously.

'One witness at the public house he visited said he was – and I quote – "rolling drunk". Does that surprise you in any way?'

'When he was relaxing,' I said, 'he would sometimes drink a fair amount. Very occasionally.'

The question niggled me. I supposed Hebburn was trying to discover if Wolfgang was showing signs of stress, such as consuming more alcohol than usual. Sometimes, in fact, he would consume an enormous amount; and then for weeks he would have nothing at all. The point was that, however much he'd had, he never became 'rolling drunk'. He lost a few inhibitions, yes, and his speech could become a little slurred; but he never, as far as I knew, lost control of his co-ordination.

'So it was in no way untypical?'

'I think we've established that,' Fräulein Klose said, turning the gold ring on her finger. 'Have you any more questions?'

Hebburn blinked at her and she glared at him. It was an oddly intimate moment; they might have been alone. The silence between them extended so long that it became uncomfortable.

'I don't think so, thank you,' Hebburn said at last.

The meeting broke up. The security man, who must have been waiting just outside the door, escorted Hebburn and Walsh away. Klose stopped me from leaving. Switching to German, she told me to sit down again. For a few seconds she stood by the door, leaving me to sweat it out.

And I was sweating. Fräulein Klose frightened me far more than the British police could ever do. The Hauptverwaltung Aufklärung is the foreign intelligence branch of State Security, an élite within an élite. Klose seemed to be in charge of their London operation, which I guessed was a key posting, ranking third after Bonn and Washington. The fact that she was a woman was another reason to be wary of her; she had come a long way in a man's world. I felt like a fish trapped in an aquarium – and the only other inhabitant was a shark who had taken a personal dislike to me.

'Do you know what that was about?' she asked abruptly.

'You mean it wasn't just routine?'

'Oh, don't be stupid. They weren't ordinary policemen.'

'Security?'

'In so many words. They call them Special Branch over here. They work with the British security service. I know Hebburn and he knows me. The point of the exercise was not to ask you questions: it was to show me they weren't satisfied.'

'Either,' I said slowly, 'it wasn't an accident, or it wasn't Wolfgang who died.'

'Nonsense. They probably think your brother was spying for us, and that for some reason we had him killed. Typical fascist paranoia. Naturally, Hebburn

96

can't prove it, because it's not true. But he wanted to show his displeasure.'

I swallowed. 'You are sure it was my brother who died?'

'Of course I am,' she snapped. 'If you really want to know the truth, I'll tell you. There wasn't much of him left. He was on a boat – I'm sure Herr Rownall told you about that. The fire was intense, there were several explosions and the tide washed most of the wreckage away. But the divers found his belt buckle, his car keys and his wedding ring.'

'Yes, but did they find *him*?'

'They found some of his body in the water. Including a left tibia.' She eyed me coldly; perhaps the shark would have liked its victim to show signs of shock. 'Most of the flesh had gone. It had a fracture. Your brother's medical records – '

'I know,' I said. 'He broke it skating.'

'They found the car he was using near the mooring, his fingerprints in the dinghy, traces of hair in the – '

'All right,' I said. 'All right. It was Wolfgang. I . . . I just couldn't help wondering, you see.'

I was just about to tell her about Wolfgang's reactions to alcohol. But she didn't give me a chance.

'Well, now you know,' she said impatiently. 'You knew your brother was dealing illegally in foreign currency?'

'Of course not.'

'But Lieutenant Arendt mentioned it to you in Schwerin.'

'That was the first I'd heard of it. I knew nothing about it before then.'

'Your brother,' Fräulein Klose said, 'abused the trust we placed in him. That's incontrovertible. The question is, how far did the abuse go? Is Hebburn right? Perhaps there is more to this than a mere criminal offence. Your brother wasn't working for us. I don't think he was working for the British. But was he working for a third party?'

FIVE

I can't claim any credit for realizing I was being followed. Ironically enough, I only noticed because of my own stupidity.

The incident, such as it was, happened at about seven o'clock on the Wednesday evening. At the time I was on my way to Ruffles, where I hoped to meet Elizabeth Allanton. I was travelling up to West Hampstead from central London because I had spent most of the afternoon at a big toyshop in Regent Street, talking to one of their buyers and wandering around the store itself.

If I hadn't been so worried about Wolfgang, I would have been feeling mildly depressed about work. Improving the East German share of the market wouldn't be easy. We were good at producing injection- and blow-moulded plastic toys but we couldn't compete with the sort of things they had on offer here. My head was full of radio-controlled model planes and programmable computer keyboards for budding musicians; I was haunted by the Porsche 956 with its two-speed gearbox and 'scale speed' of nearly 500 kph.

Afterwards the buyer took me for a drink. We sat in the upstairs bar of an old-fashioned pub near Oxford Circus. He was a tired, middle-aged man who talked gloomily of the slump in the toy trade. Kids, he said, were maturing earlier these days; they wanted quasi-adult possessions, not toys. He also blamed the slump on the impact of TV advertising, which gave a dispro-portionate share of the market to a handful of products.

'And the money some parents will spend,' he said. 'They *want* toys to be expensive – the parents, I mean. It's crazy. The world's gone mad.'

In other words, he wasn't very interested in the traditional toys I had to offer.

'We can get what we need from elsewhere,' he said. 'Let's face it, there's just not the demand there was.'

When I left him, I walked to Bond Street to get the Jubilee Line to West Hampstead. I bought a ticket from a slot machine. As I walked away I heard shouting behind me. A large, well-dressed woman was waving a furled umbrella in the direction of a small Asian.

'Can't you wait your turn like everyone else?' she screamed. 'Pushing and shoving like animals. You're all the same.'

The man, who wore a dark-blue overcoat and carried a briefcase, looked as respectable as she did. He backed away from the umbrella, his arms sketching a sort of apology.

I walked onto the escalator. The incident stuck in my mind because it was the first example I had seen of the racism that, according to the East German media, is endemic in the West. The naked hatred in the woman's face shocked me. In the GDR we don't have racial minorities, apart from the Sorbs, which is one reason why we can afford to take a high moral tone on the subject. True, the Turks who come on day trips from West Berlin to spend their Deutschmarks on the cheap alcohol aren't exactly popular. But they don't attract the blind loathing I had seen in that prosperous middle-aged woman.

A rumbling rush of wind galvanized people on the

escalator. Infected by their haste, I let myself be swept along with them. A train was just pulling into the platform. The passengers leaving the train collided with those who were trying to get on. I fought my way into a carriage just before the doors closed. There was an Undergound map above one of the windows and I counted the stops to West Hampstead.

At the next stop I glanced out of the window. Green Park. That was wrong. In a sudden panic I checked the map: I was travelling south, in the wrong direction. At the last moment I escaped from the carriage. The doors closed – all but the end door in the next carriage; a briefcase was trapped between the door and the jamb.

The platform was rapidly emptying. The doors of the train opened again and the little Asian stumbled onto the platform. He didn't look at me. He produced an Underground map from his pocket.

My mood switched from mild panic to something approaching fear. Then I told myself I was being paranoid. But after the events of the last two days there was no harm in being careful. I followed the signs to the northbound platform of the Jubilee Line.

Plenty of people were waiting there. I walked up and down, pretending to read the advertisements and telling myself I was imagining things. There was no sign of the Asian and after a while I grew calmer. True, the man had been in a hurry to get a ticket. But if I could make a mistake and get on the wrong train, so could he.

Then I glanced into the tunnel that led to the exit. The Asian was standing there, apparently engrossed in a newspaper. You couldn't have seen him from the platform unless you happened to be directly opposite him.

I was afraid. Strangely enough, there was an element of anger mixed with the fear. They were trying to frighten me, I thought, and I didn't like it. Whoever 'they' were.

When the train came in, I was only a few paces away from the man. He looked up. His eyes slid over me, as if I were just another passenger as far as he was concerned. For all I knew, his indifference was real. But so was my fear. We moved towards the train. I let him get on first and climbed into the carriage by a different door. The doors began to close. I didn't move. The Asian had folded the newspaper; I thought he might be watching me out of the corner of his eye. I leant against the glass partition and faked a yawn. The doors reached the halfway mark.

I leapt for the gap. A man swore as I cannoned into him. The Asian was trying to manoeuvre around a woman, a pushchair and a toddler lying between him and the nearest exit. I jumped sideways onto the platform. The rubber trimming on the doors brushed my arm like a pair of lips. The train pulled out of the station. I couldn't see the Asian's face. Judging by his gestures he was apologizing to the woman and the toddler. It looked as if he were having an uphill job.

The worst thing about it all was that I still couldn't be sure. It was just possible that the man hadn't been trying to get off the train. In a sense I couldn't win: I had to accept either that someone wanted to follow me or that I was behaving with the childish melodrama of the emotionally unbalanced. To cap it all, I was going to be late for dinner.

I got to West Hampstead by tube and bus. It was possible that the Asian had a colleague or even a rival,

102

so I changed direction more than once and kept a wary eye on the other passengers. I don't think I was followed but I didn't know. I wasn't an expert. By the time I reached Ruffles I was nearly twenty minutes late.

Ruffles was not so much a restaurant as a wine bar that served food. I found Elizabeth downstairs at a minute table in an alcove by the service door. She had a glass of white wine and she was scanning the jobs section in the evening paper. For a few seconds I stared without her knowing I was there. She wore a black dress, with jade ear-studs and a jade necklace. All very simple and all very stunning. Then she looked up. Her expression told me nothing. I didn't know whether she was angry that I was late or pleased to see me again. Her face was as neutral as a Swiss banker's but rather more attractive.

'You took your time,' she said.

'I'm sorry. I'm glad you waited.'

'You look terrible. What's happened?'

Suddenly I felt very tired. I sat down and said, 'I think someone tried to follow me here.'

'Oh, come on. Why?'

'It's a long story.'

'Then we'd better get a bottle of wine and some food,' she said. 'I'm starving. We have to get it upstairs.'

I bought a bottle of Californian white. While we queued for the food, I asked her if she'd found somewhere to live.

'I've got a room in a house in Kensal Rise,' she said. 'Sleazy but cheap. Most of the other lodgers are students.'

'And a job?'

'Not yet. Where do you live?'

'I've got a flat in Ealing. It goes with the job.'

'What do you do?'

'I'm a sort of salesman.'

'For a German company?'

I nodded. Then, to my relief, it was our turn to be served and she couldn't ask me any more questions for a few moments. I'd had an idea, and I wanted to think about it before I mentioned it to her. The food consisted mainly of a selection of elderly salads, over-cooked quiches and fragments of pâté.

'It seems to me,' she said when we got back to our table, 'you've got some explaining to do. Like I was glad you turned up the other night but wasn't it an odd time to call round? And the reason you gave – was that true? And how come you didn't want me to call you?'

'I don't come from *West* Germany,' I said.

'East Germany? So you're a communist?' She'd have used much the same tone of voice if I'd said I was a gorilla or a Martian.

'Not exactly,' I said. 'I'm not politically-minded.' It was too complicated to explain. 'The point is, I'm not supposed to associate with Westerners, except in the way of business.'

'So you had to sneak around after dark? Your phone's tapped? And you get someone on your tail when you go out for a meal?'

Maybe she was annoyed because I was late; maybe she'd had a rough day; maybe she hated communists. I poured us another glass of wine and asked if we could start again.

'Start where?'

'With your Mrs Issler and my Great-aunt Luise.'

'Okay. You think they knew each other?'

I guessed she was as keen as I was to change the subject. I explained how Great-aunt Luise had been first a governess and later a sort of paid companion to the von Doeneckes before the war; and how, afterwards, she promoted the family to semi-divine status.

'From what I heard,' Elizabeth said, 'the von Doeneckes were a bunch of fascist creeps.'

'But surely Mrs Issler – ?'

'Aunt Willy's father was a younger brother of the old count. He was killed at Amiens in 1918. So she was just a poor relation. Besides, they disowned her in 1937. That was when she eloped with Uncle Solly.'

'Why?'

'Need you ask? Solomon Issler.'

'He was Jewish?'

'Not just that. He was in trade. He was a jeweller, actually – not a very successful one, so he wasn't even rich. And he was American, which didn't help, and he believed in socialism and the brotherhood of man. That's how he knew my father. Over the years I've heard quite a lot about the von Doeneckes.'

She told me a little about her parents and their friendship with the Isslers. The women had remained friends when first Solly and then Elizabeth's father had died. The widowed Mrs Issler, hankering after a Europe she had once known, had moved to England; the house she rented belonged to a cousin of her husband's. Elizabeth and her mother had a standing invitation to stay with her.

'It seemed a good time to come,' Elizabeth said. 'I needed to get away from Mike.'

I waited for her to go on about her husband. She just sat there, looking past me at something that wasn't there. All I could tell from her face was that, whatever it was she saw, it wasn't a pretty sight.

'What was Mrs Issler like?' I asked.

'Finicky, I guess. If she liked you, she'd do anything for you; if she didn't, you were nowhere. She was very proud. My father wanted to help her when Uncle Solly died, but she wouldn't take a penny from him. She hated the von Doeneckes but in a funny way she liked talking about them. I don't know how to put it: she despised privilege and yet she never quite forgot she was a *lady*.'

I thought about Great-aunt Luise's interminable monologues and her library of photograph albums. Without knowing it, I had probably seen photographs of Wilhelmina von Doenecke: playing croquet perhaps, or sitting on a horse, or taking tea in the garden where eternal summer reigned, or somewhere in one of those group shots of weekend parties in the 1930s.

'What did your aunt tell you about them?' Elizabeth said. 'I'd really like to know.'

In the end we pooled our knowledge from two old ladies who had shared a life that no longer existed. I seized on the von Doeneckes with relief. They were a neutral subject, safe in the remote past.

It was disconcerting how the different sets of memories, one from Great-aunt Luise and the other from Mrs Issler, overlapped and modified each other; and finally, of course, they blended into a third set whose ambivalences made nonsense of the first two. The old count, for example, who died of a heart attack in 1941, was now far more than a distinguished general and public-spirited aristocrat: he was also a man who habitually drank more brandy than was good for him, and occasionally beat his daughters and his niece in a loosebox in the stables.

According to Elizabeth, his wife was a penny-pinching shrew; but the countess whom Great-aunt Luise had known generously supported the families of estate workers who were serving in the Wehrmacht during the war. Great-aunt Luise habitually referred to her in terms that would have done credit to a saint.

We moved on to the daughters, twins who had been killed with their mother in one of the Berlin air raids in 1944.

'Eva and Christina,' Elizabeth said. 'Spoilt little bitches who never lifted a finger for anyone else?'

'Each knitted at least twelve tons of socks for our gallant troops,' I said, knowing that I would have never dared to put it like this in a restaurant at home. 'Meanwhile, their husbands died heroically in defence of the Fatherland, one at Arnhem, the other at Stalingrad.'

By this time we had started a second bottle of wine. Like all East Germans, I have a confused view of World War II. The official line is that the Federal Republic is the descendant of Hitler's Reich; and that the workers in what is now the GDR were really fighting for our Russian liberators or – at the very least – longing for their arrival. Great-aunt Luise and other old people who lived through it tell a different story.

'One of the twins – Eva, I think – betrayed Aunt Willy's romance with Uncle Solly to their mother.'

'When they dug Eva out of the rubble, they found she was sheltering someone's baby with her body. The baby survived.'

'Oh hell,' Elizabeth said. 'Why did they have to make it so complicated? How about the son, Georg? The one who went to Oxford. The whole family came to England to visit him. I think they rented a house in London. That was when Aunt Willy met Solly. He was trying to set up a London branch of his father's business but it didn't work out.'

'Was that the time when the German Ambassador introduced the general to the Prime Minister?'

'I thought it was to the Prince of Wales.'

'Maybe both? Georg joined the Brandenburg, of course.'

'What's that?'

'It used to be the crack regiment of the German army.'

'Oh no. He was in the Waffen SS. The Russians shot him.'

I blinked. 'Are you sure?'

'Even in '36 he was a card-carrying Nazi.'

'But how would Mrs Issler know?'

Elizabeth shrugged. 'She had friends in Germany – used to get letters from them. What happened to the estates?'

'They were all in the East. They had land in East Prussia and Silesia: that went to the Poles, of course. The rest was in Neubrandenburg, and all the large land holdings were confiscated after the war.'

'Aunt Willy's grandmother – Georg's, too – brought a lot of money into the family. You heard about that? She said it was tainted.'

'What do you mean?'

'The grandmother was the daughter of an armaments dealer. Mrs Issler was ashamed of her.'

'According to Great-aunt Luise,' I said, 'the grandmother wasn't quite right in the head. Maybe Mrs Issler was ashamed of that too.'

'They're all gone now.' Elizabeth lost her smile, and suddenly we had left the security of the past behind. 'It was the funeral today.'

I touched her hand. She didn't move hers away. Then she sniffed and blew her nose.

'I wish,' she said slowly, 'I just wish they could get the bastard who did it.'

She looked at me. I knew that if I were going to say anything it had to be now.

'I don't think she was killed by a mugger,' I said. 'I think she was killed because my brother wanted to find her.'

Elizabeth straightened herself in her chair. I didn't feel tipsy any more.

'I think you'd better explain that,' she said.

'My brother was sent here to work. I think our aunt must have asked him to try and trace the surviving von Doeneckes; I told you that. He employed a private detective. Wolfgang – my brother – gave him a false name, because the Embassy wouldn't have approved. The detective found Mrs Issler. A day or two later my brother died in a fire, probably before he had time to contact her. The police say his death was an accident, officially at least. And now Mrs Issler's dead, and the police say it was just a random murder.'

'Coincidence would cover it,' she said slowly. 'I mean, if the deaths were connected, what's the reason?'

'My brother died on a boat owned by a business colleague, an Englishman called Sebastian Rownall. The British think he might have been spying for us, and maybe someone helped him die because of that. Our people think the same, except they say he wasn't spying for us but maybe for someone else.'

'Us?' She frowned. 'We've got different angles on "them and us".'

I shrugged. 'Wolfgang knew a lot about our economic planning, and about industrial technology. Or I suppose he might have been acting as a messenger, a go-between. But I don't believe it.'

'You think he was too loyal?'

'He was too intelligent.' If Wolfgang had had loyalties, they were to his family and friends. 'Spying's dangerous.' I thought of the black market activities and added: 'Or rather, I doubt if there's much profit in it. He liked money.'

'You were followed here, you said?'

'I think someone tried. Maybe the British, maybe our people. But there's a chance I imagined it.'

'It doesn't make sense. If your brother was under suspicion, why did they give you his job?'

It was a good question. I wondered, yet again, why Bochmann had chosen me and why State Security hadn't blocked the appointment. Alternatively State Security might have suggested me to Bochmann in the first place. But that led to another range of questions.

Elizabeth was staring at me, waiting for an answer.

'I don't know. I suppose the most likely explanation is that they thought I might be involved with what Wolfgang was doing. Maybe I'm living bait. But I don't know what they're trying to catch.'

'And are you involved?'

'No,' I said. 'I wouldn't be talking like this if I were.'

She fiddled with the stem of her glass. 'Okay, so your brother was in trouble with the authorities. But that doesn't mean Aunt Willy was connected. She was totally apolitical, she left all that sort of thing to Uncle Solly. And even he believed in words, not actions. It's much more likely that your brother was trying to trace her for your aunt – and it had nothing to do with the way she died.'

It was all so plausible, except for one awkward fact that wouldn't go away however much I wished it would.

'Sebastian Rownall,' I said, 'had her address.'

'So what? Maybe he was helping Wolfgang find her. It could be quite innocent.'

'No, that won't work. He didn't tell me, by the way: I found out by accident.' I explained about the shorthand pad on Rownall's desk. 'So it looks like Rownall wrote down the address *after* Wolfgang's death, and just before Mrs Issler was killed. How did he get it, and why? I've talked to the detective, and he says he's never heard of Rownall. I think I believe him. And if it was so innocent, why didn't Rownall mention it to me?'

She asked a lot of questions about Rownall: what he did, and how he fitted in with Wolfgang and me. It seemed to me that each question drew us further into a wilderness of speculation. The few facts we had pointed in all directions at once.

An accidental fire and a random mugger were somehow so much easier to cope with than the possibility of a double murder, coldly conceived and efficiently carried out.

'So where do we go from here?' she said finally. 'We can't just leave it. We need to know more.'

'I can't go to the police. We haven't the evidence. Besides, the Embassy would put me on the first flight home.'

Elizabeth hugged herself as though she were cold. 'We're both strangers here. This is a foreign country. That makes it worse.'

111

I leant forward and tapped the newspaper. 'Rownall needs a secretary. You want a job. It's worth a try, isn't it?'

In Schwerin, or even Berlin, escorting a woman back to her home is a sign of respect or friendship or romantic attachment. In London there was another reason. It is a dangerous city.

When I suggested taking her back, Elizabeth made only half-hearted objections. New York, I'd heard, was much worse than London, but no one had killed Mrs Issler in New York. Neither of us could afford a taxi. In Eastern Europe, safety on the streets is something you take for granted – the state provides it as a matter of course for all its citizens; but in the West it is a commodity like any other, available if you have the means to pay for it.

Outside Ruffles, the street was crowded. People were coming out of pubs and restaurants. There was laughter, shouting and the sound of distant music. The shop windows were brightly lit. There were buses and cars. It was very cold but at least it wasn't raining.

All I could think of was that somewhere among the scores of people might be one person who was watching us. One pair of eyes that weren't as casual as all the others. I guessed that the same idea had occurred to Elizabeth. Perhaps it was stupid for us to be seen in public together. But if I had been followed to Ruffles, it was too late to worry about that: they would already know about Elizabeth.

We didn't use the Underground. An overground line ran in a huge curve across the northern suburbs of the city and passed through Kensal Rise. When we reached the station, we found that the next train would be in ten minutes. We walked up and down the platform while we waited, partly to keep warm and partly to keep an eye on the other passengers. She was wearing a long, dark coat with a high collar. I felt shabby in her company.

'What sort of job did you do in the States?' I asked, to break the silence between us. I knew she had secretarial skills but she had given me the impression that she rarely used them.

'I worked for my father for a while after college. Then I met Mike. I worked part-time for him after we married.'

'As his secretary?'

A little shake of the head. 'In the art department.'

We walked on, down to the end of the platform. I thought that was all she was going to say. I didn't want to pry into her life. Or rather I wanted to, but had no excuse for doing so.

'Mike's the part-owner and editor of a magazine,' Elizabeth said abruptly. 'He's doing very well, and he doesn't want to lose it.'

I connected that last remark with the man I had seen – the man who was divorcing her but had pursued her across the Atlantic; the man whose interest in her was strictly business. 'Are you the other owner?'

'I've got a twenty per cent stake. My father bought it for me when we married and Mike was getting the magazine off the ground. Mike's got thirty-five himself. The other 45 per cent is owned by a guy he knew at Yale. Sam was meant to be a sleeping partner, but now he's woken up, and that's upset all Mike's calculations.'

The arithmetic was easy. So was the inference that Mike and Sam were squabbling over control of the magazine, and that Elizabeth held the balance between them.

'You don't want to sell?' I said.

'No way. Mike's offering a fair price. So's Sam. Mike thinks I turned him down because I hate him. But it's not that. It's just that — well, my shares came from my father, and they're all I've got left of him. Also, I don't like being pressurized. I want to think about it before I get rid of them. Maybe I'll decide to keep them.'

We had reached the other end of the platform again. We turned back, into the wind. We ran out of conversation. I didn't know what was going through her mind. I was thinking that I would have preferred Elizabeth Allanton to be poor. Money increased the distance between us. It was a selfish thought, and I wasn't proud of it.

A little train clattered into the station. We didn't say much on the journey. At the other end, her house was only a few hundred yards from the station.

'You want some coffee?' she said at the gate.

Most of the windows were alight. Rock music filtered into the street. A tribe of dustbins and black plastic sacks had colonized the little front garden. I pretended to myself that I didn't want to see where she lived.

'No, thanks — I'd better get back.'

'Okay. You'll call me tomorrow night?'

I nodded, said goodnight to her and walked away. I wished I had accepted her invitation. I wished that none of this was happening, that I had never left my safe, boring life in Schwerin. Most of all I wished that I could send anyone else but Elizabeth Allanton to work for Sebastian Rownall.

*

I knew my meeting with Elizabeth would have consequences. But I hadn't expected them quite so soon.

The following morning I went to Broadway. The security man inside the door looked at my pass and my face. Then he jerked his thumb towards a door and said, 'In there. The duty officer wants a word.'

The security establishment at Broadway was tiny compared to the Embassy's. It came under Klose's jurisdiction. The duty officer had a small room, but he made up for that by having four telephones and a computer. He was a thin man with an unhealthy sheen to him, as though he had recently been caught in a shower of engine oil.

'Herr Herold? You're to ring the Embassy and ask for this extension.'

He passed me a piece of paper. I thanked him and turned to leave. 'One moment, please,' he said. 'You're to use this phone.' He pushed one of his handsets across the desk towards me. 'It's a secure line,' he explained. 'Don't mind me.'

I got through to the Embassy switchboard and asked for the extension. Two seconds later Fräulein Klose was on the line.

'You were not at your flat last night,' she said. 'Where were you?'

Her booming voice must have been audible to the duty officer. He was pretending to be immersed in a folder of what looked like press releases.

'I went out for a meal,' I said.

'You were a long time.'

'I had to have a drink with a buyer in central London.' I knew she could check that if she really wanted to, so I mentioned the names of the buyer and his employer without waiting to be prompted. 'It went on for longer than I'd expected so I ate there.'

'Did your *drink*' – she gave the word a sarcastic inflection – 'result in any orders?'

'I'm afraid not, Fräulein.'

'Did you spend the rest of the evening with the buyer?'

'No – I was by myself.'

There was a grunt on the other end of the line. The duty officer turned a page. The handset was slippery with sweat from the palm of my hand. I'd taken a calculated risk: if one of Klose's men had successfully tailed me last night, she would already know about Elizabeth. I decided it was time to change the subject and perhaps earn myself a good-conduct mark.

'In fact I hoped to phone you today. I felt it my duty to report a possible incident.'

'Go on.'

'I am not sure but I think I was followed last night.' I explained about the little Asian. 'After our last meeting, I thought it best to be . . . ah . . . cautious.'

'You are sure you lost him?'

'Yes. But there might have been someone else.'

There was a silence on the other end of the line. 'I'll tell you one thing,' she said at last. 'He wasn't one of ours. Have you noticed any other signs of interest?'

'No.'

'You'd better come in and look at some photographs. I wanted to see you tomorrow, in any case – 3.30 in my office.'

'Yes, of course, Fräulein. May I ask why?'

There was a click. My only answer was the dialling tone.

SIX

After the phone call to Margarete Klose, I had a frustrating day. I tried to set up meetings with people who didn't want to meet me. If I succeeded in seeing them, I then tried to sell them things they didn't want to buy.

For the first time I was glad to get back to the flat. I planned to wade through some paperwork, have supper and then phone Elizabeth at 10.15. Just as I began to make notes for my weekly report to Bochmann, there was a knock at the door. The flat door, not the front door downstairs.

It was my neighbour, Herr Stern. He was a tall man whose suit revealed too much of his wrists and ankles. He rubbed his hands together.

'My . . . er . . . wife and I wondered if you would like to come down for a drink this evening.'

I said I would be delighted.

'Good, good. In twenty minutes, shall we say?'

I had no wish to waste half the evening making polite noises to my neighbours. But I knew that a refusal would cause me more problems than it solved. The citizens of the GDR are supposed to stick together in strange countries. Klose must have encouraged Herr Stern to be sociable, for he had almost ignored me when we were introduced at the office; he handled public relations for the trade section.

When I arrived he gave me a glass of Bulgarian wine.

'Shall I put some music on?' he said. 'I think perhaps I might. My wife is around somewhere.'

He wandered over to the stereo system in the corner and consulted a card index. Frau Stern, a small woman with coarse grey skin, bustled in from the kitchen, carrying a tray of snacks. She worked in the trade section as an interpreter and she reminded me of a well-compacted dumpling. We both turned to her with relief.

'Put on the new tape,' she ordered her husband. 'Chopin,' she said to me, 'the Etudes. How nice to meet you, Herr Herold. Have a nut.'

Before I could take one, there was a knock on the door. The new arrival was Dr Teichler, my other neighbour. He was a young man, so fair that he was almost colourless, with a prim mouth and large glasses that dominated his face. We had not met before, and I had no idea what he did.

Frau Stern disappeared into the kitchen again, and her husband fiddled with the controls of the stereo system. For two long minutes Teichler and I managed to sustain a conversation. First he said he hoped I had settled in. Then he asked if I liked London. In return I gathered that he was an historian from Leipzig; he had been given a six-month sabbatical in London to gather material for a new book.

'So sorry to hear about your brother,' he said, screwing up his face like a man getting into a cold bath on a winter morning. He took another handful of nuts. 'We had a long chat, one evening. I don't know if he mentioned it? He was most interested in my research. In fact I promised to send him a copy of the book when it is published.'

A doubt stirred in the back of my mind. But perhaps,

I thought, Wolfgang had merely feigned interest out of habit. He used to charm strangers automatically, even when there had been no reason to please them.

'And what is the book about?' I asked.

'The crisis of nineteenth-century capitalism.' Teichler's eyes gleamed like chips of blue glass. 'With particular reference to its influence on the foreign policy of the great powers. That reminds me, Herr Herold, I wanted to – '

The opening bars of the first Etude obliterated what he was trying to say. The speakers crackled in anguish. Stern fumbled for the knob that controlled the volume. Frau Stern reappeared and found it for him. Then she rounded on me. 'I'm sure you'd like to see the flat, Herr Herold.'

She took my agreement for granted and swept me from room to room, pointing out their possessions. The Sterns' flat was larger and more comfortable than mine, and also less impersonal. They had been here for nearly two years, which had given them the opportunity to acquire a variety of consumer luxuries. She lingered lovingly over a food processor and a video, their most recent purchases. Her enthusiasm touched me. She was so proud of what she and her husband had achieved with their lives. They had worked hard for the state and the Party, and this was their reward. As far as she was concerned, life was simple and life was good.

By the time we got back to the living room, Teichler had nearly finished the available food. 'Ah, Herold,' he said. 'There was something I wanted to ask you.'

'Of course.' I accepted another glass of wine from Stern. 'How can I help you?'

'I wondered if you'd come across my copy of Girving?'

'I'm sorry?'

'*The Dynastic Politics of the Munitions Industry*. By Professor Cynthia Girving.' His voice was slightly tetchy, as if I ought to have known this already. 'I lent it to your brother just before . . .'

The doubt stirred again, and this time I couldn't suppress it. There was no discernible reason why Wolfgang should have carried politeness so far. Not with Teichler.

'I'm afraid I haven't come across it.' I explained that I had checked Wolfgang's possessions myself. 'There were no books at all.'

'Oh dear. It was my own copy, you see. Rather a valuable secondary source.'

'You must let me buy you another,' I said. Presumably the book had been another casualty of the fire.

Teichler brightened up. 'That's most kind. Fortunately it's in print – I saw it in Dillons the other day.'

He helped himself to another glass of wine. On the other side of the room, Frau Stern was giving her husband a muted lecture on the operation of the stereo system. I took out my diary and a ball-point pen.

'I could pick it up myself,' Teichler said. 'If you were to – '

'I wouldn't dream of putting you to the trouble,' I said firmly. 'Just give me the details and the address of the bookshop.'

I jotted them down. Teichler said that we really must get together sometime. The Sterns rejoined us, and the four of us had one of those nostalgic, expatriate conversations about the delights of our home country.

After another half-hour I managed to get away,

pleading work as my excuse. The two men were glad to see the back of me, but I think Frau Stern would have liked me to stay; she felt sorry for me.

I bolted down some tinned soup, bread and fruit and, ignoring the paperwork, switched on the black-and-white TV. I couldn't concentrate on it. At ten o'clock I grabbed my coat and went downstairs. As I passed the Sterns' door I heard Teichler's high-pitched voice competing on favourable terms with Beethoven's Eighth.

Outside the roofs and the parked cars glinted with frost. I tried the phone box at the end of the road but that was out of order. I walked on to the Admiral Nelson. There was a payphone in the lobby between the two bars. On the way towards it I glanced into the saloon bar. Snape was sitting at his usual table by the jukebox. He didn't see me.

I dialled the number of Elizabeth's house. A man answered. I heard him shout, 'Elizabeth, the phone!' and I wondered what he looked like, how well he knew her and what she thought of him.

People sound different on the phone and it always comes as a shock, the first time you hear them. Elizabeth was cool and laconic, and her accent was more noticeably American.

'Sure I got the job,' she said. 'I start tomorrow.'

There was a rush of cold air in the lobby. I glanced over my shoulder. A man wearing a leather jacket and jeans had come in. He leant against the wall, waiting for the phone and invading my privacy.

'Are you still there?' Elizabeth said.

I lowered my voice. 'That's great. How did you do it?'

'I went to the local job centre, saying I was looking

121

for secretarial work where I could use my languages. And I said I'd worked in import-export back in the States. No luck there so I tried the same story on the secretarial agencies. The second one came up with the job at Rownall's.'

'Have you met him?'

'He interviewed me this afternoon. He's a sweetie. But his office is like a pigpen.'

'Can you handle it? The work, I mean?'

'I guess so. But Gerhard – ?'

'Yes?'

'Are you sure about this? I mean, he seemed so gentle. He showed me pictures of his wife and kid.'

'Of course I'm not sure.' I heard voices murmuring in the background at the other end of the line. 'That's what we need to find out.'

'I got to go,' Elizabeth said.

I wondered why she had to go. 'Shall I phone you tomorrow?'

'Okay. But can you call earlier – 7.30, maybe? I might be going out later.'

We left it at that. I put down the phone, trying to ignore the depression that was creeping over me. I should have been feeling elated. I hadn't really expected Elizabeth to get the job, let alone to manage it so quickly. But on the phone she had sounded remote and impersonal, and that upset me, though I had no grounds for expecting her to be any different. Nevertheless, I wished I knew what she was planning to do tomorrow evening. And with whom she was planning to do it.

I went outside and walked through the line of parked cars towards the road.

'Hey! You dropped something.'

I turned. The man in the leather jacket was standing in the lighted doorway, pointing down at the tarmac. I followed his finger but I could see nothing.

Suddenly the rear door of the car beside me swung open.

'Mr Herold,' said a familiar voice. 'Let me give you a lift.'

The man in the leather jacket moved a few paces forward, making the third side of the triangle that enclosed me; the car itself and the open door formed the other two sides.

'Come along,' said Inspector Hebburn, moving across the seat to make room for me. 'It's too cold to just stand there.'

Leather Jacket gave me a shove that sent me flying against the car. Then he manhandled me into the back and climbed in after me. There was a third man in the driver's seat.

'That's better,' Hebburn said as the door closed.

'He used the phone,' Leather Jacket said. 'It had an acoustic hood. All I could hear him saying was something about "Can you handle it?" The other party did most of the talking.'

'No doubt the phone in your flat is temporarily out of order,' Hebburn said to me. 'Or perhaps you wanted a breath of fresh air.' He tapped the man in the front on the shoulder. 'Drive on.'

'I'd rather walk,' I said. 'I'd like the exercise.'

'I don't think your preferences are terribly important at present.'

'That sounds like a typically British understatement.'

The car moved forwards and turned onto the main road. My flat was on the right. We turned left.

123

'Your English is really very good. Where did you learn it?'

'We do learn foreign languages in our schools.' I didn't tell him about Great-aunt Luise's Anglophile tendencies. Wolfgang and I often used English between ourselves when we wanted to talk privately in public places.

The car pulled into a cul-de-sac. The driver did a three-point turn and parked. He switched off the engine. Leather Jacket punched me twice in the stomach. I bent over, retching.

'The trouble is,' Hebburn said, 'your face doesn't fit. Nor did your brother's. I find that very upsetting.'

Leather Jacket yanked me up. It was too dark to see Hebburn clearly but I felt his breath on my cheek; it smelled of peppermint. I could imagine the expression of disapproval.

'We've been acting out this farce for over forty years,' Hebburn went on. 'Your people and ours and all our friends. And naturally we've evolved what you might call rules of engagement. There's a tacit consensus in these matters, you know, a professional agreement about the way these things are done.'

He paused. I had almost got my breath back. I assumed he wanted me to comment, so I said I knew nothing about all this.

Hebburn sniffed. It must have been a signal. Leather Jacket punched me again in precisely the same place. He wasn't subtle but he knew his job.

'You're not HVA,' Hebburn said disgustedly. 'You're not Stasi in any shape or form. Nor are you just what you're meant to be. According to our information, you are not a particularly valued citizen by any standard. Yet they give you a job like this. Travel to the West.

Independence. Promotion. All the good things of life. And to make it even stranger, you inherit the job from your brother. It doesn't add up, does it, Mr Herold?'

'I shall report this to the Embassy,' I said.

'I wonder if you will.'

'I've done nothing wrong. You've not charged me. You've encouraged your colleague to hit me. I shall lay an official complaint. I shall – '

'Switch him off, will you,' Hebburn said.

Leather Jacket's arm snaked round my neck and folded across my mouth.

'And search him.'

Leather Jacket went through my pockets and patted my body. The driver stared through the windscreen, apparently oblivious of what was going on behind him. Hebburn examined what Leather Jacket found in the light of a small torch.

There wasn't much. The only thing that interested them was my diary. Hebburn leafed through the pages, questioning me about everything he couldn't understand.

'Sylvia Carne. Who's she?'

'The head buyer of Morganettas.'

'Who are they?'

'A chain of toyshops.'

'Who set up the lunch?'

'She did.'

'What's this book?'

'A neighbour of mine recommended it. He's a historian.'

'Why are you seeing Fräulein Klose tomorrow?'

'To see if I can identify a face for her.'

'What face?'

'An Asian face.'

Hebburn sighed. Leather Jacket twisted my ear. Slowly the pain subsided.

'Don't try to be clever with me,' Hebburn said wearily. 'Who are you talking about?'

'The Asian who tried to tail me last night,' I said. 'The one I lost at Green Park. Was there another one?'

At the back of the diary was a list of phone numbers and a few addresses. Hebburn went through each one. I answered truthfully and as briefly as possible. Elizabeth's phone number wasn't there. I had had the sense not to write it down and fortunately it was easily memorable; the first three digits were the same as the number of a flat I'd once lived in, and the last four were the date of the October Revolution.

'You do make it difficult, don't you?' Hebburn said at last. 'It's like getting blood out of a stone. Who sent you here?'

'The job was internally advertised at the Ministry of Foreign Trade.'

Hebburn sniffed and Leather Jacket went to work again.

'Who appointed you?'

'The Special Committee for Export Procedures.'

'I mean,' Hebburn said, 'who told them to choose you?'

'I don't understand. The interview panel made the decision after seeing all the candidates.'

Leather Jacket made another contribution. The pain was almost too much to bear, but part of my mind was still operating lucidly. Nothing they had done to me would leave a mark on my body. I didn't think they were going to kill me because my death would bring too many awkward questions, and it would also mean they would never find any answers. They were just trying it on – applying a little pressure in the hope that they would squeeze something out of me.

In situations like this you have to play tricks with yourself if you want to survive. I willed myself to believe that the pain was finite, endurable and delivered with a constructive purpose in mind: I pretended that it was as necessary and as free from malice as an unpleasant experience at the dentist's. The pain was like white noise. Gradually they turned down the volume. At last we were almost back to silence. People breathing. A soft whimpering that came from me. The smell of peppermint, much stronger than before. I opened my eyes.

Hebburn's face was only a few centimetres from mine. 'Who killed your brother?' he murmured.

'As far as I know, the fire was an accident.'

'Who was he working for?'

'The Ministry of Foreign Trade.'

'Who else?'

'No one – again, as far as I know.'

And so it went on, punctuated with interpolations from Leather Jacket. After the event, my reasons for stonewalling them seemed logical and powerful. At the time it wasn't as clearcut as that. There were several points when I nearly told them everything I knew, just to stop the agony.

The only thing that prevented me was a sort of anger. They had no right to do this to me. They were behaving like animals, and I wouldn't give them the satisfaction of breaking down. Hebburn was just a British version, no better and no worse, of all the morally rotten people who had ever tried to use mental or physical force on me. I hated him. He aroused in me the same feelings that Huber did, and the other petty functionaries who used their scrap of power as a whip to beat lesser mortals into line. Great-aunt Luise used to say I had the obstinacy of Satan. I clung to my anger and my obstinacy; they were the only defences I had left.

'This is just the beginning,' Hebburn said. 'You realize that, don't you? We shall be keeping an eye on you. One step out of line, one scrap of evidence, and you'll be out on your ear.'

'Evidence of what?' I gasped.

'We don't like foreigners playing silly games on British soil. Don't push me, laddie, don't push me.'

I said I wouldn't dream of pushing him. Leather Jacket gave me another punch but it lacked the conviction of his earlier ones.

Then Hebburn said, 'On your bike.'

Leather Jacket opened his door and got out. He seized my arm in both hands and pulled me after him. I landed face down in the middle of the road. The freezing tarmac scraped the palms of my hands. Tears filled my eyes. The door slammed. The engine fired. I picked myself up and watched the car nosing out of the cul-de-sac.

There were lights behind drawn curtains in the houses on either side of me. People were only a few metres away but the road was as private as a desert. I stumbled towards the mouth of the cul-de-sac.

I had no idea where I was. I was lost in a wilderness of semi-detached houses and frost-covered cars. I walked down the road, in the same direction as Hebburn's car had taken. Eventually I came to a main road with shops, a cinema and a petrol station.

A police patrol car was parked in the forecourt of the petrol station. I walked towards it. When you have lost your way, the best thing to do is ask a policeman.

*

Margarete Klose seemed almost pleased to see me.

'Would you like a cup of tea?'

She waved me to a chair and phoned the order through to her secretary. I thought she looked tired.

'It is good news, in a way,' she said abruptly, twisting the gold ring on her right hand.

'I beg your pardon?'

'That you had a tail. It shows that someone is interested. It shows that there is something to be interested in.'

This aspect of the matter had not occurred to me. I found it difficult to feel much enthusiasm for it.

'I want you to have a look at these.' She passed me a ring-binder. 'As a rule, the British do not like employing Asians, which narrows the field. They justify their racism by saying that Asians are too obtrusive. That's nonsense. It's like saying a Turk is obtrusive in West Germany. Turn to the last section.'

I looked through the binder. It contained photographs and numbers – nothing else. The last section contained only half a dozen entries. My Asian was waiting for me on the third page.

'That's him, I think. But he looked older.'

Klose tapped a word into the keyboard on her desk and stared at the VDU. The screen was angled away from me. She grunted and made a note on the file in front of her. The secretary brought our tea.

'Have they done anything else?'

For a fraction of a second I hesitated. I had to make one of those decisions whose consequences are imponderable. If I said no, Klose might find out by other means, and I would have two enemies instead of one. If I said yes, she might think I was playing a double game; or, if she believed me, she might have me watched for my own protection, which would put Elizabeth at risk and hinder my own investigation; and in either case she might decide to send me back to the GDR. What I had before me wasn't a rational choice: it was a leap in the dark.

'Yes,' I said; and I told her exactly what had happened last night.

'The man in the leather jacket,' she said when I had finished. 'Describe him.'

I did my best. It had been dark in the car, and when I saw him in the lobby of the Admiral Nelson I hadn't taken much notice of him. 'A little shorter than me – much broader. Short greasy hair. Aged about thirty.'

She made me look through more folders of photographs. If Leather Jacket was there I didn't recognize him.

'What do you want me to do?' I asked.

Fräulein Klose stared at me. 'Do? What can *you* do? Carry on as normal, of course.'

'But what's it all about?'

'You needn't trouble yourself with that. Just report any incidents to me, if and when they occur.'

I had expected almost any reaction but this. She was neither outraged nor surprised. She expressed no regret for what I had undergone last night. It was as if, I realized with an unpleasant jolt, she had already heard the news.

'But can't we lodge an official complaint?'

'About Hebburn? Don't be ridiculous. There were no witnesses. You say they didn't even mark your body.'

'But he's a policeman,' I said weakly. 'He's meant to uphold the law, not break it.'

'He's Special Branch. They consider themselves above the law.'

'But surely – '

'This is not the GDR, Herr Herold. In this country the police are essentially a tool of repression.' She waved a hand, dismissing the subject. 'I wanted to see you about something else. Herr Bochmann will be coming to London on Monday week. Have they told you yet?'

I shook my head.

'I want you to record everything you can about his visit. I shall expect daily briefings.'

'Yes, Fräulein.'

So she expected me to spy on my superior for her. And of course I would do it. The order suggested that Bochmann was officially under investigation and that my own position was therefore at risk. For all their apparent differences, Klose and Hebburn were intent on employing me for the same purpose. They were trying to catch something, and neither seemed to know what it was.

Of course it was possible – even probable – that one or other was lying to me. The only certainty was that they both had no scruples about using me as human bait.

On my way home from the Embassy I went to Oxford Street and tried to lose a hypothetical tail in a department store. By the time I emerged onto the street I was out of breath and feeling slightly foolish, like a child trying to play a grown-up game whose rules he doesn't know. I found a payphone in another store and dialled Rownall's number.

'Sebastian Rownall and Co,' Elizabeth said.

'This is Gerhard Herold,' I said. Then I lowered my voice and spoke rapidly: 'I can't phone tonight. I'll try on Sunday. But see if you can get him to bring you to the fair on Monday.' Then, more loudly: 'May I speak to Mr Rownall, please?'

He came on the line almost at once, apparently delighted to hear from me.

'Seb – I just wanted to confirm Monday morning.'

'Delighted you can make it, old chap. I've got badges for us. Shall we meet outside the main entrance? That's Warwick Road, just opposite Earls Court tube station.'

'Fine. What time?'

'Doors open at nine. Nine-thirty suit you? Good. Oh, and by the way, I might bring my wife. She enjoys this sort of thing. Perhaps we could all have lunch afterwards.'

I said I was looking forward to it and rang off. I walked from Oxford Street to Dillons bookshop and bought a copy of *The Dynastic Politics of the Munitions Industry*. I stuffed it in my briefcase and didn't look at it until I got back to the flat.

According to the cover copy, the book dealt with arms manufacturers and dealers in the century from Waterloo to World War I. Girving believed that personal rivalries between them helped shape the patterns of warfare in the period. It seemed far-fetched to me: a typical example of the historian's tendency to magnify the importance of his speciality. I riffled through the pages until I reached the index. And there, leaping from the last page like a slap in the face, was the reason for Wolfgang's cultivation of Teichler.

VON DOENECKE, Paul Heinrich, General Count. *See* FELD-BAUSCH, Augusta Alexandra.

I turned to FELDBAUSCH. There were several index

entries for people with that surname. Augusta Alexandra had fewer references than the others. The earliest page numbers related to Hans Feldbausch, so I began with him. I worked methodically through the book, building up a picture of a family business.

The Feldbauschs were moderately successful arms dealers. They came from Nuremberg and made a respectable fortune during the Napoleonic Wars, supplying munitions, with the impartiality of their kind, to Napoleon before his Russian campaign and to the Prussians before Waterloo. Hans Feldbausch, the founder of the firm, died in 1817. His son, Karl August, was at the head of the business for over forty years. He made a comfortable living but he was severely handicapped by the lack of major wars. Also, he lacked his father's drive and devoted too much of his time to the composition of Latin poetry. He married an Englishwoman, and their son, Ludwig, gradually superseded his father.

The Feldbauschs greeted the Crimean War with a relief that proved ill-founded. Karl August made several disastrous miscalculations, which allowed his rivals to satisfy the demands of the combatants. Ludwig spent a small fortune wooing the Russians. According to Girving, he made 'clumsy attempts to bribe government contractors and civil servants, and even gave expensive presents to their families'. His ambitions were constantly frustrated by his competitors; and finally his hopes were destroyed by the death of Tsar Nicholas I, the fall of Sebastopol and the Peace of Paris. Karl August died in 1858. The War of Italian Unification and the Franco-Prussian War allowed Ludwig to regain some of the ground that had been lost. In 1872 he retired. The profits of war formed a substantial dowry for his only child, Augusta Alexandra, when she married Count Paul von Doenecke.

Professor Girving was chiefly interested in the Crimean War episode. She contended that the machinations of Ludwig and his rivals had severely impaired the performance of the Russian army, and she derived a long list of domestic and international consequences from this.

But why had Wolfgang wanted the book? He had been the last man on earth to pursue historical research for its own sake. The only possible reason was the brief paragraph about Augusta Alexandra Feldbausch, the grandmother of Mrs Issler. But this answer undermined the theory that he had traced Wilhelmina solely as a favour for Great-aunt Luise. As far as I knew, my aunt's interest was confined to the von Doeneckes she had known, not their ancestors.

Suppose, I thought for the first time, Wolfgang were interested in the von Doeneckes for his own sake, not for Great-aunt Luise's: what then? What was in it for him? I had known my brother as well as you can know anyone. He didn't want power, particularly, or even money; he valued them not for themselves but only insofar as they brought him independence. Essentially he was a solitary man whom circumstances had forced to be gregarious. In the German Democratic Republic you have to join in if you want to succeed; and the same, perhaps to a lesser extent, is true even in the West. He must have scented a promising advantage in the Feldbauschs and the von Doeneckes. It could only be something that came from that nineteenth-century union between new money and old blood.

And was it absurd to think that the something might have killed him?

*

134

That was Friday. Saturday I spent at Broadway, dictating letters and writing my report to Bochmann. On Sunday the weather changed: the temperature dropped a couple of degrees, the sky was a deep, cloudless blue and the sun shone so brightly it hurt your eyes.

When I woke up, I was dreaming of Elizabeth. It was one of those not unpleasant dreams when you want something but never quite get it, but the possibility of getting it is never ruled out either; so you remain indefinitely poised on a knife edge of anticipation.

I knew that I couldn't wait until tomorrow to see her. In any case she might not be at the fair. I cheated shamelessly, telling myself it was essential that we met to pool our information. It wasn't like that at all, but even to myself I was too cautious, and perhaps too afraid, to admit the truth.

At 8.30 I left the house and walked to the Underground. The streets were uncluttered with people and cars. I didn't think I was being followed, but as usual I couldn't be sure: it depended partly on how important Klose and Hebburn thought I was. I guessed that neither of them had unlimited manpower at their disposal.

I took a train to central London and rang Elizabeth's number from a payphone at Bond Street. I was lucky. She answered it herself.

'I thought you wanted to wait until tomorrow.' Her voice sounded fuzzy with sleep. 'But I'm glad you called. Rownall's leaving me to mind the shop so I won't see you at the fair.'

'Something's come up,' I said. 'Can I see you today?'

'You can't talk now?'

135

'I'd rather do it face to face.'

'Okay. Where?'

'I have to be careful.'

'You've still got watchers? Them or us?'

'These days I think it's them and them. And I don't know for sure.' I was stumbling over my words. 'But presumably they're professionals, so I wouldn't necessarily notice them.'

'Come here,' she said.

'But surely – '

'It's not as stupid as it sounds. The back yard runs down to the railway line. There's a footpath between the line and our fence. It's straight – you'd see if there was anyone behind you.'

'How will I know which is your bit of fence? And what about the people you live with?'

'I'll be surprised if any of them are awake before midday. Our fence has got more holes than fence. It's the only back yard with a red tent.'

'In this weather?'

'One of the students has got this thing about Antarctica.' There was a gurgle of laughter on the other end of the line. 'He's trying to acclimatize himself. He put the tent up on Friday but he hasn't gotten round to sleeping in it.'

Half an hour later I was walking along the footpath in Kensal Rise. The sun was still shining and I felt absurdly optimistic. No one was behind me. I met a man walking an alsatian and pair of teenagers sharing a can of lager. It was all so easy. I couldn't have missed the red tent if I had tried. The gap in the fence would have taken a small car. I walked up the overgrown garden, my feet crunching on the frost that still covered the long grass. Elizabeth waved from one of the ground-floor windows. She opened the back door, which led straight into the kitchen.

The squalor took me by surprise: the walls were stained with damp and grease; mould flourished on unwashed plates; the floor was gritty in places and sticky in others.

'Communal living,' Elizabeth said drily. 'I'd forgotten what it was like to be a student.'

'Messy. In more ways than one.'

'I've made some coffee. We'll take it up to my room.'

She was wearing the jeans and jersey she'd worn when I first met her. Her hair was freshly washed; she wore no make-up; and her skin looked as if she had scrubbed it. In this setting she was like a primrose in a heap of manure.

Carrying the coffee pot, I followed her into a hall and up a flight of stairs. The house was quiet and there was a powerful smell of stale beer. A woman had undressed on her way to bed, leaving a trail of clothes on the stairs. All the doors on the first landing were closed except the one to the bathroom. A man with a shaven head was sleeping in the bath; his mouth was open and he was snoring.

Elizabeth led the way up another, narrower flight of stairs. 'There was a party last night.' Something in her voice told me she wasn't enjoying this self-imposed exile. 'They asked me but I didn't go.'

At the top of the stairs she opened the door on the right. It was a small room with a dormer window overlooking the railway line. A table and chair stood beneath the window. There was a wardrobe, a chest of drawers, a single bed and, in the middle of the floor, a two-bar electric fire with a frayed flex. Everything was superficially clean, which had the effect of making

137

the underlying dirt more noticeable. She had tidied away her possessions. The room was impersonal, like my flat.

'You shouldn't be here,' I said before I could stop myself.

'Do I have a choice? You have the chair. Ten years ago I could have slotted into a house like this. You know something? These kids make me feel old.'

She sat cross-legged on the bed. I poured the coffee. Our hands touched as I gave her the mug.

'Who goes first?' I said. 'You or me?'

'You. You're the one who's got something important to say.'

'I didn't say that, not exactly.' Avoiding her eyes, I told her everything that had happened since we last met on Wednesday evening. I concentrated on the facts. When I told her about the beating I had received on Thursday night, her hands tightened around the mug. Elizabeth's face was just a white blur against the faded wallpaper. There was no point in pretending that Hebburn had given me nothing more than a fatherly lecture. I didn't want to upset her but I had to tell her. It wasn't too late for her to withdraw from this business.

I described the interview with Klose and the discovery that Wolfgang had borrowed a book that mentioned Wilhelmina von Doenecke's grandmother. I didn't comment and I didn't speculate. Nor did she.

When I had finished, she said, 'I can't match that.' Her voice sounded shaky. 'Rownall went out to lunch on Friday so I had a chance to snoop. I think he's short of money.'

'Him or the firm?'

'Both, maybe. I can read a balance sheet. I went

through all the accounts I can find. He's got an over-draft of £25,000. The utility bills for last quarter are still waiting to be paid. Not just the office ones, his home as well. And his wife called, wanting to know if he'd had time to clear her charge account at Harrods. Have you met a guy called Toughton?'

'Something to do with the warehouse Rownall uses.' A surly man with a broken nose and a lot of muscle. 'Manager or foreman, isn't he?'

'That's the one. They had a meeting in the morning and I heard some of what Toughton was saying. Wasn't very hard – he was shouting. The warehouse staff are up in arms because Rownall's been employing casual labour on the side.'

'Did you find out why?'

She shrugged. 'To avoid paying overtime? I think Toughton was in on it. What he objected to was the fact that the other guys found out. There was a lot about a man named Custer, like the general. Toughton said he'd sacked him, that the guy was a troublemaker. I don't think Rownall approved.'

A train went by. Even with the window closed it made conversation difficult. Elizabeth waited until the sound had died away.

'There was a call from a man named Howard Unsterworth. Rownall was out so he left a message with me. "Definitely Isaac Oliver". I told Rownall, and he just said "I see", but I could tell he was pleased. If he owns it, I'm not surprised.'

'You know him? It?'

She grinned at my bewilderment. 'Isaac Oliver was a British miniaturist. Elizabethan, a pupil of Hilliard's. Mainly portraits, I think. I don't know what his work is worth but it would certainly make a dent in that overdraft. I checked out Unsterworth. He deals in antiques and fine art.'

'The trouble is,' I said, 'we don't know what's connected and what isn't. We don't know who's telling us lies. Klose or Hebburn could have been behind Wolfgang's death. I'm scared.'

'You want out?'

'No.' I watched her. The morning's optimism had evaporated. This was a nasty, violent business, and it would probably get worse. I had been a fool to recruit her in the first place. I was a worse fool to want her to be more than an ally.

'What are you thinking?' she said.

'I think it would be better if you were out of this. If you found another job, went back to the States, even.'

'But gallant Gerhard soldiers on? Is that it?'

I flushed. 'Something like that.'

'You think I'm more trouble than I'm worth, huh?'

'Don't get me wrong. I'm involved in this whether I like it or not. Besides, Wolfgang was my brother. I don't have any choice. But you do. No one knows you're a part of this. You can just walk away.'

'Where?'

'What do you mean?'

'You heard. Right now it happens that there's nowhere I want to go. Okay, so Wolfgang was your brother. What about Aunt Willy? Are you saying she doesn't count, or something?' The green eyes were bright with rage. She held herself perfectly still, unnaturally so, as if only her will prevented her from quivering. And suddenly I knew I had entirely misread her mood.

Wolfgang once said that half the sorrows in the world were caused by the fact that men thought

140

women spoke the same language as they did. 'But of course they don't,' he'd said. 'If you talk to a woman you need an interpreter.'

Elizabeth wasn't so much angry as desperate. Maybe she wanted something to do, to engage her mind and emotions. In a flash of intuition I guessed that the failure of her marriage, the deaths of her father and Mrs Issler, and even the sudden descent into relative poverty had left her drifting. In this godless world we use people, ambitions and possessions as our navigation aids; take them away, and the alien emptiness of the ocean is frightening. I offered a sort of compass. Not a very reliable one but marginally better than none at all.

'There are two alternatives,' she said harshly. 'We go on with this together or we go on separately. Take your choice.'

'Then we'd better stay together.'

Another train rumbled past the house. As the sound of it diminished, so did the tension between us. My feelings were a muddle of relief, regret, worry and happiness. Elizabeth smiled at me, I smiled back.

'I was trying to think about this from Wolfgang's point of view,' I said. 'Trying to guess what he wanted. He had this – what's the word? – fantasy about a place called the Lenné Triangle.'

'Okay,' Elizabeth said. 'Let's start there.'

SEVEN

The Lenné Triangle was in the centre of Berlin: eight acres of what had once been real estate, enclosed by three streets. It was near what used to be the Potsdamer Platz. Long before Berlin was divided, history made it a place of unlikely juxtapositions.

The name came from one of its inhabitants, Peter Lenné, who was a garden planner. The Brothers Grimm lived on Lennéstrasse. In 1930 Mendelsohn, the Jewish architect, used concrete and glass to build Columbus House, an office block that astonished the city with its modernity. Even the Nazis must have admired it: three years later, the Gestapo made Columbus House their headquarters.

After the war, when the Allies divided Berlin into sectors, the Lenné Triangle was allocated to the Russians. The area had suffered badly during the war, and in 1953 many of the remaining buildings were burned out. That was in the time of the strikes, when the fascists tried in vain to halt the inexorable march of socialism. Afterwards the bulldozers went into the Triangle, flattened the rubble and left it.

In 1961 the East German government decided that an Anti-Fascist Barrier was necessary for the moral and economic health of the state. The Lenné Triangle, a wasteland, was in the Soviet sector but the Wall left it out; the enclave jutted into West Berlin, and enclosing it would have posed too many logistical problems. The Triangle remained in the Soviet sector even though it was on the wrong side of the Wall.

Nature filled the vacuum. Birch trees sprouted from the rubble and grew into a dense young wood. Rabbits colonized the Gestapo's cellars. West Berliners were afraid of the place, for the Border Brigade of the People's National Army made occasional forays across the Wall; they asserted the sovereignty of the GDR by dragging away the tramps and the lovers who had strayed into the Triangle for want of anywhere better to go.

In 1988 the interested parties decided to rationalize the position. The Lenné Triangle was to be handed over to West Berlin, as part of a complicated agreement that involved the Allies and both Germanies. The West Berlin Senate decided to use the site for the West Tangent motorway extension. The transaction was due to take place on 1 July.

All very sensible. Both East and West Berlin would benefit from the move. But a few weeks beforehand, several hundred people moved into the Lenné Triangle. Most of them were young. There were children among them, and dogs to chase the rabbits. In a corner of the site they built a rickety village: Mendelsohn used concrete and glass for the Columbus Tower; the new arrivals made do with plastic sheets and hardboard. The Lenné Triangle, they said, was their country; this was their little democracy in the shadow of the Wall. It would be a green triangle of peace in the middle of a city at war with itself.

Well, it was stupid. Unrealistic. Doomed from the start. The inhabitants were immoral layabouts from West Berlin, the rotten dregs of a rotten society. But on both sides of the Wall the affair aroused immense interest. In the West, the press called them Autonomes, Alternatives or (most accurately, perhaps) Chaotics.

The police in West Berlin reacted with water cannon and tear gas. In the East, however, the Border Brigade chatted and joked with the new inhabitants of the Lenné Triangle. They did it under orders, of course; this was a fine opportunity to make propaganda at the expense of the West. But there were rumours in East Berlin that the Border Brigade quite enjoyed the novel experience of leaning out of their watchtowers and talking to people.

At 5 a.m. on 1 July the West Berlin police invaded the Triangle. The Border Brigade, still smiling, helped about 150 villagers over the Wall; they had lorries waiting for them.

Then, as in 1953, the bulldozers moved in. Now there are no more birch trees, no more rabbits and no more Chaotics.

'The Lenné Triangle obsessed Wolfgang,' I said to Elizabeth. 'He had a video of a TV item about it — West German, of course.'

'They showed how dumb the whole thing is.'

'The Chaotics? Maybe. But they *were* clowns.'

'That's not the point, Gerhard.' She leant forward, her face eager and very beautiful. 'You've got a world divided into two armed camps. Berlin is where they meet head-on. But it doesn't have to be that way. That's what your Chaotics proved.'

I shrugged. That was what my brother had felt — though he was a European and an East German at that; and therefore his feelings were tainted with cynicism whereas Elizabeth's were tinged with enthusiasm. A difference, perhaps, between the old world and the new.

'Wolfgang didn't like the German Democratic Republic,' I said. 'But he didn't much like the West either. This affair fascinated him not because he sympathized with the Chaotics but because it wasn't part of either system.' I hesitated, groping to find the right words. 'He . . . he just wanted to be by himself in his private Lenné Triangle. That's why I don't think he was spying.'

'You make him sound very selfish.'

'He wasn't. No more than anyone else.' Defending my brother was a reflex that dated back to my childhood, to that house in Pankow. 'In the GDR everyone retreats into a little niche. Just family and maybe a few friends: a sort of self-help association. It's the only protection we've got against the state. Wolfgang was the same. Within his niche he wasn't selfish.'

'But he was up to something.'

'Wolfgang was always up to something. I wish I knew if Bochmann was involved. There must be a reason why he chose me.'

Springs creaked in the room next door. A woman moaned.

'Teichler's book,' Elizabeth said softly. 'Snape and Aunt Willy. Rownall was Wolfgang's closest associate here. Wolfgang chose him. Rownall had Aunt Willy's address. When Wolfgang died he was Rownall's guest. He's got labour problems at his warehouse and he's short of cash. If I were Hebburn – or Klose, for that matter – I'd be interested in Rownall.'

Next door, the creaks became louder and settled into a rhythm that soon picked up speed. So did the moans, which mutated into gasps and finally into shrieks.

Elizabeth grinned. 'Life goes on. Like the rabbits in the Gestapo cellars.'

The house was waking up. It was time to go. I stood up. 'What I'd like to do,' I said, 'is talk to the man Toughton sacked. What's his name?'

Elizabeth got off the bed and opened a drawer in the dressing table. She found a scrap of paper and passed it to me. *Grant Custer, 184 Ardwell House, E9.* She had scribbled the phone number underneath.

'Where did you get it?' I said.

'Rownall had to go to the john in the afternoon. He left his coat in his office. So I went through the pockets.' She paused for an instant and then said the words I was about to say. 'Maybe Rownall wants a word with Custer too.'

It was lunchtime before I got there. I travelled by bus. According to the street directory, E9 was Hackney. It was a dreary place where old and new buildings uneasily co-existed in architectural anarchy. The common features were grime and decay. It reminded me of parts of Schwerin and East Berlin, except here there was more rubbish.

I had phoned Custer from central London, saying I was a journalist writing a piece on labour relations. I heard a baby howling in the background and a woman shouting. He didn't want to talk to me. When I mentioned the word 'expenses', he changed his mind but stipulated that we meet in a pub.

'How will I recognize you?' I'd asked.

'You won't,' he said. 'Just ask for me at the bar. The public, okay?'

The Seven Bells was a sprightly survivor from another century; it looked in rather better repair than the postwar tower blocks around it. Inside, the place

146

was so packed I could hardly reach the counter. When I got there I was sweating, and my eyes smarted from the smoke. A large group photograph of the royal family was hanging on one wall, illuminated by its own spotlight. I ordered half a pint of lager and asked for Grant Custer. The landlady, a dyed blonde in her sixties, looked suspiciously at me.

'Grant who?' she said, giving me my change.

The majority of the customers began to sing 'Happy Birthday' to someone named Billy.

'Custer,' I shouted.

'Never heard of him. Who's next?'

'Me,' said at least three people.

I felt someone touch my arm. 'Mine's a pint of best with a large scotch.'

The landlady abandoned the other customers and served the man beside me. He was small, with long arms and dark, greasy hair. Bushy eyebrows above small brown eyes. A moustache that hung in a ragged fringe over his mouth, partly concealing discoloured teeth. He could have been any age between twenty-five and forty.

'Have one yourself, love,' he said. 'My friend's paying.'

'Don't mind if I do. Rum and black all right?'

'Make it a double,' he said generously.

I cleared my throat. 'You're Grant Custer?'

'So they tell me. Let's find somewhere quieter.'

I followed him to a door at the end of the counter. The crowd parted for him as it hadn't done for me: Custer was known and respected. I held his beer while he unlocked the door. We went into a small, untidy office. Custer propped himself against the desk and waved me to a chair.

'Bit basic. But nice and private, eh?' He lifted his glass. 'Cheers.'

'What was all that about?' I said.

'You what?'

'That business at the bar.'

'Oh *that*. I wanted to see you first, didn't I? So I said to Gran, "I got a business meeting on, and someone's coming to see me. But you don't know me, right?" It was Gran that served you out there. Pillar of the licensing trade, she is.'

'But why?'

'Nothing personal. I mean, you might have been a cop. Or you might have been one of John Toughton's heavy brigade.' He began to roll a cigarette but kept his eyes on me. 'Are you a Kraut or something?'

I nodded.

'Who do you work for?'

'I freelance,' I said. 'For German papers.'

'And what's all this about labour relations?'

'I'm doing a piece on unfair dismissal. A comparison between the two countries.'

'Who gave you my name?'

'A man I met in a pub last night.' This was the question I had been dreading. 'Jack? Jim? Something beginning with J.'

'Which pub?'

'It was near Canning Town. Silvertown Way, was that the road?' Rownall's warehouse was off Silvertown Way. 'One of my contacts took me there. The Something Arms, I think.'

'The Brickies?'

I shrugged. 'Perhaps.'

'Tall fellow, was he?' He lit the cigarette with a gold

148

lighter that had his initials stamped on one corner. 'Blue eyes and not much on top?'

I looked blankly at him.

He tapped his head. 'Hair, I mean.'

'Balding? Yes, maybe.'

'Sounds like Jim Thorn. What did he tell you?'

'That you'd been sacked because you'd complained about the management using casual labour. Said you might be willing to talk to me.'

'I might. If the price is right.'

'I could manage twenty,' I said.

'Fifty.'

I stood up.

'Where you off to then?'

'Do you know how many people in the UK were dismissed last week?' I said. 'Four or five hundred.' The figure sounded plausible. 'It's a buyer's market, Mr Custer.'

'You got to find them first.'

'Expenses like this come out of my own pocket.' That was true enough. 'And I'm in no hurry.'

'My figure,' he said, puffing his cigarette as though it were a Cuban cigar, 'may be open to negotiation.'

So we negotiated, settling on £25 and another round of drinks for Custer and his grandmother – £10 now and £15 on delivery.

'Tight bastards, you Krauts,' he said without rancour. 'You drive a hard bargain.'

'You worked at a warehouse, I understand.' I took out a pad and pretended to make a note. 'Who exactly are the management?'

'The place is owned by a property company in the City. They don't matter. But it's run by a bloke called

John Toughton. Proper little bleeder, he is. *Big* bleeder, I should say — used to box for the army.'

'Who uses it?'

'The warehouse? All sorts, importers mainly. The bigger firms have long-term contracts. They have so many cubic feet, see, and we reserve it for them. The small fry just rent what they need as and when they need it.'

'Is — ?' I changed the question in midstream. 'What do you handle, and where does it come from?'

'You name it, we've had it. Kitchen sinks, bags of concrete, videos. Even had a stuffed elephant once. The stuff comes up to us from the docks. We hold it for the importers, then pass it on to the wholesalers once they've done the paperwork.'

'Do you actually unpack it?'

'It depends. Most of it's containerized these days. But some loads have to be split up.'

'And what was the problem with Toughton?'

'There's always a problem with Toughton.' Custer scowled at me. 'He's a right bastard. He's on the make himself but if anyone else tries to get a piece of the action he comes down on them like a ton of shit.'

'The action? You mean stealing?'

'Stealing? Who said anything about stealing? More like natural wastage. Happens all the time. You know what I mean: a box breaks open, a microwave falls off the back of a pallet. Lost in transit. Nothing unreasonable, of course: all small-scale stuff.' He ran his fingers through his hair and perhaps recollected that I was an unknown quantity. 'Mind you, I wasn't into that sort of thing myself. I keep my nose clean. Always have' — he tapped his nose to emphasize the point — 'and always will.'

'But Toughton himself isn't as honest?'

'He's as bent as a corkscrew. To him it's a perk of the job. *His* job. No one would mind if he turned a blind eye to other people doing the same thing. But does he, hell.' A new thought occurred to him. 'Look, mate. All this is off the record, isn't it? I don't want my name in the papers.'

'Don't worry. I'll just call you "a reliable source".' I hoped that was an accurate description. 'And in any case, nothing I write will be published in the UK.'

'Just checking.' He relaxed visibly. 'Don't get me wrong.'

'Why did Toughton dismiss you?'

'It's a long story.' Custer swallowed the rest of his beer to sustain him. 'And it shows you what a devious bugger he is. Generally things slacken off after Christmas, but these last few weeks there's been more work than usual. Now that's good news for us – means we're offered overtime, see? But Mr Bloody Toughton had other ideas. He went around the pubs one night, hired a few lads out of the dole queue, cleared a whole shipment overnight. Cash in hand, know what I mean? About a dozen blokes. He could've had an army. No stamps, no tax, no insurance, no overtime. So everyone's happy except the blokes who ought to have done the work.'

'But what's in it for him? He's an employee too, surely?'

'He's on some sort of commission. The faster he shifts things through, the more space he lets, the more money he makes. As long as the money keeps coming in, no one's going to ask him questions. And that's not counting the backhander.'

'The what?'

151

'The fistful of fivers Toughton got from the importer.'

'Are you sure about that?'

He rolled his eyes towards the ceiling. 'For Christ's sake. I haven't had a guided tour of his wallet, if that's what you mean. But he wouldn't give a client preferential treatment just for the hell of it, would he?'

'Who was the importer?'

'What's that to you?' Custer was like a small, furry animal scenting danger but uncertain of its nature. 'I thought you wanted to know about me being sacked.'

'I do. But the more details, the better.'

'It'll cost you,' he said.

'I think I know already. I just want confirmation.'

'What's the name begin with, then?'

'R,' I said. 'As in Rostock, where the shipment came from.'

For an instant he looked both puzzled and disappointed. Then his face cleared. 'Jim Thorn told you, didn't he? For a moment I thought you were being clever.'

'So why did Toughton sack you?'

'Well, there was a lot of ill feeling among the lads. It went on for days. They sort of elected me spokesman so I went to see his lordship. Toughton just told me to bugger off. And the next day he sacked me.'

Spokesman, I wondered, or ringleader?

'But he was clever,' he said with a hint of envy in his voice. 'I told you he was devious. He did a spot-check on the lockers, right? Found a cordless phone in mine.' Custer sniffed and widened his eyes in simulated shock. 'Of course I'd never seen it before. "It's a plant," I said, "I been framed." But it was my locker. Toughton says he'll give me a choice: I can stay and he'll call the cops, or I can go and he'll say no more about it. "Don't want no trouble," he says. "Court appearances are too time-consuming." '

'That's terrible,' I said.

'Wicked. But what can you do? It's them and us, like it's always been. We do the work, they take the money.'

'This shipment. Do you know what was in it?'

'Toys, mainly. Jim Thorn saw the paperwork lying around in Toughton's office. Come from Rostock, like you said. That's the other Germany, isn't it? Commie bastards.'

'Where were they going to?'

'I don't know. Wholesalers, I guess. Probably about half a dozen of them.'

I asked a few more questions just to give colour to my journalistic cover story. Custer continued to play the injured innocent with such professional aplomb that I guessed it was his usual role in life.

'How did you know that Toughton had moved the shipment?'

'It was obvious. When we clocked out, there were the containers, waiting to be unloaded. Next morning they'd gone. The stuff was repacked and waiting for the trucks in the loading bay.'

'But how did you know about Toughton going around the pubs, and all those details?'

'Well, there's knowing and knowing, isn't there? More of an inspired guess, like. But I know I'm right.'

He concentrated on rolling another cigarette. This time he needed to look at what he was doing. I knew I was onto something, but I wasn't sure what. Alternatively he was a better con-man than I thought.

'There's a law of libel,' I said. 'I need more than guesswork. I need proof.' I eased my wallet out of my pocket. 'And of course I'd be willing to pay for it.'

'I might be able to give you an introduction,' he said slowly.

'To someone who was on that nightshift?'

Custer nodded. 'But I can't guarantee anything.'

'Why not?'

'The bloke's a mate of mine. He's signing on, you see. He's having a quiet drink and up comes Toughton and makes him an offer he can't refuse. But it's not an offer he'd want to talk about. There're a lot of nosy parkers in this world.'

'Guaranteed anonymity,' I said. 'All I want is a quiet chat.'

I laid the £15 I owed him on the desk. He swept it up. The wallet was still in my hands. Custer could see the edge of a £20 note.

'It won't be cheap,' he said.

'I didn't think it would be. But what can you offer exactly? That's what I want to know.'

'Tell you what,' Custer said. 'Let's have another drink while we talk about it.'

As the daylight faded, so did my enthusiasm for meeting Custer's friend. But it was too late to back out.

The bar was empty. Custer wrapped himself carefully in a dark jacket and plugged the remaining gaps in his defences with black gloves, a bobble hat and a long woollen scarf.

'Freeze your balls off out there,' he said. 'I forgot my thermal underwear this morning.'

His grandmother was washing glasses with a cigarette dangling from the corner of her mouth. She didn't look at us as we left the office. Nor did the thickset young man who was sweeping the floor. Only a Doberman showed any interest, and that was hostile. He objected to me.

'Get out of it, Rastus,' the grandmother screamed, still without raising her eyes. The dog stopped growling and slunk behind the bar. It kept watching me.

The young man put down his broom and opened the door. Two heavy bolts, a chain and two locks. There were steel shutters over the windows.

'It's a rough area,' Custer said. 'Can't take chances, especially with licensed premises.'

'It's the bloody coloureds,' the grandmother said. 'Never used to be like this.'

'Don't you believe her,' Custer whispered to me. 'It was even worse in the old days. Now. You know the way, don't you? Give me a couple of minutes, okay, and then Chris will let you out.'

He slipped outside. I waited by the door. Chris swept around my feet and the dog peered balefully at me. The old woman broke a glass and swore. I was very tired.

I still didn't know whom we were going to meet. Custer had made several phone calls and a series of complicated arrangements, and I gathered that the meeting would take place on neutral territory, at some sort of club. The place was closed but Custer knew the manager. I would have preferred to see the man alone. Custer, however, wouldn't let me dispense with his services. As far as he was concerned, I was the golden goose, and he wanted to retain a monopoly on the disposal of any eggs I might disgorge. As part of the deal, Custer had insisted that we went separately to the club. He said he didn't want to be seen with me in public; you never knew who might be watching. Who was he afraid of? The police? Toughton? I was reasonably sure that Custer had whitewashed his part in the affair at the warehouse. It might be that he was terrified of being seen with a journalist. Or perhaps the secrecy was habitual to him, a reflex like my own habit of defending my brother.

But there was another possibility I couldn't afford to ignore. I had a wallet that Custer probably thought was fuller than it really was. I was a stranger to the area and a foreigner as well.

It was time to leave. For a few seconds I stood on the doorstep, listening to the door being barred behind me. I didn't have a choice, not really. Custer's friend was the only lead I had left.

The route took me down an access road between two tower blocks. Few people were around. A knot of young men stood round the open bonnet of a thirty-year-old Cadillac. Some of them gave me curious stares as I passed. I crossed a well-lit main road that was nearly empty of traffic. Immediately opposite was a derelict chapel, its windows masked with strips of corrugated iron. A stone-flagged path led from the pavement to the door. A man wrapped in newspaper was huddled in the recessed doorway. For an instant we looked at one another. Neither of us said anything. I think he was a man; destitution makes its victims sexless.

Beyond the chapel the road rose up to a bridge. On the other side I found a flight of steps down to the towpath of a canal. The water glowed a faint yellow from the reflected lights of the city. On the right, a strip of wasteland sloped upwards to a high brick wall. There was enough light to see the path, but the ground beside it was a dark mass of vegetation. There would be bushes, I guessed, and stunted trees. A small army could be lurking in the undergrowth, waiting to spring an ambush.

'Two or three minutes' walk,' Custer had said, blowing into his shaggy moustache. 'Simple as ABC.'

So far it had taken me at least five minutes. I had to follow the towpath until I came to a footbridge. The club, which was attached to a community centre beside a recreation ground, was the first building you came to on the other bank.

If anything was going to happen to me on the way, it would be here. I hesitated at the top of the steps. The path was empty. The footbridge, a black stripe across the yellow canal, was less than 200 metres away. There were lights in some of the windows of a large, square building nearby. Almost certainly Custer was already there, looking for something to assuage his perpetual thirst.

Almost certainly. But perhaps he – or even one of his friends – was closer still. Nothing very subtle, I guessed: a heavy spanner, perhaps, or a knife.

How far would a man like Custer be prepared to go? The canal might be a temptation, especially if he could find something to weigh the body down. He might calculate that the body of a foreigner would be difficult to identify at the best of times; after a few months in that stagnant water, it would be anonymous for ever.

Another thought occurred to me, even less pleasant than the last. Suppose the affair had been an elaborate trap from the start. Suppose Rownall had left the address for Elizabeth to find; suppose Custer had been bribed, long before I had met him, to fool a gullible foreigner and lure him to the canal; suppose Custer were already miles away, building up an unshakeable alibi, and someone far more formidable were waiting for me in the shadows.

I am a coward. I've always known that, but I hated having to admit it to myself, let alone to Elizabeth or to the ghost of Wolfgang.

I picked my way down the steps. At the bottom my shoe chinked against glass. I stooped and found an empty bottle. There was a faint smell of sherry. I picked the bottle up, holding it by the neck. As weapons go, it wasn't much; but it was better than nothing.

The path stretched ahead. I walked slowly along it, pausing every few paces to watch and listen. I saw no one. Occasionally there were rustles on my right, which sounded as if they were made by small animals that were as frightened as I was. If someone were waiting for me, there would be no sound until the moment came for the final rush.

The ground beneath my feet was treacherous. The frost had hardened the ruts and potholes and turned the water they contained to ice. Once I stumbled and nearly twisted my ankle. The footbridge drew nearer. Another light came on in the building on the far side of the canal. My hand was so cold it seemed to have frozen onto the neck of the bottle. A jet passed over-head.

As I glanced up at it, I tripped again. I fell forward, my hands outstretched. The bottle slipped out of my fingers, spun through the air and landed on the bank. The palms of my hands scraped along the ground, just as they had done on Thursday when Leather Jacket threw me out of Hebburn's car. The bottle rolled into the water with a faint splash.

The fall jolted me into another frame of mind. It made me feel ridiculous, and no one likes that. I was so angry that for a moment I forgot to be afraid. I swung around. A ridge of black, frozen mud curved out of the undergrowth across the path. I couldn't distinguish which was mud and which was shadow. Or maybe it wasn't mud: it might be a branch from one of the trees. I was past caring. Whatever it was it had tripped me up, and I hated it.

So I kicked it.

Before my foot made contact, the petulance had evaporated. The tip of my shoe snagged on something yielding. I crouched, my hand outstretched. My fingers touched wool. It was knitted in a ribbed pattern. I moved my hand along to the right. There was a knotted fringe at the end, and one of the knots had caught on the corner of a brick impacted in the mud.

A scarf. It wasn't cold and it wasn't wet. My hand moved of its own volition in the opposite direction. I followed the line of the scarf across the path and into the undergrowth. It was completely dark in there. The long grass brushed my skin like damp feathers. But the scarf was dry.

Less than half a metre off the path I touched another sort of wool; it covered something rounded like a ball. The other end of the scarf was coiled around an irregular cylinder. Below it was a stiffer material, like an upturned collar. Above was a fringe of hair, just like a ragged moustache. Then my nails tapped against a row of teeth and I stopped pretending I had found a series of similes. My fingers were wet and slightly sticky.

Oh God. He was still warm.

At that moment the only thing that steadied me was the possibility that he was alive. I ran my hand down his coat until I found a pocket. I was lucky: it contained his tobacco and the gold lighter. The flame flickered for a couple of seconds before the wind blew it out.

Custer was curled up on his side. Miniature reflections of the flame gleamed in his open eyes. Panic rose inside me like water; drowning in fear, I thought, must be the worst death of all. I fought it automatically by keeping myself busy with details.

When the light died, I felt his wrist for a pulse that wasn't there. Then I undid a button and slipped my hand inside the coat. The jersey underneath was warm and moist; the jacket must have retained most of the blood. He wasn't breathing. His wallet was still in the inside pocket so he hadn't been robbed. Just stabbed or shot and tossed aside in the bushes.

I had got it all wrong: Grant Custer was the victim, not the predator. And I would never have known the truth if the end of his scarf hadn't caught on the path, if I hadn't tripped, and if I hadn't lost my temper.

I wiped my hand on the grass, trying to get rid of the blood. My stomach churned as I stood up. Nausea burned my throat. Then I remembered the long, straight towpath. I glanced back the way I had come, and forward to the footbridge. The path was still empty.

Had the killer had time to escape? There was a strong possibility that he was still there, hiding in the bushes. He might have seen me at the head of the steps, watched me walking down the path. He might even have seen my face by the flame of the lighter. Was he waiting for me to go or waiting to kill me?

This time I surrendered to the waves of panic. I was no longer rational. I wasn't a hero. I certainly wasn't a good citizen.

I was just a terrified animal, scurrying along the towpath towards the safety of the brightly-lit road.

EIGHT

Well, how do you feel when you stumble on a murdered man? When you suspect he was killed because he was willing to talk to you?

You feel guilty as well as terrified.

Everything I did seemed to move me further into the nightmare. This was the third murder. I knew the others must be connected but I couldn't prove it. The security forces of two countries were sniffing at my heels and I didn't even know why.

I still don't understand how I got back to Ealing. I think I walked most of the way. My mind was a blur. I remember buying a half-bottle of whisky at an off-licence. The man behind the counter refused to serve me until he had seen my money, and he kept his distance as though I were a dog with an uncertain temper.

Once I got inside the flat, the remnants of my self-control deserted me. I wrapped my arms round the lavatory bowl and lost the lager and what was left of breakfast. My teeth were chattering so I ran a bath. The hot water helped. Then I went to bed with a mug of sweet tea and the whisky. I cowered under the duvet for a while. Gradually I realized that curling up in the foetal position was not the most productive strategy. I sat up in bed and had some more whisky.

Who had killed Grant Custer? It was just conceivable

that his death had nothing to do with me, that he'd been killed by a stray mugger or someone with a unconnected grudge against him; but I didn't believe that. It was far more likely that he had been murdered because he was willing to talk about the labour problems at the warehouse. That gave me a shortlist of two: John Toughton and Sebastian Rownall. From what I'd seen of him, Toughton was the better bet. And the man had been a professional soldier.

The reason for Custer's death was harder to find. He knew that a shipment of East German toys had been illicitly unloaded at the warehouse. The toys were real: I'd seen the combine's manifests and the shipping documents for carriage, insurance and freight. But maybe there was something else in those containers – something worth killing for. Bochmann had to be involved at the East German end. What did the GDR have that was worth smuggling to the West, that was worth three lives? I pushed the problem aside; at present it was insoluble.

The whisky was helping. It numbed the feelings, warmed the stomach and created the illusion that I was thinking lucidly. It made a comforting, glugging noise as I refilled the mug to the halfway mark. I had three options and I didn't like any of them.

I could report Custer's death to the British police, who would inform Hebburn, who would eventually contact Margarete Klose. The British might well suspect me of having a hand in the murder. They would want to know why I hadn't reported it straightaway and why I had spent the afternoon with Custer. If I told them the truth, they had no reason to believe me; Hebburn wasn't going to give me a glowing testimonial. The British legal system was a mystery to me but, if the security forces had an interest, I couldn't expect to be treated as a respectable, public-spirited citizen. At best, I thought, they would send me out of the country in a blaze of publicity.

The most sensible course of action would be to call a taxi, get to the Embassy and pour my heart out to Fräulein Klose. She wouldn't take kindly to my private investigations but I didn't think she'd willingly hand me over to the British. State Security are possessive about their shooting rights over East German citizens; they don't like poachers on principle. But Klose would send me home in disgrace: a jail sentence perhaps, followed by a new career as a street cleaner or lavatory attendant. Toughton and Rownall would get off; the deaths of Wolfgang and Mrs Issler would never be explained; I would learn to live with my cowardice and I would never see Elizabeth again.

The third option was beautifully simple: do nothing. Finish the whisky and go to sleep. As far as I knew, no one had seen me on the towpath. The police would probably discover that Custer had spent the afternoon with a journalist; I hadn't told him my name. His grandmother, the barman and some of the customers would be able to describe me; but they hadn't seen me for long, and the collar of my coat had masked the lower half of my face. Who would connect a newspaperman in Hackney with an East German civil servant in Ealing?

Only Rownall and Toughton might make the connection if the police publicized a description of me. But they couldn't be sure. And they couldn't afford to confide their suspicions to the authorities.

With hindsight, the holes in my logic appal me. Suppose I'd been followed to Hackney by Special

Branch or State Security? At the time, however, my mind was fuddled with whisky and shock. I believed what I wanted to believe. I intended to do what I wanted. Which was, quite simply, to find out the truth about Wolfgang's death and in doing so get to know Elizabeth Allanton. Christ, we spend half our lives fooling ourselves and the other half trying to clear up the consequences.

'Gerhard!' Rownall bounced out of the taxi and waved at me. 'Over here!'

I struggled across Warwick Road, which was thick with traffic moving sluggishly north like a stream of treacle. I had come by Underground, and the Monday morning crowds had done nothing for my hangover. Rownall helped his wife out of the taxi. He looked exactly the same as usual. Somehow, after yesterday, I expected him to have sprouted horns and cloven hooves. He beamed at us both as I came up.

'My dear, this is Gerhard Herold. And this is Miranda.'

The photograph I had seen didn't do her justice. Miranda Rownall was a small, expensively-packaged woman, like an alluring elf. A lot of people were looking surreptitiously at her as they passed. Her eyes were a bright, cornflower blue. The short fur jacket was either mink or a very good imitation. She pushed a hand towards me and looked me over with interest.

'How do you do. You're very like your brother.'

'You knew him?' There was no reason why I should have been surprised but I was. 'I didn't realize.'

'Sebastian brought him to dinner. And he came over for Sunday lunch.' She had one of those crisp English voices that lend a false assurance to everything they say. 'David adored him. Our son, you know.'

'Children usually liked him,' I said.

'Let's go inside,' Rownall said. 'It's too cold to stand around on the pavement.'

He took Miranda's arm and shepherded us into the exhibition centre. The stands were arranged on two levels. I had been expecting something along the lines of the toy section at the Leipzig trade fair in September: the size, the variety and the vivid colours of the exhibits at Earls Court came as a shock. The British Toy and Hobby Manufacturers' Association were the organizers, and many of the companies represented here were their members. The companies had come to sell – retail, wholesale or export; and in some cases all three. As non-buyers, we were equipped with white badges, which gave us a similar status to that of conscientious objectors in a country at war.

We began with coffee in one of the bars. Rownall did most of the talking; the presence of his wife seemed to make him even more ebullient than usual. I didn't say much and nor did Mrs Rownall. He was such a pleasant little man that I wanted to take him at face value.

At his suggestion we separated when we left the bar. I didn't object. He wanted to cultivate potential customers and identify gaps in the market. In theory I was more interested in an overall view of the competition that faced the GDR. In practice I wanted to avoid Rownall.

'You don't mind if I look round by myself?' Mrs Rownall said to her husband. 'I'd only get in your way.'

'Of course not, darling.' He stroked her hand. 'You'd find it terribly tedious.'

She smiled at him and I looked away from his face. Rownall's eyes were hungry for her approval. For an instant he was emotionally naked. There was nothing specifically sexual about his need for her. I had seen the same look on the faces of children outside the window of a toyshop. Some hungers will never be satisfied.

I left them, and wandered along the aisles and up and down the escalators. I collected an armful of promotional literature. After an hour or so I was feeling tired and irritable – partly because the stands underlined the inadequacies of my own products, and partly because museums and exhibitions always have that effect on me.

'Cheer up,' a voice said behind me. 'What's wrong?'

I swung round. 'Mrs Rownall.'

'Miranda, please. What do you think of these?'

She was examining a display of rocking horses. They were superb animals, carved realistically in a mixture of hard and soft woods, immaculately finished and equipped with leather saddles and bridles. Despite her white badge, Miranda had the full attention of the company's rep. The rep seemed a little put out at the prospect of having to share her with another male.

'We have a sort of alcove in David's nursery,' she went on. 'A horse would be perfect for it.'

'They're beautiful,' I said. At a guess they were also almost as expensive as the real thing. 'Would he use it much?'

She shrugged, implying that value for money was not her main consideration. 'It's the look of the thing that counts. Every nursery should have a rocking horse, don't you think?'

The rep agreed enthusiastically and offered to put

her on his mailing list. She gave him her name and address.

'Let's go and have a drink or something,' she said, touching my arm. 'Then you can tell me why you were looking so gloomy.'

She had the knack of creating an atmosphere of instant intimacy. Some people have it and most don't. She swept me upstairs to what they called a bistro. I had another cup of coffee and she had some Perrier.

'Well, what's wrong?' she said.

'Oh, I loathe trade fairs,' I said lightly.

'Why?' She frowned, and then surprised me by adding: 'The competition?'

I shrugged. 'That's partly it.'

'But surely you've nothing to worry about. Sebastian says you're on to a winner.'

'I'm sure he's right – he knows the market here.'

'He's a shrewd man. That's why I married him. He'd better be right. We can't live on air.' The last two sentences were said with a smile but I don't think she was amused.

'Have you been married long?' I asked.

'Five years.' She raked me with those blue eyes. 'Does it surprise you? That I should have married him in the first place, I mean?'

The conversation had moved without warning on to another level. 'It's none of my business,' I said, more sharply than I had intended.

'I married him for security and because he makes me laugh.' She hesitated, not bothering to say why he had wanted to marry her. 'It's a flexible arrangement – within limits, naturally.'

I nodded, wondering what she was trying to say.

'Of course, I do expect – how can I put it? – certain

167

advantages in return.' She stroked the sleeve of the mink; she must have been sweltering inside it but she wouldn't take it off.

I thought about the overdraft and the utility bills. Rownall made a fifty to sixty per cent profit on the goods he got from us, and I assumed he imported from other countries, too. But it sounded as if Miranda were an expensive overhead.

'So you see,' she said wistfully, 'I wouldn't like anything to go wrong.'

'As far as I know,' I said, 'business is booming.'

'Well. That's *one* worry off my mind.'

She wanted me to ask her what else was worrying her and I resisted, automatically. I had the familiar feeling of being manipulated. Miranda Rownall was a pocket edition of Anna, my sister-in-law.

'Wolfgang mentioned you,' she said at last. 'He said the two of you were very close.'

'We were.' I paused. Would I ever be able to hear my brother's name without feeling that dull sensation of loss? Miranda was watching me carefully. Too carefully. She had a purpose in this conversation, and I had an idea what it might be. So I tested the theory with a lie: 'He told me about you, of course.'

The words could have meant almost anything. But she provided her own interpretation. Her eyes widened, and she touched her throat with the finger-tips of one hand: an absurdly theatrical gesture but it worked. She was very beautiful and she made me feel guilty for troubling her perfection.

'You haven't told Sebastian, have you?'

I shook my head.

'And you won't? You promise?'

'There is no reason why I should tell him. Is there?'

'But, Gerhard, if – '

She broke off. She was looking past me, towards the entrance. Her features rearranged themselves into a welcoming smile.

'Had enough?' Rownall said.

'Hello, darling. I was wilting, rather, and Gerhard came and rescued me. Have you seen those lovely rocking horses?'

He shook his head.

'We must get one for David.'

'But he'll want a real horse soon. A pony, I mean.'

'Not for ages. He'd get lots of use out of it. I've got a leaflet somewhere.' She delved half-heartedly into her handbag. 'Gerhard, can you remember the company's name?'

'Charton something, was it?'

'Charton Foster,' Rownall said. 'That means it'll cost a bomb.' He sounded resigned. Mink coats and de luxe rocking horses were part of the price he paid for a beautiful young wife.

Miranda had upset my thinking. If Rownall had found out that Wolfgang was having an affair with her, Wolfgang might have been killed for the most personal of reasons; his death might have had nothing to do with the East German exports at the warehouse.

'Gerhard?' Rownall was grinning at me. He knocked his knuckles on the table top. 'Anyone at home?'

'Sorry,' I said. 'I was miles away.'

'Lunch on Sunday, Miranda was saying. How about it? You can get a train from King's Cross and we'll pick you up at Luton station.'

'Yes – fine. I'd love to.'

'Why don't you ask your new floozie, darling?' Miranda said in that carrying voice. 'Make it a foursome.'

Rownall laughed. 'She means my secretary,' he explained.

'She's American,' Miranda told me. 'Have you met her?'

'I've talked to her on the phone.'

'I always get Sebastian to bring them to lunch.' She patted her husband's hand. 'I like to size up the competition, don't I?'

'You've got nothing to worry about,' Rownall said.

'Is she pretty, darling?'

'So so. Not a patch on you.'

I tried not to listen. It is unpleasant to be forced to eavesdrop on the coy cooings of a happily-married couple. It turns the stomach when you know one of them is acting out a lie.

As we were leaving the exhibition centre, I mentioned that Bochmann was arriving next Monday.

'The big white chief, eh?' Rownall said. 'You'll want to impress him with your industry.' He winked at me. 'I'll see what I can do.'

'We'll ask him to dinner,' Miranda said, serenely confident of her own powers of persuasion, 'and tell him how hard you've been working.'

'Jolly good idea, darling. Don't worry, Gerhard. We'll do our best for you.'

'Have you met him?' I asked casually.

Rownall shook his head. 'A pleasure in store. You can tell me about him on Sunday. We're going to Wheeler's for lunch. Like to come?'

'Another time,' I said. 'I've too much work to do.'

He hailed a taxi. I declined the offer of a lift and crossed the road to the Underground. Actually Rownall had a point about the importance of impressing Bochmann. The latter's position might be shaky but he was still my immediate superior. He was the man who had hired me, and he could just as easily fire me if he thought I wasn't pulling my weight. Whatever else Bochmann might be involved in, the success of the new export system was important to his career.

In the station I bought a *Standard*. I leafed through it. There was nothing about Custer, or even an anonymous body on a Hackney towpath. I didn't know whether to be relieved or worried. The absence of news could work both ways. The longer Custer's body was undiscovered, the less chance there would be of the authorities linking him with me. On the other hand, if the body *had* been found, the lack of publicity could only mean that the police were already aware that the case had a security angle.

I was hungry. Yesterday I had eaten practically nothing, and this morning I had got up too late for breakfast. Maybe I should have accepted Rownall's invitation. The thought of Rownall in his restaurant suddenly made me realize that he wouldn't be back at his office for at least a couple of hours. I found a payphone. Elizabeth answered at the second ring.

'How's it going?' I said.

There was a sharp intake of breath from the other end. Then: 'You just wouldn't believe the chaos here. It's like no one's done any filing for about three years.' She sounded tired. 'What happened yesterday?'

I gave her Custer's story about the warehouse and his dismissal.

'It figures,' Elizabeth said. 'It must be smuggling. So maybe Wolfgang got wind of it and they had to kill him. And maybe they figured he'd told Aunt Willy something about it, too, so she had to go. We need to

171

talk to one of the guys who did the unloading. Could Custer help us trace someone?'

'Custer can't do anything now.'

I told her the news. I told her about getting drunk last night, and about my whisky-flavoured ideas, which in the sober light of day seemed closer to arbitrary fantasy than rational speculation. When I finished she said nothing for a while.

'Elizabeth?' I even thought she might have put the phone down.

'I'm here. Gerhard, where's it going to end?'

'I don't know. I wish I did.' In an attempt to change the subject I mentioned the Rownalls' invitation to Sunday lunch.

'What's the wife like?' she said.

'Like the photo on Rownall's desk, but more so. And there's a complication: she had an affair with Wolfgang, and she doesn't want Rownall to find out. But what if he did?'

'That could mean . . .'

'Yes,' I said. 'It's a completely different slant, isn't it? Still, you'll see for yourself on Sunday. We could travel together, I suppose? It would seem natural.'

'Well, I guess that's something.' Her voice gave nothing away. The chance of being together on Sunday was something for me as well. What I would have liked to know was whether it was the same something for her.

'I'll work on Rownall,' I said. 'Perhaps I can get him to suggest we go together.'

'There's another thing,' Elizabeth said. 'Rownall had a letter from Howard Unsterworth this morning.'

'The antique dealer?'

'Right. It was marked "Private and Confidential". Luckily it was one of those envelopes you can get into at the side, and then reseal. The letter just asked Rownall to confirm in writing that all cheques should be made out to SJBR Associates.'

'Does that mean anything to you?'

'Not yet. But SJBR are Rownall's initials, and we know he's in financial trouble.'

'So he's siphoning off a few assets?' I said.

'Maybe. Kind of understandable. A little nest-egg. Look, I got to go. What are you going to do now?'

'Have lunch. I'm starving.'

'Me too. I wish . . .'

'What?'

'I wish you could come share my sandwich, that's all.'

'Maybe another time,' I said. 'I'd like that.'

That evening I went to the Admiral Nelson again. I took the usual precautions. Hebburn and Klose seemed to have lost interest in me for the time being, but perhaps that was only wishful thinking. I bought some food on the way to give myself a sort of alibi.

The bar was nearly empty. Alan Snape was by the jukebox, hunched over the crossword. No one came in after me so I took a chance and bought us both a drink.

He looked up as I set the glasses down on the table. 'I thought you'd come.'

'I said I would.' I gave him an envelope that contained £20, the balance of the money Wolfgang owed him. He stuffed it in his wallet. 'You're not going to count it?'

'I trust you.'

Snape took one of his professional cards from the wallet and tossed it down beside my glass. I noticed the address: he was based in a road that bisected the one where I lived. I slipped the card in my pocket.

'What's that for?' I said.

'You never know. You might need me one day.' His lips twisted. 'Anyway, they say it pays to advertise. I live in hope.'

'Could you trace a company for me?'

'Probably. Is it British?'

'I don't know.'

'Give me a ring if you'd like me to try.'

We left it at that. I liked the fact that he didn't put pressure on me to hire him. I drank my half-pint in about five minutes. Neither of us said much, but I felt easy in his company. When I'd finished he offered me another drink but I said I had to go.

I walked back to the flat, irrationally refreshed. I let myself into the house. As I passed the Sterns' door, it opened and Walter Keller came out of their flat.

'Ah, Herold,' he said. 'I was wondering where you were.'

I showed him the shopping bag. 'You could have phoned me. Saved yourself a wait.'

'I was coming to see the Sterns in any case. A social call. I thought I'd kill two birds with one stone.'

'Combining business with pleasure? What can I do for you?' A malicious impulse prompted me to add: 'I'm always ready for a little chat about the glories of English poetry.'

He flushed. 'I tried to find you this afternoon, but you were out.' His tone implied that absence from Broadway was a crime on a par with child-molesting and slandering the state. 'My section head wants a breakdown of your sales figures. He appreciates you may be working under pressure at present so I've been instructed to work with you.'

There were two ways of looking at that. Either the trade section was collecting statistical ammunition to fire at Bochmann, or Margarete Klose wanted Keller to impede my freedom of movement. I said nothing and continued up the stairs.

'Well?' Keller called after me.

'No,' I said without looking round.

'What do you mean?'

'I report to the Special Committee for Export Procedures. I need their authorization before I can pass on confidential material. You'll have to make a formal request to the Committee.'

He followed me up the stairs. 'But that could take weeks.'

'Or even months,' I said.

'We haven't the time. Be reasonable, Herold. Co-operation is – '

'Co-operation?' I swung round. 'Don't talk to me about that. I haven't had much co-operation from trade section, have I?'

Frau Stern came onto the landing, saw us on the stairs and retreated quickly into her flat. Keller stood his ground.

'You'll regret this,' he said. 'I'm warning you. I shall report your obstructive attitude.'

I climbed the last few stairs, opened my door and turned round. 'Do you have to be so pompous about it?' I smiled at him. 'It makes you sound even more of a clown than you really are.'

Keller's mouth opened and closed in silent outrage. Then he found his voice. 'I may tell you that Fräulein Klose – '

I slammed the door and leant against it. I knew it was stupid to antagonize him but I'd enjoyed it. Needling bureaucrats is one of the pettier pleasures of life, but at present I needed all the light relief I could get. I went into the darkened living room, tossed the carrier bag in the general direction of the sofa and brushed my hand against the light switch.

And there, sitting in the armchair with her eyes closed, her legs crossed at the ankles and a handbag on her lap, was Margarete Klose.

The carrier bag slithered off the sofa, disgorging two tins of soup, a packet of müesli and a tub of yoghurt. Fräulein Klose opened her eyes.

'Can I get you anything?' I said as I unbuttoned my coat. 'A cup of coffee, perhaps?'

Walter Keller had done me a favour. The adrenalin was already flowing, and I rode the shock of Klose's appearance like a wave. And for a moment my confidence was boosted by my first impression when I snapped on the light. It was the first time I had seen her outside her natural setting, the Embassy. She looked fragile: a tired, middle-aged woman with her defences down. Her hair was a mess and there was a ladder in her tights, just below the left knee. But the illusion shattered when she spoke because her voice was as strong as ever.

'You've got a point,' she said. 'He *is* pompous. And you were quite within your rights to refuse to co-operate with him. Foolish, too; but that's another matter.'

I filled the kettle while she was talking and plugged it in. I hung up my coat and drew the curtains. I had to keep busy to conceal the fact that my hands were shaking.

176

'I presume that Keller doesn't know you're here?'

The only reply was an impatient twitch of the shoulders.

I persevered with another question: 'And what about coffee?'

'A small cup. Thank you.'

'Why was I foolish not to co-operate with Keller?'

'Because it is always wise to co-operate when possible. Co-operation is the cornerstone of a socialist society, just as competition is the cornerstone of capitalism.'

The textbook answer. The great virtue of Marxist-Leninism is that it provides unassailable general answers to awkwardly specific questions.

While the water boiled, I picked up the shopping and put it away. I glanced at her once or twice: she'd closed her eyes again. Maybe it was a subtle psychological ploy to put me off balance, the sort of trick they learned on the training courses in Moscow. Or maybe she was simply tired; even Stasis need their sleep.

I made do with instant coffee. She opened her eyes when I put the cup down beside her, and asked politely if I would mind if she smoked. The silence between us lasted another minute while I found an ashtray at the back of the cupboard. My adrenalin had ebbed. I could imagine lots of reasons why she might want to see me. But why here? Why hadn't she summoned me to the Embassy?

She smoked the cigarette hungrily, as if it were a necessity she had denied herself for too long. Still she said nothing. I sipped my coffee on the sofa. If she was waiting for me to make the first move, she had underestimated my patience.

Halfway down the cigarette she had a fit of coughing

177

– so violent that it reminded me of Huber, my old section head in Schwerin. I got up and fetched her a glass of water. She nodded her thanks and I sat down again.

'You're an obstinate man,' she said, stubbing out the remains of the cigarette.

'Is that a criticism,' I said, 'or just an observation?'

'I tried to phone you yesterday. Where were you?'

'I went for a walk.' My stomach curled itself into a knot. 'It was such a lovely day.'

'You were out all day?'

'Most of it.'

'And in the evening as well?'

'I had a headache and I went to bed. I smothered the phone in cushions and spare blankets.'

She scraped a strand of hair away from her forehead. 'You spend a lot of time by yourself.' Her lips tightened, as if she'd remembered something unpleasant. 'Your brother was the same.'

That was true enough, so I said nothing. She swallowed some coffee. We had another of those silences that seemed to punctuate the evening's conversations. Had Custer's body been found? I longed for her to change the subject; Sunday was dangerous.

On the floor below the Sterns were soothing Walter Keller with Schubert's 'Death and the Maiden'. My visitor was staring at her handbag. The first time I had met Margarete Klose, I had sensed that she was personally hostile to me. Now I was not so sure. I think the hostility had been directed towards Wolfgang, and some of it had overflowed onto me.

178

She raised her red-rimmed eyes. 'Have you been followed since I last talked to you?'

'Not to my knowledge. But – as you know – I'm no expert.'

'It's difficult to tail a man who's on his guard. The only effective method is to use a lot of people so the target never has time to get used to one face. But that's expensive.'

She seemed to be in a confiding mood, so I decided to risk a question of my own: 'Does Inspector Hebburn have the resources?'

'He has access to them, which isn't quite the same thing.'

'You mean he has to convince his superiors that the expense is worthwhile?'

'Just so.' She added, without a trace of irony: 'We are all civil servants.'

She finished her coffee and lit another cigarette.

'Don't think me unwelcoming,' I said. 'But do you have duplicate keys for the other flats, too?'

'What? Oh, that. It's a matter of policy – it applies to everyone. Suppose there were an emergency. When your brother died, for example, we needed a spare key.'

It was smoothly done: not a hint of apology or defensiveness; just a confident assertion of her right to pry anywhere she wished, backed up by a little touch of personal malice.

'Have you heard from Herr Bochmann lately?' she asked.

'Not directly. I usually deal with his assistant, Herr Reichel.'

'But you know where he is?'

I frowned. 'I presume he's in Berlin.'

'So you weren't informed about his holiday?'

'But I thought you told me – ' I stopped and tried again: 'Isn't he due here on Monday?'

'This was just a short break: a week from last Tuesday. A spa holiday – his doctor advised it. To combat rheumatism and stress, I believe. He's expected back in Berlin tomorrow.'

It surprised me that Bochmann could afford the time away from the office at present. 'Where's he gone?' I asked.

'Baden-Baden.' Fräulein Klose blew a perfect smoke ring; I had not suspected she was capable of such frivolity. 'The Zum Hirsch, to be precise: they have thermal baths in the hotel itself.'

On the surface there was nothing unusual about the trip. Both of us knew that excursions to West Germany were a fringe benefit for senior officials. A week or two in an agreeable spa town is one of the privileges that make up for all those responsibilities they so selflessly shoulder on behalf of the rest of us. There are unwritten rules about it, of course: there is no point in applying unless you have the necessary money and connections; it is politic to make the trip for medical reasons, because that looks better on your record; and you leave your wife, your children and your property behind as hostages against your return. Generally State Security is able to keep a benevolent eye on you: the HVA is thick on the ground in West Germany.

But Baden-Baden is about as far from the GDR as you can get and still remain in Germany. It is in the south-west corner of the Federal Republic, close to the borders with France and Switzerland.

'I hope the treatment is working,' I said. 'It's off-season, isn't it, so at least there won't be many distractions.'

'I'm surprised he didn't mention it to you,' Klose said. 'He's something of a friend of the family, I understand.'

'Not really.' I wished people would stop trying to tie me in with Bochmann; it made me nervous. 'I hardly know him, myself. But he was very kind to my brother.'

Fräulein Klose blew another smoke ring. 'At ten-thirty yesterday morning, Herr Bochmann booked a table for lunch at the Zum Hirsch and said he was going for a walk. He hasn't come back yet.' She raised her eyebrows at me. 'Would you care to comment?'

NINE

After Margarete Klose had gone, my thoughts chased around my head like a pack of rats on a sinking ship. In this case the ship was in the middle of an ocean and there wasn't a lifeboat in sight.

That night I didn't get much sleep. I sat in the living room, drinking unnecessary cups of coffee and dozing. Meanwhile the rats scurried around and around; it made no difference to them whether I was awake or not.

In the morning I went to Broadway. On Tuesdays the accounts department doled out the weekly cash allowances. The queue stretched into the corridor. Keller came out as I waited. He glowered at me but said nothing.

The news about Bochmann hadn't broken yet. If it had, Keller and everyone else would have treated me as though I were a leper. The Stasis were stalling for a while. That might be why Klose had come to see me at the flat instead of hauling me over to Belgrave Square: to lessen the risk of unauthorized leaks.

Just after nine o'clock I rang Rownall's office. To my dismay he answered the phone himself.

'Has your secretary walked out on you?' I said. 'Couldn't stand the pace, I suppose.'

He laughed. 'I sent her out for some coffee. Actually she looks quite promising. It's early days yet, but at least she can add two and two without using a calculator.'

'I wondered what the state of play was with Morganettas,' I said. 'It would be nice if I could come up with a firm offer for Bochmann.'

'Now don't you worry. When you told me he was coming, that was the first thing I thought of. I rang Sylvia Carne yesterday afternoon and arranged to meet. We'll get something on paper in the next couple of days.'

'When are you seeing her?'

'Today. We're having lunch together in Richmond. Hope it won't be quite such a liquid affair as it was last time.'

'Last time? Oh, I remember. With her and Wolfgang.'

'Then we're going to see their sales director. Bit of a bind, really. I'm driving Sylvia back to their place in Hounslow. It'll take up most of the afternoon.'

That was better than I had hoped for. With Rownall out of the way I could contact Elizabeth.

'I'm looking forward to Sunday,' I said.

'So am I. You're getting the traditional English roast. The high point of English cuisine: beef, Yorkshire pudding, horseradish sauce, the works. You're honoured, I can tell you. Miranda doesn't do much cooking herself; most of our grub comes ready-made from Marks and Sparks. But when she does cook it's really something. She must have taken a shine to you.'

I murmured something about the pleasure being mutual.

'By the way,' Rownall went on, 'I told Beth about Sunday.'

'Beth?'

'My secretary. She's coming. Who knows? Maybe this'll be the start of something. She's quite an attractive girl, in her way. Woman, really. You need someone to – well, take you out of yourself. We all do. London's not much fun when you're single.'

I faked a laugh and diverted him by asking if he had met Morganettas' sales director before. There was a chance that the duty officer in the security section downstairs was monitoring this call. It would be unpleasantly ironic if someone took Rownall's matchmaking seriously.

Rownall rambled on cheerfully for another minute or two. Afterwards I went through the morning's mail and dictated letters for a couple of hours. A catalogue of forthcoming products had come through from the combine's export sales department. I tucked it under my arm when I slipped out of the building and headed for the Underground.

When I reached Finchley, I didn't go straight to the office. First I checked the yard at the back. Rownall's olive-green Jaguar XJS was still there, which was a blow. I'd calculated that he would be out of the way by now. If I couldn't avoid running into him, I'd pretend it was important that Sylvia Carne saw the new catalogue as soon as possible; it wasn't much of an excuse for my trek out here but it was the only one I had.

I retreated to a sandwich bar on the main road and ordered a cappuccino to have there and some sandwiches to take away. I nursed the coffee for an uneasy fifteen minutes. The next time I checked the yard, the Jaguar was gone.

The street door to Rownall's office was unlocked. I climbed the stairs and barged into the outer room. Elizabeth was on the phone. She frowned when she saw me but went on talking.

'. . . a message for Ms Sylvia Carne from Mr Sebastian Rownall,' she was saying. 'Mr Rownall was delayed, and may be a little late. Okay? Yes, Carne: C-A-R-N-E. Thanks.'

She hung up and stared gravely at me. She was dressed for work in a dark skirt and a cream, cowl-necked sweater. The drabness of the room made her green eyes glow with colour. I thought she looked worried. That made two of us.

'I've come to share your sandwich,' I said.

'Is it safe?'

'I hope so. Rownall's away, isn't he?'

'He won't be back today. So he says.'

I dumped the bag with the sandwiches on her desk. 'We need to talk. I suppose I could have phoned but I wanted to see you. Klose dropped by for a chat last night.'

'I'm starving,' Elizabeth said. 'You talk, I'll eat.'

I sat down on the visitor's chair beside the desk and told her what had happened. 'You see what it means? If Bochmann *has* defected, then everyone he knew, everyone he worked with, will come under suspicion. The new export system's his baby. It'll be discredited.'

'So you'll be recalled?' she mumbled.

'Yes.'

She swallowed what was in her mouth and pushed aside the rest of the sandwich. 'But that means – '

'It means we'll never know what happened. That it was all for nothing.' I spoke more harshly than I'd intended. I knew it also meant that I would never see Elizabeth again.

'Can't *you* defect?' she said in a jerky voice I'd never heard her use before. 'Have you ever thought of it?'

'It wouldn't help. All right, if Klose or Hebburn didn't

find a way to stop me, I'd get West German citizenship. But I'd end up drawing unemployment benefit in the Federal Republic. Besides, I don't want to defect.'

She looked blankly at me, as if I were a previously rational person who had suddenly shown traces of lunacy. 'But you can't seriously prefer the GDR to the West?'

Anger swamped me without warning. Probably worry and lack of sleep had something to do with it. I was tired of being patronized.

'Why not? It's my home,' I said. 'I owe them something. Tell me, what's so wonderful about this country? The freedom to buy things you don't need with money you haven't got? The derelicts on the streets? A plutocracy that pretends to represent the people?'

'You're talking like a textbook,' she snapped.

'But it's true, isn't it? You Westerners assume that we all want to rush to join you.'

'So you're implying the GDR's the perfect workers' state?'

'Of course I'm not. It's as flawed as anywhere else. Find me a Lenné Triangle, and I'll think about defecting.'

She looked down at her hands. I couldn't see her face. On the third finger of the left hand was a band of skin that was paler than the rest. My anger drained away. Some people say that anger has a cathartic effect on them: it 'clears the air'. I wish I could say the same. Anger just leaves me feeling slightly sick and very foolish.

'I'm sorry,' I said gently. 'I shouldn't have said that.'

'Yes, you should,' she said.

'Look, I may not be recalled – not yet. That's why Klose came to see me. She offered a deal.'

'Does she think you're involved with Bochmann?'

'She claims to believe I'm innocent, which probably means she's not sure. That's the whole point, she's not sure about anything. Bochmann's simply disappeared. The Stasis don't even know if he's really defected. Klose thinks Bochmann will head for England, that he was up to something with Rownall. She believes Wolfgang was killed because he threatened whatever they were up to.'

'She doesn't know about the warehouse? About Custer?'

'Apparently not. Nor about Mrs Issler. And I didn't tell her.'

'Why not?'

'Her priorities are different from ours. It's Bochmann she's worried about: he's got a lot of information in his head and she doesn't want it leaking out in the West. Here in the UK she hasn't got much freedom for manoeuvre. That's why she came to me. If I help her get her hands on Bochmann, she'll put in a good word for me back home. And, incidentally, she'll let me stay in London for the time being.'

The telephone rang. Elizabeth ignored it. The sound grated on me. I wanted to throw the phone out of the window.

'Shouldn't you answer it?'

'I'm out to lunch,' she said. 'What you're saying is that we haven't got much time.'

The ringing stopped.

'Once Bochmann surfaces,' I said, 'we haven't any time at all. It doesn't matter whether the Stasis find him first or he formally defects to the FRG or the

187

Americans. As soon as State Security knows where he is, I'm useless to them. Worse than useless. I'm tainted by association.'

'I'm not stopping now. We're getting somewhere. We've got leads to follow. There's Rownall's little company. There's Unsterworth. There's Rownall's home. There's . . .'

And there's us, I thought. She looked at me as though she had thrown me a challenge, which I suppose in a way she had.

'If we had money,' I said, 'we could hire someone to do some digging. Someone who knows the way this country works.' I took Snape's card from my wallet and passed it to her. 'Someone like that.'

'The guy your brother hired? Would you trust him?'

I shrugged. 'I like him. And for what it's worth I think he takes a pride in his job.'

She rubbed the pale band of skin on her finger. It is easy enough to throw away a wedding ring but much harder to discard the rest of a marriage.

'We'll use Snape,' she said. 'Will you make the arrangements?'

'How will we pay him?' I guessed the answer already and I didn't like it.

'Mike's still in London. Last time I saw him he was waving a banker's draft. I just call him and say I'm willing to sign on the dotted line.'

'Are you sure you want to?'

'It's no big deal, not really. I don't know why I didn't do it before.'

'You didn't do it because your father gave you those shares. Because your husband was hustling you.'

'The truth is, I didn't do it because I wanted to get even with him.'

'And now you don't?'

'Now it doesn't seem so important. I can do without the interrogation, okay? It's my decision.'

'All right. I'll ring Snape.' I rested my hand on the phone but didn't pick it up. 'Rownall said he'd told you about Sunday.'

She nodded.

'He called you Beth.'

'That's what I said my name was.' She lifted her chin. 'Mike calls me Beth. So does my mother. A lot of people do.'

'I'll carry on with Elizabeth,' I said. 'Okay?'

Snape worked from home, which was a small modern flat on the top floor of a five-storey block. I had made the appointment for 3.30 and I was a little late.

'Mr Herold,' he said, with a faintly interrogative air as though we had not met before. 'This way, please.'

I began to apologize for being late. Snape cut me off in mid-flow and showed me into the living room, which doubled as his office. It was clean, uncluttered and strictly functional; there were no ornaments or pictures.

'Do sit down.' He waved me to a chair that faced the window. 'Would you like some tea? I've just made a pot.'

I nodded. It turned out to be China tea with a slice of lemon in it. Snape sat down with his desk between us and the light behind him. He favoured the traditional geography of a professional consultation.

'And what can I do for you?'

'I want you to investigate a man called Sebastian Rownall,' I said. 'In particular, I – '

'Why do you want him investigated?'

I frowned. 'Do you need to know?'

'It would help if I had some idea. Besides, I have to be sure that there's nothing illegal in what you want me to do. I'm sure you understand.'

Snape's business ethics were inconvenient but I wasn't in a position to take the job elsewhere.

'My work,' I said, 'involves the promotion of East German toys in this country. Rownall is their main importer. I suspect that he is using this as a cover for something else.'

'Has this anything to do with your brother's death?'

'It may have, and that's why I'm here. It's possible that my brother realized that something was going on.'

'There are the police,' Snape said. 'And I imagine your Embassy must have someone who would be only too glad to advise you.'

'Are you saying that you don't want the job?'

He sighed. 'I'm finding out what it entails. Or rather trying to.'

'The British police think the case is closed. I've got nothing to make them change their minds. If I approach my own people, the first thing they'll do is send me back to Berlin. They don't want scandal.'

'But surely the possible murder of one of their nationals would outweigh any fear of scandal?'

'There may be East German ramifications,' I said stiffly. 'They would naturally prefer to concentrate on those.'

He sipped his tea, refusing to be hurried. Then: 'You mean they wouldn't care one way or the other about Rownall? Just what do you think was going on?'

I said nothing.

'I suppose smuggling could be one answer,' Snape said. 'Of things – or people.' He chewed his lower lip and then slid off at a tangent. 'In English, you know, the word "toys" has several slang meanings. For example, they can be the sort of appliances you see in sexshops. Or they can mean military hardware: to a gunner, his guns are "toys".'

'Fascinating,' I said. 'You must find doing crosswords quite an advantage in your job.'

'It's a possibility, you know. Western terrorists couldn't do much without the tools of their trade. A substantial proportion of them come from your part of the world and from Czechoslovakia.'

'That's just speculation. All I'm interested in is my brother.'

But if Snape were right, it would explain why Hebburn and Klose had been breathing down my neck since I arrived in London. It would also mean that the Stasis would go to almost any lengths to prevent Bochmann from talking to a Western intelligence agency. It was not a comforting thought.

'And may I ask what you expect to gain by all this? The sort of evidence that would stand up in court?'

'I suppose so.'

'You don't sound sure.'

'What I really want,' I said, 'is justice. But if I can't have that, I'd settle for knowing what happened. It's important to me.'

'I don't quarrel with that.' Snape finished his tea; mine was still untouched on the desk. 'But you wouldn't be tempted to take justice into your own hands?'

'I'm not that stupid.'

He gave me a hard stare as he reached for the teapot. 'No, I don't think you are. I do hope not. This sounds like a messy business. Dangerous, too.'

'I'm not asking you to get involved in it. All I want is some answers to specific questions. No one knows what you're doing. Your name won't come into it if I go to the police.'

'Does this have anything to do with the little job I did for your brother? With Mrs Issler?'

'I don't know.'

Snape poured himself some more tea. 'I can't help feeling that this is the sort of case I should avoid.'

I got up. 'Well, thank you for your time.'

'Do sit down, Mr Herold.'

I remained standing. 'Does that mean you'll take it?'

He nodded. 'As long as you can afford my fees.'

'Why the change of heart?'

He prodded his slice of lemon with a teaspoon. 'It's no business of yours, really. But I sympathize with your desire for justice.' His eyes met mine. 'I used to be married. My wife was killed in a car crash. The accident was caused by a twenty-four-year-old commodities broker who had two-and-a-half times the legal amount of alcohol in him. His car was a write-off but he was undamaged, apart from a broken arm. He lost his licence for two years.'

'What did you do?'

'I brought a private prosecution for manslaughter.' His voice sounded flat and resigned, as if the events had happened so long ago that the accompanying emotions had drained from his memory. 'It failed.'

'And then?'

'There was no "and then",' Snape said. 'The man has his licence back now. He's got another car. But I keep my eye on him, Mr Herold, when I can spare the time. Patience is a virtue, especially in my job. One day he'll step out of line and I'll be there to see it.'

'Justice?' I said.

'No such thing, not in practice.' He hesitated. 'But I

can't help feeling it's a desirable idea. Like democracy. The rule of law. Equality of opportunity. Peaceful co-existence.'

'Were *you* tempted to make your own justice?'

'Of course I was. But it wouldn't be justice then, would it? It'd be revenge. And that's quite a different thing. What precisely do you want me to find out about Sebastian Rownall?'

That was Tuesday. The next development came on Wednesday evening.

I was walking back from Broadway to the flat. A small, white hatchback was parked against the kerb near the end of my road. As I was passing, the driver leant across the passenger seat and rolled down the window.

'Gerhard?' The man was wearing an overcoat, a scarf and a hat; I couldn't see his face. 'I'd like to have a talk with you.' He spoke in German and casually too, as though this were a chance meeting on the Unter den Linden. 'Is there somewhere we can go?'

The voice had a slight Silesian accent and the hiss of a lisp blurred the sibilants.

'Herr Bochmann,' I said, without much surprise.

'Please get in the car.'

I stood there with my hands deep in my pockets. I said nothing.

'Please. We have to talk.'

'You may have to talk,' I said. 'But do I?'

'So you've heard the news.'

'You thought no one would notice you'd gone?'

'I thought they would have told you but I wasn't sure.' My sarcasm had irritated him; I heard it in his voice. Then he remembered we weren't in Berlin and he was no longer behind a beechwood desk in a top-floor office. 'Look, this is important for both of us. You can choose where we go. You can make any conditions you like. I'm trying to help you,' he added with a touch of exasperation. 'For Wolfgang's sake.'

'You gave me the job for Wolfgang's sake. What else did you do?'

He answered the question with another: 'Will you come?'

I opened the door and got into the passenger seat. 'Start the engine,' I said. 'And keep your hands on the wheel except when you have to change gear.'

He turned the key in the ignition. 'What exactly have they told you?'

'No talking yet. Just drive where I tell you.'

It was the evening rush hour so the roads were full. I kept him at it for half an hour, chiefly so I could make sure that there was no one on our tail. He was a bad driver, grinding his way through the gearbox and being either too cautious or too reckless; perhaps he was merely nervous. We ended up in Chiswick. I told him to find somewhere to park.

We went to a pub on the High Road. For the first time I saw Bochmann in a good light. His collar was grubby and he had a shaving-cut on his jawline. His clothes were creased, as if he had slept in them. He still looked like a chicken but a free-range existence had played havoc with the glossy plumage.

I ordered lager for myself. Bochmann wanted a large brandy.

'I thought you weren't a drinker,' I said.

He shrugged. His eyes were busy looking round the long, narrow bar. Every time the door opened he wanted to see who had come in. I paid for the drinks and steered him towards a table at the back, near the entrance to the lavatories. He sat with his back to the wall.

'Don't worry,' I said. 'This isn't a trap.'

He laid his hat on the table. For an instant there was something akin to hatred in his eyes. He took matches and cigars from the pocket of his coat. The cigars were in a packet, not in the silver case he'd used in Berlin. As he lit the cigar I noticed his fingernails were dirty.

'What are they saying about me?' he said abruptly.

'The news isn't on general release yet. You know Margarete Klose?'

'At the Embassy? I know what she does.'

'She told me you'd disappeared in Baden-Baden. That you just walked out of your hotel on Sunday.'

'Why did she tell *you*?'

'Let's take this in turns,' I said. 'Why did you appoint me in the first place?'

'You had the right qualifications. And I owed your brother for many things. It was a way of paying my debts.'

'That's not the whole story, is it? You thought I'd be easier to handle if something went wrong.'

'I don't know what you mean,' he said half-heartedly.

'Your little export business,' I said. 'Was it private enterprise or was it semi-official?'

'That's not important.'

'Are you sure? It must have needed a lot of organization at the German end. And power and money, as well: it wasn't the sort of thing your average civil servant could manage. How did it work? Did you switch an entire container for another or just re-load it?'

'A switch. It was simpler.'

'If it wasn't official, why did you bother? You had it made. In any case, what can you have in the West that you couldn't have had at home?'

'Peace of mind,' he said. 'It's nothing you would understand. Why did Fräulein Klose come to you?'

'She thinks it possible that you might try to contact me. She was right, wasn't she?'

'So she thinks you're involved? I see. I'm in limbo, eh?' He frowned as he worked out the implications. 'If I'd formally defected, they'd have sent you home. If they find me, they'll do the same. But until they know where I am, you might be useful to them. Yes, that fits.'

'Why haven't you defected?'

Bochmann finished his brandy and stared over my shoulder.

'The Americans or the West Germans would be glad to have you,' I said, groping for an answer. 'But they wouldn't give you much of a life when they'd sucked you dry, would they? An apartment somewhere, perhaps, and if you were lucky a job to go with it. But nothing like you were used to at home. I mean, it's not as if you were someone important like a general in State Security or a member of the Politburo.'

'I think I might get another drink,' Bochmann said, levering himself up from the table.

I slammed a hand down on his wrist. 'Not yet.'

He sat down slowly and licked his lips. Physical violence, I suppose, wasn't something he was used to; it simply hadn't entered his calculations. He'd suddenly remembered that I was younger and heavier than he was, and he was in no position to summon a policeman to help him. He was trembling.

'Gerhard,' he said, 'there's no need for that sort of thing. Believe me, I have only your best interests at heart.'

'I want to know about your interests, not mine. Whatever your little sideline is, it must be worth a lot of money. For you, for Rownall – maybe even for Toughton. What is it? What were you exporting?'

'I can't tell you, I'm afraid. It's – well, forgive the melodrama but it's more than my life is worth.'

'Your life may not be worth much if I tell Klose you're here.'

'She'd have to find me first; this isn't the GDR. Besides, you know what that would mean. They'd send you home, Gerhard. Is that what you want?'

'I want to know who killed my brother. It wasn't an accident, was it?'

'No, I don't think it was an accident. That's what I want to talk about, in fact. In contacting you, I have taken a considerable risk. You would do well to remember that.'

'Who did it?' I said. 'Were you involved in his death?'

'Of course not! Wolfgang was my *friend*. My dear Gerhard, what can I say to convince you?'

'That's easy. You can tell me who did it and why.'

'I don't know what happened, not yet. Wolfgang wasn't concerned with what you call my sideline. True, he may have had his suspicions about it. His curiosity may have contributed to his death. My own theory is that he was killed by someone who wasn't directly connected with my little operation.'

'Then who did it?' I said for the fourth time.

Bochmann stubbed out his cigar. 'I can find out, I promise you, and I will. But only if you do as I say.'

'And what do you want me to do?'

197

'Nothing. Leave it to me. You'll ruin everything if you carry on asking questions. You know what happened to that man at the warehouse.'

'Custer?'

'Exactly. If you'd kept away, he might be still alive.'

'Who told you about that?'

He lit another cigar. 'Just keep your head down, Gerhard, and get on with your job. Reichel, incidentally, has been quite impressed by you.'

'How very reassuring.'

'Business as usual is really your only option if you want to avoid being sent home.'

'I need to know more,' I said.

'Naturally. But first, shall I get us another drink? The same again?'

The bar was near the door. Bochmann was smiling.

'I won't try to run away, Gerhard, if that's what you're thinking.'

'I'll get the drinks.'

'Very well. Is there a lavatory here?'

'Down there.' I pointed at the alcove beside our table.

We both got up. As I stood at the bar waiting to be served, I tried to work out where I had gone wrong. Somehow I had lost the initiative. Bochmann had been scared of me at first. But later he had calmed down. Maybe I had said something that showed I was less of a threat to him than he had feared. How had he known about Custer's death and my enquiries? Did he know about Elizabeth too? That was the question that really worried me.

I ordered the drinks. I kept glancing at our table. Bochmann's hat was still there, but its owner hadn't returned. The barmaid was taking longer than I would have believed possible to change a £5 note. I left the glasses on the counter and walked quickly down the bar to the door of the lavatory.

'Do you want your change?' the barmaid called.

'Won't be a moment,' I said.

I shouldered the door open. Gents on the right, Ladies on the left; and at the end of the little corridor was a third door marked FIRE EXIT. The air smelled of disinfectant and cigar tobacco. The third door was ajar. Outside was an alleyway lined with dustbins. There was no sign of Bochmann. But there wouldn't be, would there? By now he would be safe in his car.

Just to make sure, I checked the men's lavatory; it was empty, of course. I went back to the bar and collected our drinks. I drank the lager quickly and tried to look on the bright side. I knew a little more: Bochmann was definitely involved, though possibly he was acting for a principal; he was in England and, since he knew about Custer, he must be in touch with Rownall or Toughton; and as far as I could tell his sole purpose tonight had been to dissuade me from investigating on my own behalf.

Which meant, presumably, there was still something worth investigating.

My glass was empty. What the hell? I drank the brandy I'd bought for Bochmann. It was time to go home. I walked down the bar towards the door.

'Hey, you,' the barmaid said, pointing to the table. 'You forgot your hat.'

The rest of the week dragged by. I talked to Elizabeth on the telephone and told her about Alan Snape and Bochmann; she sent Snape £500. I gave her the phone number of my flat; and we worked out a simple code

199

in case an emergency made it necessary for her to ring me there or at Broadway.

Rownall phoned me to confirm the deal with Morganettas and the arrangements for Sunday. He gave me directions that were detailed to the point of fussiness. He had talked to his secretary, he said, and she would meet me on the northbound platform of the Midland Line at King's Cross. I couldn't miss her, he assured me: Beth was a tall, elegant woman with striking green eyes and short, dark hair. '*Very* tasty.' He wished me the best of British luck with her.

I rang Snape on Thursday afternoon but he had nothing to report. I tried again on Saturday morning.

'No news, I'm afraid, Mr Herold,' he said. 'Just be patient. These things take a little time, you know.'

'I don't have time,' I said.

'I might have something for you tomorrow. But I can't promise.'

Each day I bought a newspaper. There was nothing about Grant Custer. He might never have existed.

On Saturday I had to go to the Embassy for a buffet lunch. The trade section periodically went through the motions of trying to impress British journalists; the budget prevented them from succeeding. Margarete Klose came up to me as I was fighting my way through a chicken sandwich.

'No news?' she said.

'Not yet. What do I tell Rownall? He's expecting Bochmann to turn up on Monday.'

'Don't tell him anything tomorrow.' She had obviously learned I was having lunch with him but she didn't stop to explain how. 'You can phone him on Monday and say the visit has been postponed. His secretary's going, I believe?'

I nodded.

'Talk to her – and to the wife. You never know, they might have heard something.'

'I'll try,' I said.

She slipped away. People were beginning to leave, so I abandoned the sandwich and headed for the door. On the way I bumped into Walter Keller. Literally, I mean. He was half-drunk and stepped backwards without looking where he was going.

'You again,' he said. Then, with relish and in English: '"The smooth-faced, snubnosed rogue".'

'You've been reading *Maud*,' I said. 'Is that wise?'

He blinked. I patted his shoulder and carried on. He wasn't to know that Great-aunt Luise's favourite poet was Alfred Tennyson.

On Sunday I reached King's Cross with a quarter of an hour to spare. I felt as nervous as a teenager on his first date. Five minutes later, Elizabeth arrived. Maybe she felt nervous too. More likely she was just early.

I walked up to her as she came down the steps, and she gave a little start. She was wearing a black, calf-length coat that flowed when she walked, and a sort of paramilitary beret. I hadn't seen them before.

'How did it go with Mike?' I asked.

'Okay.' She shrugged the memory away. 'Any news?'

Everyone was asking me that, or I was asking them. I shook my head.

'But Fräulein Klose has ordered me to pump you for information.'

'I wish you could,' Elizabeth said. 'But the well's run dry. The only thing I've found out is that Unsterworth's a reputable dealer.'

'You didn't visit the shop, did you?'

'Don't worry. I called a friend in New York who used to work in London; she's in the antique trade. She did a little digging and called me back. It's a husband-and-wife business – Howard and Primrose Unsterworth – based in Hampstead. They specialize in antique toys and miniatures – in practice there's a lot of overlap between them. She said they advertise, so I bought a copy of the *Collector's Guide*.'

'What sort of things did you find?'

'They're the guys to go to if you want a Third Empire hanging cradle on a gilded frame, supported by cupids and complete with the original hangings. Or a Regency high chair in mahogany.'

'Is there much money in things like that? What were the prices?'

'If you wanted them both, I doubt if you'd get much change out of five thousand. Pounds, that is, not dollars.'

The train pulled into the station. It was nearly empty. We sat side by side, our shoulders touching. The contact had a curious effect on the back of my neck: the skin felt prickly, as if it were charged with electricity.

Elizabeth stared out of the window. 'You'd think Miranda Rownall would have noticed something.'

I didn't want to concentrate on Miranda, but I did my best. 'I got the impression she wasn't very interested in the business,' I said. 'To her it's just a source of income. As long as the money's there, she won't ask questions.'

'That's not what I meant.' She turned to look at me. 'It's the Isaac Oliver miniature, and whatever else Rownall sold through Unsterworth. Family heirlooms,

202

do you think? Or a collection he built up himself? You'd expect Miranda to notice if things started disappearing.'

'Maybe she has.'

The doors closed. The train shuddered, and began to haul itself along the platform.

'Maybe. But in that case why's he doing it through the office? And why aren't the proceeds going into his private account?'

I could see where this was leading but not how it fitted in with what we already knew. 'We've got a little leverage because of Wolfgang. If she *doesn't* know anything about it at all, that suggests – '

'It's crazy,' Elizabeth interrupted.

She'd got there too. By tacit agreement we left it at that. For the rest of the journey we talked about other things. Nothing important – just silly personal details: the pet dog Elizabeth had when she was a girl; the stray kitten that Wolfgang and I adopted when we lived in Pankow; our favourite foods. It was as though we had no other reason for being together than the unacknowledged pleasure we took in each other's company. I felt we were circling one another, drawing closer and closer, and I was happy.

We got out at Luton, which was the end of the line, and the real world enveloped us again like a clammy fog. Rownall lived in a village called Abbot's Barton, about five miles east of the town. But he wasn't there to meet us.

For five minutes we hung around the station, waiting for the green Jaguar to appear. It was a grey day, much milder than it had been recently, and as we waited it began to spit with rain.

'I suppose we should phone them,' I said, looking for my diary.

It wasn't there. I'd left it in the pocket of my other jacket.

'I haven't got the number,' Elizabeth said. 'I guess we'd better call directory enquiries. Do you know the address?'

'Just the White Lodge, Abbot's Barton.'

I waited outside the station while she went to find a phone box. She was back in less than five minutes, shaking her head.

'What do you know?' she said. 'He's ex-directory. But I called us a cab.'

Ten minutes later, the taxi picked us up and took us to Abbot's Barton. I went into the pub for directions.

'Up the lane by the church,' the barmaid said. 'Fifty yards up on the right. You can't miss it.'

Our driver was late for his lunch so we paid off the taxi and walked. We passed the church and a row of nineteenth-century cottages. Immediately after the cottages was a line of conifers, in the middle of which was a five-bar gate. The gate was standing open.

The White Lodge was a substantial, L-shaped cottage in a large, bare garden. Everything seemed well-maintained. The only colours were white and green, except for the bright red burglar alarm mounted on one of the gables. Nothing was out of place. It was a blank house in a blank garden, neutral and oppressively vacant like a stage set before the actors come on. We trudged up the gravel drive to the front door, which was set in the angle of the L. I rang the bell. Nothing happened, so I tried again.

'Listen,' Elizabeth said.

Somewhere in the house a child was crying.

Then there were footsteps. The door opened. Miranda Rownall smiled uncertainly at me. The boy was clinging to her dress and staring at his feet.

'Gerhard, come in. And you must be Beth Allanton: how do you do. I'm Miranda.'

There was nothing wrong with the words, but she said them in a sort of breathless monotone. She shut the door behind us.

A smell of roasting meat filled the hall. My first impression was that the house was older than its exterior suggested. The hall was low, its ceiling held up by crudely-hewn beams that had been stripped to expose the natural wood. Turkish kilims made pools of colour on the floor. The windows were too small to let in much light. A standard lamp with a parchment shade glowed at the foot of the stairs. Beside it was a large box in dark-stained wood, with a lion's head carved in relief on the lid.

The boy sniffed and rammed his face against his mother's leg.

'It's all *right*, David,' Miranda said. 'Do let go.' She turned to us. 'Let me take your coats and then we'll get ourselves a drink.'

'We were expecting Sebastian to meet us,' I said. 'Is he all right?'

'You haven't seen him?'

I shook my head.

'I can't understand it. David, *please* let go. He went out to buy a newspaper at about nine o'clock. I haven't seen him since.'

'Was he walking?' Elizabeth asked.

'He took the car. The newsagent we use is in King's Barton . . . but he didn't go there. I rang them.'

The veneer of hospitality had peeled away, revealing the panic below. Miranda's voice was rising in pitch.

David cried more loudly. His mother stroked his shoulder without looking at him.

'Have you phoned the police?' I said. 'Don't be alarmed but perhaps he was involved in an accident.'

'Just before you came. They said they'd send someone over. I've already tried the hospitals.'

'Is there anything we can do to help?' Elizabeth said. 'Maybe we could – '

We all stopped what we were doing, even David. There was a car coming up the drive. Miranda tore open the front door.

A police car rolled to a halt. Behind it was a large saloon – a Ford, I think, painted grey with a metallic finish; it looked faintly familiar. Two men and a woman got out of the first car. One of the men was in uniform.

Mrs Rownall ran outside, dragging David along with her. 'Thank God you're here,' she said.

None of the newcomers said anything. Their faces were as blank as the side of the house. The woman glanced over her shoulder at the car behind.

One of its rear doors opened. Detective Inspector Hebburn climbed out. He walked slowly towards us.

'Mrs Rownall?' he said gloomily to Miranda. His eyes moved on. 'You must be Miss Allanton.' Then he looked at me. 'Well, laddie,' he said. 'I told you we'd be keeping an eye on you.'

TEN

Hebburn's heels left the ground. He swayed forwards and backwards. His face was ill-adapted for showing pleasure so his feet did the job instead.

David's crying subsided to a whimper. The boy sucked his thumb and stared at Hebburn with huge, round eyes.

Forwards and backwards again. Then Hebburn's heels came down on the gravel with a soft crunch.

'I'm looking for Mr Sebastian Rownall,' he said to Miranda. 'Is he at home?'

'No, he's not.' She crouched and put her arms round David. 'Who are you?'

He pulled out a warrant card and held it out for a couple of seconds. Even if she hadn't been staring at the top of David's head, she wouldn't have had time to read it.

'His name's Hebburn,' I said. Beside me, Elizabeth sucked in her breath and pretended to clear her throat. 'He's a detective inspector with Special Branch.'

Hebburn ignored me. 'Then where *is* your husband, Mrs Rownall?'

'He . . . he went out. I've already told you on the phone.'

The man I called Leather Jacket emerged from the grey car. As he walked towards us, he smiled at me; it was the sort of smile that is prompted by a happy memory. Hebburn turned to him.

'No news,' Leather Jacket said. 'The Jag's not in the garage. We've put out an alert.'

'He went to get the newspapers,' Miranda said. 'I *told* you, or one of your men. But he didn't come back.'

'When did he go?'

'Around nine – nine-thirty, perhaps. I didn't notice the time exactly. You see, I thought – '

'Any phone calls before he left?' Hebburn said. 'Any visitors?'

'No. I mean, if there were, I didn't hear.' Miranda looked at Elizabeth and me, asking silently for help we couldn't give. 'I was in the bath. And getting David dressed always takes ages. I might not have noticed.'

'You said you reported he was missing. Who did you tell?'

'I rang the newsagent's first, and they hadn't seen him. Then, after a while, I phoned the police at Luton. I thought perhaps they'd know if there'd been any accidents. But surely you must know all this?'

'Inspector Hebburn,' I said, 'isn't based in Luton.'

'Check it out,' Hebburn said to Leather Jacket, who retreated to the grey car and its radio. He turned to me. 'And I can do without your smart-arse comments. All right?'

I stared at him. There were bags under the heavy-lidded eyes, and the chin was shadowed with blue-black stubble. He was blinking more than usual; maybe the tic was more pronounced when he was tired. He sighed, implying he found me intolerably tiresome, and looked away.

'Let's go inside, Mrs Rownall,' he said. 'It's too cold to talk on doorsteps.'

Hebburn shepherded us into the house. His colleagues, none of whom had said a word, followed us in.

'You don't mind if they take a look round, do you?' he said, rubbing his hands together. 'It's freezing in here. Is there somewhere warmer we can go?'

'The drawing room – my husband lit a fire.' Miranda seemed not to have heard the first question. 'This way, Inspector.'

She opened a door on the left. David scuttled in front of her. Elizabeth and I followed. In the doorway I turned. The plain-clothes man and the woman were already climbing the stairs.

'You stay here,' Hebburn told the man in uniform. He saw me watching him and beckoned. 'Just watch it, Herold,' he said in an undertone. 'I'm getting a wee bit tired of you.'

'I was here first,' I said rather childishly, 'and by invitation.'

'Get in there, will you?'

The drawing room was square and as low-ceilinged as the hall. It occupied the whole ground floor of the house's smaller wing – the base, as it were, of the L. There were windows on three sides. On the fourth was a large hearth, big enough to walk into. The remains of a fire smouldered in the log basket. Miranda stood beside it, staring at the embers. Elizabeth, who was close to her, caught my eye as I came in. She had a cold, calculating look that took me by surprise.

Hebburn shut the door behind him.

'Can I offer you a drink, Inspector?' Miranda said in a brisk voice. 'Or coffee? Or aren't you allowed to accept drinks on duty? I must build up the fire. Sebastian usually does it. I don't know – '

She ran out of words and slumped rather than sat on one of the two sofas that stood at right angles to the hearth. David scrambled up beside her. He wasn't crying any more. It had become too serious for that. There was no doubting the strength of Miranda's affection for Rownall or their son. I liked her better than I would have believed possible a few minutes before.

'I'll do the fire,' I said. I bent and picked out a couple of small logs from the stack in the fireplace. The bark crumbled and fragments fell to the hearthrug. The logs came too late: at best they would smoke for an hour or two; at worst the fire would die.

Footsteps crossed the room above our heads. 'Someone,' a man said, his voice muffled by the ceiling between him and us but still audible, 'isn't short of a bob or two.'

Hebburn wandered around the room, staring at the marine oil-paintings on the walls. There were tempests and fishing fleets and men-of-war with blazing gunports. He seemed to have forgotten our presence.

Elizabeth looked at his back. Her mouth was tight with anger. She sat down beside Miranda, with David huddled between them; it was a gesture of solidarity.

'Inspector,' she said, 'are you planning to tell us why you're here?'

'But you know that, Miss Allanton.' He turned around and strolled across the room towards her. 'I told you. I'm looking for Mr Rownall.'

'Sure. But you haven't told us why.'

'Tell me something,' Hebburn said. 'How has Mr Rownall seemed to you this last week? His normal self?'

'I wouldn't know. I've only been working there since the Friday before last.'

'Of course,' he said. 'It'd slipped my mind.' His eyes swung from Elizabeth to me. 'How about you, Mr Herold? You've seen quite a lot of him lately, haven't you?' He made it sound as though meeting Rownall were a faintly disreputable activity, like picking one's nose in public. 'Well?'

'I've noticed nothing out of the ordinary,' I said.

'Why don't you sit down, Mr Herold?' He waited until I was sitting in the big armchair that faced the fireplace. 'Did you see him last Sunday, by any chance?'

Elizabeth shifted almost imperceptibly on the sofa. Last Sunday meant Custer.

'No,' I said. 'But I saw him and Mrs Rownall on the Monday morning.'

'Mrs Rownall?' Hebburn said.

'What? Sorry. What do you want to know?'

'Tell me about last Sunday.'

Miranda frowned. Underneath the make-up her skin was the colour of old newspaper. 'Tell you what, exactly? We had lunch at my parents'. We stayed with them until after tea.'

'And then what?'

'Well, we came home. Had supper, I suppose, after David was down. I think we watched TV.'

'I'll need your parents' names and address.' She gave the details mechanically, her mind elsewhere. The parents lived in Farnham, and her father was a retired brigadier. Hebburn wrote slowly in a small black note-book.

'And were there any phone calls or visitors *last* Sunday?'

'I can't remember,' Miranda said. 'Not at my parents', anyway.'

211

He pressed her on that point but her vagueness was unshakeable. She had gone for a ride in the morning, before the trip to Farnham. There were several phones Rownall could have used, including the one in the Jaguar. She had gone to bed before her husband in the evening.

Misery covered her like an ill-fitting overcoat. She had one arm around the boy and her fingers kneaded his forearm constantly. Her voice was dull until, when Hebburn temporarily ran out of questions, she burst out: 'But where is he? I need to know.'

'We all need to know, Mrs Rownall.' Hebburn sat down on the other sofa and leant forward, his hands on his knees. 'Tell me, has your husband any money troubles?'

'Money?' Miranda said blankly, as though the subject were one to which she had never devoted any serious thought. 'Not that I know of. Why do you ask?'

'There's a lot of valuable things in this house,' Hebburn said. 'That's obvious to anyone with half an eye. Has anything ... ah ... gone missing lately? Not stolen, necessarily, but gone to be cleaned or something?'

She shook her head. 'I'd know.'

As she spoke she looked around the room. It was as if she were seeing it for the first time in terms of the money it represented. And not just the room: the whole house and the standard of living that went with it could be translated into their sterling equivalent.

'No little economies, say? Was he worried about business?'

'Why have you come?' Miranda said. Her lips were drawn back, exposing her teeth; the pixie had become a vixen, protecting her cubs and earth. 'You're harassing me. You're nothing to do with Luton, are you? Why Special Branch? That's for spies, isn't it, and terrorists?' She swallowed, fighting back hysteria. 'I just don't understand.'

'Well, in the circumstances that's natural enough.' Hebburn gave the impression he was conceding the point out of the goodness of his heart. 'But you must — '

The front door banged. Immediately Miranda was on her feet.

'You might as well sit down,' Hebburn said. He stood up and towered over her.

'But he's come back — Sebastian.'

'It's not your husband. Sit down.'

The door opened. A large man advanced into the room. Miranda took one glance at him and began to cry. Her legs gave way and she sat down. Elizabeth put an arm around her. David peered at the newcomer from the shelter of the two women.

He was old and fat. Dirty grey curls covered his head, and his complexion was off-white, like lard. He was smoking a small cigar. When he reached the hearthrug he tossed the butt into the fireplace and broke wind. It was a loud, lingering and curiously inoffensive sound.

Meanwhile, Hebburn said nothing; he was waiting, I guessed, for a cue, which told us something about the new arrival's position in the hierarchy.

'Well, come on,' the man said in a voice like coarse sandpaper. 'We haven't got all day. Introduce us.'

With the merest suggestion of a shrug, Hebburn said to no one in particular: 'This is Mr Blaines.' He paused. 'And this is Mrs Miranda Rownall and her son David; Miss Elizabeth Allanton, an American citizen who is

213

Mr Rownall's new secretary; and Herr Gerhard Herold from the GDR.'

There was a faint stress on my first name: Gerhard rather than Wolfgang.

'How do?' Blaines said. 'Come outside a moment.'

Hebburn followed him into the hall, closing the door behind them. Miranda wept almost silently. Somewhere a clock was ticking. Footsteps tramped to and fro in the room above.

'Hey,' Elizabeth murmured to David and Miranda. 'It's going to be okay. We just have to ride this out.'

The two men came back. Hebburn returned to the sofa. Blaines came up to me. He wore a filthy raincoat; it was unbuttoned and underneath it was a shabby pinstripe suit. His shirt was too small to contain his belly. In the gap between two buttonholes I glimpsed a string vest and more of that lard-coloured skin.

'Mr Gerhard Herold,' he said, lingering over the name. 'I've heard about you.'

Miranda blew her nose. 'Are you in charge? I want to know what's happening. I *demand* to know. I want to phone my father.'

'Do you now? Who's he when he's at home?'

'Brigadier Charles Cubitt,' Hebburn said. 'Retired.'

'You can phone him later,' Blaines said. Losing interest in Miranda, he returned to me. 'Tell me what you did last Sunday, sunshine. Every last minute of your day.'

I told him the same story I had given Margarete Klose: the long, fictitious walk, the headache and the early bedtime. Unlike Klose, Blaines questioned me about the route I had taken. I gave him vague answers, which seemed to satisfy him. After all, I had only been in London for a fortnight so an ignorance of its geography was perfectly plausible. When I had finished, Blaines asked Hebburn if he had anything to add. The inspector shook his head.

'Will someone tell me what all this is about?' Miranda said. *'Please.'*

'All right, love.' Blaines dug his hands into the pockets of his raincoat. 'Ever heard of a bloke called John Toughton?'

'He's the manager of the warehouse my husband uses. I've met him once or twice.'

'How did he strike you?'

She shrugged. 'Just a man.'

'Like that, eh? Not worth noticing? Well, he was arrested this morning on a charge of murder.'

Miranda seemed to shrink. *'He's killed Sebastian?'*

All her energy went into that desperate question. David whimpered and tried to burrow into her side. For once Miranda ignored him. She was leaning forward, her eyes fixed on Blaines. 'Say something, damn you. I want an answer.'

He made her wait. He found a cigar, examined it carefully and finally lit it. 'Killed Mr Rownall?' he said slowly, trying the idea for size and seeming to find it mildly attractive. 'Not as far as we know. Of course, we can't guarantee anything. It's not as if we know where your husband is.'

Miranda hugged David until he squirmed.

'Then who did he kill?' Elizabeth said savagely.

'Custer.'

'As in Little Bighorn?'

'Not quite.' Suddenly Blaines became almost animated. 'That was George, and this bloke was called Grant. No Seventh Cavalry, either. Unless *we're* the Seventh Cavalry, and this is Wounded Knee.'

I missed the allusion and so, I think, did Hebburn.

'In 1876,' Elizabeth said to me, 'Colonel Custer and a detachment of the Seventh Cavalry were massacred by a mixed force of Sioux and Cheyenne warriors. The Seventh Cavalry got its revenge in 1890 when it slaughtered over two hundred Indians – men, women and children.'

'The Sioux Wars,' Blaines said, nodding his head. 'Nasty business, eh?' He looked at her, his face alert with curiosity. 'Are you interested in military history, then?'

'No. Who's Grant Custer? Should we know him?'

Blaines shrugged. 'You tell me.' He looked at each of us in turn, waiting for us to shake our heads. 'Custer worked at Toughton's warehouse. The week before last, Toughton sacked him for stealing. That was the official story, anyway. Plausible enough: Custer had done time for breaking and entering. But the real reason seems to have been that he was threatening to blow the whistle on something Toughton was up to. So Toughton gives him the elbow. But that wasn't good enough. Custer couldn't keep his mouth shut, see? Always a mistake, that.'

He paused, perhaps to contemplate the folly of opening your mouth. Hebburn was examining his fingernails and no doubt wishing that Blaines would follow his own advice.

'Last Sunday afternoon,' Blaines went on, 'Custer vanishes. On Monday, an old geezer walking his poodle trips over the body. He'd been stabbed. You with me so far? Well, we found a hat under the body – a dark, woolly hat with bits of hair and dandruff and God knows what inside. Very personal things, hats. To cut a long story short, the hat belonged to Toughton. And

216

Toughton had a motive and he doesn't have an alibi worth talking about. Plus, he's an ex-para – Falklands veteran, two tours in Ulster: he knows about killing people.'

'Then it's odd he left his hat behind,' Elizabeth said tartly.

'And what exactly *was* the motive?' I asked.

Blaines waved aside the questions. 'So. Where was I? This morning we had a chat with John Toughton and put some handcuffs on him.' He opened his eyes as widely as he could. 'But he says he's been framed. Well, they all say that. But Toughton says he knows who did it, and why. He puts the finger on Sebastian Rownall. He did it quite convincingly too.'

'That's stupid,' Miranda said. 'I've *told* you. Sebastian was with me last Sunday.'

'What makes you think Custer was killed on Sunday?'

'But you said he was.'

'I said he vanished on Sunday. Anyway, Toughton told us so much about your husband that we wanted to have a word with him.'

'The man's obviously a liar,' Miranda said, very much the brigadier's daughter. 'Trying to wriggle out of it by blaming someone else. Sebastian would never get involved in something like that.'

'But what do we find? Mr Rownall's vanished too. Bit of a coincidence? Suspicious, even? Don't you agree?'

He waited but no one said anything.

'Don't rush to answer,' Blaines said. 'Not now. We'll talk to you one by one, in private. Cosy little chats all round.' He raised his forefinger and panned it round the room like a gun. 'Beginning,' he said, pointing at me, 'with you.'

*

In the next two hours they interviewed us individually and continued to search the house and garden. We were not allowed to make phone calls. Occasionally the phone rang and someone answered it.

Blaines and Hebburn didn't trouble to conceal their belief that I was a third party to the deal between Toughton and Rownall. They talked to me in a small room on the ground floor. It was furnished as an office. A tape recorder whirred on the desk and Leather Jacket made notes.

The single window overlooked the lawn at the back of the house. There was a bird table a few yards away from the window. While they flung questions at me, I watched a flock of starlings squabbling over the crumbs. They were messy eaters. Beneath them on the grass, a wary robin made a decent meal from the food they dislodged.

'You might as well get it off your chest, old son,' Blaines said. 'I mean, we know most of it already.'

'That's more than I do,' I said. 'I wish I could help.'

'Your brother set up the East German end, maybe with your help. That's obvious. Something pretty substantial or you wouldn't have needed the best part of a whole container. The rest of the load was legit and the documentation's real, which probably means this is a Stasi operation; either that or you're working with someone who's got very good connections indeed. The stuff comes through to Toughton's warehouse. He doesn't know what it is but he knows enough to separate the toys from whatever else was there. Rownall whisks them out of sight. But Custer talks and he can't take a hint. So one or both of them decides to kill him. That suggests there's a lot of money involved.

Either that or they're shit-scared. Alternatively, you killed Custer yourself and maybe Rownall too. Ever gone in for journalism, Mr Herold?'

'No,' I said. 'I can't say I have.'

'We can check that, you know.'

The robin found a crust and bolted for the cover of a leafless hydrangea. I thought Blaines was bluffing. None of the people in the pub where I met Custer had seen me properly; they couldn't truthfully make a positive identification. But perhaps Blaines was prepared to bend the truth.

'Come on, Herold. Spit it out.'

'There's nothing to say. Except that I've never been a journalist and I don't understand what you mean.'

'You were right,' Blaines said to Hebburn. 'He's a pigheaded bugger, isn't he?' He looked at me. 'You're being stupid, you know. We could help you. Play fair with us and you won't regret it.'

I pretended to think about this. Then: 'May I ask you something?'

'Sure. Fire away.' He must have been expecting me to ask how many pieces of silver was my allegiance worth to him.

'Did you have my brother killed?'

Blaines just looked at me. I waited for an answer. A flat denial? Derision? A cheerful admission of guilt? Anything but the answer I actually received.

'Ah, piss off,' Blaines said. 'You're boring me. Send the next one in.'

The drawing room had become the waiting room. We were forbidden to talk, a prohibition David ignored.

'Where's Daddy?' he kept saying. 'I want Daddy.'

At two-thirty, Miranda, David, Elizabeth and I were

sent to eat overdone beef and blackened potatoes in the kitchen. The two officers who had searched the house watched us while we ate.

David bit the policewoman on the leg and then was sick. Blaines came through the kitchen as Miranda was apologizing and clearing up the mess. He said he hadn't realized that WPCs tasted that bad. After lunch Elizabeth and I did the washing up. There was a dishwasher but we wanted something to do. Miranda and David were allowed to go to bed. As I was drying the plates Inspector Hebburn came into the kitchen.

'Someone wants you on the phone,' he said to me. 'You can take it in here.'

I threw down the cloth. There was an extension on the wall above the big pine table. I picked up the handset and said my name.

'Keller's on his way to collect you,' Margarete Klose said. 'You can tell your hosts that you have to deal with an urgent problem in trade section. Was that Rownall who answered the phone?'

'No,' I said. 'It was probably Inspector Hebburn. Rownall seems to have vanished.' I half-turned, so Hebburn was behind me and I was looking straight at Elizabeth. 'You want me to come to the Embassy?' I covered the mouthpiece of the handset. 'Or to Alan's?'

Elizabeth winked.

'The Embassy, of course,' Klose said; if my news had come as a shock to her, she showed no sign of it in her voice. 'Where else?'

'Just one thing,' I said. 'There's another man here with Hebburn. His name is Blaines.'

In England the police and the security forces in general seem to make a fetish of being unostentatious. I suppose it suits the authorities for political reasons. When Keller arrived ten minutes later, there was no sign of Special Branch in the garden. They were still there, of course, inside and out.

I was waiting in the hall. Leather Jacket heard Keller's car and bundled me out of the house. Keller treated me like a parcel during the drive to London. He ignored my half-hearted attempts at conversation.

At the Embassy Fräulein Klose was waiting in her office. She was smoking and coughing. The first thing she did was to question me in minute detail about what had happened at the Rownalls'.

I told her everything I had seen and heard there – everything, that is, apart from the truth about myself and Elizabeth. She was particularly interested in Blaines.

'Who is he?' I said. 'Hebburn's boss?'

'Not exactly.' She reached for her cigarettes again. 'It's enough for you to know that if Blaines is personally involved, it means the British are taking this very seriously indeed.'

'Taking what? The container? Custer's death?'

'The container. What you've told me dovetails with a signal I've just had. There's no doubt that Bochmann arranged for one container to be diverted from the others and somehow tampered with, before they got to Rostock. Are you sure they don't know about Bochmann?'

'They didn't mention him. They seem to believe that my brother handled the German side – probably on your orders.' I added, hastily: 'I don't mean you personally. But they think this may be a State Security operation.'

'If it were,' she said, 'we wouldn't be talking about it now. Not if I'd had anything to do with it.'

She sounded convincing. But State Security is quite capable of keeping its left hand in ignorance of what its right is doing.

'I expect you can guess why I wanted to see you. You've been ordered back to Berlin.'

'Permanently?'

She shrugged.

'But why? Bochmann might still turn up.'

'It is felt that the security risk outweighs the potential benefits of keeping you here.'

'You mean you think I'm a traitor?'

'What I think is irrelevant,' she snapped. 'The matter is out of my hands. Keller will drive you back to your flat. You will pack your bags and he will take you to Heathrow.'

'*Tonight?*'

'Your ticket and your passport will be waiting at the airport. Any questions?'

Our eyes met. She had told me more than she needed, and I wondered why.

'Just one question,' I said. 'Who killed my brother?'

'I don't know. If it's any consolation to you, I wish I did. I'm as much in the dark as you are.'

Her voice hadn't changed but I felt the anger that radiated from her. It wasn't directed at me. She disliked what was happening as much as I did, albeit for very different reasons.

It was then that I made my decision. I had feared this moment and hoped it would never come. Oddly enough, when it did, the decision itself was easy. It's a pity the consequences weren't equally painless.

I got up. When I reached the door I said, 'Goodbye, Fräulein Klose.'

'Herr Herold?'

'What?'

'My report on you will not be entirely unfavourable.'

I frowned at her, trying to work out the meaning of this apparent vote of confidence.

'Oh, go away,' she said, flapping her arms. I swear she was blushing. 'Can't you see I've got work to do?'

I closed the door softly behind me. At least someone liked me.

Walter Keller was no good at keeping secrets.

Someone must have told him while I was with Klose. Her assistant? Someone in the signals section? Whoever briefed him about taking me to the airport? Any organization has an unofficial network for the dissemination of news. I was surprised that Klose had managed to prevent the Bochmann business from leaking out for so long. Keller, of course, whom the Stasis used as an errand boy, was in a better position than most for picking up gossip.

On the way back to the car, he bounced rather than walked. The street lights were on and Keller's face looked yellow. Occasionally he glanced at me. He didn't say anything until we were in the car.

'So you're leaving us,' he said as he fumbled to find the ignition. 'I didn't think you'd last long.'

'Maybe I'll be back.'

'Oh, I don't think that's very likely.' He started the engine. 'The rest of us can get back to normal again.'

I said nothing. We drove in silence to Hyde Park Corner. On Park Lane he chuckled.

'Who'd have thought it?' he said. 'Bochmann of all people. It just goes to show.'

'It just goes to show,' I said, 'that you shouldn't take people at their face value.'

'What do you mean?' The Golf veered into the inside lane and a taxi behind us hooted.

'Think about it.' I gave him no opportunity to do so. 'You know when Bochmann went?'

'Last Sunday, wasn't it?'

'Exactly. A whole week ago. Unfortunately I had to stay on.' I paused and then added: 'Margarete Klose wanted me to tie up a few loose ends.'

From Marble Arch to Ealing Keller kept his mouth shut. At this point I wasn't sure what I was trying to do. Or, rather, I knew what I wanted to do but not how I was going to do it. I hoped that I had at least gained a little more room for manoeuvre. When Keller left Belgrave Square he had been buoyed up by the comfortable superiority of a guard over his prisoner; now, with luck, he was wondering if he was merely my chauffeur. If he could moonlight for the Stasis, there was no reason why I shouldn't.

The house where I lived was in darkness; Dr Teichler and the Sterns were out. It was, I felt, a good omen. Keller reversed onto the hardstanding at the front and switched off the engine. I opened the passenger door and got out.

I stuck my head back in the car. 'Well, come on.'

'I'll stay in the car.'

'Didn't they tell you?'

'What are you talking about?'

'When you were briefed.' I sighed with exasperation. 'That's half the point of your coming here. I need you upstairs.'

'What for?'

I ignored him. I pretended to concentrate on unlock-

224

ing the front door. For a few seconds it hung in the balance. Then Keller got out of the car, stamped on his cigarette and followed me into the house.

'What do you want me to do?' he said as we walked up the stairs.

'You'll see.'

'We haven't got much time to play with.'

'Don't worry.' I fitted my key into the flat door. 'It won't take me a minute to pack.'

I opened the door and went through the hall to the living room, switching on the light. Keller shut the front door and came after me. I drew the heavy curtains across the window; there were lights in the house directly opposite.

It was no good. I couldn't think of a subtle way to do this. The blood pounded around my body. I felt remote from Keller and the flat, as though I were seeing them through the wrong end of a tele-scope.

'Why bother with the curtains?' Keller said, sounding a long way away. 'We won't be here all night.'

I shrugged. 'Can you get the bag out of that cupboard?'

His eyes followed my pointing finger. He frowned. He was looking at a blank wall.

I swung a punch at him.

And with that punch I left my past life behind. I said goodbye to my family, my friends and my country. All I had left was an uncertain future. Well, the future is always uncertain. Nothing had really changed.

Keller saw the blow coming. His mouth opened but no sound came out. He jerked his head away. My fist glanced off his jaw. He jumped back and darted behind the table.

'What the hell are you doing?' he shouted.

I shoved the table as hard as I could, trying to pin him against the wall. But a chair was in the way. Keller grabbed the edge of the table and heaved upwards. It fell on its side with a thump that shook the house. Then he picked up the chair and came for me.

By now I realized I'd underestimated him. Keller was smaller than me and I'd taken him by surprise. But he was in good condition and, unlike myself, seemed to know how to handle himself in a fight.

He swept the chair in a horizontal arc, trying to smash me into the wall. I dodged and threw the electric kettle at him. It hit his shoulder. The lid came off and water cascaded down his jacket. I leapt at him. We fell heavily, with me on top. His glasses came off. He tried to knee me in the crotch. I banged his head on the floor.

Keller stuck his thumbs in my eyes and I had to let go of him. He squirmed away and rolled to his feet. He dived towards the doorway.

I flung myself at him. He fended me off but in the process lost his balance. He keeled over. His head cracked against the edge of the open door. His body crumpled.

Once again I was on top of him. This time he wasn't moving.

I scrambled up. I trod on Keller's glasses and one of the lenses broke. I couldn't get enough air into my lungs. I wondered if he were dead. Why did he have to make it so difficult? It was an unreasonable question, but it went round and round my mind. I half-expected to hear footsteps on the stairs and police sirens outside. But everything was silent.

I pulled him over so he was lying on his back. He was much heavier than he looked – *a dead weight?* His eyes were closed. A bruise was coming up on his forehead. The water from the kettle had soaked his jacket and shirt. But he was breathing, quickly and shallowly. The relief was so great that my legs buckled. I sat in the easy chair and put my head in my hands.

Given the chance, I would have liked to put back the clock and relive the last few minutes. By now I could be on the way to the airport, with nothing worse to handle than a cool reception in Berlin. Instead the sweat was pouring down my face and soaking my body. I was shivering. I couldn't believe this had happened. I couldn't believe that I had nearly killed a man.

The rhythm of Keller's breathing changed: maybe he was waking up. I had already wasted several precious minutes. I forced myself up and stumbled over to the kitchen area.

I used the flex from the electric kettle to lash his wrists behind his back and bound his ankles with his tie. I hauled him onto the sofa and stuffed a cushion behind his head. All this wasn't his fault. The cushion and the sofa made me feel better about almost killing him. Not much but a little.

There wasn't much time. I went through his pockets, taking the car keys, all his documents and his wallet. It occurred to me that, when he woke up, he might be able to attract attention by rolling off the sofa and banging on the floor; I decided to use a couple of my own ties to anchor him to the wooden arms of the sofa. I went to fetch them from the bedroom, remembering that I also needed to pick up a few things to take with me. It was dark in there, so I switched on the light.

The scream bubbled out of me. I heard it before my brain realized what I was seeing. There was someone in my bed. The duvet was pulled up over the head.

I counted to five. I walked over to the bed. I could see a triangle of grey, greasy hair on the pillow. I took the corner of the duvet between my finger and thumb and lifted it up. Just far enough to see the face.

The tongue was forced outwards from the mouth. The lips and ears were a dark blue colour that verged on purple. The long, curving nose protruded from the face like the beak of a bird. A trickle of blood had escaped from one of the nostrils. The eyes stared at me.

But Rudolf Bochmann couldn't see me. He would never see anything again.

ELEVEN

Someone, I thought, has been playing God again.

I let the duvet fall back over Bochmann's face. The fight with Keller seemed to have anaesthetized my emotions. I felt, in an abstract way, distaste for this unsightly object in my bed, and I was impersonally angry that yet another person had been killed. But everything was one step removed, as though it were happening to someone else. In a strange way that made it worse.

At least my mind was still working. In fact it was pumping along like a river in full spate. The first thing I registered was that the authorities, whether British or East German, now had the best of reasons for keeping me out of circulation. Was someone trying to frame me? How did Bochmann get in here? I knew of only one spare key to the flat: the one that Fräulein Klose used when she paid her unscheduled visit. Maybe this was the Stasis' way of disposing of two unruly citizens at once; East Germans are economical by habit.

I had opened the door of the wardrobe. Keeping my back to the bed, I mechanically packed the lightest of the bags with a change of clothes, pyjamas and a jersey. Perhaps it wasn't Klose after all: she knew I'd spent the day at the Rownalls', which gave me some sort of an alibi. But that of course depended on when Bochmann had been killed.

I took two ties from the rack and left the room, closing the door behind me. I collected my toothbrush and shaving things from the bathroom. My face in the mirror above the basin belonged to a pale stranger: tight-lipped, with slightly bloodshot eyes; not the sort of man who had much time for smiling. At that moment the full horror of Bochmann's death burst over me. My hands were shaking so badly that I could hardly zip up the bag. But in the mirror the stranger's face was impassive.

Back in the living room, Keller was still in the same position. His eyes were closed and he was breathing through his mouth. I lashed him top and tail to the arms of the sofa. He looked so pathetic that I stuffed a second cushion behind his head. His eyelids flickered. He licked his lips, which reminded me that the man had a voice and, once he woke up, he would use it. I gagged him with a tea towel. Then I picked up the bag and took one last look at the room. I was glad to say goodbye to it.

The telephone began to ring. Keller's eyes opened. A harsh, retching noise came from the back of his throat. I guessed it was his way of saying, 'You bastard.'

The phone rang on. I wanted to leave it but I didn't dare. Elizabeth might be trying to get in touch – perhaps she couldn't come to Snape's flat for some reason. If it were Klose or someone else from the Embassy, I'd say that Keller was outside in the car. Before answering it, I carried both handset and base into the hall. I lifted the receiver.

'Who's that?' a man said at once. 'Is that you?'

An idiotic question, but I'd recognized the voice. 'Yes. Where are you?'

'No names, no packdrill, eh?' Rownall said. 'We may

have listeners. Look, I can answer your question, the big one. But we have to meet.'

'Where?'

'You remember the first time we met?' He was speaking with an unnatural lack of emphasis, as if he were reading from a script. 'I told you I fell over. Do you remember where that was?'

'Yes.'

'We'll meet there. Tomorrow at 6 p.m. Can you manage that?'

'I think so.'

'And come alone. Otherwise it's all off.'

'Why should I trust you?' I said.

'Because I'm doing you a good turn, old chap.' Rownall sounded aggrieved and for the first time like his usual self; we had departed from the script. 'You want to know what really happened, don't you? I'm trying to *help*. It's no skin off my nose if you'd rather not know.'

'I'll be there.'

He put the phone down. I pushed the street atlas into the side pocket of the bag and left the flat. I wondered how Rownall had got hold of the flat's phone number; it wasn't listed, and I had never given it to him.

I took the stairs three at a time. I was desperate to get away from this house. But when I reached the hall I stopped so abruptly that I nearly fell over. A key was rattling in the lock of the front door.

There was no time to do anything. If it was Klose, I thought, I was going to charge straight through her. The door opened. Frau Stern beamed at me. I tried to look as if I were just sauntering down the stairs.

'Going out, Herr Herold?'

I agreed that I was. She was looking at the bag on my shoulder so I said I needed some food. She said young people often forgot to eat regularly, which was so foolish of them. I agreed to that too, and took a step forward, trying to edge past her to the door.

'Did my husband give you the letter?'

'No. What letter?'

'That's typical,' she said. 'He's got his head in the clouds for most of the time. I'll get it for you now.'

Frau Stern chivvied me upstairs. Short of downright rudeness there was no escape. I suspected she treated all men as she treated her husband: as though they were slightly defective beings who needed constant guidance to function properly.

'The postman put it in our letterbox,' she said. 'He's always doing that, getting muddled, I mean. The labels are perfectly clear. I wish they'd teach the poor man to read.'

The letter was on a table just inside the door of her living room. It was an airmail envelope postmarked Schwerin; the address was in Anna's handwriting, which was minute and precise, almost like print. I put it in my pocket.

Frau Stern, with a missionary glint in her eye, asked if I would like to come for supper. I muttered something about work and almost ran down the stairs.

As I closed the front door, I realized I had left the light on in the living room. Maybe that was a mistake: it would have been better to turn it off so the flat looked unoccupied. I glanced up at the window. It was in darkness. The curtains were thick; they had been made, I think, for a much larger window. They completely masked the light behind them, even around the edges.

That should have reassured me. But it didn't. It worried the hell out of me because it made me remember something that Snape had said. I told myself there were a dozen explanations for the discrepancy. It was something to bear in mind, that was all. No point in worrying about it now.

I unlocked the car with Keller's keys and started the engine. I didn't want to advertise the fact that he hadn't driven me to the airport. I drove down to the Admiral Nelson and left it in the car park there – not on the forecourt but at the side of the pub. It would have been useful to have a car but far too risky to keep Keller's Golf.

Then at last I was free to go to Snape's flat. I walked quickly through the quiet streets, making a slight detour to avoid my own road. It was a residential area, and cars were parked bumper to bumper along the roads. On the way I passed a Jaguar XJS, just like Rownall's. It even looked as if it might be olive green; but the yellow glare of the street lamps made it impossible to be sure.

Coincidence, of course: that's what I thought.

When I reached the block of flats where Snape lived, I tried to find out if there were any watchers in the parked cars nearby. All of them were empty, apart from one that contained an obviously courting couple. Too obvious? The trouble with paranoia is that it feeds on itself. Once you become suspicious, everything around you confirms your suspicions.

Snape answered the door. His face was as deadpan as ever. He was dressed casually in a brown roll-neck jersey and corduroy trousers; it was the first time I'd seen him out of a suit.

'Good evening,' he said, glancing at my bag. 'Miss Allanton's waiting.'

Relief hit me like a shower of cold water. 'I hope you don't mind my telling her to come here?'

'Not at all, Mr Herold. I'll just put it on your account.'

'Of course,' I said. 'Time's money.'

Elizabeth darted towards me as soon as I went into the living room-cum-office. She kissed my cheek. For an instant her warmth and her perfume wrapped themselves around me. I was so surprised, and happy, that I lacked the presence of mind to return the kiss.

'Have you been here long?' I said.

'Five minutes.' She took a step backwards and looked at me. 'Are you okay?'

I nodded and smiled in what I hoped was a reassuring way. We couldn't talk openly with Snape in the room. But there was no immediate need to talk. Just looking at her was like taking a long, warm bath. She was wearing the same clothes she'd worn at the Rownalls'; I guessed she hadn't had time to go back to Kensal Rise.

Snape cleared his throat. 'No luck, I'm afraid.'

I swung round. 'What do you mean?'

'With SJBR Associates, of course.' He raised his eyebrows. 'What did you think I meant?'

I shrugged. I had almost forgotten about Rownall's other company. I said: 'I was surprised you hadn't been able to trace them – that's all.'

'Well, they aren't registered in the United Kingdom. Do you want me to check the Channel Islands and the Isle of Man?' He saw my frown and added, 'It's the obvious next step. They're offshore Crown dependencies, not part of the UK.'

I looked at Elizabeth, who nodded. 'Do you need more money?' I said to Snape.

'It depends how long this goes on for and how far afield you want me to look. The search fees and so on can be quite a considerable item in an enquiry like this.'

'Keep on looking till you find it,' Elizabeth said. 'We'll send you another five hundred in the morning. Will that do?'

Snape looked gravely at her. 'Indeed it will. Can I get you a drink? Or some tea?'

'Tea, please,' I said, before Elizabeth had a chance to answer.

'It'll take a few minutes,' he said. 'Do sit down.' He left the room. I heard him moving around in the kitchen.

'We could ask him to check out the Unsterworths,' Elizabeth whispered. 'Maybe he could find out exactly what Rownall's been selling.'

I shook my head. 'Stand by the door,' I said. 'Tell me when he's coming back.'

She was puzzled but did what I asked. I had no time for explanations. I moved behind the desk and started opening drawers at random. I knew from Snape's bill that he was registered for VAT. I knew from Rownall's frequent complaints on the subject that registration for VAT required you to keep detailed accounts. In the bottom drawer on the lefthand side I found two lever-arch ring-binders. I picked out the one labelled 'Current Output Invoices'.

I flicked through the contents. There were only a dozen invoices there, covering the last ten months; business hadn't been brisk recently. They were carbons, of course, not the originals. Wolfgang's was the third from the top; it was made out to Peisker and marked 'Paid in Full'. The payment included expenses and VAT. Snape had scribbled the date of the payment underneath: three days before Wolfgang's death.

'He's coming,' Elizabeth hissed.

I threw the binder in the drawer, and shut the drawer with my knee. Even so, I was too late. He'd catch me on my feet and on the wrong side of the desk.

Elizabeth saw the problem. She caused a diversion by meeting Snape in the hall and asking if she could use the bathroom. That gave me twenty seconds to get back to my chair.

For the next ten minutes we drank Lapsang Souchong and tried to make conversation. I wasn't much use: the invoice confirmed the discrepancy I'd noticed as I was leaving my flat, and I had enough to do trying to cope with the implications.

The ability to make small talk wasn't among Snape's talents; he sipped his tea and contributed the occasional grunt. Elizabeth soldiered on, dealing in turn with loose tea versus tea bags, the weather, British Rail and the differences between London and New York. In short, she played the part of an ingenuous American visitor who liked the sound of her own voice.

We left as soon as we decently could, promising to phone Snape in the morning. Elizabeth took my arm as we went down the stairs.

'What the hell was that about?' she said.

'Later. We need to find somewhere to talk.'

'What's got into you, Gerhard?' When I didn't answer, she added, 'I've got a car.'

'How did you manage that?'

'I meant to tell you: I hired it yesterday, just in case.'

'Could be dangerous if Hebburn runs a check on car-hire firms.'

'Stop worrying.' She gave my arm a little shake. 'My licence is still in my married name.'

The car, a Honda Accord, was parked a couple of streets away. Elizabeth put the keys in the ignition but didn't start the engine.

'So,' she said. 'Something's bugging you about Snape. You going to tell me about it?'

'I'll tell you while we drive.'

'It would help if I knew where we were heading.'

'Anywhere. I just want to find out if we've got a tail.'

'No one followed me here.'

'Maybe not,' I said. 'But they could have *met* you here.'

She shrugged, perhaps a little angrily, and twisted the key in the ignition. She drove well, especially for someone who was new to the car, to London and to driving on the left. She handled the Honda far better than I'd handled Keller's Golf. We zigzagged in a westerly direction, away from the centre of town. I got a crick in my neck from peering out of the rear window.

'Satisfied?' Elizabeth said at last.

'I'm not sure.' I wasn't just talking about the possible tail. 'I think Snape may have gone to the police.'

'When?'

'Good question. Probably around the time of Wolfgang's death.'

'How do you figure that out?'

'Snape came to see me on my first evening in London – the night I met you. He said he thought I was Wolfgang; he said there was a light in the window of the flat. That's how he knew I was in. But tonight I found out that the curtains block off all the light.

They're really thick, and they overlap the sides of the window frame. I reckon they were made for another window. I remember I drew the curtains. So how did Snape know I was there?'

'No problem. That night you must have left a crack between them, and the light showed through.'

'That's not all: I found a copy of the invoice Snape gave Wolfgang. Paid in full, it said – the lot; including VAT and expenses.'

Elizabeth cornered too fast and I swayed against the door. 'Sorry,' she said. 'You know, there's a simpler explanation.'

'Try me.'

'Maybe Snape was short of money. So, when he heard Wolfgang was dead, he thought why not try and get a bonus out of it?'

'That means he lied about not knowing Wolfgang was dead.'

'People do tell lies.' Elizabeth's voice had a hint of amusement in it. 'Every now and then.'

'Not Snape,' I said obstinately. 'He's not the type.'

'That's your intuition speaking. If you're right about him going to the police, he must have lied to you from the start. All I'm saying is that it's more likely he lied to make some money.'

'I don't believe it. He'd lie if he thought there was a principle at stake. Something like patriotism. I think he went to the police when he found out who Wolfgang really was.'

'Bullshit,' Elizabeth said crisply. 'You're being naive.'

Before we knew it, we were in the middle of a quarrel. I think it surprised both of us. We were tired and under considerable strain. She wasn't to know that the word 'naive' had touched a nerve. We East Germans labour under the terrible suspicion that, shut off from the rest of Germany, we are provincial and unsophisticated. In consequence we strain to prove to the world how successful we are as a nation, how shrewd we are, and how cosmopolitan. And in consequence we are all too ready to suspect that Westerners are sneering at us behind our backs.

Elizabeth pulled over to the side of the road and cut the engine. We soon left Snape behind. We were arguing about her cynicism and my inability to understand the subtleties of the capitalist mind; about her tendency to reduce everything to money and my childlike faith in masculine intuition; about her recklessness and my unwillingness to trust her.

'This is stupid,' I said miserably.

'Crazy,' Elizabeth agreed. 'What the hell are we doing?'

'I'm running away.' I glanced at her profile, which was dimly outlined against the window: like a face on a coin. 'I should have told you this before – Bochmann's dead.'

She listened in complete silence while I told her the rest of it: Klose ordering me back to Berlin; the fight with Keller; Bochmann's body in my bed; and Rownall's phone call.

When I'd finished, Elizabeth said, 'I can see why you don't want to take a chance on Snape. Who do you think killed Bochmann?'

'How do I know? Klose and Rownall are on the shortlist.' I mentioned the XJS I'd seen on my way to Snape's flat. 'Whoever it was, I'm implicated.' I hesitated. 'You know what Klose might do? Ask the British police to find me.'

I could expect no mercy from Hebburn or Klose. The irony was, I thought I'd burned my boats when I attacked Keller, but Bochmann's killer had already burned them for me. I didn't even have a choice in the matter.

Elizabeth touched my shoulder. 'But you still want to know who killed Wolfgang, don't you?'

'Of course I do.' My voice shook. 'More than ever.'

I clung to that like an article of faith. It *was* a matter of faith, not reason: Wolfgang had been murdered and it was my responsibility to do something about it. I owed it to him and I owed it to myself. The thought that someone had killed my brother generated a dull anger in me. I almost welcomed the obstacles people threw in my way: they kept the anger alive and hardened my determination.

'And what then?' Elizabeth said softly. 'Suppose you can stay out of sight for twenty-four hours. Suppose you talk to Rownall. Suppose he gives you the answer. What *then*?'

'I don't know. I wish I did.'

She took my right hand in both of hers and peered at my face. 'We'll figure that out later. Right now we need to find a hotel with room service and a private bathroom. Okay?'

'No,' I said. 'It's not. You've done enough. I'll write to you if I find out anything about Mrs Issler. I promise you that. But I don't want you involved. It's all too dangerous.'

'Shut up, will you?' she said gently.

She cupped my face in her hands and suddenly we were kissing.

*

It wasn't much of a place. There was no room service. The nearest we got to a private bathroom was the wash-basin at the end of the bed.

The Myrtle House Hotel was in Isleworth; we'd agreed that it would make sense to be reasonably close to Richmond, where I was due to meet Rownall. It was a large Victorian semi with modern wings tacked on at the side and at the back. The lobby throbbed with canned music, the sort that makes you wish can-openers had never been invented.

Elizabeth strode up to the desk and demanded a room.

'No twins left,' the receptionist said, raising her voice to make herself heard above the racket. 'But I can do you a double. Forty-five pounds, with breakfast. That includes VAT and service.'

She was a skinny, middle-aged woman with a perm like a blue helmet; she patted it every few seconds to make sure it was still there.

'That'll be fine,' Elizabeth said. 'Has it got its own bathroom?'

'No bath, dear. Not if you want a double.' She added defensively, 'But it's got a television and tea-and-coffee-making facilities.'

Elizabeth registered us as Mr and Mrs Gerald Pirrall and rattled off an address in Manchester. The receptionist warned us that only sandwiches were available because it was Sunday evening. Neither of us felt like going out again. We asked for a plate to be sent up to the room.

The woman gave us a key and asked if we could find our own way upstairs. 'I can't leave the desk,' she said. 'It's Sunday evening, you see.' That seemed to be her explanation for everything.

'Pirrall?' I said as we climbed the stairs.

'It's Mike's name. I'm still entitled to use it.' Elizabeth glanced back at me, her face inscrutable. 'Anyway, I have to. It's on my credit cards.'

The room was small and modern. The window overlooked the back. There was so much furniture you could hardly move without bumping into something. There was a picture of a sickly-looking kitten with a pink ribbon round its neck on the wall opposite the bed. The curtains were pink, too. I drew them across the window. I heard the rumble of traffic and saw headlights, but most of the road behind the hotel was screened by a block of flats and a row of Lombardy poplars.

The double bed took up most of the space. I tried not to look at it and failed miserably. Left to myself in Reception, I would probably have asked for two singles. I didn't know what Elizabeth's choice implied: it might be merely that she thought sharing a room would be safer and cheaper; or maybe, like me, she had something else in mind. How much do you read into a kiss?

We both wanted baths. We talked awkwardly about who should go first. In the end we tossed a coin, and Elizabeth won. While she was away I unpacked my bag. Then I sat on the bed and read the Gideon Bible I found on the bedside table. Or rather I turned the pages and the print blurred into a grey, meaningless stream. I was thirsty but I lacked the energy to make myself a drink. Sleeping was about all I was fit for.

When Elizabeth came back from the bathroom, she was swathed in towels because she had with her only the clothes she'd been wearing.

'Can I borrow your toothbrush?' she said. 'That is, if you don't mind.'

'Sure. It's on the basin.'

I edged past her to the door. We avoided one another's eyes. Intimacy isn't an easy habit to achieve: you need practice.

As I lay in the bath the events of the day rolled through my mind in a surreal pageant. I knew there was something I had missed, something that might be important. A fact I should have noticed? An inference I should have drawn? Anna's letter? No, not that: I still hadn't opened it because I knew she could have nothing to write that I wanted to read. I was too tired to bother with it now. All I could do was lie there with only my knees and my head above the water. I tried to ignore the pageant and after a while I succeeded. Everything was very peaceful.

A knocking on the door brought me awake. The water had cooled around me. For a moment I didn't know where I was.

'Gerhard?' Elizabeth said. 'Are you okay? You've been in there for nearly an hour.'

I said I was fine and struggled out of the bath. My skin was corrugated with wrinkles. I rubbed some of the water off me, pulled on my pyjamas and staggered along the corridor to our room.

Elizabeth was sitting on the stool in front of the dressing table, eating a sandwich. She was wearing my jersey, which just covered her bottom. I couldn't stop looking at her.

'I got some scotch,' she said.

There was a half-bottle of whisky and a toothmug beside her plate. She poured a couple of inches in the other toothmug and passed it to me.

'You went downstairs like that?' I said. My mouth was dry and my voice sounded strange.

'Don't be a prude.' She laughed at me. 'Don't worry. I bribed the woman who brought the food.'

I drank half the whisky and got into the bed with a sandwich. Elizabeth came to join me. As she slid under the covers, the jersey rode upwards. She was wearing nothing underneath. I stretched out my hand. She pushed it gently away.

'Food first,' she said.

The first mouthful of sandwich seemed to take about a week to chew. I don't remember the second. You see, I fell asleep.

I woke up as a child wakes: suddenly and completely, as though someone has thrown a switch from OFF to ON.

The room was dark and also chilly, and I guessed that the heating had been off for some time. The sounds of traffic had died away. This was the dead time of the morning.

I felt refreshed and stupid. I remembered going to bed with Elizabeth. For the first time, and possibly the last. The woman I loved. The woman I wanted as you want a toothache to stop or a cold drink in the middle of the desert. And I'd fallen asleep.

She was breathing softly and regularly. I knew she had been as tired as I was. She wouldn't thank me for waking her.

I turned my head on the pillow. It was too dark to see anything. My hand crept towards her. I touched warm skin: the outside of her thigh. My fingers swept upwards. She was lying on her back. I marvelled at how smooth and soft she felt. The rhythm of her breathing accelerated slightly. I lifted my hand away, feeling guilty: she needed her sleep. The breathing returned to normal. I waited. The temptation grew. It swelled until I could no longer resist it. Holding my breath, I touched her again, this time higher up her body. The sickle-shaped hollow, I thought, at the base of a breast. My fingers traced the curve above the hollow. The nipple was hard and dry.

'Stop it!' she said. 'You're tickling me.'

She lunged towards me. The bed creaked like a rusty hinge. Our arms flailed in the darkness. Something fell to the floor with a clunk: a toothmug perhaps, or the Gideon Bible. We were both laughing.

That's how it was, the first time. Not so much grand passion as loving slapstick.

After the kiss in the car, I think we'd both been prepared for something like a sexual earthquake. Then I fell asleep, which ruined that. What happened afterwards flowed out of the anticlimax, surprising us both. It was not exactly a seismic upheaval. We went through the motions but technically neither of us put on a sophisticated performance. We were laughing too much.

'The trouble with women,' Wolfgang once said, 'is that they've got no sense of humour in bed. They take it all too seriously.'

But he was wrong. Or maybe Elizabeth was just an exception to the general rule. After all, she was exceptional in other ways too.

We switched on the light and had some more whisky.

'I should have asked,' I said. 'Are you . . . were you taking precautions?'

'Don't worry.' She rested her head on my shoulder. 'I don't know why I laughed so much. I don't usually.'

'No. Nor do I.'

One of her eyelashes brushed against my skin. 'I wish you could stop time,' she said. 'Just hold it on one instant. For ever.'

'Like a photograph. Photographs fade.'

'This one wouldn't.'

I said nothing. It was an academic question. There were no still photographs, just moving pictures that stretched from the womb to the tomb. Soon it would be tomorrow. Already was. Usually you can predict with a fair degree of accuracy where the plot of your personal movie is taking you, at least in the next few days. I couldn't. The utter uncertainty of the rest of my life oppressed me. I wanted to stay with Elizabeth. I wanted the truth about Wolfgang's death. They were the two fixed points of the present; the rest was chaos.

'Tell me,' Elizabeth said, her voice muffled by my shoulder. 'If you had to go back to the GDR, and then you wanted to get out again, could you do it?'

'Not officially. The only people they let out are those they trust and those they want to get rid of.'

'Who do they want to get rid of?'

'Dissidents. Artists, intellectuals, people like that. People who can make enough noise to be heard in the West or cause trouble at home. Or people who are no use to the state like the elderly and criminals. You can always *apply* for an exit visa. About half a million people have. They let out about ten or twelve thousand a year. In the meantime they harass you and your family. Even your children are discriminated against at school. In a way you can see their point. There's no reason why they should favour the disloyal.'

'It doesn't shock you?'

'It's the way things are.' These were restrictions I had grown up with, just as she had grown up with

246

unemployment, violence on the streets and a so-called democracy, that was run like a soap opera.

'Do people still try to escape?'

'Illegally? A few. But the border police are very efficient and they've had a lot of practice. It's increasingly dangerous for those who try.'

'So how would you do it? If you wanted to, that is.'

What was she doing? Surveying the options in front of us?

'Go abroad – to Hungary, maybe,' I said. 'And hope I could find a friendly truck-driver going across the border. Or go to Rostock.'

'The port? You could go by sea?'

'Wolfgang gave me a name and an address. Of course, it may not still be possible. And whichever way you did it, you'd need a lot of hard currency. Why do you want to know?'

Elizabeth sat up and reached for the whisky bottle, which was on her side of the bed. 'If the Brits get hold of you, you might be forcibly repatriated, assuming you don't end up in a British jail. That guy Hebburn doesn't like you. But you won't get a hero's welcome in the GDR.'

She sloshed whisky into the toothmugs.

'If I tried to come back,' I said, 'it wouldn't be because I want to live in the West.'

The green eyes studied me. Her face was solemn; without make-up on it, it wasn't so very hard to see the little girl she had once been. Something turned over inside me. The urge to protect, I suppose, not that I was capable of protecting anyone, least of all myself.

'Would you come back for my sake?' she said. 'I'm not asking for a commitment. It's just – well, I'd kind of like to know.'

'I'd try,' I said; and I meant it.

She leant back against the pillows. My right arm entangled itself with her left.

'Suppose you get your answer from Rownall tomorrow,' she went on. 'What will you do with it?'

'That depends on the answer. If there's no more I need to find out, I'd try to get to the West German Embassy or a consulate. Maybe. I don't know.'

'We could find a Lenné Triangle,' Elizabeth told her whisky. 'A small one. We could *make* it.'

'Lenné Triangles,' I said brutally, 'are a myth. They don't exist. People pretend they do for the same reason they pretend there's a god.'

Wolfgang had chased after that myth, and look what had happened to him.

'My Uncle Jack,' Elizabeth said, 'was an architect in New York City. He rushed around and made a lot of money. Then he had a coronary. The doctors gave him six months, maybe a year if he was lucky. So he sold up and went to live in Canada, in British Columbia. Bought some land and built himself a house. He's got a river, mountains, woods. Nearest neighbour's a mile away. He got married again. Their eldest daughter's coming up to her fifteenth birthday. Even now, there's a lot of empty land in BC.'

'How does he pay for paradise?' I asked. 'American Express?'

'They don't need much. Low overheads. He writes articles sometimes. Sells his woodcarvings.'

'But he had capital to start with.'

'*I've* got capital.'

'I'm not old enough to be a pensioner,' I said. 'Even yours.'

'Don't be so stupid,' she snapped. 'If the roles were

248

reversed, you wouldn't mind my living off your money. It's an old-fashioned double standard, and I don't like it.'

It was a fair point, and I said so.

'Besides,' she said, 'you're happy enough to use my money now. For Snape. This hotel. The car. What am I supposed to think that means?'

It took me a few seconds to identify the bitterness in her voice for what it was: jealousy. That she was jealous of a ghost was no consolation to either of us. I was prepared to sponge off her to find out what had happened to Wolfgang; yet I wouldn't do it to make her – and me – happy. Assuming, of course, that happiness was what we would have.

'Okay,' I said. 'You're right. If all goes well, I'll be your pensioner and we'll look for a Lenné Triangle. How's that?'

She kissed me and then drew back. 'Do something else for me, Gerhard. Forget about Rownall. Go to the West Germans tomorrow. Tell them everything.'

'No,' I said.

'They're the only people who can protect you from Special Branch and the Stasis.'

'No,' I said.

'Please. For me.'

I kissed her, which was the kindest way of saying no. We got rid of the toothmugs and slithered down the bed. This time everything was in slow motion and we didn't laugh.

At one point she freed her mouth and said, 'You obstinate son of a bitch. You make everything so complicated.'

This time we had our earthquake. We made the tremors last for as long as possible. The springs of the bed creaked and groaned at every sudden movement on the mattress. Fear of waking other people forced us to be gentle and almost furtive. In a strange way that increased the pleasure: sharing anything can be enjoyable, even secrecy. When I think of that bedroom now, I think *that* was our Lenné Triangle – and at the time we didn't even notice.

Afterwards we huddled together in the darkness. The sound of traffic was seeping back into the room. The birds were waking up.

'Gerhard?' Elizabeth whispered.

'What?' I was almost asleep.

'It doesn't matter. Go to sleep, sweetheart.'

I slept. Now I wish I'd stayed awake.

TWELVE

On Monday morning I woke with the taste of fear in my mouth.

Elizabeth was already up, stooping over the basin and splashing water on her face. Her naked body was beautiful, and also unbearably vulnerable. She glanced around as I got out of bed.

'You know how I feel?' she said. 'It's like the first day I went to grade school. But worse.'

During breakfast, we made what plans we could. The dining room was half full. The other guests, most of whom were male, shovelled their food as though someone were timing them. The solitary waitress swayed among the tables, rolling her hips in time with the muzak. We sat by the window, watching the rain sliding down the glass and blurring the traffic on the road outside.

Afterwards, when Elizabeth had gone shopping, I went back to our room and skimmed through the newspapers. Next, I wrote a letter to the West German Ambassador to the United Kingdom. I introduced myself to His Excellency as a potential citizen of the Federal Republic, and therefore one of his responsibilities; I outlined what had brought me to England and what had happened to me here; I explained what we proposed to do today and requested him, if something happened to prevent me from reaching the safety of the Embassy, to make the matter public.

The letter might never be sent. It was an attempt to ensure that no one – Rownall, Blaines, Hebburn or Klose – could smother the affair in a blanket of silence. I realized that, if the letter reached the Embassy, the Ambassador himself was unlikely to read it; his staff would divert it to the London section of the BND, the Federal Intelligence Service. That wouldn't matter. I just wanted someone to know the truth, even if the truth were left to gather dust in the BND archives.

As I sealed the envelope, I remembered the letter from my sister-in-law. I had nothing else to do, so I read it.

Gerhard,
By the time you get this, Great-aunt Luise will probably be dead. The people at the nursing home seem to think she's my responsibility now. It's stupid, she always hated me. Anyway, I told the Director I would write to you. There's nothing anyone can do. She doesn't recognize people any longer. Most of the time she's unconscious.

How are you? Are you enjoying England and the job? I think of you often, and wish we hadn't said goodbye like that. But there are other memories, aren't there? I remember those most of all.

Everything's much the same at home. Thank you for sending back Wolfgang's things. Is there anything that was his you would like? Just let me know. Will keep you informed about Great-aunt Luise. Looking forward to seeing you when you're back home.

Love
Anna

There was a complimentary book of matches in the ashtray. I opened the window and burned the letter on the sill. The ashes fluttered away in the direction of the Lombardy poplars.

My family. The trouble was, Wolfgang had been the glue that held the rest of us together. His death dissolved all the links between us: me, Anna and Great-aunt Luise.

It was true that I still felt slightly sorry for Anna. There were two inferences to be drawn from her letter. First, that she was desperate to attach herself to someone who could assure her at least a reasonable standard of living. Second, the fact that she was interested in me implied that the news of Bochmann's defection had not been released in the GDR.

Everyone was keeping quiet, in the UK as well as the GDR. I shut the window and glanced at the pile of newspapers on the bed. No mention there of Toughton's arrest or the search for Rownall. If the police wanted Elizabeth or me to help them with their enquiries, they weren't publicizing the fact. By now someone must have found Bochmann's body in my flat; it wouldn't be easy for Klose to conceal that from Hebburn.

The silence was ominous. It was like a barrier insulating us from the rest of the world.

When Elizabeth came back, she had a new suitcase in one hand and three carrier bags in the other. Her hair glistened with rain as though it had been lacquered. She swept the newspapers off the bed and showed me what she had bought.

The case was full of clothes, mainly for her. What was suitable for Sunday lunch with your boss was not suitable for life with a fugitive on Monday morning. She'd bought jeans, running shoes, a jersey, a woolly hat and a heavy coat that came down to her knees. She'd bought me a hat, too, and a long waxed jacket with big pockets.

There were two folding knives with four-inch blades that could be locked into place. Those were more for morale, I hoped, than for use. There was a fishing line of heavy-duty nylon in case we caught a fish that wanted to get away. There were large-scale maps not only of the Richmond area but of London. There was a road atlas. There were two piles of cash, each containing £100. She had also bought a tape recorder small enough to fit in a pocket, with a separate microphone and two blank tapes.

Elizabeth dried her hair and changed her clothes. Meanwhile I fiddled with the tape recorder, installing it in the jacket and checking that it actually worked. I practised operating the controls and switching tapes when the recorder was in my pocket.

In jeans and jacket Elizabeth looked like a slim boy. The hat concealed her hair. Rownall still didn't know of the connection between his secretary and me. We wanted it to stay that way for as long as possible.

I pressed the record button. 'Say something,' I said. 'I want to test the recorder.'

'Now,' she said. 'Let's go take a look around.'

A few weeks before Wolfgang died, he and Rownall had lunch with Sylvia Carne of Morganettas. Sylvia took a fancy to Wolfgang, and they all had a lot to drink. Outside Richmond station, on their way back to the car, Rownall fell over.

'I just lay there like a stranded whale,' he'd told me,

smiling his jolly smile. 'We were laughing so much it took me about half an hour to get up.'

Elizabeth and I spent a couple of hours driving round Richmond and its environs. On the way we tested the recorder again, and played back the tape on the deck in the car. Then we parked in a multi-storey car park, had lunch in a pub and covered the area around the station on foot. From Rownall's point of view, Richmond was a good choice. Bus routes and railways, both overground and underground, converged on the station. The town was also within easy reach of three motorways.

They say that all the best plans are simple. But ours was simple for the wrong reason: it had to be because we didn't know enough to make it complicated. I was to meet Rownall; Elizabeth was to keep us under observation; if he and I moved away, she would follow, if she could; and afterwards, assuming that Rownall was willing and able to tell me what had happened to Wolfgang, we would go to the West German Embassy and try to persuade someone to listen to us.

If we got separated, we would meet at the hotel, where we had booked in for another night. If I hadn't returned by midnight, she would take my letter to the Embassy and contact the police. If neither of us got back to the hotel, the chambermaid would find an envelope addressed to the manager on the dressing table. It contained enough money to cover our bill, the letter to the Ambassador, and a note asking the manager to forward it.

There were too many unknowns.

What neither of us could understand was why Rownall was sticking his neck out to satisfy my curiosity.

*

At five to six I was waiting by the entrance to the station concourse, pretending to read a newspaper.

Elizabeth was only a few yards away in the Honda, which was parked illegally on the station approach road. The time of day improved Rownall's chances of remaining unobserved: the evening rush hour was in full swing, and commuters were surging up from the platforms.

At five past six a traffic warden sauntered towards the Honda. Elizabeth wound down the window. She must have told him a convincing story because he let her stay there.

By ten past six I was convinced that Rownall had changed his mind. Two minutes later a teenager ambled up to me and asked if I'd got a light. I shook my head, irritated by the interruption and expecting him to move on. But he stayed there, looking up at me.

'Your name Harry or something?' he said, mumbling because of the unlit cigarette that dangled from his mouth.

I nodded.

'You got to walk round Richmond Green.'

'What?'

'You heard.'

He wandered into the station. I stood there for a few seconds, following him with my eyes. Rownall was just making sure of me, I thought: change the rendezvous and then watch to see if I were followed or made contact with someone on the way.

I pressed the record button and murmured, 'I'm going to walk round Richmond Green.'

A woman nearby looked strangely at me and hurried away; probably she thought I'd made her a proposition.

I pressed eject. By the time I started walking the tape was in my hand. I drew abreast of the Honda. The driver's window was open a crack and out of the corner of my eye I saw a blur of movement on the other side of the glass. I flipped the tape out of my pocket and let go. It fell to the ground with a faint clatter. With luck the drop had been masked from a possible watcher by my body and the car. With luck Elizabeth had seen it fall.

I walked slowly along the Quadrant. It was still drizzling, and there were gusts of wind to drive the rain into unexpected places. I had to give Elizabeth time to listen to the tape and to work the car through the heavy traffic to the Green. On the way I slotted the second cassette into the recorder. At the Square I hesitated for as long as I dared before turning down Duke Street. As far as I could tell, no one was following me on foot.

Richmond Green is shaped like a lozenge. I arrived at the eastern corner. The pavements were full of people hurrying home. A few dogs were tearing about on the Green itself. I crossed the road and walked slowly around the perimeter of the grass in an anti-clockwise direction. I felt dreadfully exposed. At the back of my mind lurked the possibility that Rownall had lured me here not to talk but to kill me.

Halfway around the Green I saw the Honda. It passed within a few paces of me and I was no longer entirely alone. I plodded on, one hand resting on the recorder, the other curled round the knife.

'Gerhard?'

The voice was behind me and barely more than a whisper. I stopped and turned. My finger pressed the record button.

'Over here,' Rownall said.

He was sitting in a small van. A moment earlier I had watched the van pull out of the traffic and park. As I approached, Rownall opened the door and struggled out.

'That awful youth actually did what he was paid for? I was beginning to wonder.'

I said nothing. He was wearing dark overalls and a flat cap. Together with the van he looked like a plumber on his way home.

'Sorry to be so – well, tortuous about this. Unavoidable, really.'

'If you say so,' I said.

He moved nearer. 'Tell me, how were Miranda and David when you saw them? I presume you *did* see them yesterday?'

'Unhappy,' I said. 'Miranda thought you might be dead. She wouldn't believe what the police were saying about you.'

His face crumpled for an instant. He said, 'Look, would you mind getting in the van?'

'Can't we talk here?'

'Afraid not. I need to show you something.'

'Why should I trust you?'

'Because you've got no earthly reason to think I'll do you any harm.' Rownall's voice rose in volume as he spoke, betraying the strain he was under. 'Because I'm trying to help you. Because I'm the only person who can tell you the truth about Wolfgang.'

'Did you kill him?' I said.

'No. *No.* I swear it. I've never killed *anyone*. I wouldn't be here if I had.' God knows why, but he convinced me. Or maybe my need to talk to him overrode my natural scepticism. I took a step towards

258

the van. It was painted white or perhaps cream. There was no lettering on the side.

Rownall opened the rear doors. 'You don't mind riding in the back, do you? More discreet, you see. It won't be for long. I put some cushions in there.'

'Even so, I think I'll ride in front,' I said.

'I'd rather you went in the back,' he said quietly.

'No.'

'Look at this.' His right hand came out of his coat pocket. He was holding an automatic. 'Just get in.'

We were standing very close together, enclosed by the back of the van and its open doors. The gun seemed out of place: it didn't belong in the hand of a cheerful little man like Rownall.

'You wouldn't dare use it. Not here.'

Rownall said, 'It makes less noise than a car back-firing. You'd fall back in the van. I'd just close the doors and drive away.'

I clambered inside. He slammed the doors. There were no windows. The darkness was absolute, like a coffin. I heard a scrape and a click, which suggested that the lock on the doors had been reinforced with a hasp and padlock.

The engine fired and we moved off. Rownall drove jerkily, cornering too fast and fumbling the gears; he was used to the automatic transmission in the Jaguar. The first sharp corner took me by surprise: I careered headfirst into one of the sides. After that I kept my centre of balance low. I used my hands to explore my surroundings. At the front a panel had been bolted over what was presumably a window to the driver's cab, and there were similar panels at the back, one on each door. The doors didn't have handles on the inside. There wasn't enough room to stand up, and barely

259

enough to lie down. Rownall had given me three small cushions – too few for comfort. It was very cold.

I was in a small metal prison.

Much later I looked at a map and worked out the distance we travelled. Rownall's idea of a short journey was well over 100 kilometres, more like 120 or 130. At first it was relatively easy, once I'd learned to cope with the corners. The traffic was so heavy that Rownall went slowly and was often forced to stop.

Soon, however, we were on a faster road. We picked up speed gradually. I reckoned we must be on a motorway, which meant the M3, the M4 or the M25. It was here that my troubles really began. It was like being trapped inside a drum that was swaying and rolling, while the drummer was pounding vigorously and irregularly on the skin. Add to that the roar of engines, not just the van's but those of the vehicles around it. It was impossible to distinguish between noise and vibration. Every cell in my body seemed to be breaking away from its neighbours.

At first I tried to keep active. I blunted the blade of the penknife on the panels over the windows. I estimated times and speeds, and calculated the distance we would have travelled if my estimates were correct. I told the tape recorder where I thought we might be going and exactly what I thought of Sebastian Rownall. I thought a good deal about Elizabeth, wondering if she were somewhere behind the van. Part of me wished that she had lost us, that she was safely out of this mess.

Later I wedged myself and the cushions in a corner

and huddled there, with my hands over my ears. I was no longer thinking coherently.

I didn't notice when we left the motorway. Gradually I realized that everything was much quieter. Once or twice we stopped for several minutes – at traffic lights, perhaps. I began to recover. I was stiff and bruised, and I had cramp in one leg. Systematically I flexed my muscles.

There was another halt. This time Rownall cut the engine and got out of the van. All I heard were footsteps and two metallic clangs. He started the engine, drove a few metres in first gear and then repeated the process. Gates, I thought: we'd arrived.

'Seb.' A pause. 'Seb.'

It was Rownall talking, which didn't make any kind of sense.

'Seb?' he said again, now with a rising inflection. 'Seb? Seb? Oh, damn it.'

The rattle of keys. A rumbling sound. Rownall returned to the van and drove a little further. He stopped and slammed the van door. The rumbling sound again. More footsteps, this time with a hollow ring to them, as if we were under cover. A door banged. Then silence.

I shuffled to the back of the van and opened the knife. I lay across the doors, hunched on my side. What seemed like hours slowly slipped away. Rownall came back, his feet dragging on the ground.

'Gerhard?' he said. He cleared his throat. 'Gerhard? Look, I'm sorry about this. It can't have been a comfortable ride.'

I said nothing.

'There's a good reason for it, I promise you.' He sounded genuinely upset. 'You'll understand every-

261

thing soon. You'll be *pleased* . . . Can you hear me all right?' He waited for an answer that didn't come. 'Just a little bit longer and we'll have you out.' A pause. 'Are you okay?'

Another minute crawled by. I hoped he was thinking about the carbon monoxide that could leak from the exhaust, about cornering techniques that could slam the head of an unwilling passenger against the side of the van. I hoped he was imagining me bleeding to death. I wondered whether to try the effect of a groan. On the whole, silence seemed wiser: it left more to Rownall's imagination.

'Gerhard? Gerhard?' He fumbled at the padlock. Urgency made him clumsy and he swore. He pulled open the offside leaf of the doors. Light poured into the van. I squinted through half-closed eyes. I could see a hand with a gun in it.

Rownall stuck his head inside and peered at my face. He yanked open the other door. My right arm, which had been supported by the door, fell out of the van. He lurched backwards.

His left hand, the one that wasn't holding the gun, touched my face and quickly withdrew. I held my breath. Rownall's breathing was rapid and noisy. He took a step back and frowned down at me, obviously trying to work out what to do. He had three options: he could pretend this wasn't happening, lock me up again, or help me.

In the end he decided to help me, which I can see now is a point in his favour; at the time I was merely glad because I thought it gave me the best chance of the three. He edged towards me. The gun was still in his hand but it was pointing at the ground. He studied my face and my body. He looked very anxious. It was not the sort of expression you'd expect a murderer to have when he confronted his victim.

First he felt for my pulse on the wrist that dangled out of the van. It took him a while to find it, during which he bit his lip and made a continual clucking noise with his tongue. Next, he pawed at my jacket with his free hand; he needed the other for the gun. The zip defeated him. He grunted and tried another idea. His left arm worked its way under my right armpit. I guessed that he decided I'd be more comfortable flat on my back, along the length of the van. He failed to shift me one-handed. Still holding the gun, he stretched his right hand out to my shoulder and pushed while trying to lift me with the left.

I flopped over. The movement took him by surprise, and he pitched forward. My legs shot out of the van. My right arm grabbed him round the waist. He toppled onto me. My left hand swept up from behind my back. The blade of the knife flashed in the light. I gripped his neck in the crook of my elbow and dug the tip of the blade into the back of his shoulder. The gun barrel grated against the floor of the van. He squirmed, but he couldn't escape my arms.

'Don't fire,' I said. 'The bullet could go anywhere.'

I increased the pressure on the knife. The blade slid forward perhaps half a centimetre, so quickly that I guessed the tip had finally penetrated Rownall's clothing. He jerked convulsively, like a fish out of water. A thin squeal wrenched its way out of his throat.

And then he was still.

But I couldn't take any chances, even then. I disentangled the gun from his hand. The butt was warm and slightly slippery from his sweat. Once that was safe I wriggled out of the van.

He was lying on his front, with his legs trailing through the doors. His breathing was rapid. Part of the face was visible: in this light the skin looked predominantly grey; the high colour of good living had fled, leaving a few unhealthy blotches.

A faint? A minor epileptic fit? Whatever it was, it had been triggered by fear: fear of me. I turned him over on his back, lifted his legs and pushed him into the van. I put one of the cushions behind his head, which was another unwanted reminder of yesterday evening and Keller, and loosened his collar. I checked the wound on his shoulder as best I could. There was very little blood. The knife had barely broken the skin.

Rownall stirred. He muttered, 'No, really – I promise.'

There was a bunch of keys in one of the side pockets of the overalls. I grabbed them and backed out of the van. I would have liked to have searched him properly but that would have to wait. I locked him in.

I leant against the van. My legs felt as though the bones had melted under pressure and become viscous: they supported me merely out of habit; any moment they would bow beneath the weight. I was conscious of a pain in my groin and a burning need to empty my bladder.

I was in a loading bay: concrete floor, concrete-block walls and a roof of corrugated asbestos supported by an iron framework. Strip-lighting hummed overhead. The floor was spattered with oil and needed sweeping. Nearly a third of the space was occupied by a drunken pile of wooden pallets and empty cardboard boxes.

There were two exits. The big metal doors, tall enough to allow a high-sided truck to pass through them, must lead to the outside world; there was a wicket in one of the leaves. Directly opposite them was a smaller set of double doors, raised like a stage a metre above ground level.

In the van, Rownall stirred and moaned.

The wicket seemed more attractive. I walked across to it on legs that were beginning to feel almost normal again. Two bolts, which were already drawn back, and a Yale. I glanced down at the gun, noticing the safety was on. It was an ugly thing: a Colt .45 Government Model with a black rubber stock; it was over twenty centimetres long and weighed more than a kilo; you couldn't stuff it in a pocket and forget it was there.

Keeping the gun in my hand, I put the Yale on the catch and slowly pulled open the door.

Outside was a tarmac yard, lit by a single light above the doors and bounded by a chain-mesh fence topped with strands of barbed wire. A pair of gates gave access to a deserted road. Beyond it were darkened buildings and more fences. There was no sign of the Honda. In a way I was glad of that.

A stiff, salt-smelling breeze swirled round the yard. As I watched, it flattened a sheet of newspaper against the fence. It was no longer raining. Somewhere in the distance a siren hooted. We were near the sea, or perhaps a tidal estuary. There were other, fainter sounds: a dog barking, a lorry changing gear.

I picked my way across to a row of wheeled dustbins. I relieved myself against the side of one of them; the verb is apt. The sky was charcoal grey except at the horizon, which was tinged with yellow. No stars or moon. There were some lights around, but too few of them, and too little traffic, for a city. I guessed we were on some sort of industrial estate.

The loading bay was attached to an oblong, two-storey building with a flat roof. No lights were on, apart from the one above the double doors. The windows were blank.

What had Rownall said? *Something I need to show you* . . .

I went back inside. Rownall wasn't making a noise: either he was still unconscious or he was too scared to open his mouth. I opened the driver's door and removed the keys from the ignition. In the glove compartment I found a torch and a walkie-talkie. Maybe the radio explained Rownall's performance in the yard: 'Seb? Seb?' He'd been identifying himself to someone who wasn't there, probably repeating himself because he was trying a pre-set series of channels.

Something I need to show you . . . Or someone?

I knew from my national service that the range of those walkie-talkies wasn't more than a few kilometres, even in optimum conditions. And the ones I'd used had been military issue, much more sophisticated than this little Citizen's Band radio.

But the someone wasn't *here*: that was the point, surely; or Rownall wouldn't have tried the radio.

For a moment I thought of trying to make him talk. But first I needed to know where I was, to gather as much information as possible. To be honest, I had no particular desire to wave a gun in his face or anyone else's. I leapt at the excuse to postpone it.

I left the radio and went over to the doors on the loading platform. Half-hidden by the pile of rubbish was a flight of concrete steps that led up to the side of the platform. The nearer leaf of the doors was ajar. I pushed it open. Rownall must have disabled the alarm system already. There was darkness beyond, but the air felt warmer. Enough light came through from the

loading bay to show that this was a storeroom. Wooden
shelves on a steel framework stretched from floor to
ceiling. They were arranged in aisles on either side of
a broad central passage. I shone the torch on the
nearest shelf. There was a row of cartons, filmed with
dust.

THIS SIDE UP, I read. I raised the beam a fraction. DURSLEY.
THE DIPPY DOGLET PEOPLE.

That nudged something in my memory. It took me
back to one of the briefings Reichel had arranged in
Berlin, just before I left for England. It was with a man
who directed the research and development programme of our toy manufacturers. A pompous type
who liked the sound of his own voice, he'd explained
that the Western market was increasingly dominated
by promotional toys linked to TV series: My Little Pony,
Cabbage Patch dolls, Postman Pat.

It cut both ways, he'd said: Western companies
scrambled for exclusive concessions, invested heavily
when they got them, and then were forced to file for
bankruptcy if the TV series went under. Character
merchandizing was an immensely lucrative but high-
risk business for the manufacturers. His argument was
that we should avoid all promotional toys and concentrate on a variety of staples that would go on selling
steadily, if not spectacularly. This, I'd thought at the
time, was just as well, because East German toy manufacturers lacked the resources to handle new, fast-
turnover ventures; he was merely recommending the
inevitable. The man had mentioned some of the character merchandizing ventures that had failed to come
off: among them were the Dippy Doglets.

As I moved down the store, I glanced along some
of the other shelves. Packaging. Granules of plastic:

high-impact polystyrene, polyethylene and polypropylene. Acetone, of course; they'd need a lot of that. Pigment. Spare parts for the machinery. It was all unexpectedly familiar to me.

Why the hell had Rownall brought me to a toy factory?

There was another door at the far end of the storeroom. It was unlocked. Beyond it was a corridor that ran the length of the building. I tried every door that opened onto it in turn. Some were locked; but Rownall had keys for all but the one at the end of the corridor. This was marked NO ENTRY and had two locks.

I dared not switch on the lights, and the torch had to be used with caution. I didn't want to advertise my presence to Rownall's friend. It was possible that the factory had a watchman or was on the rounds of a security patrol. My movements were furtive, like a thief's.

The nearest door led to the plastic moulding shop. It stank of acetone solvent. There were huge yellow silos for the plastic granules that fed the Krauss Maffei moulding machines. The machines – tool-steel sandwiches that look like field howitzers and cost upwards of £100,000 each – mix the granules with pigment, macerate them and heat them to 180 degrees centigrade: the resulting mixture is fired into steel moulds at a pressure of 23,000lb per square inch. Once there had been six machines in this room; now there was only one. The more complicated the toy, the more machines you need to make the components. The missing machines underlined the point that Dursley was struggling to survive.

The assembly shop told the same story of retrenchment. It was a wilderness of rotating tables and conveyor belts, many of which were obviously out of service. Dust, dirt and rubbish hinted at a slackly-supervised work force with low morale. I wandered on, through the quality control and packing departments, past lavatories, restrooms and storage areas.

The offices were upstairs. Some of them no longer had tenants. I wanted to find out who owned Dursley's but there I drew a blank; I was in too much of a hurry to search methodically.

In the marketing manager's office, there was a case displaying toy kennels and a family of miniature dogs; I presume they were dogs – each had four legs, a head and a tail; but the modelling was too primitive for conclusive identification. In the bottom drawer of the desk I found sales literature for the Dippy Doglets range, which was the obvious ancestor of the much less sophisticated models in the display case; it was an example of evolution in reverse. In the same drawer was an old fly sheet advertising THE TOYSHOP ON THE THAMES: 'Dursley's, the Dippy Doglet People . . . Low, low prices, direct from the manufacturers. Stacks of parking. Full range of Dippyville accessories. Duane, Dumbo, Duncan, Daisy, Derek and Dodo say "*Please* come and see us! Wuf! Wuf! WUF!"'

The address was in Kent and the postal town was Rochester, which was nothing more than a name to me. The phone number on the fly sheet was the same as the one on the marketing manager's phone. It looked as if they'd tried retailing direct from the factory, probably in a desperate attempt to get rid of surplus stock.

I used the phone to ring the Myrtle House Hotel. No, the receptionist told me, Mrs Pirrall had not returned. I left a message for Elizabeth – just the name of the company and the phone number. It made me feel slightly better.

I headed for the stairs. I had learned nothing beyond the fact that this was a small, ailing toy factory. By now I had been everywhere except through the one door at the far end of the corridor. It was time to persuade Rownall to talk.

The loading bay seemed dazzlingly bright. Nothing had changed in my absence. The van was silent. I walked over to it and tapped on the side.

'Rownall?'

There was no answer.

'I'm going to let you out,' I said. 'I'll use the gun if I have to.'

I unlocked the door, pulled it open and jumped back. Maybe he was trying the same ploy I had used on him. I levelled the gun at the van.

'Come on,' I said. 'Out you come.'

For a second my mind went on strike, refusing to believe the information my eyes transmitted. I saw a pair of legs inside. They weren't wearing overalls but jeans. There were running shoes on the feet, and the ankles were tied together with what looked like a tow-rope.

A whisper came out of the van: 'Gerhard.'

Elizabeth. It was more than a shock: it was an impossibility.

Behind me someone chuckled. I swung round, flicking off the Colt's safety catch.

Rownall was leaning against the wall, almost hidden by the pile of rubbish. He had one of those jolly smiles on his face. At that moment I hated him.

'I didn't know about Beth,' he said. 'That was clever of you.'

'If you've hurt her – '

'She's all right.' He levered himself away from the wall and took a step towards me.

'You stay there,' I said, 'or I'll put a bullet in you.'

'Haven't you noticed?' Rownall gave a little snort of amusement. 'That Colt's a model – a *toy*.'

I pulled the trigger. *Click*. Everything came back to toys.

'I told you so,' Rownall said. 'By the way, there's someone to see you.'

The wicket was opening as he spoke. A tall, middle-aged man came through. He was wearing a trenchcoat. He smiled at me. I knew his face better than I knew my own.

It was my brother Wolfgang.

THIRTEEN

When I was a child, I believed my brother reserved a special smile for me. Later, in my teens, I realized this unique configuration of his facial muscles was my invention, not his. He smiled in precisely the same way at Great-aunt Luise or the current girlfriend or colleagues from the office. God knows, that should have warned me of the dangers of wishful thinking.

'Gerhard,' he said softly.

Rownall chuckled, perhaps at the expression on my face.

Wolfgang strode across the loading bay and hugged me. I hugged him back. He was both familiar and strange, like a recurring dream. I was too shocked to feel happy: for a bystander, a return to life is in many ways more difficult to cope with than the death that preceded it.

His hands on my shoulders, he pushed me back and looked at me.

'We must talk,' he said. 'There's not much time.' He looked past me to Rownall and switched to English. 'Bring the Fiesta in here, will you, Seb? The keys are in the ignition. And then would you get the Honda that's parked on the road?'

Rownall hurried to open the doors that led to the yard. My brother's tone and Rownall's response to it told me all I needed to know about their relationship: master and man.

'Let's go inside,' Wolfgang said. 'I want to show you something.'

'No,' I said, walking towards the van.

'Leave her. I take it she's working for you?'

'In a manner of speaking.'

I opened the other door of the van. Elizabeth was lying on her side with her head on a cushion. Her eyes were open.

'I need to talk to you alone,' Wolfgang said, and the warmth had left his voice. 'She'll be all right.'

I fumbled at the rope around her legs.

Wolfgang gripped my arm, partly to restrain me and partly, I think, to reassure me. 'Look, we need to talk in private. It's important.'

The Fiesta reversed into the loading bay. It was the same white hatchback that Bochmann had driven on the evening he picked me up in Ealing. Rownall parked it beside the van and went back outside.

'Are you okay?' I said to Elizabeth. 'Has he hurt you?'

'I'm fine.'

'Which is more than I am,' Wolfgang said, sounding amused. 'She bit me.'

'Go talk with him,' Elizabeth said. 'The sooner you do that, the sooner we can sort out what to do.'

'I'm not leaving you there,' I said.

Wolfgang looked curiously at me, his head on one side. He was used to himself leading and me following; so was I.

'I agree it's a little undignified,' he said. 'Why don't you untie your friend? We'll leave her here with Seb. Would that suit you?'

I nodded reluctantly.

'I'm not going to run away,' Elizabeth said.

'I'm sure you won't,' Wolfgang said.

While I untied Elizabeth, Rownall returned with the Honda. Wolfgang had a word with him and then locked the doors that led to the yard. Elizabeth scrambled out of the van and rubbed her wrists and ankles.

'When did it happen?' I said.

'Just outside. Your brother must have tailed me from Richmond.'

'Come on,' Wolfgang said. I followed him up the steps into the storeroom. He was carrying Elizabeth's black leather shoulder bag, which he had collected from the Honda.

'You've already had a look around, I imagine?' he said.

'There was one door I couldn't unlock.'

'The toyshop. It used to be stuffed with Dippy Doglets.'

'And now?'

'You don't know?'

I shook my head.

'We'll go there in a moment. Upstairs first.'

He led the way to the managing director's office. Behind the desk there was a photograph of what I assumed was the front of the factory. He lifted it down, exposing the door of a safe with a combination lock.

'Seb thinks we're safe here,' he said as he twirled the knob to and fro. 'Me, I'm not so sure.'

He swung the door open and lifted out two small rucksacks.

I said, 'So it was you who fixed the fire on Rownall's boat?'

He shut the safe. 'Yes – with a little help from Seb.

He picked me up in a rubber dinghy, and we had a car waiting a couple of miles downstream. I'd heard from Bochmann that the Stasis were asking questions. Not just about this – there were other things.'

'Like the currency-dealing?'

'Yes.' He held out one of the rucksacks. 'Would you carry this? I was going to vanish anyway, of course. The Stasis just hurried things up. I'd hoped to be able to see you first.'

'To say goodbye.'

'Nonsense. To arrange for you to join me. That was always the plan. In the event it worked out rather well: it was easy to persuade Bochmann to appoint you in my place.'

'I might have preferred to stay,' I said, leaning against the desk.

'In that godawful country?'

'Is this one any better?'

'That's not the point.' Wolfgang was opening the drawers of the desk, one by one. 'The point is, it's in the West. If you're in the West and you've got money, you can do anything. You're *free*.'

'Free to find a personal Lenné Triangle?'

'Precisely.' He glanced up, smiling what I used to think was the special smile; he looked so grateful, too, which puzzled me. 'I knew you'd understand. No one else does.'

Trust me, that smile said, just as it had said so many times before. *Trust me and everything will be all right.* I felt like an iron bar confronted with a magnet.

'Then whose body was it?' I said harshly. 'The one who died in the fire?'

'A man named Beadlow. Henry James Beadlow. He was a lucky accident: same colouring as me, roughly

275

the same height and age.' Wolfgang bent across the desk and touched my cheek. 'Don't get me wrong. You don't think *I* killed him, do you?'

I flinched from the hand. It is a terrible thing to doubt someone you have trusted all your life. It undermines all certainties.

'That's the obvious conclusion,' I said. 'If you didn't, who did?'

'Pneumonia, perhaps? Exposure? Thirty years of alcohol doesn't leave you with much resistance. He was just a tramp, you know. One of those derelicts the West doesn't know what to do with. I found him in an outhouse near the mooring when I got down there. The place where Seb kept the oars and things. He must have broken in. I reckon he'd been dead for at least a day.'

'His left tibia was fractured.'

'They found that? Good.'

'You just broke it – in case someone noticed?'

'Well, Beadlow didn't mind: he was dead. Why not? Come on, Gerhard, it was crucial. Imagine if they'd found a left tibia that *wasn't* broken.'

They hadn't found the head. I wondered if that had been luck, too, or whether my brother had once again made his own luck. I knew him too well. He was always a careful planner, and I don't think he would have left to chance something as important as his own corpse. My imagination produced a grotesque picture of Wolfgang working on Henry James Beadlow with a panel saw.

'And it worked the other way,' he went on. 'How many people have a fracture in their left tibia? The fire must have made it impossible for the autopsy to show whether the break happened before or after death. It meant the next best thing to a positive identification.'

'It was a callous thing to do.'

'I know.' Wolfgang stuffed a handful of papers in his inside pocket. 'But he was dead. No use to himself or anyone else. Except me. Let's go. I'll show you the toyshop.'

I didn't move. 'Other people died.'

'Custer, for instance?' He shrugged. 'Nothing to do with me. That was Toughton's doing. You met him, I think? He spent twenty years in the army: a professional sadist, if you ask me. Using him was Seb's idea. Toughton panicked when Custer started talking. It was as simple as that.'

I doubted that. Toughton was no longer important in the scheme of things: he was a natural scapegoat. His hat had been found under Custer's body. It would have been easy enough for Rownall to get hold of it and give it to Wolfgang.

I said, 'So the police got the right man?'

Wolfgang nodded. 'Seb was due to meet Toughton yesterday morning, for the final pay-off. When Toughton didn't turn up, Seb rang him at home. A strange man answered the phone. Toughton was yelling in the background. Seb had the sense to get out while he could. He knew Toughton wouldn't keep his mouth shut. Luckily he hasn't got much to say. He doesn't know what we were bringing in, or about me, or about this place. Seb told him as little as possible.'

'Why's he doing this?' I said. 'Rownall, I mean. He's got a wife and a kid – a nice house, a business.'

'Because he wants to keep them. His firm's been losing money, and he's on the verge of bankruptcy.'

'But he's risking everything,' I said.

Wolfgang shrugged. 'It didn't seem like that when

we started. I was the one who was taking all the risks. He was just organizing the warehouse side. If something went wrong, he probably thought he could blame it on Toughton.' He smiled wryly. 'But one thing led to another.'

'It's tough on his wife,' I said.

'But that's why he's doing it. Not for himself; it's Miranda and David who concern him. Of course we didn't know it was going to turn out like this. You don't, do you? Yesterday morning, he knew he had two alternatives in front of him: either lose everything and go to jail, or disappear and be rich. No choice, really. Seb's a realist.'

'He won't have Miranda and David if he's on the run.'

'If he went to jail, he'd lose them for sure and for ever. This way he's in with a chance. A good chance, I'd say. Money opens a lot of doors. And there *is* a lot of money at stake.'

Perhaps he was right about Rownall: with money, he could buy a new identity, a new country and a comfortable standard of living. From what I'd seen of Miranda, I suspected she'd settle for the old trinity of household gods: her husband, her son and enough money not to have to worry about money.

'She'll join him,' Wolfgang said. 'Come on. Let's go downstairs.'

'I was forgetting,' I said. 'You've got inside knowledge about Miranda, haven't you?'

I levered myself away from the desk and picked up the rucksack Wolfgang wanted me to carry.

'Ah.' My brother rubbed his cheek, which he often did when embarrassed. 'I'm surprised she told you.'

278

'It was an accident. She thought *you'd* told me, and that I might be tempted to tell Rownall.'

'Well, for God's sake, don't. It was stupid. I was spending the evening with them, and Seb had to go out for a couple of hours . . . Meant nothing on either side. I don't want to hurt Seb.' Wolfgang opened the door and turned back, grinning. 'That reminds me. How did you get on with Anna?'

I realized I was rubbing my own cheek with the side of a forefinger; these things can run in families.

'Not the sort of experience you want to repeat in a hurry?' He was still grinning. 'Well, don't worry about it – it was my idea. How does she like being a widow?'

I told him that Anna's grief hadn't struck me as being excessive; I also mentioned that she thought she might like to marry me. What I didn't say was that I had been in bed with her when they came to tell me he was dead.

Anna's offer amused Wolfgang, and even now I found myself smiling back at him. His good humour was infectious; some people are like that, and it makes it hard to resist them.

'And Great-aunt Luise?'

His amusement vanished when he heard what Anna had written. 'Did she miss me?'

'Of course she did. But when I went to see her she thought I was you, which must have been some consolation. You care about her, don't you?'

He shrugged. 'Look, we really should get moving.'

I waited until we were on the stairs. 'Bochmann was involved from the start, wasn't he?'

Wolfgang nodded and carried on.

'Why?'

'He needed money, I suppose. We all do.'

It sounded thin to me. Bochmann had had power and privilege, which were better than money for a man like him, but I let it go for the moment. 'Who killed him?'

Wolfgang didn't answer until he reached the corridor. Then he stopped and looked gravely at me.

'I killed him. It was self-defence. Can't we talk about this later?'

'No, we can't. How did it happen?'

As I waited for his answer, I caught myself wishing my brother had really died; not a pleasant thought to live with, but it would have been so much simpler that way.

'Bochmann panicked,' Wolfgang said at last. 'Just like Toughton did. In his case, the Stasis were digging out the container business; you heard about that. He was implicated up to his neck. So he got out while he could. That was never part of the original plan. And when he got here, he panicked about Custer, and about Special Branch and Klose, and about your asking awkward questions. That's why he came to see you: to try and shut you up.'

'You should have come yourself,' I said. 'That might have worked.'

'I underestimated you.' He patted my shoulder. 'I didn't think you'd be so ... so tenacious. In fact I underestimated you all along. I should have told you what I was going to do.'

'Then why didn't you?'

'I thought it would be safer if you didn't know. Safer for you, as well as for me. You might have given something away without meaning to.'

He was trying to change the subject. I reminded him he was telling me about Bochmann.

'Well, when he got to England, he phoned Seb. We brought him down here. Tried to work out what to do with him. He was obviously cracking up. Drinking like a fish, which he hadn't done since — well, not for years. Yesterday morning, when Seb turned up, his nerve broke. He ran away, to London. He was going to blow the whole thing wide open. It was strange, really: he couldn't cope with the responsibility of being on his own.'

It wasn't strange at all. The Ministry and the Party were like support systems for Bochmann, and he couldn't survive long without them.

'If he'd gone back, they'd have crucified him,' I said.

'Yes. He must have known that. Maybe he felt he deserved it. Maybe it didn't matter what they did to him as long as they took him back.'

'Anyway,' I said. 'You followed him up to London?'

'In the Jaguar. That wasn't much fun because we guessed the police had an alert out for it. We caught up with him in Ealing. Not Broadway; he was standing on the doorstep of your house, ringing all the bells. Luckily no one was in.'

As he was speaking, Wolfgang moved along the corridor towards the locked door at the end. He had lowered his voice, and the next words came out in rapid bursts.

'I told Seb to dump the Jaguar and went into the house with Bochmann; I'd made copies of my keys. I tried to calm him down. I said I'd wait with him till you came back, and we'd tell you everything. I meant it, I swear. We waited maybe half an hour. Then he got it into his head that you'd been arrested at Seb's house. He wanted to ring Klose. I had to stop him. It was him or us, after all. He went crazy. He tried to kill me. I had no option. You understand?'

He glanced back at me, his eyebrows raised. He wanted me to say yes. He wanted me to tell him that everything was all right, just as he used to tell me when I was a child. I said nothing.

Wolfgang shrugged, as if to say he didn't need anyone's reassurance. His face was blank, neither hurt nor hostile. Then he smiled at me. 'There's nothing we can do about it now, is there?' He unlocked the door, pushed it open and switched on the light inside. 'There,' he said, and I heard a world of pride in that one word. 'Astonishing, isn't it?'

Everything came back to toys. Not guns or explosives or people; politics didn't enter into it. Just toys.

We were in a high-ceilinged room at the end of the building. It was almost as large as the loading bay, and it had a concrete floor. There the resemblance ended. Just inside the door was a counter with shelves behind it. The walls had been freshly whitewashed. The windows were covered with heavy blinds. There was a pile of wooden crates in one corner. In the centre a number of pallets had been pushed together to form a low platform, about four metres square.

On the platform was a dolls' house.

The phrase gives the wrong impression: it suggests a battered box, peopled with dolls and furnished with matchboxes; something for a child's imagination to work on. But this house had been made for adults. The central block had five bays and three storeys above a basement; it was nearly two metres high. Two flights of steps, which together made a perfect semi-circle, curved up to the front door in the middle bay of the *piano nobile*. Ionic pilasters carried the eye up to the pediment, which was decorated with a coat of arms.

The wood had been painted to simulate stone, and the paint had faded to a soft green-brown.

From both sides of the house, low, colonnaded wings ran forwards at an angle of forty-five degrees; each ended in a pavilion with a domed roof. A wall linked the pavilions in front of the house, and in the centre it was broken by a pair of magnificent gates that rose to twice the height of the wall. The gates had been painted black to resemble wrought iron, and they were surmounted by the imperial eagle of the Romanovs.

The triangular space enclosed by the buildings was carpeted with green baize, which had been tacked to the pallets; and someone had painted a drive from the gates to the steps. Those details, unlike the others, had a makeshift air about them. The baize was wrinkled at the edges and a few drops of paint had been spilled near the gates. The defects were endearing, for they hinted that someone's imagination had been at work: in this case a grown-up child's. They also threw into relief the perfection of the buildings.

Wolfgang was watching me. He looked fond, stupid and possessive: just like Dieter did when he introduced me to his first baby. And equally anxious to see his feelings reflected in my face.

'You did all this for a *dolls' house*?'

'A dolls' house?' He lifted a flap in the counter and moved towards it. 'It's no more a dolls' house than — than the Stadt Berlin is a fifty-pfennig dosshouse. This should be in a museum. It's unique. The only rival worth mentioning belongs to the Queen of England.'

I waved the distinction aside. 'You do realize that the Stasis and Special Branch are convinced you're a threat to national security? Are you really telling me that the whole business comes down to a dolls' house?'

He laughed. 'That's their mistake. Anyway, I wouldn't call it a dolls' house. Not exactly.'

'What do you call it then?'

'The main block is an eighteenth-century "baby house" ' – he used the English words – 'a term which includes models built for adults. There are very few survivors in this condition and with the original contents. No more than two really – Nostell Priory and Uppark, and they aren't in the same league. If it was just that, it would be priceless. But there's more. The colonnades and pavilions were added a hundred years later, along with the wall and the gates. They form a triangle, did you notice?'

He gave me no chance to answer.

'It was carefully done, thank God. The additions just lift into place; the main structure wasn't touched. And of course they practically double the value, what with their contents and the historical associations. The alterations were made to please a czar. Not that he ever saw it.'

Wolfgang was unstoppable. His face alight with excitement, he paced up and down, waving his arms to emphasize a point or direct my attention to a particular feature of the house. He showed me three of the rooms: each of them had a separate, hinged flap in the façade. A tide of information rolled over me. I absorbed only a fraction of it.

'Vanbrugh's design is authenticated; that's most unusual ... There's a Hilliard in the long gallery ... Chippendale made the chairs and table in the dining-room ... In the library there's a holographed poem by Goethe – a line a page, the book's no more than a couple of centimetres high. God knows how they got

hold of it. The poem's not in the collected edition . . .
The locks are brass and they all work . . . A lot of early
American items, including a complete fireplace set in
pewter, probably by Robert Boyle; very rare, very
collectable . . . The dinner service is gold, of course . . .
One of the pavilions is a music room – it's got a grand
piano that actually works, all seven and a half octaves;
just a bit out of tune. We've got most of the documentation: the piano was made in the Fischer workshop at
Moscow in the 1830s – it cost 1500 roubles even then.
There's some Russian porcelain, too: a lot of Popov
stuff. In fact it wouldn't surprise me if some of the
pieces were originally made for the Nachtchokine
house in the Pushkin Museum . . . The chandelier in
the drawing room is made of diamonds; that's French,
Louis Seize, probably an adapted pendant . . .'

The subject was new to me but the enthusiasm
wasn't. I'd heard him like this so often before: the
dolls' house had joined a select group that included
sailing, the Lenné Triangle and the best way to import
Western music to East Berlin. Something fascinated
him and he attacked it like a starving man attacks a
plate of food.

'According to one source, there's a miniature ghost
who wrings her hands in the lying-in room. That's in
the main house, of course; the ghost is older than the
wings. It's meant to be a previous owner who died
young: an English lady whose lover died. It was her
sister who took it to Germany. She – '

'The Feldbauschs' English heiress,' I said firmly.
'Then your dolls' house, with the additions, was going
to be a *douceur* in a Crimean arms deal that fell through.
And finally it went by marriage to the von Doeneckes.'

Wolfgang stared at me with his mouth open. It gave

me a grim satisfaction; in the past I had so rarely managed to astonish my brother; it was usually the other way round.

'How did you know that?' he said, taking a step closer to me. 'Who told you? Come on, tell me.'

'You remember Teichler? The historian in Ealing? You borrowed a book from him, and forgot to return it.' I gave him a second to recall *The Dynastic Politics of the Munitions Industry*. 'I saw Count Paul von Doenecke in the index, and that gave me the Feldbausch connection.'

Wolfgang relaxed. He surged into a historical digression about Augusta Alexandra Feldbausch and her long, miserable marriage with Paul von Doenecke.

'These great dolls' houses,' he said, 'often go down the female line. It's the women who cherish them, you see, who maintain them and add to them. And that's what Augusta did, for nearly sixty years. She bought scores of miniatures for it. Most of them never went inside, because there just wasn't room. An amazing woman. She lavished all the love she had on that house; von Doenecke didn't want anything from her except her money and a male heir.'

His voice was bitter. He was angered by a wrong done to a woman he had never met, who had lived more than a hundred years before. The reason, I suppose, was almost as strange as it was simple: my brother shared with Augusta a passion for this imposing pile of wood and paint, metal and fabric.

A passion worth killing for. That reminded me of Mrs Issler.

After Augusta's death, Wolfgang told me, the dolls' house had gathered dust in the von Doeneckes' home in Neubrandenburg.

'From our point of view,' he said, 'the beauty of it is that it's always been in private hands. It was never exhibited. No one photographed it or recorded the contents. Augusta allowed hardly anyone to see it.' His eyes strayed towards the house and lingered on it. 'I can understand that. It was like a private world to her. You feel possessive about – well, your private retreat, don't you?'

We were back to the Lenné Triangle again. But the Lenné Triangle meant different things to my brother and me. I don't think he ever realized that.

In 1944 the old countess, Augusta's daughter-in-law, had the dolls' house crated up; she intended to send it to the Schloss Museum in Berlin for safekeeping. But Allied bombing put paid to that idea: the museum was badly hit, and she decided instead to brick it up in a cellar beneath a barn on the estate. The von Doenecke steward and two elderly estate workers laboured at night to fulfil her wishes.

'There's over fifty cases,' Wolfgang said. 'Everything comes apart – it was designed that way. All in all, it must weigh at least five tons. You can see why we needed to use a container.'

The countess – and her daughters, who were also in the secret – died a few months later in one of the Allied bombing raids on Berlin. The three old men were killed during the Russian advance in 1945. The country was in chaos. If anyone had remembered the Feldbausch house, which is unlikely, they would have assumed that it had been destroyed, along with so many other treasures, at the Schloss Museum; either that or that the Russians had looted it or burned it. The house had been due to go to the museum, and there was no evidence to show that it hadn't. It was convenient,

Wolfgang added, that the museum's records had also been lost in the bombing.

Only one person knew where the dolls' house was: Great-aunt Luise. And she had told Wolfgang.

'I knew that was my chance,' Wolfgang said. 'If it was still there, if I could get it out of the country. Have you any idea what something like that is worth? Christie's auctioned a dolls' house called Titania's Palace way back in 1978, in London. That was only about eighty years old – nothing like this. Even so, it went for £150,000. This one must be worth at least several million dollars; more, if we sell the contents in batches.'

'Isn't that what you're doing already?' I said. 'Through Unsterworth? There's the Isaac Oliver, for instance.'

Wolfgang frowned. Then his face cleared. 'The secretary – what's her name? – must have heard something. Am I right?'

'Yes. And her name's Elizabeth Allanton.'

'Who is she?'

'She's American,' I said carefully. 'An old friend of Mrs Issler's.'

He looked hard at me for a moment. He was trying to guess, I think, what I might know and what I merely suspected.

'Mrs Issler?' he said at last, giving nothing away.

'Born Wilhelmina von Doenecke. The one surviving grandchild of Augusta Alexandra Feldbausch. Probably her last descendant, and presumably her heir.'

'How did you get on to her?'

'The same way as you did,' I said. 'Through Alan Snape.'

'Why did you go to him?'

'I didn't. He came to me. Said you owed him money.'

288

'That's rubbish.'

'I know it's rubbish now. But I didn't then.'

'It's immoral,' Wolfgang said, apparently shocked. 'I could have sworn he was on the level.'

'That's the trouble. He is. He checked up on you as a matter of routine. Where you lived, who you were, where you came from. He found you'd told him a pack of lies. Naturally he'd wonder why an East German official should give him a false name and pretend to come from the Federal Republic. And at some point, probably after you disappeared, I think he got in touch with Special Branch.' I hesitated. 'He's an old-fashioned man. A patriot.'

My brother leant against the counter. I guessed what was going through his mind because the same thoughts had gone through mine. If Snape had gone to Special Branch, they must have had their suspicions early on about Wolfgang's fatal accident and its possible link with Mrs Issler's murder. They must have thought that I was in the conspiracy from the moment I arrived in London. They must have wanted Snape to contact me.

And then, while he was working through the obvious implications, I thought of another, subtler possibility I should have seen before. I didn't want to see it. It was the one thing I couldn't cope with. I ignored it.

Wolfgang stirred. 'I traced Mrs Issler,' he said. 'But that was all. I haven't met her. Have you? What's she like?'

He did it brilliantly. Wolfgang was never less than plausible.

'I've never met her either,' I said. 'Someone stabbed her to death, the day before I arrived in London.'

'Who?'

'The police think it was a mugger. Apparently.'

'Oh, for God's sake,' Wolfgang exploded. 'You don't think it was me, do you? Of course I didn't kill her. I swear it.'

I looked at him, waiting for something more.

'Look,' Wolfgang went on, 'I knew about Wilhelmina from Great-aunt Luise. She might have been able to – to make some sort of claim on the Feldbausch house. So I wanted to find out if she was still alive. And that's all I did. She was obviously no threat to us as long as we sold the contents bit by bit. As long as we didn't publicize the fact we'd got the *Feldbausch* house, and we weren't going to do that.'

'Then who killed her?'

He rubbed his cheek. 'Maybe it *was* a mugger. Otherwise, the only person who could have done it is Seb. But I just can't believe it.'

Rownall as the murderer made a kind of sense. I'd found Mrs Issler's address on the pad in his office, and he had as much to gain – and lose – from this business as anyone. But I didn't believe it, either. *Master and man?*

'Does Snape know about Elizabeth?' Wolfgang said.

'He met her yesterday.'

'So Special Branch will know about her too. Why's she here? Are you in love with her?'

I told him how we'd met, and how we'd developed a shared interest based on the deaths of people close to us. I left his second question unanswered.

'What are you going to do with her?' he said.

'I don't know what *we're* going to do, yet.'

'You should ditch her. She's excess baggage.'

I shook my head.

Wolfgang lowered his voice. 'I've got a boat moored a few kilometres from here. A converted lifeboat. I've already loaded some of the crates onto it. We can drive down with more. Altogether, the contents make up about five per cent of the weight, and maybe sixty per cent of the value. I've rented a cottage in Brittany. Seb doesn't know about it. We can go there and wait. See what happens.' He tapped one of the rucksacks. 'We've got plenty of money to live on.'

'And then what?'

'We can move on.' He shrugged. 'Wherever you like.'

'What about your friend Sebastian? And Elizabeth?'

'It's a matter of priorities,' he said. 'You and I would be safer out of the country. If all goes well, Seb can carry on selling the rest of the stuff. As for Elizabeth, she's an encumbrance. Surely you see that? It'll be much better if it's just you and me.'

The words seem bald and unconvincing. The impact came from the tone of voice and the look on his face. He was coaxing me to agree, with all the considerable charm he could muster; he was appealing to our shared past; he was reminding me of everything I owed him and could never repay.

'I . . . I need a little time,' I said. 'Okay?'

He swooped towards the counter and picked up Elizabeth's bag. He unstrapped the flap and turned out the contents.

'Just checking,' he said, and then changed the subject with uncharacteristic clumsiness. 'You know, it's almost a wrench to sell this stuff. I wish I could keep it intact. So far we've disposed of a few of the things that Augusta acquired but never used for the house. We had to: we needed working capital. All this' – he waved both hands in a gesture that embraced the factory around us – 'wasn't cheap.'

As he talked, he sorted through Elizabeth's belongings. I watched him, half-wanting to protest but half-fascinated, too; this was a part of Elizabeth. Handkerchief, make-up, a key ring, a wallet, a cheque book, a folder full of credit cards in the name of Pirrall. He spread out the cards on the counter: American Express, Diner's, Access, Barclaycard: the plastic passports to consumer credit in the West.

'It says Pirrall here,' he said pointing to the Barclaycard, 'not Allanton.'

'That's her married name. She's divorcing him.'

'I see. What did she think of Seb as a boss?'

'She liked him.'

'So do I,' Wolfgang said. 'And he's been very useful, I must admit. Especially with the Unsterworths. They think he's a country gentleman who's had some business setbacks; now he's trying to make ends meet; discreetly selling off the treasures from his attic; doesn't want the neighbours to hear about it. They sell for us on commission – a high one, but it's worth it: they've got a lot of contacts and their reputation enhances the value.'

Meanwhile he had found the folding knife, the length of nylon fishing line and a ball-point pen. I watched him so closely that I'm surprised he didn't comment on it. He poked at a packet of tissues, and examined a pink driving licence, also in the name of Pirrall, receipts from this morning's shopping spree, the £100 in cash and a railway ticket left over from yesterday. There was nothing else. He put the knife, the cash and the fishing line in his pocket.

The possibility I couldn't cope with had hardened into a certainty. Suddenly I wanted nothing better than to talk about inessential details. 'All cheques,' I said quickly, 'are made out to SJBR Associates? Is that you and Rownall?'

'We're registered in Jersey. It's a front, actually, for a couple of Liberian companies; the money goes straight through. SJBR bought the end of the lease on the factory from Dursley when they folded, and some of the stock; we're leasing the machinery. We've kept the place ticking over, but no more than that. We needed a base, you see. The factory's made a good cover while we sorted ourselves out.'

'You've been here all the time?'

'Most of it.' Wolfgang shovelled Elizabeth's belongings back into the bag. 'There's an office through there where I sleep, and a little washroom. Quite self-contained. I keep out of sight in the daytime.' He paused, frowning at me. 'Are you all right? You look a bit pale.'

'I'm just tired.'

'Have you made up your mind? Are you coming with me?'

I think he was sure what my answer would be. Otherwise he wouldn't have told me so much. His confidence was based on the experience of a lifetime: he had always led, and I had always followed.

It was quiet in that big room, with just me, my brother and that great, useless patrician plaything. Normally you hate people and things in different ways because you can attach blame to people, not to things; but I hated the dolls' house as though it were an alien and malevolent person.

A car was passing along the road in front of the factory, the first I'd heard since we came into the toyshop. It was travelling very slowly. Wolfgang switched off the lights. He moved towards the nearest window and pushed aside a corner of the blind. I followed him.

The road outside was well lit, to deter thieves. The tail lights of a car were disappearing around the corner at the end of the block. The sound of its engine didn't die away: it cut out.

Out of the silence came footsteps. A man walked along the frontage of the factory, in the same direction as the car. He was in some sort of uniform, and an alsatian ran quietly beside him.

'Police?' I whispered.

'No. Just the security man from the place next door. But I don't like that car stopping. It's unusual at this time of night.'

As the man was passing directly beneath a lamppost, he glanced towards the factory; we must have been invisible to him but I saw his face very clearly.

I'd seen him before. I'd seen him at Rownall's house, yesterday morning, when he'd smiled at me as if at a happy memory; I'd seen him wearing his leather jacket in the lobby of the Admiral Nelson; and afterwards, in Hebburn's car, I'd felt his fists in my stomach and his fingers twisting my ears and probing my weak places. You don't forget the face of a man who has caused you so much pain.

'What is it?' Wolfgang asked.

'I don't know his name,' I said. 'But he's a Special Branch officer.'

FOURTEEN

Love, the Christians say, is infinite: fear isn't. We have a limited capacity for fear, and at that moment I had no room for more.

I felt unnaturally calm – and almost relieved. Leather Jacket was such a straightforward enemy; I knew where I was with him. Beside me, Wolfgang was whistling tunelessly through his teeth.

'Are you sure?' he said.

'Of course I'm sure.'

A high-pitched buzzer began to whine, quietly and persistently, somewhere nearby.

'Someone's broken the circuit.' He rearranged the heavy blind over the window. 'We installed our own alarm system here. Switch on the lights, will you?'

Wolfgang walked around the back of the dolls' house and opened a door I hadn't noticed before; the house towered between it and the counter. A second later, the buzzing stopped. I caught a glimpse of three black-and-white TV monitors mounted on the wall inside.

The bank of switches was beside the door to the corridor. I brushed my hand against them and flooded the toyshop with light.

'They're by the back gates,' my brother said. 'I can only see three of them. They're still trying to be discreet about it. We've got a little time.'

'What are you going to do?'

'See that box on the end of the shelf? We'll take that and the rucksacks, and leave the rest.'

He crossed the room and pulled down half the pile of crates in the corner. Underneath were three drums of acetone. There's always plenty of acetone in a factory that makes plastic products. He lowered the drums onto their sides. As he was manoeuvring the last one into position, he glanced up at me.

'If I'm not having the house,' he said, 'no one is. Besides, it'll give them something else to think about.'

'I want to get Elizabeth,' I said.

'Just give me a minute. We'll go together.'

'Can we get out of here?'

'Trust me.'

I slid the box he wanted off the shelf. It was small but heavy enough to make it awkward to carry. I rested it on the counter and watched Wolfgang.

He had unscrewed the caps most of the way. Starting with the drum farthest from the door, he gave each cap a final anti-clockwise turn. His movements were precise and rapid, though there was no impression of haste; it was as if this were a drill he had practised until it had become second nature.

The contents swept the caps out. The liquid gurgled out of the drums and poured across the concrete floor. It was colourless like water, and the ripples glinted in the light.

'Open the door,' Wolfgang said, coughing. He jumped back, just before the flood reached his shoes. 'God, this stuff stinks.'

I kept the door ajar with my foot while I slung Elizabeth's bag over my shoulder and picked up the box and one of the rucksacks. I knew what was going to happen, and I had no regrets whatsoever.

The tide of acetone swept under the pallets. A few seconds later it emerged on the other side of the platform. The Feldbausch house was an island on an inflammable sea. In a few more seconds the acetone would reach the door.

There was a Dippy Doglet leaflet on the counter. Wolfgang crumpled it up and lit it with his cigarette lighter. For an instant he stared at the little palace. It was unnerving to think of him laying down the baize grass and painting in the drive, to think of him *playing* with a wretched dolls' house.

A toy for the lonely? I thought. *The English girl who lost her lover; the unwanted wife; and now my brother.*

But his face was empty of emotion; perhaps I imagined it all. In that case, why did he squander those precious minutes on the dolls' house? He picked up the second rucksack and grinned at me. Still smiling, he tossed the little ball of flame over the counter. It floated gently downwards.

Wolfgang pushed me into the corridor and slammed the heavy door. There was a noise like a bursting balloon. It was succeeded, almost at once, by a fierce crackling. The sound was so savage that it seemed alive: no mere series of chemical reactions, but something with a conscious purpose to drive it on. On the other side of the door there was a monster, crazy with hostility and hunger, its claws ripping through skin and flesh.

And I was on the monster's side.

My brother broke into a stumbling run. I followed him down the corridor. Another, much louder bell began to ring continuously: the fire alarm. Elizabeth and Rownall must have been able to hear it. Where the hell were they?

I glanced back as we turned into the storeroom. Tendrils of smoke were already oozing through the gap between the door and its frame.

Wolfgang opened the door to the loading bay. The clangour of the bell was deafening. On the steps he stopped so sharply that I bumped into him.

Rownall was lying on his back near the van. Elizabeth was standing beside him. She looked over her shoulder and saw us. Something in the yard crashed into the gates of the loading bay; it sounded like a sledgehammer.

'This way,' Wolfgang shouted to her. He stuffed his free hand in the pocket of his trenchcoat and jumped down to the floor.

Her eyes widened. My brother had a gun in his hand. It was an automatic, like Rownall's, but much smaller. I had to do the small-arms course in the People's Army: I think the gun was the West German Walther TPH, probably the .25 ACP version – remarkably accurate for nearly a hundred metres if you're a good shot; and Wolfgang was. I don't know how he got hold of it. Maybe Rownall wheedled it out of John Toughton.

'This one,' he went on, 'isn't a toy.'

'Do as he says,' I shouted.

I didn't want either of them to get hurt. And I didn't want to meet Leather Jacket and his friends again; I had absolutely no faith in Hebburn's goons or, indeed, in anyone else.

The sledgehammer hit the gates again. They buckled inwards, the metal frames twisting under the pressure. Glass shattered somewhere in the factory behind us: probably one of the toyshop windows, blown out by the heat.

Elizabeth ran towards us. Wolfgang gave her his rucksack.

'Up the stairs,' he said. 'You first, Gerhard.'

Elizabeth and I stumbled through the storeroom and into the corridor, which by now was filling with black, oily smoke. Behind us I heard a sound like a smack on bare skin; it was swamped by the bell, the sledgehammer and the noise of the fire; and at the time I didn't realize its significance.

Wolfgang locked the door to the loading bay. Flames were licking around the door to the toyshop. Despite the box in my arms, I shot up the stairs, three at a time. Up there the air was clearer, though smoke was beginning to build up at the far end of the landing, above the toyshop. Automatically I moved in the opposite direction. Wolfgang was just starting on the stairs.

'What did he tell you?' Elizabeth muttered.

'Later.' Our shoulders touched. 'This'll be dangerous. You don't have to come with us.'

'And wait for them instead? No way.'

It was her decision.

'What happened to Rownall?'

'I hit him,' she said; and left it at that.

Wolfgang caught up with us. 'The door on the left,' he said.

We burst into a room the cleaners used for storing their tools. There were floor-polishers, Hoovers, brooms, mops and buckets. There was also a stepladder. Wolfgang pulled it open and placed it immediately below a hatch in the ceiling.

'Up you go,' he said to Elizabeth.

She glanced at me, shrugged and obeyed. The hatch folded back. She wriggled through it and disappeared into the blackness beyond. Wolfgang jerked his head at me.

'Keep an eye on her,' he mouthed.

As I reached the top of the ladder, Elizabeth took the box from me and hauled me upwards. The hatch gave access to a sort of cabin – a flimsy wooden structure that contained a massive tank. There was a door in one wall. It was locked, but I booted it open.

Suddenly we were outside, on a flat roof sprinkled with loose chippings that crunched underfoot. The night sky was heavy with clouds and the air smelled salty. Rows of lights separated by a great slice of darkness marked the estuary of the Thames.

A column of smoke rose from the broken windows of the toyshop up the side of the factory. The alarm bell was still ringing. I heard the seesawing racket of sirens in the distance.

Wolfgang left the shelter of the cabin. Elizabeth followed. I lingered for a few seconds, trying to get a better grip on the crate.

'Stop!' a man shouted. 'Just take it easy. Hands in the air.'

I put down the crate and straightened up. My fingers curled around the knife in my pocket. I edged out of the cabin.

'Lean against the wall. Feet apart.'

The newcomer was behind the cabin, so he could see only Wolfgang and Elizabeth. His voice trembled with excitement.

I lobbed the knife, still closed, over the cabin roof. It smacked against the loose chippings a few metres beyond. There was an instant of silence: it was the briefest of diversions. Just time enough for me to have second thoughts about the wisdom of what I'd done.

A *crack*. A grunt of surprise. The chink of metal. A scrape that merged with the faintest of thuds and the rattle of chippings.

'No . . .'

It was the same voice, reduced to a shocked whisper.

Wolfgang and I converged on the body of a man lying on his back. There was a rifle with a telescopic sight beside him. His face was just a white blur. As I knelt down, he started to whimper.

Wolfgang scooped up the rifle. 'I got him in the right shoulder, I think.'

I found the entry and exit wounds. The man squirmed. It had been good shooting in the semi-darkness.

'Give Gerhard your rucksack,' Wolfgang told Elizabeth. 'Then get the crate.'

'How did he get up here?' I said suddenly.

'The fire escape, I think. It's too public for us — it comes down at the front of the building. I've made alternative arrangements.' He lowered his voice. 'Gerhard, listen: do you trust her?'

'As I trust you,' I said.

Elizabeth joined us; she was staggering under the weight of the box. In the end Wolfgang carried the rifle as well as his rucksack, and I traded burdens with Elizabeth. The wounded man moaned.

'We can't leave him here,' Elizabeth said. 'He'll burn.'

'The fire brigade'll be here any moment,' Wolfgang snapped. 'They'll deal with him. It's their job.'

'No,' I said. 'It's too risky. Where's the head of the fire escape?'

Unwillingly, Wolfgang pointed it out. It was at the opposite end of the building from the toyshop, at a reasonable distance from the fire.

'But what's to stop him from shouting for help?' he said. 'Or even crawling down?'

I remembered the fishing line. 'We'll tie him up and gag him.'

Wolfgang didn't prevent us from dragging the man over there, but he didn't help either. He was too busy unstrapping an aluminium extension ladder fixed to the inner wall of the parapet. It was at the same end of the building as the fire escape but at the back.

I imagine that, like the alarm system, the ladder was one of Wolfgang's innovations at the factory. He laid it flat on the roof. By the time we rejoined him, he had pulled it out to a length of about four metres.

'And now,' he said, 'for the difficult bit.'

I'd guessed what he planned to do. A wing projected from the next factory. It had a monopitch roof, glistening with rain, that sloped gently towards us. The gap between the two buildings was not much more than a couple of metres. But at that point the roof of the wing was considerably lower than the roof on which we were standing. Pushing even a lightweight ladder across such a gap wasn't going to be easy, especially as we needed to be as quiet as possible.

With Elizabeth as an extra counterbalance, we slid the ladder over the parapet and gradually allowed the end to descend under its own weight towards the roof below. The first time it missed, jarred against the guttering and slipped onto the wall beneath. We hauled it back a little and tried again. This time it hit the roof with a double clunk.

The sirens were drawing closer, the smoke was getting thicker and the flames were nibbling at the far end of the roof.

The ladder now formed the hypotenuse of a right-angled triangle whose other sides – the gap between the two buildings and their difference in height – were roughly equal: in other words, the ladder was standing, precariously, at about forty-five degrees to the horizontal. Below it was the dimly-lit ravine that separated the factories, bisected at the bottom by a chain-mesh fence topped with barbed wire.

'You first,' Wolfgang said to Elizabeth. 'And hurry. I want you to hold the ladder steady at the bottom. Gerhard can pass the bags down to you.'

She peered over the parapet. 'Sorry, you guys. No way am I going over there.' Her voice was unsteady, and she kept licking her lips.

'Then you'll have to stay here,' Wolfgang said.

'Let me help you,' I said. 'You'll be okay. I promise.'

'No. No – I'm sorry.' She took a step backwards and glanced at the flames behind us. Reflections of the fire glowed in her eyes. For an instant I was infected by her fear: I saw the ravine as a dark pit lined with steel teeth, and I felt the fascination it exerted on her.

'Oh, for Christ's sake,' Wolfgang said. 'Coming or staying, it's all one to me. Just make up your mind.'

'You're coming with us,' I said softly, as though to a child in the grip of a nightmare. 'I'll tell you exactly what to do. It'll be very easy.'

She stretched out her hand and allowed me to lead her back to the parapet. Her eyes were on my face, not on the drop below.

'I'm going first,' I said. 'Wolfgang will hold the ladder at the top. When I say the word, follow me down. I'll guide your feet from rung to rung.'

I scrambled onto the parapet. The wind hit me and

303

I swayed. The smell of salt was much stronger. I swung myself onto the ladder and felt for the next rung.

At first it was easy. The parapet kept the ladder reasonably steady. But as I moved down my weight distributed itself along the unsupported central section of the ladder. The aluminium flexed itself beneath me. Involuntarily I looked down. The pit was much deeper, and the teeth much sharper. I wanted to throw my arms around the ladder and never let go.

I looked up at the two blurred faces above the parapet. 'Help her up,' I said.

Elizabeth moaned. A tiny, wordless sound with a world of terror trapped inside it. But she allowed Wolfgang to help her onto the wall.

I reached up and gripped her left ankle. 'Turn your body,' I said, 'and hold onto the top of the ladder with both hands. Good girl. Keep your eyes on Wolfgang. Now, let your leg go loose and I'll put your foot on the ladder . . . good. Keep looking at Wolfgang. Now swing the other leg over. That's right.'

By now she was entirely on the ladder. Her head was still above the level of the parapet.

'Down we go.' I moved her right foot onto the rung beneath. 'And the next one.'

We crept lower and lower. I kept talking: nonsense probably – anything to fill her mind. The three-metre stretch of ladder became thirty. The ladder swayed more and more, partly because of our combined weights and partly because Elizabeth was trembling so much. I felt like shouting with relief when my foot touched the roof at the bottom.

'Don't look down!'

Three things went wrong simultaneously. As I reached the safety of the roof, I unconsciously relaxed my grip on Elizabeth's ankle. Then one of the ladder's uprights slipped – only a centimetre or two, but it was enough. And Elizabeth looked into the pit.

She whimpered. Her arms and legs went limp. She was no longer holding on; I guessed she'd blacked out. Her whole body began to buckle, unbalancing the ladder. At the top Wolfgang was swearing as he tried to keep it steady.

I lunged forward and got my right arm around her legs. I was leaning over the gap between the buildings, supported only by my left arm on the ladder. I heaved myself backwards.

It was a forlorn hope. I knew it couldn't work. I landed heavily on the roof – on my side, because of the drag of Elizabeth's weight. She half-slithered, half-fell. Her body twisted as it left the ladder. There was a thud.

Her waist was resting on the plastic guttering at the edge of the roof. I clung to her legs. The rest of her was hanging over the pit, straining to get away from me.

I pulled desperately, trying to get my other arm around her knees. But I couldn't get enough purchase.

Then she said: 'No . . .' And her hand came up and gripped the guttering. The plastic creaked and twisted.

'Hold on,' I said. 'Don't move. I'm coming.'

It wasn't my voice. There was a calm stranger up on the roof with me.

I wriggled down the wet slope towards her. I was still on my side, with one arm wrapped around her legs. One jerky movement could send both of us toppling over the edge. The ladder vibrated: Wolfgang was coming down.

My left hand crept closer to hers. I grabbed her wrist. It was cold and the tendons felt as hard as rock.

'I've got you now,' I said. 'We can pull you up. You're safe.'

Wolfgang stumbled over my legs and I nearly lost my grip.

The guttering cracked and gave way. Elizabeth screamed. She slipped a little further into the pit, and I moved with her. My head was over the edge of the roof. I shut my eyes. All my strength was concentrated in my left hand. It felt as though it were burning.

'All right,' Wolfgang said. 'I've got her.'

He was lying on his stomach with both hands around Elizabeth's arm.

'Stay there,' I said to him. 'I'll pull the legs.'

I let go of Elizabeth's wrist and edged up the slope of the roof, away from the pit. I used the ladder to give me leverage and hauled her backwards. As she came up, Wolfgang went hand over hand up her arm until he could get a grip on her shoulders.

I don't know how long we lay there: a huddle of bodies, gasping for air. One of those eternities that probably last no more than a couple of seconds. I shall never forget the smell of salt, the wailing sirens and the wind on the back of my hand.

It was Wolfgang who recovered first. He ordered Elizabeth to hold the ladder steady. Then he and I went up. My muscles obeyed me but I was barely conscious of what I was doing. There was no time to think about what had happened. Maybe that was just as well.

I waited on the ladder as he climbed back onto the roof of the toy factory. He passed me the first rucksack. I clambered down until I reached the point where Elizabeth could take the rucksack from me. I repeated the journey twice more. The crate was the worst: I needed both hands to hold it, and had to bump it down from rung to rung. Finally Wolfgang came down with the rifle slung across his back.

He led us away in single file. It was a slow, lopsided journey across the slope of a roof that was slippery with rain. 'Please God,' Elizabeth kept murmuring, 'Please God.'

At the end of the roof there was a sharp drop to the factory's loading bay. Wolfgang pointed to our right, down towards the pit. We worked our way almost to the guttering. Here the roof of the bay was only two or three metres below the one we were on. Getting from one to the other was easy enough if you clung to the guttering and lowered yourself feet first; easy enough as long as you remembered not to glance into the pit.

I touched Elizabeth's arm. 'Can you manage?'

'Child's play,' she said; and I think she tried to smile at me.

Wolfgang went first. I held Elizabeth's wrists as she wriggled over the edge and into my brother's arms. She managed.

Down there the going was much easier. The bay had a shallow, double-pitched roof, and crossing it was like walking up a gentle hill and down the other side. Some of the lights were on in the main block of the factory.

'They don't usually have a nightshift,' Wolfgang said.

On the far side of the bay we repeated the process: lowering ourselves onto the roof of a shed that had been built against it. For the first time I had a clear view of the yard below. The gates were open and the outside lights were on. Three cars were parked between us and the gates. From that angle, I couldn't see if they were occupied. One of them was a marked police car.

The nearest was only ten metres away from us; it was a large Ford – grey, with a metallic finish.

The trouble with fear is that it comes in so many shapes.

'That's Hebburn's car,' I whispered to Wolfgang. 'The Special Branch inspector.'

Leather Jacket had come from the direction of this factory, and he'd been wearing the uniform of one of their security people.

Wolfgang swore softly. I think he'd hoped that, once away from the burning building, we'd have a clear run for it. But it was much too late to change course. We slid down the roof and dropped to the ground. The shed was an open store and it didn't face the gates: once inside we were unlikely to be seen.

And that was just as well because there were footsteps coming into the yard. A car door opened and closed.

'The Fire Brigade want us to evacuate this place as well,' Leather Jacket said. 'Otherwise they say they won't be responsible.'

'Not yet.' Hebburn's voice. 'I want no firefighting at all until we've found the rest of them.'

'They won't like that.'

'Tough. They'd like it even less if they caught a stray bullet. You've kept them outside the road blocks?' Leather Jacket must have nodded because Hebburn asked: 'Where the hell's the Mobile Incident Van?'

I peered around the edge of the shed. Both men were standing by the Ford. One of them had probably got out of the car as the other entered the yard. There was no sign of anyone else.

'Somewhere on the M25, I guess.' Leather Jacket

sounded on the defensive. 'But the Anti-Terrorist Squad is due at any moment.'

Hebburn snorted. 'They should have been here half an hour ago. You'd better get Standish down from the roof. Otherwise he'll get roasted too. It's a bloody inferno in there.'

'Okay. I'll use the car radio. You know, sir, the odds are they're dead already.'

'I'm not risking any more lives to find out. We'll wait. If they're alive they'll have to make a break for it.'

As Hebburn was speaking, I nudged Wolfgang. 'Unless you've got a better idea, we need that car. And Hebburn to drive it.'

There was a flash of white in the gloom as Wolfgang smiled. 'Perfect.'

He passed me the rifle and we charged.

It was as simple as that: no planning, no discussion and certainly no finesse. I think both of us sensed that the moment was too valuable to lose: a man getting into a car is vulnerable. An effective attack needs to be fuelled by aggression, and it was lucky that our targets were the two Special Branch men I knew best. I had their treatment of me to avenge and also I was terrified of them. As a result, I felt extraordinarily vindictive. I'm not proud of that.

Leather Jacket was half in, half out of the car. I lunged with the rifle, using it as though it had a bayonet on the end.

The muzzle smacked into his cheekbone. He screamed. The impact flung him backwards across the passenger seat. He tried to shield his face with both hands. His legs were still out of the car. I reversed the rifle and hammered the butt into his belly. Then I dragged him out.

He curled up on the tarmac. He was gasping and groaning at the same time; the sound reminded me of a friend's dog that had been fatally wounded in a hunting accident. The friend put the dog out of its misery with a bullet. I would have liked to do the same with Leather Jacket.

'That'll do,' my brother said gently.

He was standing on the other side of the car, just beyond Hebburn's reach. The inspector was looking at the Walther. Leather Jacket's predicament did not appear to concern him unduly.

The fury oozed away, leaving me exhausted. My self-loathing was directly proportional to the hatred I'd felt for Leather Jacket. I think Wolfgang guessed how I was feeling, because he suddenly unleashed a string of orders at me. Anything to keep me busy.

We were in a desperate hurry. At any moment someone could come looking for Hebburn. Wolfgang and I searched our captives; each of them was carrying an automatic. I loaded our rucksacks, the rifle and the box into the boot of the Ford. Elizabeth helped but didn't speak to me. Meanwhile, Wolfgang made Hebburn drag Leather Jacket into the shed. The inspector used his own tie and belt to truss his subordinate, and his handkerchief to gag him.

'Into the car,' Wolfgang said.

Hebburn was to drive; Wolfgang sat beside him; and Elizabeth and I went in the back. I kept Hebburn's gun in my hand.

'Start the car.'

The inspector obeyed. 'Are you Wolfgang Herold, by any chance?'

It was the first thing he'd said since the attack. His voice was precisely the same as ever: gloomy and weary. I've never met a man who seemed less prone to panic.

'Drive out of the gates,' Wolfgang said, ignoring the question, 'and turn left.'

'There's a road block, you know.'

'And you're going to get us through it.'

'That may not be possible. But I'll try, of course.'

'If you don't succeed,' Wolfgang said, 'I'll kill you. I mean that.'

'Oh, I believe you. But first – have you considered the other options? A negotiated surrender, for example.'

'Don't talk: drive.'

Hebburn put the car into gear and moved slowly through the gates and onto the access road. There was a series of explosions from the toy factory; perhaps the fire had reached the acetone in the storeroom or the fuel tanks of the cars in the loading bay. Half the building was in flames. I wouldn't have believed a fire could spread so fast. The neighbouring factories were bathed in a flickering orange glow.

We drove away from the blaze. The road was lined with light-industrial units, similar in size and appearance to the toy factory. Armed policemen lurked in doorways or crouched behind walls.

The road block was at the end of the access road, on the boundary of the industrial estate. Two cars had been parked horizontally across the road, leaving a gap in the middle plugged by a crash barrier. Men with rifles clustered behind it. On the main road beyond, three fire engines and a couple of ambulances were waiting.

Hebburn slowed as he approached the barrier and wound down his window.

'No heroics,' Wolfgang said. 'Turn right once we're through.'

The men had recognized the car. They were moving back the barrier before we stopped.

'Everything all right, sir?' a sergeant said. 'Any news?'

Hebburn grunted. 'The next time a car comes down here, don't move the barrier until the car's stopped and you've checked it. Is that clear, sergeant?'

'Yes, sir. Sorry, sir.'

We turned right and accelerated away.

'Good,' Wolfgang said. 'You're being sensible. Drive as fast as you can within the speed limits.'

'Kappa One,' the radio said, so loudly that all of us jumped. 'Kappa One.'

'Turn it off,' Wolfgang said.

'Wait,' I said suddenly. 'Is Standish your man on the roof?' Hebburn nodded.

'He's at the top of the fire escape. Bullet in the shoulder. Tell them to fetch him.'

Wolfgang muttered something under his breath. Then, aloud: 'All right. Do it, Hebburn. Just say this: "Hebburn. Collect Standish from the top of the fire escape." Nothing more.'

He rammed the Walther into Hebburn's side to re-inforce the point. Hebburn repeated the authorized message, word for word, into the microphone.

'Roj,' said a disembodied voice. 'But sir – '

Wolfgang switched off the set.

'I'm afraid they'll suspect something's up,' Hebburn said, almost apologetically.

'They'll do that anyway, with you leaving,' I said.

'It won't take long for them to put out an alert for us,' he went on. 'We should really – '

'Quiet,' Wolfgang said.

'I'm only trying to help.'

'Don't give me that. You're trying to ingratiate yourself. You're trying to suggest your interests are identical with ours. Textbook procedure.'

'It's really just common sense,' Hebburn said, unruffled. 'For both of us. Don't you agree?'

'Shut up or I'll shoot you,' Wolfgang said.

'Just as you like, Mr Herold.'

After that we drove in silence, apart from Wolfgang's directions, for about fifteen minutes. Elizabeth stared out of her window. She'd said nothing for a long time, and I missed the sound of her voice.

Wolfgang rummaged in the glove compartment. He found a pair of handcuffs, which he stuffed in his pocket. But the gun and most of his attention were fixed on Hebburn.

At first there were buildings and streetlights; people were coming out of pubs, and there was a good deal of traffic; TV sets flickered behind curtained windows; for most people, life was going on as usual.

Later the lights dropped away and we were rushing through the darkness. Occasionally we met a car coming in the opposite direction, and we passed through one or two villages. I got the impression that we were travelling through flat, open countryside.

'Slow down,' Wolfgang said. 'There's a turning coming up. Easy to miss it – it's just a track.'

As we turned, the headlights raked across a painted sign: SWAMPTON YACHT CLUB. MEMBERS ONLY. The car bumped down a rutted lane that seemed even narrower than it was because of the high hedge on either side. We stopped by a five-bar gate made of tubular steel.

Wolfgang passed a key back to me. 'There's a pad-lock,' he said. 'Relock it once we're through.'

The car's headlights, which were on full beam, created an artificial day in the middle of the night. A yacht club conjures up pictures of affluent people in an affluent setting: but beyond the gate were nothing more than two wooden sheds set in an expanse of scrubby grassland.

The hinges squealed as I opened the gate. The Ford slid through the gap. Hebburn drove around the nearer of the two sheds and, once the car was out of sight from the gate, cut the engine and the lights.

Head down against the wind, I followed the car. It was parked parallel to one of the long sides of the shed. The others had already moved on to the double doors that faced the estuary. A concrete slipway ran steeply down from the shed to the black, heaving water.

'We're lucky,' Wolfgang said as he watched Hebburn open the door, 'the tide's up; we'll catch it on the ebb. There's a light just inside the door, Inspector. On your left.'

Inside, half a dozen dinghies had been stored for the winter; they were upside down and raised off the ground; all but one were sheeted with canvas. The place smelled musty. At the back of the shed were the racks that held oars, sails, masts and outboard motors.

Wolfgang stood well back with the gun while the three of us manhandled the uncovered dinghy out of the shed. It was wooden, clinker-built and surprisingly heavy. We got it onto the slipway and dragged it down to the water. There was just enough light from the open doors to see what we were doing. I tied the painter to one of the rings set in the concrete.

Wolfgang beckoned Hebburn back inside. I followed them in. Elizabeth lingered in the doorway as though she were a sentry; her shoulder bag was slung across her chest like a sword belt or a bandolier. My brother handcuffed Hebburn to one of the uprights that supported the racks.

'You're going to leave him here?' I said.

'I can't think of a better place. Can you?'

'Does anyone ever come here in winter?'

Wolfgang grinned at Hebburn, who blinked back at him. 'At weekends. Sometimes. Depends on the weather.'

'We're not going to leave him to die.'

'He wouldn't give you much consideration if the positions were reversed.'

That might be true, but it was beside the point. I said: 'We could use the radio in the car.'

Wolfgang shook his head. 'That would mean telling them where we were.'

'Is there a radio on the boat?'

He nodded.

'Then we can use that, can't we?'

'We'll talk about it later.'

'I mean it,' I said.

Wolfgang shrugged, and with that shrug my last doubts vanished. I ran out of excuses and mitigating circumstances for him. It was ironic that it should have happened now, when the point at issue was the life of a man I disliked as much as Hebburn.

The inspector was a threat to our security. Apart from that Wolfgang was indifferent to whether the man lived or died. Like Standish on the roof, Hebburn was a problem that needed solving. Bochmann, Custer and Mrs Issler had all posed similar problems: they were possible dangers. In each of those three cases, without me to restrain him with my scruples, my brother had chosen the simplest, most effective solution.

Three cases or four?

Beadlow hadn't been a problem: merely a man no one would miss and whose body Wolfgang could use. An unwanted by-product of this affluent society, like the beggar woman at Bond Street station and the man wrapped in newspaper in the doorway of the chapel near the canal. I knew my brother had lied to me, that he'd killed Beadlow just as surely as he had killed the other three.

Four cases? Or five?

I remembered the sound I'd heard just before Wolfgang left the loading bay at the toy factory for the last time. The *smack* that had been almost drowned by the bell, the fire and the sledgehammer.

'You shot Rownall,' I said, 'just before you left.'

'Through the head, to be precise,' Hebburn said, his face twitching. 'We got the body out.'

'He would have talked,' Wolfgang said, as if stating the obvious. 'He knew about this boat. I had to buy it through SJBR.'

I thought of Miranda and David. My brother must have realized the pain he had caused. I don't think he enjoyed inflicting it; possibly he even regretted what he saw as the necessity for it. He wasn't evil in the traditional sense that Great-aunt Luise would have understood: he didn't make a conscious decision to choose the opposite of good. It was just that for him the greatest good was his own well-being; and any supreme good requires sacrifices. In this case, the sacrifices had to be other people.

Why was I the exception? He'd run all sorts of risks to get me here. I knew the answer to that as well: I was still the little brother. I was his shadow, his familiar. I was part of him, part of his niche. In his mind the logic went: *what's good for Wolfgang is good for Gerhard.*

I'd known that all my life, and I'd been grateful for it too. I used to think how lucky I was to have a brother like Wolfgang; he'd done so much for me. But nothing is free. Everything comes with a price tag.

'We'll need the outboard and a pair of oars,' Wolfgang said briskly. His eyes were on Elizabeth, not me. 'Over there, at the end of the rack. Can you put them in the boat? I'll get the stuff from the car.'

She picked up the oars and I took the motor. Wolfgang left the shed and I heard him opening the boot of the Ford. There was a faint buzzing in the sky that I identified a few seconds later as the rattle of a helicopter's rotors.

Elizabeth waited until we were well down the slipway, out of sight of Wolfgang. 'I think he's going to kill me,' she whispered.

'No. There's been enough killing.'

I lowered the motor into the stern of the dinghy and took the oars from her. I straightened up and unbuttoned the side pocket of my jacket. Hebburn's gun, warm from my body, was there. It was too dark to see Wolfgang's lifeboat or any of the other boats in the mooring. The light from the shed reached only the dinghy and a small semi-circle of shifting water.

The helicopter was louder now. I saw its lights overhead. It was flying down the estuary towards the sea.

'So what are you going to do?' Elizabeth said.

Wolfgang's footsteps prevented me from answering. My hand wrapped itself round the butt of the gun. He

317

came down the ramp, grunting with the strain because he was carrying the crate and both rucksacks.

'Would you get the rifle?' he said to me. 'Then we'll be off.'

'You can go,' I said. 'We're staying here.'

'Don't be stupid.'

I pulled out the gun, holding it towards the light so he was able to see it. His hands were fully occupied by the crate.

'I'm sorry,' I said. 'If I were you, I'd get in that boat and go.'

'If it's the woman who's changed your mind – '

'No,' I said. 'It's you.'

It was as if time had stopped, just for an instant. The three of us were frozen in a tableau: *The Prodigal's Farewell*, perhaps, or *Am I My Brother's Keeper?*

Then Wolfgang scrambled aboard the dinghy. It rocked but he kept his balance. He put down the box. I stood there watching him, wishing I had something to say. He swivelled round and sat in the stern so that he was facing us. He looked up at us, and the light, feeble though it was, bounced a gleam off the Walther in his hand.

'Get in the boat,' he said. 'No, not you, Gerhard. I want your friend – she'll make a better hostage. Come along, Miss Allanton.'

I took a step forward and stopped. To me he was just a lighter blur in the darkness. To him, we were silhouettes against the light from the shed.

'I'll shoot,' I said.

He laughed. He actually laughed. 'No, you won't. But I will, if necessary. You know that.'

I moved between Elizabeth and Wolfgang. 'Run,' I said to her, 'get out of the light.'

'No,' she said. 'I'm going with him.' She touched my arm and then walked down the slipway. I stretched out my hand, but I was too late: my fingertips merely brushed the side of her shoulder bag.

Wolfgang said to her: 'You can row. Make yourself useful.'

She turned back to me. 'Trust me, sweetheart,' she said. 'Please.'

Elizabeth clambered carefully into the boat and sat down. As I watched she slid the oars into the rowlocks. At the back of my mind I was aware that Wolfgang would probably kill me; I had forfeited my privileged position and become yet another possible danger to his well-being. It no longer seemed to matter very much.

'Untie the painter, Gerhard,' Wolfgang said, 'and push us off.'

I obeyed him. Despair and cold made my fingers clumsy. The tide or perhaps the current whipped the boat downstream. Elizabeth was pulling hard with one oar, trying to bring the bows round.

'Goodbye,' Wolfgang said. But he didn't shoot me.

The dinghy slipped out of my sight almost immediately though I could hear the creak of the rowlocks. The sound of the helicopter was fading. As it faded, I realized the clatter of the rotors had masked another sound: the soft throb of engines on the water. At least one boat was travelling without lights, and it wasn't far away. On the landward side I heard the chink of metal: someone was beside the five-bar gate.

On the boat, Elizabeth screamed out: 'Over here!'

'You bitch,' Wolfgang said.

There was a shot. Then a splash.

Even before the splash I was ripping off my coat. A searchlight came on. It was unbearably brilliant. The

319

beam panned around the mooring. I had a confused impression of masts, hulls, and buoys; I doubt if there were more than ten boats there, but it seemed as if a whole navy were lined up in the little inlet. Someone – Hebburn, I think – was shouting. Another searchlight burst out of the darkness and sliced across the beam of the first. I kicked off my shoes. There were running footsteps behind me.

'THIS IS THE POLICE.' The amplified voice bellowed across the water from one of the boats. 'WE ARE ARMED. YOU ARE ADVISED – '

I didn't hear any more. I was under the water. I surfaced from the dive and broke into a swift crawl. When I was a child, I was so afraid of water that I made myself learn to swim; I learned sufficiently well to swim for my school in the Berlin Indoor Championships. But water still scares me. Facing a fear doesn't necessarily destroy it. More's the pity.

The river was colder than anything I'd ever swum in. There was a vicious undertow. I aimed in the direction of the splash. The searchlights swung to and fro. Suddenly they locked on the dinghy.

It was no more than a few metres away from me and rocking violently. It was empty. When Elizabeth went overboard, Wolfgang must have lost his balance. One oar was gone; the other was still in its rowlock. Luckily the current, the boat and I were all moving in the same direction.

A head bobbed up beside me. The searchlight was full on my brother's face.

'Gerhard – please – '

Wolfgang, you see, had never learned to swim. I think that in his own way he was afraid of the water too. 'If you're a good enough sailor,' he used to say,

'you don't fall in. When in doubt, wear a life jacket.'
No life jacket this time: just a heavy trenchcoat.

I swam on.

The helicopter was coming back.

Elizabeth was lying face-down. She was on the shoreward side of the dinghy, away from the search-lights. The blade of the oar had entangled itself with the strap of her bag: otherwise I doubt I would have found her. Her body rose and fell with the surface swell. Even in a bad light, Wolfgang was a good shot. I knew she must be dead.

I trod water and forced the strap down the oar. The undercurrent tried to tug me down. When she was free I rolled her body over. I hooked my left arm over the gunwale of the dinghy and supported her with my right. I concentrated all my energy on keeping Elizabeth's head above the water.

There was nothing else I could do. My arm ached. The cold devoured me. I wondered how much of the Thames she'd sucked into her lungs already. How long had she been there? Seconds? Minutes? I had no way of knowing.

Somewhere nearby my brother was drowning.

FIFTEEN

The water was hot and prickly. My head hurt. It was dark.

I tried to swim to the surface. Without air I would die. My limbs failed to obey me. Ah well, I thought, this is death. When you drown, the whole of your past life is meant to flash through your mind. Silly, really: it couldn't be the whole of your life because in that case you'd take as long to drown as you'd taken to live; or two-thirds, perhaps, if they meant the whole of your waking life. No, surely they must mean you had a condensed version, not the whole thing? Excerpts, as it were. Highlights.

I waited but nothing happened. The second showing of my life obstinately refused to begin. It was so damned hot. And those prickles made me increasingly uncomfortable. In tropical rivers, weren't there tiny parasitic insects that bored into the skin of unwary swimmers? That must be the explanation.

God, I was thirsty. Ironic: all this water and nothing to drink. I opened my mouth. No water came in.

'He's coming round.'

A man's voice. English. What was he doing in the river? The English had lost their empire years ago, including all their tropical rivers. Should never have had them in the first place.

I opened my eyes. A white pillow. White tiled walls. A man in a white coat. His face was white, too. Too much white altogether. Another man behind the first, staring down at me. A navy-blue uniform tunic. A pink face. Black hair. That was much better.

'Water,' I said.

I hoped they would get me a drink and also explain about the river. Perhaps they could do something about the insects. They didn't hear me, or perhaps I thought the word 'water' but forgot to say it. I waited a little longer. Nothing happened. So I went to sleep.

I never found out where they took me.

Not a hospital: the staff were all male and there were no windows. A TV camera was mounted in one of the corners of the ceiling. No doubt there was a microphone somewhere. The door had a judas window, and I heard the click of a bolt or a lock when people came in or out.

The next time I woke up, two men in white coats brought me a cup of sweet, milky tea. They helped me empty my bladder. One of them examined me and took my temperature. They sponged the sweat off me, changed the coarse, prickly sheets and gave me a pair of pyjamas.

They made observations and suggestions that were really commands: 'You can get onto the bed'; 'If you open your mouth . . .' Otherwise they didn't talk to me. I said nothing to them, and I was glad when they went away.

Time passed. I'd lost my watch with the rest of my clothes. The stubble on my chin suggested it was between twenty-four and forty-eight hours since I'd last shaved: that was in the bedroom at the Myrtle

House Hotel; as I shaved, I'd watched Elizabeth pulling on her clothes behind me.

My body felt heavier than usual. I examined myself under the bedclothes. A few bruises on my shoulders. A variety of dull aches in my muscles. A plaster on the forehead, just above the left eyebrow. There appeared to be nothing seriously wrong with me. In the physical sense, I mean.

My visitors came in pairs. The next shift brought me breakfast on a tray. The cutlery was plastic. The men waited while I ate, avoiding my eyes. The chairs they sat on had been bolted to the floor. I was ravenous, which compensated for the elderly cornflakes, the cold, rubbery egg, the brittle bacon and the brown liquid that was neither tea nor coffee. When I'd finished, they left me alone.

I lay on the unyielding bed and looked at the white ceiling. My mind was perfectly clear. I remembered everything that had happened. Now, at last, I had almost all the answers. I knew who had done what, and why; and what I didn't know I could guess. Only Bochmann's motives remained mysterious.

I knew that two people I had loved were dead. We Germans are said to be prone to mournful moral speculations, and I had my share of those. I thought that if I had been betrayed, I too had betrayed; and that if you recognize an overriding loyalty, then you must recognize the need to betray your lesser loyalties. I thought that nothing comes free: everything has its price: and the price of loyalty is the risk of betrayal.

Curiously enough, I was not unhappy: I was relieved. At the time I thought that was because most of the uncertainties had gone. Now I wonder if they gave me a sedative. My mind seemed to work lucidly but I felt nothing sharply; my emotions were mercifully padded in cotton wool. The grief came later.

I dozed off. The scrape of the judas window awoke me. The door opened and Inspector Hebburn came in, followed by a small man I didn't know. Hebburn blinked furiously at me.

'Hullo, Mr Herold. Sleep well?'

I said nothing. The inspector's tic was more pronounced; his skin was grey, and the bloodshot eyes were almost submerged in puffy folds of skin. There was another change in him: he gave me a small but unmistakable smile. I attributed the smile to the fact that I had tried to save his life.

'I'd like to ask you a few questions,' he said.

'I am a citizen of the German Democratic Republic,' I said. 'I wish to contact my Embassy.'

'That's not possible at the moment.'

'Why not?'

He shrugged and changed tack. 'Have *you* got any questions?'

'Two of them.'

'Yes.' He didn't ask what they were. 'Your brother . . . missing presumed drowned. His body's not been recovered.'

'He couldn't swim,' I said.

Hebburn nodded, acknowledging the information. 'Elizabeth Allanton, the secretary. She's alive, laddie. But it was touch and go. Another minute under the water and she'd have been a goner. You saved her life.'

They kept me there for two days. They asked questions; I refused to answer. I demanded my legal rights; they denied them. They worked in relays. Sometimes Hebburn was there but more often not. Once there was a woman, who I think was a psychologist. I learned something from the questions they asked.

They behaved with more restraint than I'd expected. No one laid a finger on me. They didn't deprive me of sleep or food. My possessions were not returned to me, but I was given clothes and a toothbrush; once a day they let me use an electric razor.

On the morning of the third day, Hebburn arrived with three men in tow. Two of them were in uniform. They escorted me down a long, institutional corridor, up some stairs and into a yard. It was a dank, grey day; but the sight of the sky overhead and the feel of the drizzle on my cheeks were the best things that had happened to me in a long while.

A plain van was waiting for us. In the front I glimpsed a driver and another man; the engine was already running. Hebburn said goodbye to me. His colleagues followed me into the back of the van. There were seats and, once the doors were closed, the only source of light was a panel of frosted glass in the roof. I must be important, I thought: I had five men to look after me.

I was still without a watch, so I don't know how long the journey took. Perhaps three hours? The guards read their newspapers, smoked, ate and played cards. I tried to make conversation, but that didn't work. The men were by no means hostile, any more than Hebburn had been. They offered me their newspapers; one of them gave me some chocolate; another tossed a cigarette onto my lap; and all the while, none of them said a word.

Journey's end was a Palladian mansion, a gigantic first cousin once removed to the Feldbausch dolls' house. I didn't have time to look closely at it. My escorts hustled me out of the van, across a gravelled forecourt and through a side door. In the hall beyond, they handed me over to a pair of middle-aged men with hard, well-muscled bodies.

My new friends wore sports jackets and cavalry twill trousers; they had Old Soldier written all over them. I was taken upstairs to a room on the second floor: a comfortably-furnished bedroom with a bathroom attached. The window was barred but it overlooked parkland that rose gently to a belt of oaks on a ridge. The oaks masked other, more modern buildings.

'Where is this?' I asked.

'Someone'll be along in a minute. Now, there's some sandwiches here and a flask of coffee. Help yourself.' And they left me alone with the view. There was nothing to show that I was under surveillance but eavesdroppers are under no obligation to make their activities obvious.

It was early afternoon, I guessed. There were two armchairs and a coffee table by the window. I sat in one of the chairs and watched the parkland and the sky for hours. I saw no one outside, though I heard the occasional car. Slowly the light faded. Perhaps they hoped the waiting and the uncertainty would wear down my resistance; but both conditions had long since lost their novelty for me. The armchair was comfortable, and eventually I dozed off.

The door opened with a crash. The overhead light came on.

'Moping in the gloaming? This'll never do.'

I swung around, screwing up my eyes against the light. Blaines, the man I thought of as Hebburn's boss, was standing in the doorway. He had a bottle of Johnny Walker Black Label in one hand and two glasses in the other.

'Bugger me.' He advanced into the room, preceded by his belly. 'You look twenty years older than you did last Sunday.'

'I feel it.'

'They've not been mistreating you?'

'No. But you've no right to keep me from getting in touch with my Embassy.'

Blaines put the bottle and the glasses on the table, and sank into the other chair. He took a letter from his pocket and flicked it across the table. It landed face downwards.

'Which Embassy had you in mind, son?'

A trap of my own making had opened in front of me. THE MYRTLE HOUSE HOTEL was printed in purple capitals across the flap of the envelope. It was the letter I'd written to the West German Ambassador on Monday morning: my insurance policy against something going wrong. Something had gone wrong; but not in the way I'd anticipated.

'The Allanton woman told us where you were staying,' Blaines said. 'We got the rest of your stuff and paid your bill.'

'I want the Embassy of the GDR,' I said.

Blaines splashed whisky into both glasses and slid one of them across the table to me.

'Could be awkward, couldn't it? Suppose Old Ma Klose saw that letter? Might lead to a bit of a misunderstanding.'

I sipped the whisky to give me time to think. It exploded in my mouth and ran down my throat in a smooth trickle of liquid fire.

'At the time I wrote that letter,' I said, 'I had a mistaken view of what was happening. I retract it.'

Blaines snorted. 'You can try, I give you that. But

would it do you any good, that's the question? Eh? Would pigs fly?'

I drank some more whisky.

'Jesus,' he said. 'Hebburn's right about you. It's like talking to a bloody stone wall.'

Another silence. Blaines retrieved the letter, returned it to his pocket and lit a cigar. All the while he stared at me.

'Look,' he went on. 'I don't want to fart about. I'm going to put my cards on the table and make you an offer. From our point of view, this business has been a right cock-up from start to finish. We've spent a lot of money and a lot of time. At our end, everyone thought the Stasis were doing something devious, as per usual. Everything pointed that way. And what do we get at the end of it? A bloody dolls' house, that's what. Plus half a dozen corpses, don't forget those, and' – he jabbed the cigar at me – 'one live Kraut. All it adds up to is a bloody waste of time.'

'In that case,' I said, 'you might as well cut your losses and let me go home.'

'Okay. Say we do that. Pack you off to the workers' paradise. Trouble is, it won't be a paradise for you, will it?' His voice sank to a rasping whisper. 'The Stasis have got egg on their faces, and they won't be happy about that. Bochmann wasn't just anybody, you know, and your brother's embarrassed a lot of his friends. Oh yes, they're going to want a scapegoat. And who better than you?'

I was terribly afraid that Blaines was right.

'Let's face it, you fit the bill. You've lied to them. You beat up that bloke Keller. You tried to defect.' He patted his breast pocket. 'They'll have documentary proof of that, remember? The State Prosecutor will argue that you were involved in the conspiracy from the start.'

'I was never involved,' I said.

'You know that; I know that; but do they? And even if they do, they'd prefer you to be guilty. *You* can't prove you're innocent. And don't forget: we're not going to let them sweep this under the carpet as they usually do. We can raise such a stink that they'll have to do something about it.'

I guessed what was in his mind. The GDR has always been vulnerable to Western propaganda.

Blaines rammed the point home. 'According to our estimates, fifteen to twenty per cent of the GDR's population tune in to the BBC's German Language Service. *Hier ist England. Live aus London.* And then there's West German TV and radio. We're not without influence in the Federal Republic. All we'd have to do is plant a few stories and wait. Nothing easier, right? You must see that.'

I finished my whisky. My mouth was dry so I got some water from the bathroom. Blaines smoked in silence; he wasn't trying to force the issue, not yet. While I was away he refilled my glass.

'That's one alternative,' I said. 'What was the offer you were going to make?'

He squirted smoke at me. 'Ah. That's a rather different story. With the first option, everyone's a loser. But this one's what you might call mutually advantageous. We can offer you a very attractive package.' He ticked off the benefits one by one on fingers like uncooked English sausages. 'A new identity; full citizenship in one of several Western countries, including Britain and the States; a house or flat of your own; personal security if and when needed; the sort of job you'd

330

feel happy with – and if you wanted we'd provide retraining; plus a substantial tax-free sum in the currency of your choice.' He bared two jagged rows of yellow teeth in what I could only assume was a smile. 'Though I say it myself, it's a pretty generous offer. It's the sort of thing we'd come up with for a top-level defector.'

'And what do you want in return?' I said.

'Nothing to it, really. A couple of TV appearances. Bit of radio, maybe. We'd write your scripts for you, of course. A few newspaper interviews; might even get someone to ghost your memoirs. Luckily your English is excellent, and you've got the sort of face that people trust.'

'What lies would you want me to tell?'

He laughed so much he swallowed smoke the wrong way and started to cough. When he'd recovered he said: 'At least you're straightforward to do business with, I give you that. Makes a change in my neck of the woods.'

Blaines paused, as if expecting me to contribute something to the conversation. I drank the whisky slowly, savouring it as I had savoured the view this afternoon.

'All right,' he said at last. 'We'd want you to tell the truth, basically. With one little addition: that your brother and Bochmann persuaded Margarete Klose to co-operate with them.'

'I don't understand,' I said; which was not altogether true.

'I'll be honest with you, son. We've got a minor disaster on our hands. This could make up for it, and more. That Klose woman's a pain in the arse. If we throw this at her, they'll have to send her home. Or

331

we could play it carefully and dangle a few carrots in front of her at the same time: then there's a chance she'd defect herself. That would make us very happy.'

'You want me to frame her – that's it, isn't it?'

'You could put it that way.' Blaines shrugged. 'Come on, it's not much to ask. Remember who she is: I've never met an East German who *liked* the Stasis.'

I finished the whisky and put the glass down on the table.

'Well?' Blaines said. 'Have we got a deal?'

'I am a citizen of the German Democratic Republic,' I said. 'I insist on contacting my Embassy.'

'Jesus bloody Christ,' Blaines said gently. 'Have you heard a word I said? I'll spell it out again.'

The level in the whisky bottle sank lower and lower. Blaines talked, sometimes softly, sometimes loudly. He ordered food for us; he talked with his mouth full while we ate, and though I said nothing I still finished the meal a poor second.

Next day, other people came to talk to me. They all said the same thing in different ways. It was a fine, mild day and one of them took me outside for a walk. He introduced himself as Charles and he was very good at the soft sell. Two Old Soldiers trailed behind us.

I got the impression that our route had been carefully planned to avoid showing me anything they didn't want me to see. The great house and the grounds had the air of a dilapidated private home; but private homes don't have a battery of radio masts on the roof, Nissen huts in the back garden or a large population of ex-servicemen.

'Your attitude doesn't make sense, you know,' Charles said as we walked down a long, overgrown kitchen garden with a ruined range of greenhouses on its south wall. 'You've got everything to lose by going back to the GDR. And everything to gain by staying here. It's not as if you're a communist. It's not as if you've got a wife and kids waiting for you. So why is it? I'd like to know. Really.'

I just smiled at him. He was a nice young man: charming, civilized, exquisitely dressed; he reminded me of Reichel, Bochmann's assistant in Berlin. But I didn't try to tell him why I wanted to go back: he wouldn't have understood. And in any case silence was strength.

Charles tried another line of attack. 'Maybe you think you couldn't cope with the West? I was looking up the figures: every year, about fifteen hundred East German emigrants *return* to the GDR. Can't stand the pace, I suppose – and the competitiveness, and the unfriendliness. Understandable, really: the West must come as a shock if you've been spoonfed by the state all your life. Is that the problem?'

'No,' I said.

'I was going to say, there's no need for *you* to worry. I've seen the psychological profile they did for you. Lots of jargon: you know what these people are like. But you could sum up what they said in two or three words.'

'And what words were they?' I couldn't resist it – everyone likes to know what the world thinks of him.

'Self-motivating,' Charles said. 'Obstinate. A survivor.'

'If that's the case, I think I can cope with the GDR.'

In a way I felt sorry for him and his colleagues. It must have been so frustrating for them. And an obstacle you can't understand is always irritating as well. I knew they could have got me to agree that the moon was made of green cheese if they had really set their minds to it. I'm no hero: I couldn't stand up to sustained physical torture. Or they could have pumped me full of drugs and turned me into an obedient zombie.

But that wouldn't have served their purpose. If I were to be of any use to them, it had to be of my own free will. They wanted me to put up a sustained and convincing performance for the media. There were no short cuts.

We emerged from the kitchen garden and walked around a roofless octagonal dovecote and into an artificial glade. There was the park on one side, separated from the glade by an iron fence, and the wall of the kitchen garden on the other. A stream ran through the glade, widening at the bottom to form a pond about four metres across. In the centre of the pond was an island; and on the island was a little summerhouse like a miniature pagoda.

'This was originally laid out as a sort of Chinese water garden, I think,' Charles said. 'Must have been lovely in – in the old days. Shame it's gone to seed.'

We ambled down the path with the Old Soldiers at a respectful distance behind us. Magnolia trees and rhododendron bushes. Weeds in the stream and a fallen branch across the path. A smell of gently-rotting vegetation. There were many trees I couldn't identify. Crocuses, winter aconites and snowdrops were pushing themselves up through the earth. Our footsteps made no sound on the dead leaves. It was very peaceful.

Charles paused by the pond. 'There are some rather pretty tiles in the summerhouse,' he said. 'Like to take a look?'

I nodded, partly to humour him and partly to prolong our time in the pale afternoon sunshine. The pond was shallow and stepping stones led across it to the island. Charles waved his hand in a gesture that invited me to help myself.

I glanced back when I reached the island. Charles was still standing where I had left him; he was smiling encouragingly. That's when I realized the tiles were only an excuse. I went into the summerhouse.

As I'd half-expected, Elizabeth was waiting inside with her hands outstretched to me.

I don't know how long we clung together.

She stood back, still holding me, and stared into my face. There were tears on her cheeks. She looked older and thinner than I remembered – more beautiful, too.

'Gerhard, please stay.'

I didn't let go of her; I couldn't: 'I thought they'd use you sooner or later.' My voice was as shaky as hers.

'This is our chance,' she said. 'Don't you see that? You needn't even be my pensioner.'

'I'd be someone's pensioner.'

'Does it matter? Do *they* matter? They . . . they're nothing to do with us. In a month or so we could forget them all. Sweetheart, it's worth it. You won't regret it.'

'There'll be regrets whatever I do.'

'Don't you remember what we agreed?'

Of course I remembered. We were going to build ourselves a refuge from the rest of the world: our own Lenné Triangle. *If all goes well*, I'd said. But it hadn't gone well. Anyway, Lenné Triangles are a myth.

'On Sunday night,' I said, 'you wanted me to go to the West German Embassy. You said it was the only way to avoid the Special Branch and the Stasis. Do you remember *that*?'

She nodded.

'I wish I'd taken your advice,' I said.

I kissed her on the forehead and lifted her hands from my shoulders. The tears were streaming down her face. I walked out of the summerhouse. The sun was still shining. There were rainbows on my eyelashes and Charles was just a blur to me.

'They said you saved my life,' Elizabeth said. 'But I don't want it back if you're not here.'

Charles took me back to my room. Half an hour later, Blaines came in. He tried once more to persuade me to stay, but his heart wasn't in it. What he really wanted to do was to throttle me.

In the evening two of the Old Soldiers took me outside. The van was waiting for us. The Old Soldiers handed me over to the Special Branch escort.

This time nobody offered me any newspapers, cigarettes or chocolate. It was a shorter drive than before. When we stopped I heard big jets screaming in the sky.

They took me to a little office where Inspector Hebburn was sitting with Fräulein Klose. There was a big desk between them. The room was charged with the sort of atmosphere you get after an unresolved quarrel. Klose didn't look at me. The ashtray beside her was littered with butts. The desk was empty except for the bag I'd left at the Myrtle House Hotel and two official forms.

'I'll need your signature for the bag,' Hebburn said to me, tapping one of the papers. 'And the other one's your deportation order.'

SIXTEEN

Security services, psychoanalysts and the Catholic church have one thing in common: the belief that confession is good for you.

In their wisdom they have incorporated the practice of confession into their different professional procedures. They know what everyone who keeps a journal knows: that putting your past into words is a way of relieving yourself of its burdens.

On the flight home, Margarete Klose said nothing to me: nothing at all. When we reached Berlin-Schönefeld, we were met by two men in plain clothes. I was driven to a building in a road off Prenzlauer Allee; it looked like a converted office block. They took me down to the basement and put me by myself in a room that was nearly but not quite a cell.

Next morning, I was visited by a colonel from State Security. He had drooping jowls, bulging eyes and a voice that came out as a croak.

The Ministry, he said, had decided to institute an internal enquiry into this complicated affair. The results of the enquiry would be sent to the State Prosecutor, who would then decide whether or not I was to be put on trial. The enquiry was scheduled for May, nearly three months after my return. Once it began, I would be entitled to legal representation. In the meantime I was a sort of prisoner. With great condescension the colonel told me the reason for the delay.

'We need time, you see,' he said, blowing out his cheeks, 'for the preliminary investigation. Time to gather materials, take depositions and so forth. It's a laborious business. And we shall require your assistance.'

I said I would be delighted to help in any way I could.

He frowned at the interruption, for he had obviously taken my co-operation for granted. 'You'll be interviewed, of course. On top of that, we'd like you to describe what happened in your own words, in your own time. I'll send in a tape recorder and a typewriter. It'll give you something to do.'

'Thank you,' I said, for he seemed to expect it. 'Where do you want me to begin?'

The frown returned. 'At the beginning. Where else?'

It began with adultery and a knock on the door . . .

For ten weeks I talked and wrote. They wanted everything: all the details I could remember, the precise words, the nuances, even what I thought at the time. I did my best. I left out nothing of importance and included much that must have been irrelevant. Germans are very thorough.

Somewhere, I knew, a group of officials was transcribing the tapes, marrying them to the pages I'd typed and linking the result to the tapes of the interviews. The material would be shaped into a narrative, which would then be checked against the depositions from other witnesses. Expert opinions would be sought. Précis would be made. No doubt a committee had been appointed to discuss the affair.

Suddenly, on the third Sunday in May, it was all over. The first I knew about it was when the colonel sent a car to bring me to his office. He was not in a good mood, probably because he didn't like working at the weekend. Like Hebburn, he needed my signature before he could let me go. His secretary brought me my belongings and a rail pass to Schwerin.

'But what do you want me to *do*?' I said.

'Go home.'

'But the enquiry – '

'It's over. It was held last week. Your appearance wasn't required.'

'Will there be a trial?'

'I'm not authorized to tell you that,' he croaked.

'But – ' I stopped, realizing that comrade colonel was enjoying my anxiety. I said, in a calmer voice: 'Do I go back to my old job?'

'You'll be notified in due course. Good morning, Herr Herold.'

When I got to Schwerin, I had my next surprise. Dieter was waiting on the platform.

He was plumper and sleeker than I remembered. When he saw me he grinned with such obvious pleasure that tears pricked at my eyes. We shook hands, and then he took my bag and led the way to my own car.

It was a brilliant day, unusually warm for the time of year. I still felt shaky. I wasn't used to the crowds, the colours and the sheer variety of life. Coping with freedom is a skill, and I was out of practice.

'How did you know I was coming?' I said.

'The Stasis phoned me this morning.'

'What?'

Dieter shrugged. 'That's what happened. They told me what train you'd be on and suggested I met you.'

'I don't understand.'

'Nor do I, but it's good to see you. You're coming to dinner tonight, by the way. Edith insists.'

'I forgot to bring her any perfume.'

'She'll get over it.'

The Wartburg was if possible rustier than before but it started first time.

Dieter revved the engine dangerously high. 'We had the Stasis around at the office,' he said in my ear. 'A lieutenant called Arendt.'

'I know him,' I said. 'He's got a wife who likes pot plants.'

'He wanted – well, a sort of character reference for you. And he asked if I thought you'd been up to something with Wolfgang. Something illegal.'

'What did you tell him?'

'I said you were a model citizen, as far as I knew. What else? He saw Huber and Manfred Schmude, too; but I don't know what they said.'

'Have they seen Anna? My sister-in-law?'

'I don't know. What have you been up to?'

'I'll tell you later.' I was struggling with the realization that Dieter knew nothing of what had happened. 'Has . . . has there been anything about it on the news?'

He shook his head.

'Even over *there*?' I knew Dieter watched West German TV and occasionally tuned in to the BBC.

'Not a thing.' He scraped his fingers through his sandy hair: my questions were making him nervous. 'Maybe it would help if I knew what you were talking about.'

'How are the kids?' I said.

It was hardly surprising that the East German media had not been allowed to use the story. But the silence of the West was curious. Blaines must have changed his mind. But perhaps not: perhaps his threat of publicity had been a bluff from the start; however he presented it, the affair hardly reflected well on the British.

Dieter dropped me outside the block where I lived. I arranged to walk over to his place that evening. He offered me the car but I told him he might as well keep it for a while.

I walked upstairs and unlocked my front door. Gustav's TV was booming away downstairs. The air was warm and stale. There were dead flies on the table. The flat felt like someone else's home.

I dropped my bag on the floor and opened a window. Immediately, as if opening the window had been a signal, the telephone began to ring.

'Herr Herold? You don't know me but I wonder if we could meet. I have some news for you.'

'Can't you tell me now?'

'I'd rather do it face to face.'

It was a man's voice, and German wasn't his first language. His reluctance to talk on the phone was understandable; you never know who might be listening.

'I thought perhaps I could buy you a beer,' he went on. 'Or a cup of coffee.'

'All right. Where and when?'

'Five o'clock this evening? I'll leave the meeting-place up to you. You know this city, I don't.'

'You know the central square? With the cathedral and the restored houses?'

'I'll find it. How will I know you?'

'You won't,' I said, seizing the opportunity. 'It's a case of how I'll know you.'

There was a long pause. Then: 'I'll walk round the square in an anti-clockwise direction. I'll be wearing a check shirt, I'll have a camera slung around my neck and I'll be carrying a guidebook. I'm an old man, and I'm bald as the day I was born.'

I put the phone down. I stood by the window for a few moments, staring down at the railway. Then I got out the directory and looked up a number. The phone was answered on the second ring.

'Good afternoon,' I said. 'Frau Eichler? This is Gerhard Herold. May I speak to Anna?'

We met in the public gardens near the former palace of the grand dukes. The location was her suggestion. The gardens are popular on a fine Sunday afternoon. We were just two people in the crowd, and that suited me very well. It's not the sort of place you'd choose for an amorous encounter.

I hardly recognized Anna. She wore no make-up and she'd had her hair cut short. There was a sturdy briefcase in her hand. Someone had been making an honest socialist out of her.

'Gerhard.' She pecked me on the cheek. 'You look pale. I'm afraid we haven't much time – I'm meeting someone.'

'How are you?' I said.

She ignored that. 'What on earth's been going on in England? The Stasis have been crawling all over us these last few months. It's Wolfgang's fault, isn't it?'

'What happened to Great-aunt Luise?' I asked.

She made patterns in the gravel with the toe of her

shoe. 'You haven't heard? That's when the problems started. After she died, Lieutenant Arendt went through her belongings. You remember him? It was most embarrassing, all those fascist mementos. But he found something that was much worse: did you know that she and Wolfgang were blackmailing Rudolf Bochmann?'

'I didn't know,' I said; but I'd guessed there had to be something to explain Bochmann's willingness to co-operate with Wolfgang. 'It went back to the house in Pankow?'

'There was a signed confession. Bochmann had a son who died there. A baby.'

I nodded. 'A fall on the stairs.'

'It wasn't an accident,' Anna said. 'And the wife had nothing to do with it. Bochmann was drunk and under a lot of pressure at work. The baby kept crying . . .'

'Oh God.'

'It was Great-aunt Luise who saw it happen. You know what she was like with Wolfgang. A cat with one kitten. She'd do anything for him.'

For a while neither of us said anything. We walked down to the edge of the water. No wonder Bochmann had been such a wonderful friend to Wolfgang for over twenty years. No wonder Great-aunt Luise had ended her days in a nursing home normally reserved for the Party faithful and their spouses. No wonder Bochmann had been willing to run all sorts of risks to get Wolfgang and the Feldbausch dolls' house into the West: he hadn't been doing it for profit but to get a blackmailer out of his life. And no wonder, when the Stasis began to close in on him, he abandoned everything and made a bolt for Wolfgang. For this is a puritan country, true to its Lutheran roots: the private

343

lives of our public officials have to be beyond reproach.

Anna and I stood in the shade of a silver birch. Children were running along the bank, shrieking at the tops of their voices. Lovers strolled by, arm in arm. A brass band was playing in the distance. Sailing dinghies swooped across the lake. Old people sat in the sun. This is a good country, I thought, in its way.

But Great-aunt Luise never came to terms with it. She was one of those Christians who know all about good and evil. The Socialist Unity Party was evil because it had destroyed almost eveything she valued. So Bochmann had been fair game. She helped Wolfgang and she had her revenge: that was the secret she shared with him. Maybe she saw herself as an agent for divine retribution. I wouldn't put it past her.

'But what was it all about?' Anna said. 'Were you involved? Are you going back to England?'

'I wasn't involved, and I'm not going back to England.'

'So you'll be staying here? In Schwerin?'

'I'm not sure.'

She fumbled in her bag for a cigarette and made a great fuss about lighting it. 'Did you get the letter I sent you?' she said in a voice that wasn't quite casual enough.

'Yes.'

'I was a bit, well, overwrought when I wrote it. That business with Great-aunt Luise . . . in fact, I can't really remember what I said.'

Anna, my brother once told me, believed in magic. And now she wanted a spell to remodel the past.

'Nor can I,' I said, hoping my relief wasn't too obvious. 'Just that Great-aunt Luise was on the verge of death. That was the only important thing in the letter.'

For the first time she smiled at me. 'I hope – ' She broke off, looking over my shoulder. 'There's Manfred,' she said and darted away from me.

They came towards me arm in arm: Wolfgang's widow and the human weasel. She'd jilted me in favour of Manfred Schmude.

'Ah, Gerhard,' Manfred said. 'Has Anna told you? We're engaged.'

'Congratulations,' I said, with an enthusiasm that surprised them both. 'I'm sure you'll be very happy.'

I watched the man while he made a complete circuit of the square. I was sitting on a bench in front of the cathedral, pretending to read a newspaper.

His clothes marked him out as a Western tourist. He was elderly but he walked easily, and the bald head was healthily tanned. He looked with great interest at the buildings and from time to time consulted the guidebook. His mouth was tight and determined; and his head was tilted back so the chin jutted out, which gave him an arrogant appearance. As far as I could tell, neither of us was under observation.

After he had passed the bench for the second time, I got up and followed him. I tapped him on the shoulder. He turned without haste.

'Herr Gerhard Herold?' He held out his hand. 'I thought it was you.' As we shook hands, he went on: 'My name's Verner. John Verner.'

I took him to a bar with tables that spilled onto the pavement. We sat outside and ordered beer. I had no intention of skulking in the shadows.

'Do you mind if we talk in English?' he said. 'By the way, my friends usually call me Jack.'

'And your niece calls you Uncle Jack?'

The waiter came with the drinks.

'Elizabeth asked me to come and see you,' Verner said.

'Is this official?'

He frowned. 'What do you mean?'

'I think you know very well.'

Verner took his time. He swallowed some beer and glanced over his shoulder. No one was within earshot.

'So she was right,' he said quietly. 'She thought you knew. How did you find out?'

'There were a lot of things,' I said. 'I didn't put them together until near the end. In the toy factory. You know about that?'

'She told me everything. So how did you guess?'

'Snape – the private detective – was working for Special Branch. He gave me Mrs Issler's address as soon as I got to London. That means Hebburn wanted me to go there. Why? It led me straight to Elizabeth, and to that performance with the man who was meant to be her husband. It was very carefully stage-managed, wasn't it?'

The contempt in my voice stung him: Verner poked his chin at me as though daring me to hit it. But for a moment he said nothing. His Adam's apple bobbed up and down. Then he sighed.

'The play-acting was designed to make you feel protective, I guess: it's a great way to disarm suspicion. But she is divorced – that was true.'

'How did she know so much about the von Doeneckes? She was word-perfect. Almost too well-informed.'

'Mrs Issler had written her memoirs,' Verner said. 'It was all there in her desk: a dog-eared typescript, along with about thirty rejection letters. What else?'

346

'She was so keen to help me, right from the start. And everything turned out so conveniently – for her, for us. She got the job at Rownall's. When we needed money she was able to get it. She had this useful friend who could tell us all about the Unsterworths. When we needed a car, she'd already hired one. Outside Richmond station she was parked on a double-yellow line, and the traffic warden didn't even give her a ticket.'

'Is that all?'

I shook my head. 'She knocked out Rownall in the loading bay at the toy factory: I suppose she wanted to open the gates for the police, and he tried to stop her. Then there's the fact that Hebburn got there almost as soon as we did. Had they arranged to tail her? Or was there some sort of homing device in the Honda?'

'A bug,' Verner said. 'It was in the lining of her shoulder bag.'

'Yes, the shoulder bag. That's where she really slipped up. I was there when my brother searched the bag. That's when I knew for certain that she wasn't what she claimed to be. She said she'd just come in from the States, the day before I arrived in London. But she had no passport. She had a driving licence – not an American one, not an international one: hers was British, like her credit cards.' I stared at Elizabeth's uncle and I couldn't keep the bitterness out of my voice. 'Everything I told her, everything I did, went straight back to Special Branch.'

'Have you told the authorities about this? *Your* people, I mean.'

I nodded.

'And yet you let your brother drown and saved Elizabeth's life.'

I said nothing. It had been one of those impossible choices that hit you once or twice in a lifetime. You make the decision knowing that, whichever you choose, the consequences will haunt you for ever. Wolfgang had been a killer who killed for his own profit and convenience; but he was my brother. Elizabeth was doing a dirty little job, but doing it for a reason that wasn't selfish and to the best of her ability; and also I loved her.

'She nearly told you the truth,' Verner said. 'Several times. She said she tried to get you to go to the West German Embassy.'

'I know. But that last time, in the summerhouse – '

'For God's sake, that little scene had an audience. The summerhouse was wired for sound and vision. They drummed it into her that you were not to know she was working for them: they figured you'd go crazy if you found out: reject her, reject the deal.'

'They were right,' I said.

Verner put his elbows on the table. 'Now you listen to me. Okay, so Elizabeth lied to you. In fact, she's a British citizen, though her mother's American and she was raised in New York. And she was also a Special Branch officer – '

'Was?'

'She resigned at the end of last month. For God's sake, man, they told her to get close to you: but the point is, she *did* get close – for real. Can't you understand she's in love with you? That's why she resigned; that's why she tried to get you to go to the West Germans; and that's why she's fourteen weeks' pregnant with your child.'

I couldn't speak. I watched my knuckles whiten on my lap.

'She's in Canada now,' Verner said softly. 'At my place. You once told her you could get out of this country if you had the money. Something about Rostock and containers. Would twenty thousand dollars cover it?'

'No,' I said. 'It's too late.'

'Gerhard, she was only trying to do her job. So she made a mistake about what was important to her. Now she wants to put it right. Okay? It's very human, right? We all make mistakes. It's – '

'No, I'm staying here. It's over.'

'So you don't want to be with her and your child, huh? You just walk away? You just pretend it hasn't happened. What the hell *do* you want?'

'I want you to tell her,' I said, 'that I'm glad she sent you, that I'm glad I was more than a job for her. I want you to give her my love. And I want you to go away.'

'Is that your last word?' he snapped. The colour in his cheeks was darkening.

I had nothing left to say to him. My thoughts were a jumble. Integrity had something to do with it: a fine notion that I didn't really understand. The Lenné Triangle is a myth. *This is a good country.* Loyalty and betrayal. *My dearest Elizabeth.* Nothing is free and everything has its price.

Verner's chair scraped back. He stood up. 'You're a fool, Herold. If you change your mind, I'm staying at the Stadt Schwerin. Just for one night.'

'Remember to give her my love,' I said. 'That's the important part of the message.' I watched him walk away. His brown scalp gleamed with sweat. He was rigid with anger.

I asked the waiter if there was a phone and, as an afterthought, ordered another beer and a brandy to go with it. The phone was at the back of the bar. I dialled the number for the local State Security bureau and asked to speak to Lieutenant Arendt.

'The Lieutenant isn't in the building today,' the receptionist said. 'I can pass you on to the duty officer or take a message.'

'Would you ask him to call me?' I gave her my name and home number.

'Is it urgent?' she said.

'No. There's no hurry.'

When I got back to my table, there was no sign of Jack Verner. The beer and the brandy were waiting for me. So were Fräulein Klose and Lieutenant Arendt. They looked like an old married couple: a social worker and a poet on a Sunday outing.

'Good afternoon,' I said politely. I shook hands with them.

Wolfgang would have been proud of my detachment. But there was nothing particularly creditable about it. I was still grappling with the knowledge that in rejecting Elizabeth I had also rejected our child, and that cushioned me from this latest shock. In any case, I'd expected the Stasis to take an interest. I was beginning to understand the way their minds worked.

'I just tried to phone you, Lieutenant,' I said as I sat down.

Arendt raised his eyebrows and glanced at Klose, as if requesting permission to speak. 'What about?'

I told them about Jack Verner and his offer.

'But you knew all that, didn't you?' I said at the end. 'Is that why I was released today? Because you'd heard that Elizabeth Allanton's uncle was heading for Schwerin?'

Fräulein Klose lit a cigarette. 'It's true that we monitored your conversation with Verner. Did you know that Elizabeth Allanton wrote to me?'

I stared dumbly at her.

'It was in March. She told me about the deal that Blaines proposed. And about the pressure that was put on you to agree. She was anxious that we should appreciate what you'd done.' Klose sniffed. 'A remarkable young woman, in her way.'

'And what happens now?' I said.

'To some extent, that's up to you.' She hesitated. 'The enquiry has established your loyalty to the state. You've resisted a great many temptations. You've also shown a regrettable tendency to act on your own initiative. Nevertheless, if you wanted it, I think your Ministry could find you a job in Berlin, on the same grade as you had here. But perhaps you've had enough of export statistics.'

'Could I find a job elsewhere?'

Klose shrugged. 'I think another Ministry might be persuaded to take you on. The work would be more varied. You'd have more to do with people and less to do with figures. You'd be able to use your languages. You would have a reasonable chance of promotion, assuming your work was satisfactory. There would also be a possibility of foreign travel.'

'May I have a little time to think about it?' I said.

'Until midnight,' she said. 'You can phone us when you get back from your friend Dieter's.'

'Tell me something,' I said. 'Was Verner really – ?'

But Arendt and Fräulein Klose were already on their feet. To this day I don't know whether Jack Verner was what he said he was. We have devious minds in State Security. We are quite capable of devising and acting out a little charade as the final test of a person's loyalty. Klose gave me the ghost of a smile.

'Until midnight,' she said.